Women

Also published by Handheld Press

HANDHELD CLASSICS

HANDHELD MODERN

HANDHELD RESEARCH

Women's Weird

Strange Stories by Women, 1890–1940

edited by Melissa Edmundson

Handheld Classic 12

This anthology published in 2019 by Handheld Press.
72 Warminster Road, Bath BA2 6RU, United Kingdom.
www.handheldpress.co.uk

ISBN 978-1-912766-24-6

1 2 3 4 5 6 7 8 9 0

Series design by Nadja Guggi and typeset in Adobe Caslon Pro and Open Sans.

Printed and bound in Great Britain by Ashford Press, Hampshire.

Contents

Acknowledgements

I would like to express my gratitude to Kate Macdonald of Handheld Press, for asking me to select the stories for this book, as well as for allowing such a generous word limit.

My thanks go as well to Eleanor Fitzsimons for sending me an advance copy of her biography of Edith Nesbit.

For helping to secure the republication rights to stories still in copyright, I appreciate the help of: Georgia Glover of David Higham Associates for permission to reprint Margery Lawrence's 'The Haunted Saucepan'; Sharon Rubin of Peters, Fraser & Dunlop for permission to reprint Margaret Irwin's 'The Book'; and Alice Johnstone of Random House and Frank Gargent, bursar of St Hilda's College, Oxford, for permission to reprint D K Broster's 'Couching at the Door'.

I also wish to thank Jeffrey Makala for his feedback on the introduction and for using his librarianship skills to help secure some elusive first editions.

As always, thanks to Murray, Maggie, and Kitsey for their furry support.

Melissa Edmundson

Melissa Edmundson researches and publishes on nineteenth and early twentieth-century British women writers, with a particular interest in women's supernatural fiction. She is the editor of a 2011 critical edition of Alice Perrin's *East of Suez* (1901), and author of *Women's Ghost Literature in Nineteenth-Century Britain* (University of Wales Press, 2013) and *Women's Colonial Gothic Writing, 1850–1930: Haunted Empire* (Palgrave Macmillan, 2018). She edited *Avenging Angels: Ghost Stories by Victorian Women Writers* (Victorian Secrets, 2018).

Introduction

BY MELISSA EDMUNDSON

Women have long been associated with having special powers and intuitive connections with the natural and supernatural worlds. The Old English 'wyrd', meaning 'fate' or 'destiny', gradually came to mean 'the power to control destiny', a power that has been linked with the feminine since the Fates of Greek mythology. These weaving goddesses – Clotho, Lachesis, and Atropos – created an individual destiny for each person at birth. In Norse mythology, the Norns controlled the past, present, and future. They are closely associated with the Sisters of Fate in German folklore. William Shakespeare further solidified the connections between the idea of destiny and the feminine, adding a supernatural quality to the three Weird Sisters in *Macbeth* (1606), characters rooted in Scottish folklore and inspired by his reading of Holinshed's *Chronicles of England, Scotland, and Ireland* (1587). Also popularly known as the Three Witches, these women are associated with Hecate, the Greek goddess of magic, witchcraft, and supernatural beings such as ghosts. They combine a reimagining of the role of women in Greek mythology with European folklore about witches and wise women who have the power to control the natural world, heal people through the use of folk magic, predict the future, and summon otherworldly spirits. It is perhaps only natural that women would eventually build on this tradition to create their own visions of the supernatural world, summoning spirits through their writing.

Women's early supernatural fiction was largely centered around the figure of the ghost. The first decade of the seventeenth century saw the publication of Sarah Malthus's pamphlet *King William's Ghost* (1704). Towards mid-century, Elizabeth Boyd contributed to the ballad tradition with *Altamira's Ghost; Or Justice Triumphant* (1744). Throughout the Romantic period and into the nineteenth century, women published ghost stories in magazines, in collected editions of poetry, and in newspapers. Many of these tales are traditional ghost stories and feature spirits who return from the dead to right some wrong done to them. However, as the nineteenth century progressed, women began to experiment with other forms of supernatural fiction. Charlotte Riddell, in her collection *Weird Stories* (1882), created spectres whose stories reflected economic inequalities, property disputes, and stolen inheritances. Other writers, such as Mary Elizabeth Braddon, Rhoda Broughton, Mary E Wilkins Freeman, and Margaret Oliphant, wrote about hauntings caused by family disputes, domestic abuse, doomed love affairs, and murder. By the final decade of the nineteenth century, Vernon Lee, in her collection *Hauntings* (1890), was using European art and history as an inspiration for her spectral protagonists, eschewing the modern world that was such a part of ghost fiction in the work of Riddell and others.

During the late Victorian period and into the twentieth century, women's supernatural fiction became much darker as newer, more ominous presences emerged beside the traditional figure of the ghost. Women's Weird fiction in these decades incorporated other themes besides the primarily domestic concerns of earlier supernatural fiction, and, while many later stories are still concerned with gender, they also explore more universal imaginings of fear, unease, and dread. This collection surveys some of these experimental forms to show how these authors moved beyond the traditional ghost story and into areas of Weird fiction and dark fantasy.

Defining Weird fiction

Throughout the twentieth century, there have been numerous attempts to define and classify the Weird tale. H P Lovecraft, in *Supernatural Horror in Literature* (1927), described the Weird tale as something more than a traditional ghost story: 'The true weird tale has something more than secret murder, bloody bones, or a sheeted form clanking chains according to rule'. For Lovecraft, the feeling inspired while reading is important:

> A certain atmosphere of breathless and unexplainable dread of outer, unknown forces must be present; and there must be a hint, expressed with a seriousness and portentousness becoming its subject, of that most terrible conception of the human brain – a malign and particular suspension or defeat of those fixed laws of Nature which are our only safeguard against the assaults of chaos and the daemons of unplumbed space. (Lovecraft 1973, 15)

He continues by saying, 'Atmosphere is the all-important thing' (16) and that '[t]he one test of the really Weird is simply this – whether or not there be excited in the reader a profound sense of dread, and of contact with unknown spheres and powers' (16). Lovecraft was not the only writer to attempt to describe the effect of the Weird tale. In the Foreword to her collection *Randalls Round* (1929), Eleanor Scott describes the nightmarish dreams that inspired her supernatural fiction:

> in dreams there is a kind of connecting thread so frail that no art can ever reproduce it – it is not possible to put it into the language and associations of waking life; and only in the first awakening, when one is, as it were, in the borderland between the world of dreams and the world of every day, remote from both yet understanding both as one never does when fully awake or fully asleep, can one remember the thread and try, however vainly, to translate it into terms of every day. (Scott 2010, 7)

Mary Butts's essay, 'Ghosties and Ghoulies: Uses of the Supernatural in English Fiction', serialized in *The Bookman* in January to April 1933, echoes Scott's description of a writer's sources of inspiration by saying, 'A writer must, if only half consciously, believe in what he is writing about. Details he can invent, and setting; terror and wonder he must have known and may have reflected on' (Butts January 1933, 388).[1] Butts's examination of the effect of the supernatural tale also recalls Lovecraft's description of the Weird tale. She remarks that these types of stories must elicit 'a stirring, a touching of nerves not usually sensitive, an awakening to more than fear – but to something like awareness and conviction or even memory' (386). Like Lovecraft, Butts stresses that these types of stories must have an otherworldly feel, while she also uses the concept of the 'border' between the natural and supernatural described by Scott:

> Their borders are sometimes indistinct, but the first order, implicitly or explicitly, assume theories of life existing beyond, or generally beyond our perception; theories which, in different make up some hideous, some lovely, some awful, some idiotic – are immeasurably old; and not *all* accounted for by our increased scientific knowledge of the world. Theories which suppose laws, a range of beings from gods and bogies to daimones and God, an atlas of unknown worlds, physically existing regions beyond the senses of man. (386)

More recently, scholars have debated over what Weird fiction actually is and which writers should be credited with writing it. Ann and Jeff VanderMeer, in their collection *The Weird* (2011), continue in the tradition of Lovecraft, Scott, and Butts, remarking, 'The Weird acknowledges that our search for understanding about worlds beyond our own cannot always be found in science or religion and thus becomes an alternative path for exploration of the numinous' (VanderMeer & VanderMeer 2011, xvii). It represents 'the impulse to remind readers of the strangeness of the world and the limits of our understanding of it' (xvii). The VanderMeers provide one of best summations of the Weird, precisely by focusing on the indefinability of the term: 'The Weird is as much a *sensation* as it is a mode of writing, the most keenly attuned amongst us will say 'I know it when I see it', by which they mean 'I know it when I *feel* it' (xvi). Every fan of the Weird does indeed know this feeling – the feeling of something being 'off', not quite right. Roger Luckhurst and James Machin prefer the term 'mode' rather than 'genre', with both citing previous work by Veronica Hollinger, who has discussed these classificatory terms in relation to science fiction (Hollinger 2014). Machin also acknowledges the difficulties inherent in trying to define the Weird, a type of fiction that 'is intrinsically problematic for critical discourse' (Machin 2018, 13).

Machin has published the most comprehensive history of the Weird to date, but his discussion of the Weird leaves out what he terms 'the Victorian Ghost Story' (26). The inclusion of 'Victorian' becomes a reductive, problematic term itself, one which invariably haunts later iterations of ghosts in fiction – particularly ghosts as imagined by women – and obscures the more fruitful ways in which supernatural fiction and the Weird entwine in the early decades of the twentieth century and into the interwar period. Perhaps Elizabeth Bowen said it best when she commented on the continuing relevance of the ghost in fiction, remarking that 'they adapt themselves well, perhaps better than we do, to changing world conditions – they enlarge their domain, shift their hold on our nerves and, dispossessed of one habitat, set up house in another' (Bowen 1956, vii).

Women's Weird: Themes, issues, anxieties

The stories included in *Women's Weird* showcase a wide variety of themes and represent the various ways women interpret the Weird in their writing. Some themes are connected to real world social concerns that become even more frightening when placed in a Weird context. Claustrophobic spaces, nightmarish worlds, and otherworldly entities come to represent traumatic pasts that are impossible to escape. Other stories reach beyond specific cultural issues to take on universal human fears and the dark inner selves that we try to overcome and keep hidden. The shadow in the corner, the possessed object, the almost-human creature: all these manifestations lay bare our shared fears and anxieties.

Gender issues relating to abuse and trauma are apparent in Charlotte Perkins Gilman's 'The Giant Wistaria' (1891), published a year before her seminal work of feminist fiction, 'The Yellow Wall-paper'. The story is a comparison of two different eras and the treatment of women in both. The first section, set in Puritan times, makes a victim out of a young, unmarried mother – in social terms, and quite literally in her confinement and death in the cellar well underneath the house. The wisteria covers secrets and keeps a firm grasp on the house, becoming a controlling, disruptive presence that mirrors the woman's puritanical father. The roots continue to 'strangle' her bones even after her death. Yet the women who rent the house in more modern times are still caught between freedom and male control. They are often infantilised by their husbands. In a scene that prefigures 'The Yellow Wall-paper', one character is given bromide by her physician husband to help calm her nerves and make her sleep. In Gilman's story, the stranglehold of patriarchy has lessened, but its roots run deep.

Edith Wharton's 'Kerfol' (1916) likewise presents a woman whose life is lived under the complete control of a patriarchal figure – her husband – who keeps the woman a virtual prisoner in his remote estate of Kerfol. Like many other authors in this collection, Wharton uses a male narrator. Yet unlike other stories, where the once skeptical narrator becomes enlightened to the presence of an unknown supernatural world, Wharton's narrator refuses to give credit to Anne de Cornault's testimony, thus denying her claim of sympathy and understanding. Despite his wish at the beginning of the story to know more about Kerfol, 'not to *see* more,' as he says, 'but to feel more: feel all the place had to communicate' (70), the narrator is unfeeling toward Anne's mental abuse and suffering. Kathy A Fedorko writes that the narrator's 'arrogant judgment' of

Anne points to Wharton's desire to show 'the unreliability of the male narrator who rejects his empathy and intuitive knowledge for sole reliance on control and rationality' (Fedorko 1995, 66). The eerie silence of the spectral dogs in 'Kerfol', who give the sense 'of having in common one memory so deep and dark that nothing that had happened since was worth either a growl or a wag' (74), mirrors the enforced silence of Anne, who fights to free herself from a domineering husband, but who is, like the dogs, irrevocably damaged by a 'deep and dark' traumatic memory of a life of imprisonment and abuse.

Other stories in *Women's Weird* are reminiscent of those written by M R James in the early twentieth century. In 'The Twelve Apostles', Eleanor Scott, who Richard Dalby calls 'one of the best, but ultimately least known, writers in this genre during the 1920s' (Dalby 2010, 169), reworks Jamesian motifs such as the curious-but-naïve narrator who seeks answers – through the study of old manuscripts and religious texts – to questions about the life of a former occupant of a supposedly haunted house. Scott's story contains a degraded priest in league with the devil, a secret chamber, and religious iconography that provides clues to the mystery. It was inspired by the author's very real nightmares.

The prevailing attitude of critics and the public in this period routinely denied women creative agency and asserted that women relied on adapting stories written by men in order to have their own work published. Yet Mary Cholmondeley's 'Let Loose', first published in *Temple Bar* in April 1890, predates James's stories of haunted churches and crypts, so that it could legitimately be said that James's tales were in the style of Mary Cholmondeley. As well as 'Let Loose' frequently being overlooked or disregarded by those preferring James, Cholmondeley had to defend herself from accusations of plagiarism. In a note at the beginning of the 1902 American publication of the story, Cholmondeley addresses those who claim that it is a retelling of F G Loring's story 'The Tomb of Sarah', published in *Pall Mall* magazine in December 1900, ten years after Cholmondeley's story had appeared. Other than being set in a church crypt and involving a vengeful spirit, Loring's vampire story has little connection to Cholmondeley's story.

Family legacies and cycles of suffering and death play a part in several stories. Louisa Baldwin's 'The Weird of the Walfords' (1889) presents a haunted object that leads to the doom of an entire family line. Humphrey Walford is obsessed with the family (death) bed and his obsession grows until it becomes a type of monomania. He mistakenly thinks that he can somehow control fate and overcome death by destroying the bed. Instead, the bed returns to revenge itself on Walford. Like a ghost, the object takes a different shape: it is itself and yet changed into another form. The past cannot be destroyed, and returns to haunt the present and harm the living.

Edith Nesbit's 'The Shadow' (1910) complicates the ghost story formula in two significant ways: the narrator claims that the entity 'wasn't exactly a ghost' (59), and the supernatural events take place in a new house without any prior history of violence or misdeeds. The mysterious, ominous shadow figure is somehow linked to one of the main characters, yet we never find out why. This leads to even more mystery: what has the man done in the past to have this shadow follow him? From where did this shadow come? Is it a curse? Despite these unanswered questions, the supernatural presence literally follows the family through generations and attaches to the man's descendent, who 'inherits' it with disastrous consequences.

The darker side of human nature and its own revenants – jealousy, greed, ambition, morbid curiosity, and prejudice – are at the heart of these narratives. For every external force of evil represented by the supernatural creatures and haunted objects across these tales, there are internal forces that also threaten safety and stability. In Margaret Irwin's 'The Book' (1930), what happens to Corbett could happen to anyone; he is not special, just bored, restless, and ambitious, like so many of us. Corbett's obsession with the possessed book exposes his vulnerability to the evil forces within it, but the matter-of-factness of the tragedy makes the story even more chilling. The narrator says, 'his deep interest in [the book] should have convinced him that from his humanity at least it was not altogether alien' (234). Yet for all its insistence on the nearness of evil in our everyday lives, Irwin's story manages to make a powerful statement about the enduring quality of free will amidst such evil. No matter how powerless we may seem, there are consequences to the choices we make, and Corbett chooses to fight against the demonic influence that resides in the book before it can do further damage.

Francis Stevens in 'Unseen – Unfeared' (1919) presents racist thoughts as a sickness, the thoughts of one who is deranged in mind, not a part of normal human feeling. These thoughts are reflected in the strange creatures seen by the protagonist Blaisdell, but also by Blaisdell's misinterpretation of Pietro Marini's 'evil' look. The Italian Marini is, in many ways, the hero of the story. Stevens refuses to make him into the stock 'dark foreigner' who appears so often in literature, supernatural or not. The treatment of racist views in Stevens's story provides an important counterpoint to the more blatant racism in the fiction of Lovecraft. For instance, here is a description of a New York street in Lovecraft's 'The Horror at Red Hook', which appeared in *Weird Tales* in 1927:

> Red Hook is a maze of hybrid squalor near the ancient waterfront opposite Governor's Island, with dirty highways climbing the hill from the wharves to that higher ground where the decayed lengths of Clinton and Court Streets lead off toward the Borough Hall. [...] The population is a hopeless tangle and enigma; Syrian, Spanish, Italian, and negro elements impinging upon one another, and fragments of Scandinavian and American belts lying not far distant. It is a babel of sound and filth, and sends out strange cries to answer the lapping of oily waves at its grimy piers and the monstrous organ litanies of the harbour whistles. (Lovecraft 2005, 128)

In Lovecraft's fiction, the racism is not redeemed. According to this narrative and so many other Lovecraft stories, minority and ethnic groups are the root cause of evil instead of that evil being caused by hatred and bigotry. As in Irwin's story, Stevens blends the knowledge of the evil that surrounds us with an affirmative message. After his traumatic experience, Blaisdell refuses to pursue forbidden knowledge and chooses instead to take something positive away from his near-death experience. This is rare in Weird fiction. Stevens is issuing the same challenge to the reader as she does to Blaisdell: knowing what we now know, knowing what we have seen/not seen, which worldview are we going to choose in our own lives? Should we give in to evil, or fight against it? Stevens, 'the woman who invented dark fantasy', shows how the Weird can engage in real world concerns while at the same time opening up monstrous new worlds to entertain and frighten its readers (Hoppenstand 2004, xxiv).

Apart from the grotesque creatures that populate many of these stories, there are other narratives that convey a sense of dread based on the threat of continued emptiness and nothingness, in both life and death. May Sinclair presents the hell of an emotionally empty life in 'Where Their Fire Is Not Quenched'. One of the more experimental stories in *Uncanny Tales* (1923) – Mary Butts said of Sinclair's collection that she 'has gone further than most others in our time [and] has written one very remarkable book' (Butts April 1933, 13) – this story tells of a purely sexual relationship that is destined to fail but must be relived over and over again for eternity. Originally propelled by an intense lust which turns to an equally intense boredom, the couple cannot escape their fate. Death is not the end, but for the readers of Sinclair's story, this is no comforting thought.

Curiosity, obsession, and misunderstanding resurface in Elinor Mordaunt's 'Hodge' (1921) when the past literally comes back to life. As a prehistoric being, Hodge is not separate from the natural world, as many Weird creatures usually are, but is instead an ancient being out of deep time. He is a temporal other, belonging to the place, but not to the time. The narrator describes this distance between prehistory and modernity when describing Hodge:

> Silhouetted against the sea and sky, white in contrast to its darkness, it had the aloofness of incredible age; drawn apart, almost sanctified by its immeasurable remoteness, its detachment from all that meant life to the men and women of the twentieth century: the web of fancied necessities, trivial possessions, absorptions. (131)

Hodge is never allowed to become fully a part of the world he is reborn into and thus is not allowed to completely come back to life, as the narrator says, 'for all its new-found life, it was as far away as any ghost' (133). Hodge is an exception to the typical Weird creature in another respect – he is a sympathetic figure. Perception is a persistent problem in 'Hodge' and readers are left wondering whether the 'bestial' qualities that begin to overwhelm the Fane siblings' view of Hodge were always there, or never. Their reaction to (and eventual fear of) Hodge is coloured by their failure to fully humanise a creature who clearly does not fit in their modern world but whose 'rebirth' is a direct result of their actions. This vacillation is represented in the changing representation of Hodge, as he goes from a primitive 'it', then to a man, and finally back to an animalistic 'it' again as he becomes more threatening towards Rhoda and Hector near the end of the story. Their refusal to see Hodge as a sentient being, to treat him as something less than human, is also used as an excuse for Hector's final act against Hodge at the end of the story.

The descriptions of the supernatural entities in these stories are truly remarkable and should be placed among the most memorable creatures Weird fiction has to offer. Many of these manifestations seek revenge. In 'Unseen – Unfeared', the narrator witnesses a 'great round blob of a body on tottering tentacles', 'centipedish things, with yard-long bodies', 'detestable, furry spiders', and 'things with human faces' (106). Other stories feature the return of people who once lived deplorable lives. This type of Weird body comes back, as Mary Butts described, 'hideously changed, and charged with a vitality due to its evil life on earth; in one form or another, beast, pest and ghost' (388). The violently severed hand of Sir Roger Despard in 'Let Loose' and the 'tentacle, both slimy and hairy' (223) that reaches for Matthews in 'The Twelve Apostles' were once debauched men. Their hatred does not die with them but extends beyond the grave, taking terrible new forms.

In addition to changed physical bodies, the authors in this collection also use traditionally feminine objects to haunt and to enact revenge on the living. This particular trope seems to appear more frequently in the stories from the 1920s onwards as the conveniences and luxuries of modern life take on frightening new forms and energies. In Margery Lawrence's 'The Haunted Saucepan' (1922), the domestic space of the kitchen becomes a nexus of evil, as an unassuming object becomes an instrument of death and a symbol of a *femme fatale's* lust for luxury and comfort. Though the woman is still alive, her destructive spirit is linked to the enamel saucepan which makes a 'hateful little purring noise' and sits 'grinning to itself, planning new evil' (189). Seemingly harmless articles of clothing likewise become dangerous. In D K Broster's 'Couching at the Door' (1933), the hedonistic Augustine Marchant is terrorized by a seemingly harmless fur boa. The terror in Broster's story slowly builds as the boa enters uninvited into Marchant's house, a reminder of an unnamed, terrible act committed by Marchant against a woman (most likely a sex worker) during a 'glamorous, wonderful, abominable night in Prague' (250). The boa purrs and nuzzles against him in bed, turning the once confident Marchant into a nervous and frightened coward who is prepared to sacrifice someone else in order to rid himself of the unwelcome 'familiar'. Broster's shock ending shows readers that Marchant only manages to trade one horror for another, greater horror.

The ladies' gloves in Mary Butts's 'With and Without Buttons' (1938) are worn and rotten. This story, with its tactile descriptions, is very much in the Jamesian tradition. In a 1932 letter to M R James, Butts mentions writing 'With and Without Buttons' and acknowledges her debt to his supernatural fiction, saying, 'I've at last managed to write a ghost story myself which should come out soon [...] & given any quality it may have it owes to your influence' (Blondel ed. 2002, 401). Louis Adeane calls the story 'equal to almost anything written by the master himself' (Adeane 1995, 105). Yet there is an emphasis on gender anxiety and female power in Butts's tale that is missing from James's work, an emphasis which makes this story come full circle from the cultural beginnings of women's involvement with concepts of the wyrd/weird. The two sisters, tired of their male neighbour Trenchard's 'calling the bluff, in inaccurate language, of God, the arts, the imagination, the emotions', decide to 'haunt' him and 'give him a nightmare' (273). Their repetition of 'with and without buttons' becomes a sort of witch's chant, but the sisters also unwittingly summon an older and more ominous female spirit that manifests through old clothing.

Establishing a women's Weird tradition

The historical and literary associations women authors have with the Weird, sometimes empowering and sometimes not, have not served them well in the study of the history of supernatural literature. In Margaret Irwin's 'The Book', the narrator describes the bookshelf in the Corbett family home, noticing that the 'gap between two books seemed the most hideous deformity, like a gap between the front teeth of some grinning monster' (227). I would like to adopt this image as an analogy for recognising women's contributions to Weird fiction, and as an answer to the question, 'Why do we need a collection devoted to women's Weird fiction?' Despite participating in the development of the Weird tale since its beginnings, there is still a 'gap' between the books. This represents a failure to read and appreciate women's supernatural writing equally alongside that of men. Though recent critical studies of the Weird have helped to bring this mode of writing the respect it deserves, these studies tend to examine the work of the same group of men: Arthur Machen, H P Lovecraft, Algernon Blackwood, M R James, John Buchan, M P Shiel, Ambrose Bierce, William Hope Hodgson, and Lord Dunsany. The tendency to focus on this limited group is spurred by anthologies of the supernatural which continue to include those authors while ignoring women's involvement with the Weird. This oversight makes the work of male authors more readily available and allows the early writing by women from the late 1800s until 1940 – a period that some term the 'Old Weird' – to be more easily forgotten. This is not to say that these male-authored works do not deserve scholarly attention, but by only focusing on this group of (white) men, we perpetuate a very incomplete picture of the history of Weird literature.

Joanna Russ, in How to Suppress Women's Writing (1983), calls Irwin's 'The Book' 'one of the most interesting stories of the supernatural I ever read' (Russ 2005, 129). Russ corrects the noted anthologist and bibliographer E F Bleiler for his dismissal of nineteenth-century women writers of the supernatural in the introduction to his Best Ghost Stories of J S LeFanu (1964)[2] by positing that women authors' tendency to paint less-than-complimentary portraits of male characters and tropes are at the root of women's dismissal from the history of supernatural fiction, a history that has, until very recently, been predominantly written by white, male scholars. She says:

> Margaret Irwin's collected works are not, it seems, in print anywhere today, though LeFanu's are. This is not to deny LeFanu's achievement. Yet I suspect that LeFanu's father-son conflict, his theme of the 'disinherited hero', would interest critics more than Irwin's portrayal of the corruption of masculine values. (129)

Russ's feminist study was published in 1983, and yet, sadly, her observation remains true. Irwin's work, along with many other supernatural collections by women, remains out of print, while collections of LeFanu's writing, and many of his male contemporaries, abound.

Although her point about thematic issues being a major cause for women's critical dismissal is important, Russ identifies only part of the problem. Women are indeed often criticised when they 'only' write about gender and the domestic, or when they confront 'the corruption of masculine values' in their ghost stories. However, women have also not received enough credit for writing about things other than gender, and it is through the Weird tale that we can begin to see the true range of their work in supernatural fiction.

It is my hope that *Women's Weird: Strange Stories by Women, 1890–1940* helps to spotlight women's involvement in Weird fiction. Though this collection focuses on a representative selection of stories that covers fifty years, there are many other women authors and stories who could have been included, for a much broader range of years. The stories in this current collection will hopefully inspire readers to seek other writers including Marjorie Bowen, Mary E Wilkins Freeman, Ellen Glasgow, Violet Hunt, Eleanor Smith, Edna W Underwood, and many others. Like the unseen worlds that populate Weird fiction, these writers and their works are out there, just waiting to be discovered.

Notes

1 Although her short stories have not yet been the subject of sustained critical reappraisal, Mary Butts is now regarded as an important novelist within the modernist era. Roslyn Reso Foy reintroduced Butts's work to a modern audience in *Ritual, Myth, and Mysticism in the Work of Mary Butts: Between Feminism and Modernism* (2000). In *Step-Daughters of England: British Women Modernists and the National Imaginary* (2003), Jane Garrity includes a chapter on Mary Butts along with chapters on Dorothy Richardson, Sylvia Townsend Warner, and Virginia Woolf.

2 In his introduction to the edition, Bleiler compares the work of LeFanu with that of Charlotte Riddell, Rhoda Broughton, and Amelia B Edwards.

Though he calls this selective group 'excellent practitioners in the ghost story' (Bleiler 1964, v), Bleiler does tend to be dismissive of these three women in favor of LeFanu, calling their work 'typically Victorian' and 'competent' (ix) in comparison with what he considers the greater artistic skills of the one male writer in the group. To Bleiler's credit, he did publish a collection of Riddell's ghost stories for Dover Press in 1977.

Further reading

Adeane, Louis, 'An Appraisal of Mary Butts,' *A Sacred Quest: The Life and Writings of Mary Butts*, Christopher Wagstaff (ed.) (McPherson & Company, 1995), 97–106.

Adrian, Jack, 'Introduction,' *Couching at the Door*, Jack Adrian (ed.) (Ash-Tree Press, 2001), ix–xxxi.

Bleiler, E F, 'Introduction,' *Best Ghost Stories of J S LeFanu*, E F Bleiler (ed.) (Dover, 1964), v–xi.

Blondel, Nathalie (ed.), *The Journals of Mary Butts* (Yale University Press, 2002).

Bowen, Elizabeth, 'Introduction,' *The Second Ghost Book* (1952), Lady Cynthia Asquith (ed.) (Pan Books, 1956), vii–x.

Butts, Mary, 'Ghosties and Ghoulies: Uses of the Supernatural in English Fiction,' *The Bookman* (January 1933), 386–389.

—, 'Ghosties and Ghoulies: Uses of the Supernatural in English Fiction,' *The Bookman* (April 1933), 12–14.

Dalby, Richard, 'Afterword,' *Randalls Round* (Oleander Press, 2010), 169–175.

—, 'Introduction,' *Nights of the Round Table* (Ash-Tree Press, 1998), ix–xix.

Edmundson, Melissa, 'Buyer beware: Haunted objects in the super-natural tales of Margery Lawrence', in *The Female Fantastic: The Gendered Supernatural in the 1890s and 1920s*, Elizabeth McCormick, Jennifer Mitchell, and Rebecca Soares (eds.) (Routledge, 2018), 50–64.

Fedorko, Kathy A, *Gender and the Gothic in the Fiction of Edith Wharton* (The University of Alabama Press, 1995).

Fitzsimons, Eleanor, *The Life and Loves of E Nesbit* (Duckworth, 2019).

Flanders, Judith, *Circle of Sisters: Alice Kipling, Georgiana Burne-Jones, Agnes Poynter, and Louisa Baldwin* (W W Norton, 2001).

Hartley, Cathy (ed.) *A Historical Dictionary of British Women* (Routledge, 2003).

Hollinger, Veronica, 'Genre vs. Mode,' in *The Oxford Handbook of Science Fiction*, Rob Latham (ed.) (Oxford University Press, 2014, 139–51.

Hoppenstand, Gary, 'Francis Stevens: The Woman Who Invented Dark Fantasy,' *The Nightmare and Other Tales of Dark Fantasy*, Gary Hoppenstand (ed.) (University of Nebraska Press, 2004), ix–xxv.

Lovecraft, H P, *Supernatural Horror in Literature* (1927) (Dover, 1973).

—, 'The Horror at Red Hook' (1927), *H P Lovecraft: Tales* (The Library of America, 2005), 125–140.

Machin, James, *Weird Fiction in Britain, 1880–1939* (Palgrave Macmillan, 2018).

Russ, Joanna, *How to Suppress Women's Writing* (1983) (University of Texas Press, 2005).

Scott, Eleanor, 'Foreword,' *Randalls Round* (Oleander Press, 2010), 7.

VanderMeer, Ann and Jeff, 'Introduction,' *The Weird: A Compendium of Strange and Dark Stories*, Ann and Jeff VanderMeer (eds.) (Tor, 2011), xv–xx.

Biographical notes

Louisa Baldwin (1845–1925) was born in Wakefield, the fourth surviving daughter of George Browne and Hannah Jones Macdonald. Her older sisters were Alice Kipling (mother of Rudyard Kipling), Georgiana Burne-Jones (wife of the artist Edward Burne-Jones), and Agnes Poynter (wife of Sir Edward John Poynter). In 1866, Louisa married Alfred Baldwin, and after the birth of her son, the future prime minister Stanley Baldwin, the following year, was stricken with a mysterious debilitating illness that lasted for the reminder of her life. Despite this, Baldwin published her first novel, *A Martyr to Mammon*, in 1886, followed by *Where Town and Country Meet* (1891), *Richard Dare* (1894), and *The Story of a Marriage* (1889). *The Shadow on the Blind* (1895) was her only supernatural collection and contains stories that had previously appeared in magazines. In addition to 'The Weird of the Walfords', which was published in *Longman's Magazine* in November 1889, 'The Uncanny Bairn: A Story of the Second Sight' appeared in *The Cornhill Magazine* in September 1892, followed by 'The Shadow on the Blind' in September 1894. 'My Next Door Neighbour' and 'How He Left the Hotel' were published in *The Argosy* in June 1892 and October 1894, respectively. 'The Ticking of the Clock,' with its ominous ending, appeared in *Longman's Magazine* in July 1894.

Dorothy Kathleen Broster (1877–1950) was born in Garston, near Liverpool, to Thomas Mawdsley and Emily Kathleen Broster. She attended Cheltenham Ladies' College before gaining a scholarship to attend St Hilda's College, Oxford. In 1898, she earned an Honours degree in Modern History, but the degree was not officially awarded until 1920. Prior to 1920, Broster worked as the secretary for Sir Charles Firth, Regius Professor of Modern History at Oxford. During this time, she also began writing historical fiction and is most well known for her bestselling Jacobite trilogy, *The Flight of the Heron* (1925), *The Gleam in the North* (1927), and *The Dark Mile* (1929). During the First World War, Broster volunteered as a nurse, and in

1915 she went to France with the British Red Cross. The next year she was sent home with a knee infection. Broster never married but had a close friendship with Gertrude Schlich which lasted from the time of the First World War to Broster's death. Most of her supernatural fiction appears in two collections: *A Fire of Driftwood* (1932) and *Couching at the Door* (1942).

Mary Butts (1890–1937) was born in Parkstone, south Dorset, to Frederick John and Mary Jane Briggs Butts. She attended Westfield College in London from 1909–1912 but did not complete her degree. Butts then entered the London School of Economics, graduating in 1914 with a certificate in social science. She then worked with the Children's Care Committee in the East End. During the First World War, Butts was a committed pacifist. She married the publisher John Rodker in 1918, but the two divorced in 1926. Her first novel, *Ashe of Rings* (1925), was set during WWI. She married the artist Gabriel William Aitken in 1930, and the couple moved to Cornwall. Butts published *Death of Felicity Taverner*, one of her most well-known novels, in 1932. This was followed by *The Macedonian* (1933) and *Scenes from the Life of Cleopatra* (1935). Butts's short stories were collected in *Several Occasions* (1932) and the posthumous *Last Stories* (1938). She was also an active reviewer and published on the work of Aldous Huxley and M R James, among others. Her autobiography *The Crystal Cabinet* was completed in 1937.

Mary Cholmondeley (1859–1925) was born at Hodnet Rectory, Shropshire, the daughter of the Reverend Richard Hugh and Emily Beaumont Cholmondeley. She left school at sixteen to help her father with parish work. In 1896, she moved to London with her father and began publishing in major periodicals such as *The Graphic* and *Temple Bar*. She published her first novel, a detective story titled *The Danvers Jewels*, in 1887. Her other novels include *Sir Charles Danvers* (1889), *Diana Tempest* (1893), and *A Devotee* (1897). In 1899, Cholmondeley published the bestseller *Red Pottage*. She continued publishing into the twentieth century and after her father's death lived with her sister. Her collections include *The Lowest Rung* (1908) and *The Romance of His Life* (1921). In 1918, Cholmondeley published her memoir, *Under One Roof.*

Charlotte Perkins Gilman (1860–1935) was born in Hartford, Connecticut, to Frederic Beecher and Mary Ann Fitch Wescott Perkins. Considered a pioneering American feminist, Gilman is best known for her story 'The Yellow Wall-paper,' which appeared in the *New England Magazine* in May 1892. After her divorce from her first husband, Charles Walter Stetson, Gilman supported herself, her daughter, and her mother by running a boarding house. During this time, she also began her career as a professional writer while also lecturing across the United States. Her non-fiction works include *Women and Economics* (1898), *Concerning Children* (1900), *The Home: Its Work and Influence* (1903), *Human Work* (1904), *Man Made World: Or Our Androcentric Culture* (1911), and *His Religion and Hers: A Study of the Faith of Our Fathers and the Work of Our Mothers* (1923). In 1935, her autobiography *The Living of Charlotte Perkins Gilman* was published. Gilman edited the monthly magazine *The Forerunner* from 1909 to 1915. She returned to feminist themes in her later fiction with her feminist utopian novel *Herland* (1915) and its sequel *With Her in Ourland* (1916). In addition to 'The Giant Wistaria,' Gilman wrote two other ghost stories: 'The Rocking-Chair,' published in *Worthington's Illustrated* in May 1893, and 'The Unwatched Door,' which appeared in *Impress* in December 1894.

Margaret Irwin (1889–1967) was born in London to Andrew Clarke and Anna Julia Irwin. After the deaths of her parents when Irwin was still a child, she lived with her uncle. At Oxford, she read English, and in 1924 published the time-slip fantasy novel *Still She Wished for Company.* Irwin married the author and illustrator J R Monsell in 1929. She won a historical novel competition prize for *None So Pretty* (1930), which launched her career as a popular historical novelist. Her longer fiction includes the Queen Elizabeth trilogy: *Young Bess* (1944), *Elizabeth, Captive Princess* (1948), and *Elizabeth and the Prince* *of Spain* (1953). Irwin also wrote a biography of Sir Walter Raleigh titled *That Great Lucifer* (1960). Her supernatural fiction appears in the collections, *Madame Fears the Dark* (1935) and *Bloodstock* (1953).

Margery Lawrence (1889–1969) was born in Wolverhampton, Staffordshire, to Richard and Grace Banks Lawrence. She began her career working as an artist and illustrator and lived in Chelsea for a time while an art student. She described her experiences among the artistic community in the somewhat controversial novel *Bohemian Glass* (1928). Lawrence married the hotel magnate Arthur Towle in 1927, and they remained together until his death in 1948. Throughout the 1920s, Lawrence published short stories in popular magazines, eventually collecting her supernatural fiction in *Nights of the Round Table* (1926), *The Terraces of Night* (1932), and *The Floating Café* (1936). She contributed to occult detective literature with her portrayal of Dr Miles Pennoyer in the short story collections *Number Seven, Queer Street* (1945) and *Master of Shadows* (1959). A self-professed 'ghost hunter', Lawrence was a lifelong believer in Spiritualism and wrote about the subject in several novels, including *The Bridge of Wonder* (1939), *The Rent in the Veil* (1951), *The Yellow Triangle* (1965), and *A Residence Afresh* (1969). She recounted her psychic experiences and her belief in life after death in *Ferry Over Jordan* (1944).

Elinor Mordaunt is a pseudonym of Evelyn May Mordaunt (1872–1942), born at Cotgrave, Nottinghamshire to St John Legh and Elizabeth Caroline Bingham Clowes. She traveled to Mauritius in 1897 and married the sugar-planter Maurice Wilhemn Wiehe. The marriage was unhappy, and Mordaunt returned to England. In 1902, she arrived in Melbourne, Australia, supporting herself and her infant son by taking in sewing and working as a decorative painter. She returned to England in 1909 and began to pursue a career as a professional writer. She published several novels, including *The Garden of Contentment* (1902), *Lu of the Ranges* (1913), *The Rose of Youth* (1915), *Father and Daughter* (1928), and *Traveller's*

Pack (1934). Her short stories appeared consistently in major magazines throughout the 1910s to the 1930s and were collected in *The Island* (1914), *Old Wine in New Bottles* (1919), *Short Shipments* (1922), *And Then—? Tales of Land and Sea* (1927), and *The Tales of Elinor Mordaunt* (1934). Mordaunt continued to travel throughout her life. In addition to Australia, she visited Africa, Central and South America, and the Pacific. In 1923, she sailed around the world via sail and cargo steamer. Mordaunt published her autobiography *Sinabada* in 1937.

Edith Nesbit (1858–1924) was born in Kennington, London, to John Collis and Sarah Alderton Nesbit. She is best known for her children's books, including *The Story of the Treasure Seekers, Being the Adventures of the Bastable Children in Search of a Fortune* (1899), *The Wouldbegoods, Being the Further Adventures of the Treasure Seekers* (1901), *Five Children and It* (1902), *The Phoenix and the Carpet* (1904), *The Railway Children* (1906), and *The Story of the Amulet* (1906). From the 1880s to the 1920s, Nesbit also wrote novels for adults, as well as poetry and drama. She was a founding member of The Fabian Society and served as editor of the society's journal. In 1880, she married Hubert Bland, but the marriage was not successful due to Bland's numerous extramarital affairs. Nesbit relied on the profits from the sale of her published work to support her family, which included children from Bland's affairs. Nesbit's contributions to supernatural literature are extensive. The majority of her Gothic stories appear in the collections *Grim Tales* (1893), *Something Wrong* (1893), *Man and Maid* (1906), and *Fear* (1910).

Eleanor Scott is a pseudonym of Helen M Leys (1892–1965), born in Hampton Hill, Middlesex, to John and Ellen Leys. Scott had a lifelong interest in history and attended St Hilda's College, Oxford. During the 1930s, she worked as a teacher, eventually becoming Principal of an Oxfordshire teacher training college. Her ghost story, 'The Room,' appeared in the *Cornhill* in October 1923 under the name H M Leys, but she switched to 'Eleanor Scott' for the publication of her novel *War Among Ladies* (1928). Her other novels include *The Forgotten Image* (1930), *Swings and Roundabouts* (1933), *Beggars Would Ride* (1933), and *Puss in the Corner* (1934). Scott returned to her interest in history with two non-fiction books for the Nelsonian Library: *Adventurous Women* (1933) and *Heroic Women* (1939). She lived with her elder sister Mary (a noted historian) in Oxford for many years before moving to Devon. *Randalls Round* (1929) is Scott's only collection of supernatural fiction.

May Sinclair (1863–1946) was born in Thorncote, Cheshire, to William and Amelia Hind Sinclair. She read widely from volumes in her father's extensive library and later attended Cheltenham Ladies' College. Sinclair's early interests were in poetry and philosophy. She published *Nakiketas and Other Poems* in 1886 using the pseudonym Julian Sinclair. She followed this with *Essays in Verse* (1892) and became the first woman member of the Aristotelian Society after the publication of *A Defence of Idealism* (1917). After her father's death due to alcoholism, Sinclair became responsible for the care of her mother. She later assumed the care of children from two of her deceased brothers. Her early novels include *Audrey Craven* (1897), *Mr and Mrs Nevill Tyson* (1898), and *The Divine Fire* (1904). She was a member of the Women Writers' Suffrage League and wrote *Feminism* (1912) for the organization. She was also a member of the more radical Women's Freedom League and the Society for Psychical Research. Sinclair was a leading modernist writer and supported the Imagist and Vorticist movements. Her friends included H G Wells, Ford Madox Ford, Wyndham Lewis, W B Yeats, Ezra Pound, T S Eliot, Violet Hunt, H D, and Charlotte Mew. Sinclair's later novels were influenced by her growing interest in psychoanalysis and the aftermath of the First World War. These include *The Three Sisters* (1914), *The Tree of Heaven* (1917), and *The Romantic* (1920). Her two experimental modernist novels, *Mary Olivier: A Life* (1919) and *The Life and Death of Harriett Frean* (1922), are considered some of her best work. Sinclair's supernatural fiction is collected in *Uncanny Stories* (1923) and *The Intercessor, and Other Stories* (1931).

Francis Stevens is a pseudonym of Gertrude Barrows (1883–1948), who was born in Minneapolis, Minnesota, to Charles and Carrie Hatch Barrows. She married the British newspaper reporter Stewart Bennett and moved to Philadelphia. In 1910, less than a year after giving birth to a daughter, Bennett drowned during a storm. Stevens supported herself and her daughter by working as a secretary at the University of Pennsylvania. After assuming the care of her mother after her father's death, Stevens began to write fiction for pulp magazines, including several novel-length pieces. The first of these was *The Citadel of Fear*, which was serialized in the *Argosy* from September 14 to October 26, 1918. This was followed by *The Heads of Cerberus*, published in the *Thrill Book* in 1919, and *Avalon*, published in the *Argosy* the same year. Her novel *Claimed* also appeared in the *Argosy* the following year. Her short stories include 'The Nightmare', 'The Labyrinth', 'Friend Island', and 'Behind the Curtain', all published in *All-Story Weekly* between April 1917 and September 1918. Two more stories appeared in the *Argosy*: 'The Elf Trap' in July 1919 and 'Serapion' in June–July 1920. Her last recorded story is 'Sunfire', published in *Weird Tales* in July–October 1923. Little is known about Stevens's later life apart from a move to California.

Edith Wharton (1862–1937) was born in New York City to George Frederic and Lucretia Rhinelander Jones. In 1885, she married Edward Robbins Wharton, but the union was not a happy one and the couple divorced in 1913. Her husband, much like her parents, did not appreciate Wharton's interest in intellectual pursuits and her desire to become an author. Her early writing consisted of accounts of her travels through Europe, as well as collections of short stories. Her novels include *The House of Mirth* (1905) *Ethan Frome* (1911), *The Custom of the Country* (1913), and *The Age of Innocence* (1920). Wharton became the first woman to win the Pulitzer Prize for Fiction in 1921 for *The Age of Innocence*. During the First World War, Wharton toured the front lines and wrote in support of America entering the conflict in a series of essays titled *Fighting France* (1915). She wrote about the impact of the war in her novel *The Marne* (1918) and established schools and orphanages for Belgian refugees in Paris. From October 1933 to April 1934, Wharton published a series of autobiographical essays for the *Ladies' Home Journal*, and these essays later appeared as *A Backward Glance* (1934). Her Gothic fiction is included in *Tales of Men and Ghosts* (1910) and *Xingu and Other Stories* (1916). Wharton's supernatural fiction was later collected in *Ghosts* (1937), which contains a Preface summarizing Wharton's views on writing ghost stories.

Bibliographical details

'The Weird of the Walfords' first appeared in *Longman's Magazine* in November 1889 and was published in Baldwin's collection *The Shadow on the Blind and Other Ghost Stories* (J M Dent & Company, 1895). The current text is based on the 1895 publication.

'Let Loose' was first published in *Temple Bar* in April 1890 and was later included in the American edition of Cholmondeley's collection *Moth and Rust* (Dodd, Mead & Company, 1902). The current text is based on the 1902 publication.

'The Giant Wistaria' was published in *The New England Magazine* (Boston) in June 1891. The current text is based on the 1891 publication.

'The Shadow' was originally published as 'The Portent of the Shadow' in the London magazine *Black and White* in December 1905 and was republished in *The Index* (Pittsburgh) in January 1906. The story was later included as 'The Shadow' in Nesbit's collection *Fear* (Stanley Paul & Co, 1910). The current text is based on the 1910 publication.

'Kerfol' was originally published in Wharton's collection *Xingu and Other Stories* (C Scribner's Sons, 1916) and was later included in her collection of supernatural fiction, *Ghosts* (D Appleton-Century Company, 1937). The current text is based on the 1916 publication.

'Unseen – Unfeared' originally appeared in *People's Favorite Magazine* (New York) in February 1919. The current text is based on the 1919 publication.

'Hodge' was originally published in *Metropolitan Magazine* in April 1921 before being included in Mordaunt's *Short Shipments* the following year. The story was later collected in *The Tales of Elinor Mordaunt* (Martin Secker, 1934). The current text is based on the 1934 publication.

'Where Their Fire Is Not Quenched' was first published in the *English Review* in October 1922 and later appeared in Sinclair's collection *Uncanny Stories* (Hutchinson & Co, 1923). The current text is based on the 1923 publication.

'The Haunted Saucepan' originally appeared in *The Tatler* in December 1922 and was later collected in Lawrence's *Nights of the Round Table* (Hutchinson, 1926). This collection was reprinted in a popular edition as part of Hutchinson's Readers' Library series in 1947. The current text is based on the 1947 publication.

'The Twelve Apostles' was published in Scott's collection *Randalls Round* (Ernest Benn, 1929). The current text is based on the 1929 publication.

'The Book' was originally published in *The London Mercury* in September 1930 and was later collected in Irwin's *Madame Fears the Dark* (Chatto & Windus, 1935). The current text is based on the 1935 publication.

'Couching at the Door' was originally published in *The Cornhill Magazine* in December 1933 and later republished as the title story in Broster's collection *Couching at the Door* (William Heinemann, 1942). The current text is based on the 1942 publication.

'With and Without Buttons' was published posthumously in *Last Stories* (Brendin Publishing Company, 1938). The current text is based on the 1938 publication.

Obvious typographical errors and inconsistencies have been silently corrected. American spellings have been altered to British, and some punctuation has been modernised where it would not affect meaning.

1 The Weird of the Walfords

BY LOUISA BALDWIN

On a summer's day in the year 1860, I, Humphrey Walford, did a deed for which I should have been disinherited by my father and disowned by my ancestors. I laid sacrilegious hands on the old carved oak four-post family bedstead and destroyed it.

Alone I could not have accomplished the work of destruction. The massive posts, canopy, and panels would have resisted my single efforts; but I compelled two reluctant men to lend me their aid, and by the help of saws and hatchets we reduced the whole structure to billets of wood such as one might kindle a cheerful flame with in the parlour grate on a damp summer evening.

It was a bed with a history to me so unspeakably melancholy that I had resolved when I was my own master I would destroy the gloomy structure, and rid me of the nightmare-like feeling with which the sight of it never failed to inspire me.

The bed itself was upwards of three hundred years old, carved in oak grown on our land, while the heavy dark-green hangings, faded and musty-smelling, dated only from the time of my great-grandfather Walford. I have the dimensions of the huge hearse-like thing by heart. It was ten feet long by eight feet wide, and ten feet high; and when as a small child I was brought to see my young mother die in the recesses of the vast bed, I looked up at its tall posts with something of the awe with which I should now regard the loftiest tree.

For three centuries this bed had been the cradle and grave of our family. Its heavy drapery had deadened the sound of the first cry and the last groan of the generations of Walfords who had been born or died in Walford Grange. In its solemn depths the newly-wedded brides of the family lay the first few nights in their new home, till the wedding festivities were ended, and the squire and his wife began their every-day married life by occupying a less stately but more comfortable bed. I knew the history of the gloomy old piece of furniture as family tradition had preserved it for three centuries. Ten Squire Walfords had either died in that bed or had lain on it after death awaiting their burial. I was the eleventh squire dating from the epoch of the bed, and I would neither die in it nor be laid upon it after my death. And to make sure of this there was no way but now, in my youth and strength, to fall upon it with hatchet and saw and utterly destroy it.

I did not fear death more than my forefathers, but I resented being bidden by family tradition and custom to die in a given spot. I rebelled at having a definite place assigned to me to lie down in and die – a place so fraught with dismal associations as the ancient, hearse-like bed. I could not endure to think that, wander wide as I would, I must return to this bed of death at last, and here, among stifling pillows and heavy curtains, end my life precisely where it began.

Must this ghastly horror of my childhood be the goal towards which I tend? When I am sailing on mid-ocean, the ship ploughing her way through the furrows of the sea, shall I only be speeding, sooner or later, towards this dismal bed? When I climb mountains and breathe the keen air of the heights, is it but to end in the exclusion of light and air? must every step I take, every journey I make, be but a stage on the road that ends in the stifling pillows of this bed of death? No, a thousand times no, and I brought my axe down on the footboard with a crash.

How vividly both the dead and living who had occupied this ancient bed rose before my mind's eye! Here had lain Ralph Walford, killed in the Civil Wars, fighting for the king, and his wounded body was brought home and stretched on what had been his bridal bed to await his burial. And here died Squire Ralph's young widow, who, a short time after her husband's sad home-coming, gave birth to his posthumous child, and never again left this ill-omened bed till they carried her out feet foremost. Ralph Walford's brother Heneage, the next Squire, thought to make the old bed festive with gold and crimson hangings, to forget that his brother's corpse had lain on it, his orphan child been born in it, and his widow died in it, and by the upholsterer's wit to convert a hearse into a bridal bower.

Brighter times came to our family with the Restoration. We had spent our blood and treasure in the king's cause, for which he did not suffer us to go unhonoured; for shortly after his joyful restoration his gracious majesty was travelling within ten miles of Walford Grange, and, the weather proving stormy, and there being no other Royalist house of consideration near, he made shift to pass a night under the roof of his faithful servant Heneage Walford.

My father often told me the history of that memorable visit, as it had been handed down from generation to generation. How gracious and witty was the king's majesty, how merry and light-hearted, as little troubled by the murder of his royal father and the heavy misfortunes of his house as by the brave lives lost and families impoverished in his cause!

Squire Heneage was as loyal a man as ever drew sword for the king, yet he was heard to say that it was a cursed day for him when his gracious majesty honoured him by being his guest, for it turned his wife Mistress Johanna's head, and she was never again the woman she had been. She grumbled and bemoaned herself that the king had not knighted her husband, so that she might have ruffled it a step above the squirearchy. But one abiding comfort remained with her from the royal visit. And this was that both at coming and going the king had saluted her, and she ever after prettily described the royal manner of kissing, which she affirmed to differ from that practised by ordinary men. Mistress Johanna's serving woman, Anne Grimshaw, said that the king had saluted her too; but this her mistress would not hear of, and when she appealed to Squire Heneage he set the vexed question at rest by giving his opinion that, judging it as a matter of probability, it was more likely that a vain woman should lie, than that his sacred majesty should kiss Anne Grimshaw, who had a foul face of her own.

If I have somewhat enlarged on the fact of the king's visit to Walford Grange, it is not so much on account of any tokens of his royal favour that he was pleased to bestow on my ancestors, as because he lay in the best chamber, in the great oak bed with its brave new hangings. But the king was tormented by terrible dreams, and woke in the morning haggard and weary, as though he had been ridden by witches. And that I attributed to a malign influence in the hearse-like bed itself, and with that I crashed into it afresh.

I had long promised myself this fierce destructive joy, when I in my turn should be master of Walford Grange. My father had died in this bed three years ago, and I had been travelling in the south of Europe ever since, urged partly by the restless curiosity of youth, and partly by the belief that no Squire Walford had ever crossed the seas before. Some younger sons and thriftless members of our family, in pursuit of the fortune denied them at home, had ventured into foreign lands, but the head of the house never. My father met any wishes or arguments I advanced on the subject of travel by a statement that seemed to him conclusive – that a man sees enough in his own country that he can't understand, without going abroad to complete his confusion. But now on my return home I hastened to carry out my design on the hated ancestral bed.

What consternation prevailed in the house when it was understood what I was about, and when I and Gillam the carpenter and his man, having stripped the great bed of its drapery, proceeded to take to pieces the panels of the carved oak canopy! Mrs Barrett, the old housekeeper, stood wiping her honest eyes and bewailing my impiety.

'Don't 'ee do it, squire, don't 'ee do it! You may come to know the want of a good feather bed to die in yet! Such a bed as it's been for lyings in and layings out, and I'd hoped to ha' seen you laid in it, like your poor father before you.'

What Mrs Barrett's expectation of life may have been I know not, but she was sixty-five, and I twenty-four years of age.

'My good Barrett, I have determined that this bed shall utterly perish. We will not contribute one more corpse to its greedy maw. But if it be its feathers that you bewail, you are welcome to its pillows to line your nest with, but the bed itself must perish.'

'What, squire, the bed that your great uncle Geoffrey was found dead in, when he'd gone upstairs over-night as well and as hearty as ever man was, and making his ungodly jokes, the Lord forgive him! The very bed as your grandfather lay in two whole years before he died, and all the house heard his groans; and where your Aunt Hester was laid with the water drip, drip, from every limb, just as they brought her in drowned from the brook!'

'Yes, my good Barrett, because of these very things the bed must perish.'

Then Gillam began, as he took off his paper cap and wiped his brow:

'If it's as the bed don't seem nateral like to sleep in after so many o' your kin has laid stiff and stark in it, won't you sell it, squire, to them as knows nothing of its ways? That there panel with the berried ivy on it is a deal too pretty a bit of carving to make firewood on.'

'No, Gillam, I shall not sell it. The man who would take money for the bed his ancestors died in, would sell their bones to make knife-handles of. Besides, the bed has existed long enough; it has served my family to die in for ten generations. It's my own property, Gillam; mayn't I do what I will with my own?'

'Ay, surely, squire; there's no law to hinder a man making any fool of hisself as he pleases wi' what's his own. But I sides with the chap as made the bedstead, and I shouldn't like to think as in a matter o' two or three hundred years a bit o' my work 'ud be chopped up for firing.'

'Be under no uneasiness, Gillam; you and I do not live in an age that produces lasting work. Our glue-and-tintack carpentry is not done with a view to posterity.'

'Well, squire,' continued Gillam, returning to his first idea, 'if you won't sell the bedstead whole nor piecemeal, you might give me them panels with the carved ivy on 'em. I could find you some bits o' wood as 'ud burn brighter and better.'

'I don't mind giving you the old ivy carving, Gillam,' I said, 'but only on condition that I shall never see anything more of it, in any shape or form.'

'That's easy promised, sir, and thank you kindly. I'll make it up into something as'll surprise itself.'

Having weakly consented to his request, I saw him lay aside two or three beautiful panels, richly carved with branches of berried ivy, as salvage from the general wreck. If the gloomy horrors of the old bed had not eaten into my very heart, I could never have lent a hand at such a work of destruction. I should at least have saved the footboard with its carving in high relief of Adam and Eve under the tree, a man-headed serpent twining round the trunk, and the branches bending beneath their load of fruit. But I could not look at it without thinking of the dying eyes that had fixed their fading gaze on it, so my axe and saw made havoc of a work of art. When the floor was littered over with billets of wood, and the men were wiping their hot faces, I felt a strange lightness of heart, a comfortable sense of work postponed at length happily accomplished.

'Gillam,' I said, 'there was timber enough in that huge thing to build a man-of-war, drapery to make her sails, and rope enough for all her rigging.'

'Ay, there was a'most;' and, hastily throwing his tools into his basket, he added, sarcastically I thought, 'there'll be nothing else I can help you to pull down or to smash up, squire?'

I soon found that my destructive toil had benefited me in more ways than one. Not only had it freed me from an intolerable oppression of spirit, but it had established for me in the neighbourhood a reputation for eccentricity, which I maintained afterwards at the smallest cost, and found of great service. The carrying out of my long-cherished purpose was regarded as evidence of a wild and lawless disposition, bordering on mental derangement. Night after night at the alehouse Gillam recounted to a breathless audience the story of the scene of destruction at which he had assisted professionally. And it grew in the telling till, without the slightest intention of lying, he added that the squire's rage against the old place was such, that he had been obliged to menace him with the screwdriver to keep him from tearing down the mantelshelf and wainscot.

I was evidently a man whom it was not wise to thwart or contradict. My servants flew at my least word with an alacrity I had not before observed. My bidding was promptly done, my orders were not disputed, and whatever I said was agreed to with servility. While enjoying the sweets of mental health, as my neighbours voted me on such insufficient grounds on the borderland of insanity, I availed myself of the liberty it gave me to speak and act as I chose. Their hasty judgment had made me free of the wide domain of conduct. There was nothing I could do, however extravagant, but was clearly shadowed forth in the destruction of the ancestral oak bed.

I began to grow lonely in Walford Grange. My good Barrett died suddenly, and in my solitude I wanted someone to sit and talk with me in the long evenings, for even the bright wood fire flickering on the hearth could not satisfy all my desires for cheerful companionship. I should not have wished to marry if I had had a brother to live with me, to share my thoughts and occupations, and who would himself marry and preserve the name. But I was the last of the family, and I did not mean to let an ancient race die out.

I began seriously to think of marrying, though whom, I had not an idea, for so far I had not seen the woman I should care to marry, nor could I suppose that anyone looked with an eye of favour upon me. But when a man makes up his mind to marry, and sets out on his travels by land and sea, resolved never to return to his home till he brings a wife with him, it would be hard if he could not effect his purpose.

It happened that I met with my wife unexpectedly, and where I should have thought I was least likely to meet her – in a log house in the far west of America. Her name was Grace Calvert, and she was only eighteen years old, fair and fresh as an unfolding flower, and full of the high spirits and delight of life suited to her age and her free and simple bringing up. I fell in love with her at first sight, and we were married after a short courtship, for I had obtained the object of my travel, and my little wife was wild with curiosity and impatience to see England. She had a most romantic conception of the land of her forefathers, and delighted me by her belief that every village in England contained a church, vast and venerable as

Westminster Abbey, and was engirt with hills crowned by frowning fortresses.

Grace had never seen houses built either of brick or stone, and had I not been able to show her a photograph of Walford Grange, it would have been impossible to give her any idea of an object so strange that there was nothing within the narrow limits of her experience with which to compare it. Her imagination was greatly stirred by the picture of the old house. Not a detail escaped her, from the fluted chimneys to the stone seats in the wide porch. The oriel windows, with their diamond panes, pleased my young wife more than anything, and especially she admired the broad windows of the best bed-chamber, in which some two years before I had wrought my destructive will on the ancestral bed. The room was now bare and stripped of furniture, and since Mrs Barrett's death I had kept it constantly locked.

Grace was fascinated with the position of the room, with its large window over the porch, looking down the avenue of limes by which the house was approached, to the open country, and the line of low hills that bounded the horizon.

'That room must be lighter than those on the ground floor,' she said, 'see how the upper story projects and throws a shadow over the lower rooms. We will make it our sitting-room, will we not?'

The request gave me a strange sinking of heart, and I felt that not even the society of my young wife could induce me to live in the room that had so long contained the hearse-like bed. I temporised with her in a vague manner, neither granting nor denying her request. I begged her to wait till she could see for herself how much better adapted to the comfort of daily life were the rooms on the ground-floor than those on the upper story.

In all her short life, Grace had not been further than twenty miles from the spot where she was born, and I feared lest taking her away from all she loved, and from everything with which she was familiar, might prove too keen a pain.

There was a brief tempest of tears at parting with the dear ones she was never to meet again, but it was an April shower succeeded by smiles. Each outburst of weeping was of shorter duration, and the sunny intervals between them were longer, till in a few days Grace was her bright self again. The excitement of the journey was so overwhelming as to swallow up every other feeling.

We reached our home one November afternoon, as the setting sun looked out through a rift in the clouds, and his level beams lighted up every casement with a red glow. As we drove up the leafless avenue, heavy drops fell from the bare boughs overhead, and Grace, clinging to my arm, said in a frightened whisper –

'O Humphrey, that light in the window is not like sunshine! It looks as if your old house was on fire!' and raising my eyes I caught for one moment the full effect of the illusion. But, the sun sinking into his bed of cloud, the red glow faded from the windows and left them dark and dim. 'Welcome, my darling, to your English home!' I said, and I took my little wife by the hand and led her up the wide oak staircase; and before we sat down to our evening meal I had taken her over the house from garret to basement, preceding her, candle in hand, through the darkening rooms.

She expressed unbounded admiration for the house and its furniture, but the old family portraits and pictures excited her utmost enthusiasm, for Grace had never seen anything more venerable or older than her grandparents and the log house in which she was born. When her raptures had toned down sufficiently to allow her to eat a little, and we were seated at supper in the oak parlour, my little wife suddenly said: –

'Humphrey, there ought to be a ghost in a house like this.'

'Why should there be?' I asked, while I smiled at her extreme gravity.

'Because so many generations of men and women cannot have been born and died in this house without leaving some trace of themselves for us who come after,' and I saw that works of fiction had penetrated into the far west, for Grace had certainly been reading romances.

'I object to talking about ghosts at supper,' I said; 'breakfast is the best time for such conversation, and not a word should be uttered on the subject later than twelve o'clock at noon,' and I rose, and taking one of the candles with me, and holding it so as to throw the light on a dark painting over the mantelshelf, I asked –

'Do you know who that is?'

My little wife looked earnestly at the portrait, with her head inclined dubiously, and with a puzzled expression of face.

'I am not surprised that you do not know who that dark sinister-looking man is, for the backwoods of America are not hung with portraits of Charles the Second. Yes, that is King Charles; and the melancholy cast of his features must be merely an inherited expression – certainly nothing in his nature answered to it – for he passed through grief and tragedy with a light heart. He once spent a night in this very house; we have the tradition of his visit, with many quaint details, preserved to this day.'

'Oh how wonderful to think of it!' said Grace eagerly; 'and would the king sup in this very room where you and I are now?'

'Yes, in this very room, and would you like to know what he had for supper?'

'No, that is not the kind of thing that makes me curious. I want to know how the king looked, how he was dressed, and in which of those solemn-looking old bedrooms upstairs he slept. No doubt you still have the bed the king slept in?'

'No,' I replied with decision, 'that I am sure we have not.'

'Then to-morrow, Humphrey, you will shew me the room the king slept in, and the bed I can imagine for myself.'

The bed she could imagine for herself! My little wife did not know what she was talking about. The next day the event occurred which might have been expected. I was walking in the garden, when Grace came to me, and slipping her hand through my arm, drew me towards the porch.

'You see that large window,' she said, pointing towards it as she spoke; 'that is the one I admired so much in the picture of the house. I have looked out of every window but that, and I fancy the room must be locked, for I cannot open it, so I have fetched you to unlock it for me.'

I walked in silence by her side while she led me into the house and upstairs to the door of the hated room, talking with so much animation herself that she did not notice that I had not spoken a word.

'This is the room,' she said gaily, and she turned the latch of the door to and fro, saying as she did so, 'You see it is locked.'

'I know it is,' I said sullenly.

'Then fetch the key and open it,' and Grace gave the door handle a little impetuous shake.

'My dearest, don't ask me again to open that door, for I shall not do it.'

'Not do what I ask you to do? How cruel of you!' and her eyes filled with tears.

I knew that my young wife thought me brutal, but I could only say 'Anything else in my power I will do for you, only this one thing, this one little thing, I beg you will not ask me to do.'

'If you admit that it is such a very small thing, there can be no reason why you should refuse to grant me such a trivial request,' persisted Grace; 'when I ask you simply to unlock a door in your own house, and you refuse to do it, I can only think that you do not love me, or else that there is some horrid mystery about the room that you wish to keep hidden from me;' and she wiped away a hasty tear, that proceeded rather from indignation than from grief.

'My dear Grace, do not let us be tragic about nothing. There is no secret connected with this room that I have ever heard of, and I love you so much that I cannot bear to see you troubling yourself with absurd imaginations. The fact is this. I have a feeling – call it superstition, what you will – but I have a feeling that would make it very painful to me to open this door and take you into the room. And what pleasure could there be in seeing a bare, unfurnished room, precisely like any other empty room?'

'But I should set about furnishing it at once.'

'Let us come away,' I said, gently removing her dear obstinate hand from the lock. 'I repeat, I have a feeling about that room that would prevent my ever being happy in it,' and, I added lightly, 'Don't let my Eve spoil our paradise by longing after the forbidden fruit.'

But Grace said quickly, 'It was not Adam who forbade Eve to eat of the fruit. If it had been, I can't see that there would have been any great harm in disobeying him.' And we said no more about the locked door, but a cloud had come between us, and the unalloyed sweetness of our first happiness was lost.

One day, a few weeks after this folly, when I was beginning to hope that my little wife had forgotten her curiosity, I saw from her constrained and uneasy manner that something had happened to disturb her.

'My dear Grace, you certainly are not happy this morning – will you not tell me what ails you?' I asked.

Her voice trembled and her face flushed as she replied. 'Humphrey, I did not think you could tell me an untruth.'

'My child, what do you mean? We are playing at cross purposes. Be so good as to explain your meaning, that we may not misunderstand each other for a moment.'

'You told me that the big bed-room you keep locked was empty.'

'So it is,' I said, growing impatient at this childish scene, 'but what is the untruth I have told you?'

'Why, the room is not empty. I can prove what I say.'

'The room not empty! Nonsense! I keep the key, and none but myself has entered it these two years.'

'How can you persist in such an untruth, Humphrey? I am not ashamed to confess that I looked through the keyhole – I wonder I did not do it before – and I saw in the middle of the room, between the door and the window, an enormous old bed. I could only see the two foot-posts, but they went up to the ceiling, and the footboard was high and richly carved, and the curtains a gloomy, dark green. So you have deceived me about the room, and I am afraid there is some secret connected with it that you dare not tell me. What ails you, Humphrey?' and my wife rose with a terrified exclamation, for I thought I was fainting, and all the life seemed to have gone out of the air.

'Grace,' I said, when I had shaken off the sense of oppression, 'let us go at once to that unlucky room, and settle this preposterous dispute. You say that the room has furniture in it – I say that it is empty. We will see which of us is right, and then we will never mention the subject again,' and I asked my wife to come with me and assure herself that the room was, as I said, absolutely bare and unfurnished. My hand shook as I turned the key, and, flinging the door open till it strained on its hinges, we entered the room together.

Grace shrank back with a low cry, and covered her face with her hands.

'Where is it gone to, the great bed that I saw standing on this very spot? I cannot have been deceived. O Humphrey! why do you play me such cruel tricks? You terrify me.'

'My little wife,' I said, assuming an air of cheerfulness I was far from feeling, 'this comes of what I must call your overweening curiosity. If my dear girl had been content to let me keep this door locked, she would not have grown so curious that her little brain is almost turned, and she has taken to seeing housewifely spectral illusions of domestic furniture. Depend upon it, what you think you saw was nothing but the creature of your own imagination, that has dwelt so long on the idea of furnishing the room that you have only to peep through the keyhole, and, hey, presto! the thing is done, and beds and tables start forward at your bidding. But henceforward you can enter the room as often as you like, only we will not live in it, and I will not have it furnished.'

This appeared to satisfy Grace, and though I could not fully persuade her that the great bed she had seen when she peeped through the keyhole was an illusion begotten of curiosity and a lively imagination, yet with the door of the room unlocked, she felt that she had some control over any tricks I might play her in the future.

I was deeply disturbed by what she had told me. I had not breathed a word to my wife about the destruction of the ancestral bed. Mrs Barrett was dead before we were married, and I had changed my servants since her death, and, as we saw nothing of our neighbours, Grace could not have heard from anyone of the ghastly old bed, which nevertheless she had accurately described to me.

I could never tell her the truth now. It would shake her nerves, and impress her with the idea that there was something weird about the house. I wished I had not destroyed the old bed. Better far that she should have known the gloomy reality than behold a presentment of it that was neither an embodiment of memory nor a vivid picturing of it from imagination. I tried if I could summon up a like hallucination, but in vain. Though my memory of the ancient bed was perfect, and every detail stamped on my mind, never could I call it up before my external vision, however earnestly I tried to do so.

Grace completely regained her accustomed cheerfulness, and in the spring was busy making a thousand little preparations for the expected arrival of an infant, which was to surpass any yet born into this world. I could hardly believe the gentle obstinacy of my wife, when, after all I had said about the empty room, she asked one day if she might not make it into a nursery.

'Do you not remember, dear, that I said we would not furnish that room?' I said.

'Oh, of course, not furnish it; a nursery needs no furniture; but it is much the most cheerful and sunny room in the house.'

And again I had to appear inhuman and refuse my little wife a trivial request.

One morning as I sat in my room busy with my accounts, Grace came to tell me that she was going to drive to the county town, some eight miles distant, for a round of shopping, such as her soul loved. I said that if she would wait till the next day I should be able to take her myself, but she tapped the barometer on the wall, that had stood for some time at 'set fair', and assured me it would rain to-morrow, and that she must avail herself of the fine weather to-day. So away drove my self-willed darling, nodding a gay farewell as the carriage drove away from the house.

Grace returned late in the afternoon in the best of spirits, bringing with her an enormous package, such as none but a country woman, or one, like my little wife from the far west, would dream of bringing with her in an open carriage. It must have broken the coachman's heart to drive with it through the streets of the county town.

'What in the name of wonder have you brought home with you?' I asked.

'Ah!' she said, laughing, 'it is a trial for your curiosity now! Anything else you may ask me I will tell you, only I cannot let you know anything about this mysterious package.'

'Then have it put out of sight,' I said, 'or depend upon it I shall find some hole in the wrapper to peep through. You ought to know what a devouring passion curiosity is.'

As the unwieldy bundle was carried upstairs, its cover slipped aside and revealed a pair of black oak rockers. But I said nothing; Grace should tell me her little secret in her own way, and at her own time.

We thought ourselves the happiest creatures in the world when our little son Heneage was born. The gloom that brooded over the house from the death of many generations was lessened by the joy of birth, and my young son's life was like the sprouting acorn that sends up its vigorous shoot through the earth, fed by the fallen leaves of a hundred autumns. On the third day of our happiness my wife sent for me, and told me she had a very pretty surprise for me.

'I can tell you all about the big mysterious package now. It was a beautiful old-fashioned cradle that I bought in Carlyon from a man called Gillam, who keeps an old furniture shop here. I fell in love with it at once, for I knew how well it would suit this house with its old oak. Gillam said he could swear it was old work; in fact, he said it was originally part of a fine old bedstead a poor mad gentleman in the neighbourhood actually destroyed in a fit of frenzy, but he was lucky enough to secure a portion of the wreck, and made it up into that cradle, and baby looks lovely in it. I'm afraid I gave a great deal of money for it, but one does not meet with such a beautiful thing every day,' and the nurse removed a screen from before the cradle, that its beauties might burst upon me suddenly and with the more effect.

Cold drops stood on my brow as I recognised, in the high sides and head of the cradle, the carving of ivy branches and berries I had so madly given Gillam when I destroyed the old bed.

'I thought you would have been so pleased,' said Grace, disappointed by my silence as I stood spell-bound, my eyes following every line of the hated carving. 'I thought you would have been so pleased to see baby in a cradle really worthy of him.'

But I could not speak; I was oppressed by a sense of coming doom.

'It is very unkind of you,' said Grace. 'I had prepared a pretty surprise for you, and instead of being pleased, you stand and sigh and look as if you saw a ghost. Nurse, take baby out of his lovely cradle; we must get him a common wicker thing to lie in instead!' And the nurse did as her mistress bade her, and lifted little Heneage from his cradle of death, for while we talked the child had slept his feeble life away.

I have no memory of what happened day by day during the few weeks following. It was one consuming fear lest my wife too should die. Six weeks after our child's death I carried her downstairs, and this was the only progress made towards recovery. She remained at the same stage of convalescence, made wayward by grief, with shattered nerves, and so weak in mind and body that I dared not thwart her in anything. As the dim, sunless days of autumn drew on, my little wife said to me as though we had never spoken on the subject before –

'I want the big empty room furnished for my sitting-room, Humphrey. I shall have a little sunshine there sometimes to cheer me in your dismal English winter, and it will amuse me to furnish it.'

As I looked at her white wishful face, I felt that nothing mattered to me now, and I said, 'Do exactly as you like, dear, in everything,' and she was too listless to thank me.

But the work of transforming the sombre room into a bright boudoir proceeded rapidly, for Grace said with a shudder, 'I will have no more old oak furniture.'

My little wife always went to extremes, and now, in her antipathy to old oak, she filled the room with tawdry chips of furniture, chairs made of gilded match-sticks tied together with ribbons, that must sink into feeble ruins if a cat so much as jumped on them.

I entered into all her little fancies, and feigned excessive admiration of each fresh idea she had on the subject of decoration. I did her bidding, even to placing her couch on the very spot where the hated bed had stood. Thus was my resistance broken down, and I, who three years ago had tried by sheer physical force to thwart destiny, was now unconsciously working to bring about its fulfilment. It did not tarry long.

One gloomy November afternoon, Grace lay on her couch covered with soft shawls, and the window curtains were drawn back to give as much light as possible. The glow of the setting sun illuminated the room, and lent a more living hue to the grey pallor of her face.

'How like the day when I first came to Walford Grange!' she said; 'the sun is setting with the same fiery light. Do go into the garden, Humphrey, and see if the windows are aglow with red light as they were then.' And I left her to do as she asked me.

Seen from the garden, the house looked precisely as it had done on the day of our homecoming. From garret to basement every window glowed red in the light of the setting sun, as though from fire within. Everything that my eyes rested on was as it had been a year ago. Grace and I only were changed – changed in ourselves and changed to each other. I felt impatient of the changeless aspect of nature and of inanimate things around me, and I entered the house, now dark in contrast with the twilight without, and returned to my wife's room with a heavy heart.

'The house looks as it did when you first saw it,' I said. 'Till the sun sank behind the hill, the windows were lighted up with the same strange effect of fire that you noticed a year ago,' and I threw a fresh log on the embers as I spoke, sending a bright train of sparks up the wide chimney. 'Shall I light the candles?' I asked, turning towards my wife's couch; 'the room is growing dark.' But there was no reply. I was speaking to the dead.

In vain I had baulked the old bed of its prey, for there on the very spot where it had stood for three centuries and generations of my ancestors had died, the wife of the last of the Walfords lay dead.

I buried my sweet Grace by our little son, and on the night of the funeral, alone in my desolate home, I conceived the idea of freeing myself for ever from the horror of darkness that had fallen on Walford Grange. I sent every servant away. I would have the house and my sorrow to myself.

When I was assured that I was alone in the house, I went rapidly from room to room in a strange exultation, speaking aloud and flinging open doors and windows till the cold night air rushed through chambers and passages, and curtains and hangings flapped in the wind.

'When I destroyed the old bed of death,' I said, 'I thought to restore joy and brightness to Walford Grange. But I should have destroyed not it alone, but the room in which it stood, and the very house of which it formed a part. Never more shall man dwell in this house glutted with death. Never more shall the voice of the bride and bridegroom be heard in its chambers, or footsteps of children be heard on its stairs. Never more shall fire, subdued to harmless household use be kindled on its hearth, but fire untamed in its ferocity shall devour the accursed pile.' And I seized the burning log from the hearth and threw it on the couch where Grace had died.

Carrying a lighted brand, I sped from room to room of the doomed house, leaving in each a fiery token of my presence, and then, descending the wide staircase, where flickering shadows were cast from every open door, and the silence was broken by the crackling sound of flames, I let myself out into the darkness, closing the heavy door behind me with a crash.

On through the cold damp air I ran, the moon through a rift in the clouds guiding me by her fitful light, till, drawing her shroud around her, she left me again in darkness. Not once did I turn to right or left or look behind me till I had gained the summit of the hills that bounded the valley. Then I stood and turned to take a last look at the home of my fathers. Just then the moon, issuing forth in cold splendour from her bed of cloud, shed a solemn lustre far and wide. And I saw for the last time the house of my birth, the cradle and grave of my race, and every window from basement to garret glowed with fire, no mere reflected glare, but red from the raging fire within, and keen flames darted from the casement of the room above the porch.

I stood long to watch the fire of my own kindling, till when a sudden burst of light and leaping splendour of flame showed me that the gabled roof had fallen in, I shouted, took off my hat, and waved a last farewell to Walford Grange.

2 Let Loose

BY MARY CHOLMONDELEY

> The dead abide with us! Though stark and cold
> Earth seems to grip them, they are with us still.

Some years ago I took up architecture, and made a tour
through Holland, studying the buildings of that interesting
country. I was not then aware that it is not enough to take
up art. Art must take you up, too. I never doubted but that
my passing enthusiasm for her would be returned. When
I discovered that she was a stern mistress, who did not
immediately respond to my attentions, I naturally transferred
them to another shrine. There are other things in the world
besides art. I am now a landscape gardener.

But at the time of which I write I was engaged in a
violent flirtation with architecture. I had one companion on
this expedition, who has since become one of the leading
architects of the day. He was a thin, determined-looking
man with a screwed-up face and heavy jaw, slow of speech,
and absorbed in his work to a degree which I quickly found
tiresome. He was possessed of a certain quiet power of
overcoming obstacles which I have rarely seen equalled. He
has since become my brother-in-law, so I ought to know; for
my parents did not like him much and opposed the marriage,
and my sister did not like him at all, and refused him over
and over again; but, nevertheless, he eventually married her.

I have thought since that one of his reasons for choosing
me as his travelling companion on this occasion was because
he was getting up steam for what he subsequently termed 'an
alliance with my family', but the idea never entered my head

at the time. A more careless man as to dress I have rarely met, and yet, in all the heat of July in Holland, I noticed that he never appeared without a high, starched collar, which had not even fashion to commend it at that time.

I often chaffed him about his splendid collars, and asked him why he wore them, but without eliciting any response. One evening, as we were walking back to our lodgings in Middleberg, I attacked him for about the thirtieth time on the subject.

'Why on earth do you wear them?' I said.

'You have, I believe, asked me that question many times,' he replied, in his slow, precise utterance; 'but always on occasions when I was occupied. I am now at leisure, and I will tell you.'

And he did.

I have put down what he said, as nearly in his own words as I can remember them.

✕

Ten years ago, I was asked to read a paper on English frescoes at the Institute of British Architects. I was determined to make the paper as good as I could, down to the slightest details, and I consulted many books on the subject, and studied every fresco I could find. My father, who had been an architect, had left me, at his death, all his papers and note-books on the subject of architecture. I searched them diligently, and found in one of them a slight unfinished sketch of nearly fifty years ago that specially interested me. Underneath was noted, in his clear, small hand – *Frescoed east wall of crypt. Parish Church. Wet Waste-on-the-Wolds, Yorkshire (via Pickering).*

The sketch had such a fascination for me that I decided to go there and see the fresco for myself. I had only a very vague idea as to where Wet Waste-on-the-Wolds was, but I was ambitious for the success of my paper; it was hot in London, and I set off on my long journey not without a certain degree of pleasure, with my dog Brian, a large nondescript brindled creature, as my only companion.

I reached Pickering, in Yorkshire, in the course of the afternoon, and then began a series of experiments on local lines which ended, after several hours, in my finding myself deposited at a little out-of-the-world station within nine or ten miles of Wet Waste. As no conveyance of any kind was to be had, I shouldered my portmanteau, and set out on a long white road that stretched away into the distance over the bare, treeless wold. I must have walked for several hours, over a waste of moorland patched with heather, when a doctor passed me, and gave me a lift to within a mile of my destination. The mile was a long one, and it was quite dark by the time I saw the feeble glimmer of lights in front of me, and found that I had reached Wet Waste. I had considerable difficulty in getting any one to take me in; but at last I persuaded the owner of the public-house to give me a bed, and, quite tired out, I got into it as soon as possible, for fear he should change his mind, and fell asleep to the sound of a little stream below my window.

I was up early next morning, and inquired directly after breakfast the way to the clergyman's house, which I found was close at hand. At Wet Waste everything was close at hand. The whole village seemed composed of a straggling row of one-storied grey stone houses, the same colour as the stone walls that separated the few fields enclosed from the surrounding waste, and as the little bridges over the beck that ran down one side of the grey wide street. Everything was grey. The church, the low tower of which I could see at a little distance, seemed to have been built of the same stone; so was the parsonage when I came up to it, accompanied on my way by a mob of rough, uncouth children, who eyed me and Brian with half-defiant curiosity.

The clergyman was at home, and after a short delay I was admitted. Leaving Brian in charge of my drawing materials, I followed the servant into a low panelled room, in which, at a latticed window, a very old man was sitting. The morning light fell on his white head bent low over a litter of papers and books.

'Mr er—?' he said, looking up slowly, with one finger keeping his place in a book.

'Blake.'

'Blake,' he repeated after me, and was silent.

I told him that I was an architect; that I had come to study a fresco in the crypt of his church, and asked for the keys.

'The crypt,' he said, pushing up his spectacles and peering hard at me. 'The crypt has been closed for thirty years. Ever since –' and he stopped short.

'I should be much obliged for the keys,' I said again.

He shook his head.

'No,' he said. 'No one goes in there now.'

'It is a pity,' I remarked, 'for I have come a long way with that one object,' and I told him about the paper I had been asked to read, and the trouble I was taking with it.

He became interested. 'Ah!' he said, laying down his pen, and removing his finger from the page before him, 'I can understand that. I also was young once, and fired with ambition. The lines have fallen to me in somewhat lonely places, and for forty years I have held the cure of souls in this place, where, truly, I have seen but little of the world, though I myself may be not unknown in the paths of literature. Possibly you may have read a pamphlet, written by myself, on the Syrian version of the Three Authentic Epistles of Ignatius?'

'Sir,' I said, 'I am ashamed to confess that I have not time to read even the most celebrated books. My one object in life is my art. *Ars longa, vita brevis*, you know.'

'You are right, my son,' said the old man, evidently disappointed, but looking at me kindly. 'There are diversities of gifts, and if the Lord has entrusted you with a talent, look to it. Lay it not up in a napkin.'

I said I would not do so if he would lend me the keys of the crypt. He seemed startled by my recurrence to the subject and looked undecided.

'Why not?' he murmured to himself. 'The youth appears a good youth. And superstition! What is it but distrust in God!'

He got up slowly, and taking a large bunch of keys out of his pocket, opened with one of them an oak cupboard in the corner of the room.

'They should be here,' he muttered, peering in; 'but the dust of many years deceives the eye. See, my son, if among these parchments there be two keys; one of iron and very large, and the other steel, and of a long and thin appearance.'

I went eagerly to help him, and presently found in a back drawer two keys tied together, which he recognized at once.

'Those are they,' he said. 'The long one opens the first door at the bottom of the steps which go down against the outside wall of the church hard by the sword graven in the wall. The second opens (but it is hard of opening and of shutting) the iron door within the passage leading to the crypt itself. My son, is it necessary to your treatise that you should enter this crypt?'

I replied that it was absolutely necessary.

'Then take them,' he said, 'and in the evening you will bring them to me again.'

I said I might want to go several days running, and asked if he would not allow me to keep them till I had finished my work; but on that point he was firm.

'Likewise,' he added, 'be careful that you lock the first door at the foot of the steps before you unlock the second, and lock the second also while you are within. Furthermore, when you come out lock the iron inner door as well as the wooden one.'

I promised I would do so, and, after thanking him, hurried away, delighted at my success in obtaining the keys. Finding Brian and my sketching materials waiting for me in the porch, I eluded the vigilance of my escort of children by taking the narrow private path between the parsonage and the church which was close at hand, standing in a quadrangle of ancient yews.

The church itself was interesting, and I noticed that it must have arisen out of the ruins of a previous building, judging from the number of fragments of stone caps and arches, bearing traces of very early carving, now built into the walls. There were incised crosses, too, in some places, and one especially caught my attention, being flanked by a large sword. It was in trying to get a nearer look at this that I stumbled, and, looking down, saw at my feet a flight of narrow stone steps green with moss and mildew. Evidently this was the entrance to the crypt. I at once descended the steps, taking care of my footing, for they were damp and slippery in the extreme. Brian accompanied me, as nothing would induce him to remain behind. By the time I had reached the bottom of the stairs, I found myself almost in darkness, and I had to strike a light before I could find the keyhole and the proper key to fit into it. The door, which was of wood, opened inwards fairly easily, although an accumulation of mould and rubbish on the ground outside showed it had not been used for many years. Having got through it, which was not altogether an easy matter, as nothing would induce it to open more than about eighteen inches, I carefully locked it behind me, although I should have preferred to leave it open, as there is to some minds an unpleasant feeling in being locked in anywhere, in case of a sudden exit seeming advisable.

I kept my candle alight with some difficulty, and after groping my way down a low and of course exceedingly dank passage, came to another door. A toad was squatting against it, who looked as if he had been sitting there about a hundred years. As I lowered the candle to the floor, he gazed at the light with unblinking eyes, and then retreated slowly into a crevice in the wall, leaving against the door a small cavity in the dry mud which had gradually silted up round his person. I noticed that this door was of iron, and had a long bolt, which, however, was broken. Without delay, I fitted the second key into the lock, and pushing the door open after considerable difficulty, I felt the cold breath of the crypt upon my face. I must own I experienced a momentary regret at locking the second door again as soon as I was well inside, but I felt it my duty to do so. Then, leaving the key in the lock, I seized my candle and looked round. I was standing in a low vaulted chamber with groined roof, cut out of the solid rock. It was difficult to see where the crypt ended, as further light thrown on any point only showed other rough archways or openings, cut in the rock, which had probably served at one time for family vaults. A peculiarity of the Wet Waste crypt, which I had not noticed in other places of that description, was the tasteful arrangement of skulls and bones which were packed about four feet high on either side. The skulls were symmetrically built up to within a few inches of the top of the low archway on my left, and the shin bones were arranged in the same manner on my right. *But the fresco!* I looked round for it in vain. Perceiving at the further end of the crypt a very low and very massive archway, the entrance to which was not filled up with bones, I passed under it, and found myself in a second smaller chamber. Holding my candle above my head, the first object its light fell upon was − the fresco, and at a glance I saw that it was unique. Setting down some of my things with a trembling hand on a rough stone shelf hard by, which had evidently been a credence table, I examined the work more closely. It was a reredos over what had probably been the altar at the time the priests were proscribed. The fresco belonged to the earliest part of the fifteenth century, and was so perfectly preserved that I could almost trace the limits of each day's work in the plaster, as the artist had dashed it on and smoothed it out with his trowel. The subject was the Ascension, gloriously treated. I can hardly describe my elation as I stood and looked at it, and reflected that this magnificent specimen of English fresco painting would be made known to the world by myself. Recollecting myself at last, I opened my sketching bag, and, lighting all the candles I had brought with me, set to work.

Brian walked about near me, and though I was not otherwise than glad of his company in my rather lonely position, I wished several times I had left him behind. He seemed restless, and even the sight of so many bones appeared to exercise no soothing effect upon him. At last, however, after repeated commands, he lay down, watchful but motionless, on the stone floor.

I must have worked for several hours, and I was pausing to rest my eyes and hands, when I noticed for the first time the intense stillness that surrounded me. No sound from *me* reached the outer world. The church clock which had clanged out so loud and ponderously as I went down the steps, had not since sent the faintest whisper of its iron tongue down to me below. All was silent as the grave. This *was* the grave. Those who had come here had indeed gone down into silence. I repeated the words to myself, or rather they repeated themselves to me.

Gone down into silence.

I was awakened from my reverie by a faint sound. I sat still and listened. Bats occasionally frequent vaults and underground places.

The sound continued, a faint, stealthy, rather unpleasant sound. I do not know what kinds of sounds bats make, whether pleasant or otherwise. Suddenly there was a noise as of something falling, a momentary pause – and then – an almost imperceptible but distant jangle as of a key.

I had left the key in the lock after I had turned it, and I now regretted having done so. I got up, took one of the candles, and went back into the larger crypt – for though I trust I am not so effeminate as to be rendered nervous by hearing a noise for which I cannot instantly account; still, on occasions of this kind, I must honestly say I should prefer that they did not occur. As I came towards the iron door, there was another distinct (I had almost said hurried) sound. The impression on my mind was one of great haste. When I reached the door, and held the candle near the lock to take out the key, I perceived that the other one, which hung by a short string to its fellow, was vibrating slightly. I should have preferred not to find it vibrating, as there seemed no occasion for such a course; but I put them both into my pocket, and turned to go back to my work. As I turned, I saw on the ground what had occasioned the louder noise I had heard, namely, a skull which had evidently just slipped from its place on the top of one of the walls of bones, and had rolled almost to my feet. There, disclosing a few more inches of the top of an archway behind was the place from which it had been dislodged. I stooped to pick it up, but fearing to displace any more skulls by meddling with the pile, and not liking to gather up its scattered teeth, I let it lie, and went back to my work, in which I was soon so completely absorbed that I was only roused at last by my candles beginning to burn low and go out one after another.

Then, with a sigh of regret, for I had not nearly finished, I turned to go. Poor Brian, who had never quite reconciled himself to the place, was beside himself with delight. As I opened the iron door he pushed past me, and a moment later

I heard him whining and scratching, and I had almost added, beating, against the wooden one. I locked the iron door, and hurried down the passage as quickly as I could, and almost before I had got the other one ajar there seemed to be a rush past me into the open air, and Brian was bounding up the steps and out of sight. As I stopped to take out the key, I felt quite deserted and left behind. When I came out once more into the sunlight, there was a vague sensation all about me in the air of exultant freedom.

It was already late in the afternoon, and after I had sauntered back to the parsonage to give up the keys, I persuaded the people of the public-house to let me join in the family meal, which was spread out in the kitchen. The inhabitants of Wet Waste were primitive people, with the frank, unabashed manner that flourishes still in lonely places, especially in the wilds of Yorkshire; but I had no idea that in these days of penny posts and cheap newspapers such entire ignorance of the outer world could have existed in any corner, however remote, of Great Britain.

When I took one of the neighbour's children on my knee – a pretty little girl with the palest aureole of flaxen hair I had ever seen – and began to draw pictures for her of the birds and beasts of other countries, I was instantly surrounded by a crowd of children, and even grown-up people, while others came to their doorways and looked on from a distance, calling to each other in the strident unknown tongue which I have since discovered goes by the name of 'Broad Yorkshire.'

The following morning, as I came out of my room, I perceived that something was amiss in the village. A buzz of voices reached me as I passed the bar, and in the next house I could hear through the open window a high-pitched wail of lamentation.

The woman who brought me my breakfast was in tears, and

in answer to my questions, told me that the neighbour's child, the little girl whom I had taken on my knee the evening before, had died in the night.

I felt sorry for the general grief that the little creature's death seemed to arouse, and the uncontrolled wailing of the poor mother took my appetite away.

I hurried off early to my work, calling on my way for the keys, and with Brian for my companion descended once more into the crypt, and drew and measured with an absorption that gave me no time that day to listen for sounds real or fancied. Brian, too, on this occasion seemed quite content, and slept peacefully beside me on the stone floor. When I had worked as long as I could, I put away my books with regret that even then I had not quite finished, as I had hoped to do. It would be necessary to come again for a short time on the morrow. When I returned the keys late that afternoon, the old clergyman met me at the door, and asked me to come in and have tea with him.

'And has the work prospered?' he asked, as we sat down in the long, low room, into which I had just been ushered, and where he seemed to live entirely.

I told him it had, and showed it to him.

'You have seen the original, of course?' I said.

'Once,' he replied, gazing fixedly at it. He evidently did not care to be communicative, so I turned the conversation to the age of the church.

'All here is old,' he said. 'When I was young, forty years ago, and came here because I had no means of mine own, and was much moved to marry at that time, I felt oppressed that all was so old; and that this place was so far removed from the world, for which I had at times longings grievous to be borne; but I had chosen my lot, and with it I was forced to be content. My son, marry not in youth, for love, which truly in that season is a mighty power, turns away the heart from study, and young children break the back of ambition. Neither marry in middle life, when a woman is seen to be but a woman and her talk a weariness, so you will not be burdened with a wife in your old age.'

I had my own views on the subject of marriage, for I am of opinion that a well-chosen companion of domestic tastes and docile and devoted temperament may be of material assistance to a professional man. But, my opinions once formulated, it is not of moment to me to discuss them with others, so I changed the subject, and asked if the neighbouring villages were as antiquated as Wet Waste.

'Yes, all about here is old,' he repeated. 'The paved road leading to Dyke Fens is an ancient pack road, made even in the time of the Romans. Dyke Fens, which is very near here, a matter of but four or five miles, is likewise old, and forgotten by the world. The Reformation never reached it. It stopped here. And at Dyke Fens they still have a priest and a bell, and bow down before the saints. It is a damnable heresy, and weekly I expound it as such to my people, showing them true doctrines; and I have heard that this same priest has so far yielded himself to the Evil One that he has preached against me as withholding gospel truths from my flock; but I take no heed of it, neither of his pamphlet touching the Clementine Homilies, in which he vainly contradicts that which I have plainly set forth and proven beyond doubt, concerning the word *Asaph*.'

The old man was fairly off on his favourite subject, and it was some time before I could get away. As it was, he followed me to the door, and I only escaped because the old clerk hobbled up at that moment, and claimed his attention.

The following morning I went for the keys for the third and last time. I had decided to leave early the next day. I was tired of Wet Waste, and a certain gloom seemed to my fancy to be gathering over the place. There was a sensation of trouble in the air, as if, although the day was bright and clear, a storm were coming.

This morning, to my astonishment, the keys were refused to me when I asked for them. I did not, however, take the refusal as final – I make it a rule never to take a refusal as final – and after a short delay I was shown into the room where, as usual, the clergyman was sitting, or rather, on this occasion, was walking up and down.

'My son,' he said with vehemence, 'I know wherefore you have come, but it is of no avail. I cannot lend the keys again.'

I replied that, on the contrary, I hoped he would give them to me at once.

'It is impossible,' he repeated. 'I did wrong, exceeding wrong. I will never part with them again.'

'Why not?'

He hesitated, and then said slowly:

'The old clerk, Abraham Kelly, died last night.' He paused, and then went on: 'The doctor has just been here to tell me of that which is a mystery to him. I do not wish the people of the place to know it, and only to me he has mentioned it, but he has discovered plainly on the throat of the old man, and also, but more faintly on the child's, marks as of strangulation. None but he has observed it, and he is at a loss how to account for it. I, alas! can account for it but in one way, but in one way!'

I did not see what all this had to do with the crypt, but to humour the old man, I asked what that way was.

'It is a long story, and, haply, to a stranger it may appear but foolishness, but I will even tell it; for I perceive that unless I furnish a reason for withholding the keys, you will not cease to entreat me for them.

'I told you at first when you inquired of me concerning the crypt, that it had been closed these thirty years, and so it was. Thirty years ago a certain Sir Roger Despard departed this life, even the Lord of the manor of Wet Waste and Dyke

Fens, the last of his family, which is now, thank the Lord, extinct. He was a man of a vile life, neither fearing God nor regarding man, nor having compassion on innocence, and the Lord appeared to have given him over to the tormentors even in this world, for he suffered many things of his vices, more especially from drunkenness, in which seasons, and they were many, he was as one possessed by seven devils, being an abomination to his household and a root of bitterness to all, both high and low.

'And, at last, the cup of his iniquity being full to the brim, he came to die, and I went to exhort him on his death-bed; for I heard that terror had come upon him, and that evil imaginations encompassed him so thick on every side, that few of them that were with him could abide in his presence. But when I saw him I perceived that there was no place of repentance left for him, and he scoffed at me and my superstition, even as he lay dying, and swore there was no God and no angel, and all were damned even as he was. And the next day, towards evening, the pains of death came upon him, and he raved the more exceedingly, inasmuch as he said he was being strangled by the Evil One. Now on his table was his hunting knife, and with his last strength he crept and laid hold upon it, no man withstanding him, and swore a great oath that if he went down to burn in hell, he would leave one of his hands behind on earth, and that it would never rest until it had drawn blood from the throat of another and strangled him, even as he himself was being strangled. And he cut off his own right hand at the wrist, and no man dared go near him to stop him, and the blood went through the floor, even down to the ceiling of the room below, and thereupon he died.

'And they called me in the night, and told me of his oath, and I counselled that no man should speak of it, and I took the dead hand, which none had ventured to touch, and I laid it beside him in his coffin; for I thought it better he should take it with him, so that he might have it, if haply some day after much tribulation he should perchance be moved to stretch forth his hands towards God. But the story got spread about, and the people were affrighted, so, when he came to be buried in the place of his fathers, he being the last of his family, and the crypt likewise full, I had it closed, and kept the keys myself, and suffered no man to enter therein any more; for truly he was a man of an evil life, and the devil is not yet wholly overcome, nor cast chained into the lake of fire. So in time the story died out, for in thirty years much is forgotten. And when you came and asked me for the keys, I was at the first minded to withhold them; but I thought it was a vain superstition, and I perceived that you do but ask a second time for what is first refused; so I let you have them, seeing it was not an idle curiosity, but a desire to improve the talent committed to you, that led you to require them.'

The old man stopped, and I remained silent, wondering what would be the best way to get them just once more.

'Surely, sir,' I said at last, 'one so cultivated and deeply read as yourself cannot be biased by an idle superstition.'

'I trust not,' he replied, 'and yet – it is a strange thing that since the crypt was opened two people have died, and the mark is plain upon the throat of the old man and visible on the young child. No blood was drawn, but the second time the grip was stronger than the first. The third time, perchance –'

'Superstition such as that,' I said with authority, 'is an entire want of faith in God. You once said so yourself.'

I took a high moral tone which is often efficacious with conscientious, humble-minded people.

He agreed, and accused himself of not having faith as a grain of mustard seed; but even when I had got him so far as that, I had a severe struggle for the keys. It was only when I finally explained to him that if any malign influence *had* been let loose the first day, at any rate, it was out now for good or evil, and no further going or coming of mine could make any difference, that I finally gained my point. I was young, and he was old; and, being much shaken by what had occurred, he gave way at last, and I wrested the keys from him.

I will not deny that I went down the steps that day with a vague, indefinable repugnance, which was only accentuated by the closing of the two doors behind me. I remembered then, for the first time, the faint jangling of the key and other sounds which I had noticed the first day, and how one of the skulls had fallen. I went to the place where it still lay. I have already said these walls of skulls were built up so high as to be within a few inches of the top of the low archways that led into more distant portions of the vault. The displacement of the skull in question had left a small hole just large enough for me to put my hand through. I noticed for the first time, over the archway above it, a carved coat-of-arms, and the name, now almost obliterated, of Despard. This, no doubt, was the Despard vault. I could not resist moving a few more skulls and looking in, holding my candle as near the aperture as I could. The vault was full. Piled high, one upon another, were old coffins, and remnants of coffins, and strewn bones. I attribute my present determination to be cremated to the painful impression produced on me by this spectacle. The coffin nearest the archway alone was intact, save for a large crack across the lid. I could not get a ray from my candle to fall on the brass plates, but I felt no doubt this was the coffin of the wicked Sir Roger. I put back the skulls, including the one which had rolled down, and carefully finished my work. I was not there much more than an hour, but I was glad to get away.

If I could have left Wet Waste at once I should have done so, for I had a totally unreasonable longing to leave the place; but I found that only one train stopped during the day at the station from which I had come, and that it would not be possible to be in time for it that day.

Accordingly I submitted to the inevitable, and wandered about with Brian for the remainder of the afternoon and until late in the evening, sketching and smoking. The day was oppressively hot, and even after the sun had set across the burnt stretches of the wolds, it seemed to grow very little cooler. Not a breath stirred. In the evening, when I was tired of loitering in the lanes, I went up to my own room, and after contemplating afresh my finished study of the fresco, I suddenly set to work to write the part of my paper bearing upon it. As a rule, I write with difficulty, but that evening words came to me with winged speed, and with them a hovering impression that I must make haste, that I was much pressed for time. I wrote and wrote, until my candles guttered out and left me trying to finish by the moonlight, which, until I endeavoured to write by it, seemed as clear as day.

I had to put away my MS, and, feeling it was too early to go to bed, for the church clock was just counting out ten, I sat down by the open window and leaned out to try and catch a breath of air. It was a night of exceptional beauty; and as I looked out my nervous haste and hurry of mind were allayed. The moon, a perfect circle, was – if so poetic an expression be permissible – as it were, sailing across a calm sky. Every detail of the little village was as clearly illuminated by its beams as if it were broad day; so, also, was the adjacent church with its primeval yews, while even the wolds beyond were dimly indicated, as if through tracing paper.

I sat a long time leaning against the window-sill. The heat was still intense. I am not, as a rule, easily elated or readily cast down; but as I sat that night in the lonely village on the moors, with Brian's head against my knee, how, or why, I know not, a great depression gradually came upon me.

My mind went back to the crypt and the countless dead who had been laid there. The sight of the goal to which all human life, and strength, and beauty, travel in the end, had not affected me at the time, but now the very air about me seemed heavy with death.

What was the good, I asked myself, of working and toiling, and grinding down my heart and youth in the mill of long and strenuous effort, seeing that in the grave folly and talent, idleness and labour lie together, and are alike forgotten? Labour seemed to stretch before me till my heart ached to think of it, to stretch before me even to the end of life, and then came, as the recompense of my labour – the grave. Even if I succeeded, if, after wearing my life threadbare with toil, I succeeded, what remained to me in the end? The grave. A little sooner, while the hands and eyes were still strong to labour, or a little later, when all power and vision had been taken from them; sooner or later only – *the grave*.

I do not apologise for the excessively morbid tenor of these reflections, as I hold that they were caused by the lunar effects which I have endeavoured to transcribe. The moon in its various quarterings has always exerted a marked influence on what I may call the sub-dominant, namely, the poetic side of my nature.

I roused myself at last, when the moon came to look in upon me where I sat, and, leaving the window open, I pulled myself together and went to bed.

I fell asleep almost immediately, but I do not fancy I could have been asleep very long when I was wakened by Brian. He was growling in a low, muffled tone, as he sometimes did in his sleep, when his nose was buried in his rug. I called out to him to shut up; and as he did not do so, turned in bed to find my match box or something to throw at him. The moonlight was still in the room, and as I looked at him I saw him raise his head and evidently wake up. I admonished him, and was just on the point of falling asleep when he began to growl again in a low, savage manner that waked me most effectually. Presently he shook himself and got up, and began prowling about the room. I sat up in bed and called to him, but he paid no attention. Suddenly I saw him stop short in the moonlight; he showed his teeth, and crouched down, his eyes following something in the air. I looked at him in horror. Was he going mad? His eyes were glaring, and his head moved slightly as if he were following the rapid movements of an enemy. Then, with a furious snarl, he suddenly sprang from the ground, and rushed in great leaps across the room towards me, dashing himself against the furniture, his eyes rolling, snatching and tearing wildly in the air with his teeth. I saw he had gone mad. I leaped out of bed, and rushing at him, caught him by the throat. The moon had gone behind a cloud; but in the darkness I felt him turn upon me, felt him rise up, and his teeth close in my throat. I was being strangled. With all the strength of despair, I kept my grip of his neck, and, dragging him across the room, tried to crush in his head against the iron rail of my bedstead. It was my only chance. I felt the blood running down my neck. I was suffocating. After one moment of frightful struggle, I beat his head against the bar and heard his skull give way. I felt him give one strong shudder, a groan, and then I fainted away.

When I came to myself I was lying on the floor, surrounded by the people of the house, my reddened hands still clutching Brian's throat. Someone was holding a candle towards me, and the draught from the window made it flare and waver. I looked at Brian. He was stone dead. The blood from his battered head was trickling slowly over my hands. His great jaw was fixed in something that – in the uncertain light – I could not see.

They turned the light a little.

'Oh, God!' I shrieked. 'There! Look! Look!'

'He's off his head,' said some one, and I fainted again.

✕

I was ill for about a fortnight without regaining consciousness, a waste of time of which even now I cannot think without poignant regret. When I did recover consciousness, I found I was being carefully nursed by the old clergyman and the people of the house. I have often heard the unkindness of the world in general inveighed against, but for my part I can honestly say that I have received many more kindnesses than I have time to repay. Country people especially are remarkably attentive to strangers in illness.

I could not rest until I had seen the doctor who attended me, and had received his assurance that I should be equal to reading my paper on the appointed day. This pressing anxiety removed, I told him of what I had seen before I fainted the second time. He listened attentively, and then assured me, in a manner that was intended to be soothing, that I was suffering from an hallucination, due, no doubt, to the shock of my dog's sudden madness.

'Did you see the dog after it was dead?' I asked.

He said he did. The whole jaw was covered with blood and foam; the teeth certainly seemed convulsively fixed, but the case being evidently one of extraordinarily virulent hydrophobia, owing to the intense heat, he had had the body buried immediately.

✕

My companion stopped speaking as we reached our lodgings, and went upstairs. Then, lighting a candle, he slowly turned down his collar.

'You see I have the marks still,' he said, 'but I have no fear of dying of hydrophobia. I am told such peculiar scars could not have been made by the teeth of a dog. If you look closely you see the pressure of the five fingers. That is the reason why I wear high collars.'

3 The Giant Wistaria

BY CHARLOTTE PERKINS GILMAN

'Meddle not with my new vine, child! See! Thou hast already broken the tender shoot! Never needle or distaff for thee, and yet thou wilt not be quiet!'

The nervous fingers wavered, clutched at a small carnelian cross that hung from her neck, then fell despairingly.

'Give me my child, mother, and then I will be quiet!'

'Hush! hush! thou fool – some one might be near! See – there is thy father coming, even now! Get in quickly!'

She raised her eyes to her mother's face, weary eyes that yet had a flickering, uncertain blaze in their shaded depths.

'Art thou a mother and hast no pity on me, a mother? Give me my child!'

Her voice rose in a strange, low cry, broken by her father's hand upon her mouth.

'Shameless!' said he, with set teeth. 'Get to thy chamber, and be not seen again to-night, or I will have thee bound!'

She went at that, and a hard-faced serving woman followed, and presently returned, bringing a key to her mistress.

'Is all well with her – and the child also?'

'She is quiet, Mistress Dwining, well for the night, be sure. The child fretteth endlessly, but save for that it thriveth with me.'

The parents were left alone together on the high square porch with its great pillars, and the rising moon began to make faint shadows of the young vine leaves that shot up luxuriantly around them; moving shadows, like little stretching fingers, on the broad and heavy planks of the oaken floor.

'It groweth well, this vine thou broughtest me in the ship, my husband.'

'Aye,' he broke in bitterly, 'and so doth the shame I brought thee! Had I known of it I would sooner have had the ship founder beneath us, and have seen our child cleanly drowned, than live to this end!'

'Thou art very hard, Samuel, art thou not afeard for her life? She grieveth sore for the child, aye, and for the green fields to walk in!'

'Nay,' said he grimly, 'I fear not. She hath lost already what is more than life; and she shall have air enough soon. To-morrow the ship is ready, and we return to England. None knoweth of our stain here, not one, and if the town hath a child unaccounted for to rear in decent ways – why, it is not the first, even here. It will be well enough cared for! And truly we have matter for thankfulness, that her cousin is yet willing to marry her.'

'Hast thou told him?'

'Aye! Thinkest thou I would cast shame into another man's house, unknowing it? He hath always desired her, but she would none of him, the stubborn! She hath small choice now!'

'Will he be kind, Samuel? Can he –'

'Kind? What call'st thou it to take such as she to wife? Kind! How many men would take her, an' she had double the fortune? And being of the family already, he is glad to hide the blot forever.'

'An' if she would not? He is but a coarse fellow, and she ever shunned him.'

'Art thou mad, woman? She weddeth him ere we sail to-morrow, or she stayeth ever in that chamber. The girl is not so sheer a fool! He maketh an honest woman of her, and saveth our house from open shame. What other hope for her than a new life to cover the old? Let her have an honest child, an' she so longeth for one!'

He strode heavily across the porch, till the loose planks creaked again, strode back and forth, with his arms folded and his brows fiercely knit above his iron mouth.

Overhead the shadows flickered mockingly across a white face among the leaves, with eyes of wasted fire.

⚹

'O, George, what a house! What a lovely house! I am sure it's haunted! Let us get that house to live in this summer! We will have Kate and Jack and Susy and Jim of course, and a splendid time of it!'

Young husbands are indulgent, but still they have to recognize facts.

'My dear, the house may not be to rent; and it may also not be habitable.'

'There is surely somebody in it. I am going to inquire!'

The great central gate was rusted off its hinges, and the long drive had trees in it, but a little footpath showed signs of steady usage, and up that Mrs Jenny went, followed by her obedient George. The front windows of the old mansion were blank, but in a wing at the back they found white curtains and open doors. Outside, in the clear May sunshine, a woman was washing. She was polite and friendly, and evidently glad of visitors in that lonely place. She 'guessed it could be rented – didn't know.' The heirs were in Europe, but 'there was a lawyer in New York had the lettin' of it.' There had been folks there years ago, but not in her time. She and her husband had the rent of their part for taking care of the place. Not that they took much care on't either, 'but keepin' robbers out.' It was furnished throughout, old-fashioned enough, but good; and 'if they took it she could do the work for 'em herself, she guessed – if *he* was willin'!'

Never was a crazy scheme more easily arranged. George knew that lawyer in New York; the rent was not alarming;

and the nearness to a rising sea-shore resort made it a still pleasanter place to spend the summer.

Kate and Jack and Susy and Jim cheerfully accepted, and the June moon found them all sitting on the high front porch.

They had explored the house from top to bottom, from the great room in the garret, with nothing in it but a rickety cradle, to the well in the cellar without a curb and with a rusty chain going down to unknown blackness below. They had explored the grounds, once beautiful with rare trees and shrubs, but now a gloomy wilderness of tangled shade.

The old lilacs and laburnums, the spirea and syringa, nodded against the second-story windows. What garden plants survived were great ragged bushes or great shapeless beds. A huge wistaria vine covered the whole front of the house. The trunk, it was too large to call a stem, rose at the corner of the porch by the high steps, and had once climbed its pillars; but now the pillars were wrenched from their places and held rigid and helpless by the tightly wound and knotted arms.

It fenced in all the upper story of the porch with a knitted wall of stem and leaf; it ran along the eaves, holding up the gutter that had once supported it; it shaded every window with heavy green; and the drooping, fragrant blossoms made a waving sheet of purple from roof to ground.

'Did you ever see such a wistaria!' cried ecstatic Mrs Jenny. 'It is worth the rent just to sit under such a vine – a fig tree beside it would be sheer superfluity and wicked extravagance!'

'Jenny makes much of her wistaria,' said George, 'because she's so disappointed about the ghosts. She made up her mind at first sight to have ghosts in the house, and she can't find even a ghost story!'

'No,' Jenny assented mournfully; 'I pumped poor Mrs Pepperill for three days, but could get nothing out of her. But I'm convinced there is a story, if we could only find it. You need not tell me that a house like this, with a garden like this, and a cellar like this, isn't haunted!'

'I agree with you,' said Jack. Jack was a reporter on a New York daily, and engaged to Mrs Jenny's pretty sister. 'And if we don't find a real ghost, you may be very sure I shall make one. It's too good an opportunity to lose!'

The pretty sister, who sat next him, resented. 'You shan't do anything of the sort, Jack! This is a *real* ghostly place, and I won't have you make fun of it! Look at that group of trees out there in the long grass – it looks for all the world like a crouching, hunted figure!'

'It looks to me like a woman picking huckleberries,' said Jim, who was married to George's pretty sister.

'Be still, Jim!' said that fair young woman. 'I believe in Jenny's ghost as much as she does. Such a place! Just look at this great wistaria trunk crawling up by the steps here! It looks for all the world like a writhing body – cringing – beseeching!'

'Yes,' answered the subdued Jim, 'it does, Susy. See its waist – about two yards of it, and twisted at that! A waste of good material!'

'Don't be so horrid, boys! Go off and smoke somewhere if you can't be congenial!'

'We can! We will! We'll be as ghostly as you please.' And forthwith they began to see bloodstains and crouching figures so plentifully that the most delightful shivers multiplied, and the fair enthusiasts started for bed, declaring they should never sleep a wink.

'We shall all surely dream,' cried Mrs Jenny, 'and we must all tell our dreams in the morning!'

'There's another thing certain,' said George, catching Susy as she tripped over a loose plank; 'and that is that you frisky creatures must use the side door till I get this Eiffel tower of a portico fixed, or we shall have some fresh ghosts on our hands! We found a plank here that yawns like a trap-door – big enough to swallow you – and I believe the bottom of the thing is in China!'

The next morning found them all alive, and eating a substantial New England breakfast, to the accompaniment of saws and hammers on the porch, where carpenters of quite miraculous promptness were tearing things to pieces generally.

'It's got to come down mostly,' they had said. 'These timbers are clean rotted through, what ain't pulled out o' line by this great creeper. That's about all that holds the thing up.'

There was clear reason in what they said, and with a caution from anxious Mrs Jenny not to hurt the wistaria, they were left to demolish and repair at leisure.

'How about ghosts?' asked Jack after a fourth griddle cake. 'I had one, and it's taken away my appetite!'

Mrs Jenny gave a little shriek and dropped her knife and fork.

'Oh, so had I! I had the most awful – well, not dream exactly, but feeling. I had forgotten all about it!'

'Must have been awful,' said Jack, taking another cake. 'Do tell us about the feeling. My ghost will wait.'

'It makes me creep to think of it even now,' she said. 'I woke up, all at once, with that dreadful feeling as if something were going to happen, you know! I was wide awake, and hearing every little sound for miles around, it seemed to me. There are so many strange little noises in the country for all it is so still. Millions of crickets and things outside, and all kinds of rustles in the trees! There wasn't much wind, and the moonlight came through in my three great windows in three white squares on the black old floor, and those fingery wistaria leaves we were talking of last night just seemed to crawl all over them. And – O, girls, you know that dreadful well in the cellar?'

A most gratifying impression was made by this, and Jenny proceeded cheerfully:

'Well, while it was so horridly still, and I lay there trying not to wake George, I heard as plainly as if it were right in the room, that old chain down there rattle and creak over the stones!'

'Bravo!' cried Jack. 'That's fine! I'll put it in the Sunday edition!'

'Be still!' said Kate. 'What was it, Jenny? Did you really see anything?'

'No, I didn't, I'm sorry to say. But just then I didn't want to. I woke George, and made such a fuss that he gave me bromide, and said he'd go and look, and that's the last I thought of it till Jack reminded me – the bromide worked so well.'

'Now, Jack, give us yours,' said Jim. 'Maybe, it will dovetail in somehow. Thirsty ghost, I imagine; maybe they had prohibition here even then!'

Jack folded his napkin, and leaned back in his most impressive manner.

'It was striking twelve by the great hall clock –' he began.

'There isn't any hall clock!'

'O hush, Jim, you spoil the current! It was just one o'clock then, by my old-fashioned repeater.'

'Waterbury! Never mind what time it was!'

'Well, honestly, I woke up sharp, like our beloved hostess, and tried to go to sleep again, but couldn't. I experienced all those moonlight and grasshopper sensations, just like Jenny, and was wondering what could have been the matter with the supper, when in came my ghost, and I knew it was all a dream! It was a female ghost, and I imagine she was young and handsome, but all those crouching, hunted figures of last evening ran riot in my brain, and this poor creature looked just like them. She was all wrapped up in a shawl, and had a big bundle under her arm – dear me, I am spoiling the story!

With the air and gait of one in frantic haste and terror, the muffled figure glided to a dark old bureau, and seemed taking things from the drawers. As she turned, the moonlight shone full on a little red cross that hung from her neck by a thin gold chain – I saw it glitter as she crept noiselessly from the room! That's all.'

'O Jack, don't be so horrid! Did you really? Is that all? What do you think it was?'

'I am not horrid by nature, only professionally. I really did. That was all. And I am fully convinced it was the genuine, legitimate ghost of an eloping chambermaid with kleptomania!'

'You are too bad, Jack!' cried Jenny. 'You take all the horror out of it. There isn't a "creep" left among us.'

'It's no time for creeps at nine-thirty AM, with sunlight and carpenters outside! However, if you can't wait till twilight for your creeps, I think I can furnish one or two,' said George. 'I went down cellar after Jenny's ghost!'

There was a delighted chorus of female voices, and Jenny cast upon her lord a glance of genuine gratitude.

'It's all very well to lie in bed and see ghosts, or hear them,' he went on. 'But the young householder suspecteth burglars, even though as a medical man he knoweth nerves, and after Jenny dropped off I started on a voyage of discovery. I never will again, I promise you!'

'Why, what *was* it?'

'Oh, George!'

'I got a candle –'

'Good mark for the burglars,' murmured Jack.

'And went all over the house, gradually working down to the cellar and the well.'

'Well?' said Jack.

'Now you can laugh; but that cellar is no joke by daylight, and a candle there at night is about as inspiring as a lightning-bug in the Mammoth Cave. I went along with the light, trying not to fall into the well prematurely; got to it all at once; held the light down and *then* I saw, right under my feet – (I nearly fell over her, or walked through her, perhaps) – a woman, hunched up under a shawl! She had hold of the chain, and the candle shone on her hands – white, thin hands – on a little red cross that hung from her neck – *vide* Jack! I'm no believer in ghosts, and I firmly object to unknown parties in the house at night; so I spoke to her rather fiercely. She didn't seem to notice that, and I reached down to take hold of her – then I came upstairs!'

'What for?'

'What happened?'

'What was the matter?'

'Well, nothing happened. Only she wasn't there! May have been indigestion, of course, but as a physician I don't advise any one to court indigestion alone at midnight in a cellar!'

'This is the most interesting and peripatetic and evasive ghost I ever heard of!' said Jack. 'It's my belief she has no end of silver tankards, and jewels galore, at the bottom of that well, and I move we go and see!'

'To the bottom of the well, Jack?'

'To the bottom of the mystery. Come on!'

There was unanimous assent, and the fresh cambrics and pretty boots were gallantly escorted below by gentlemen whose jokes were so frequent that many of them were a little forced.

The deep old cellar was so dark that they had to bring lights, and the well so gloomy in its blackness that the ladies recoiled.

'That well is enough to scare even a ghost. It's my opinion you'd better let well enough alone!' quoth Jim.

'Truth lies hid in a well, and we must get her out,' said George. 'Bear a hand with the chain?'

Jim pulled away on the chain, George turned the creaking

windlass, and Jack was chorus.

'A wet sheet for this ghost, if not a flowing sea,' said he. 'Seems to be hard work raising spirits! I suppose he kicked the bucket when he went down!'

As the chain lightened and shortened there grew a strained silence among them; and when at length the bucket appeared, rising slowly through the dark water, there was an eager, half reluctant peering, and a natural drawing back. They poked the gloomy contents. 'Only water.'

'Nothing but mud.'

'Something –'

They emptied the bucket up on the dark earth, and then the girls all went out into the air, into the bright warm sunshine in front of the house, where was the sound of saw and hammer, and the smell of new wood. There was nothing said until the men joined them, and then Jenny timidly asked:

'How old should you think it was, George?'

'All of a century,' he answered. 'That water is a preservative – lime in it. Oh! – you mean? – Not more than a month; a very little baby!'

There was another silence at this, broken by a cry from the workmen. They had removed the floor and the side walls of the old porch, so that the sunshine poured down to the dark stones of the cellar bottom. And there, in the strangling grasp of the roots of the great wistaria, lay the bones of a woman, from whose neck still hung a tiny scarlet cross on a thin chain of gold.

4 The Shadow

BY EDITH NESBIT

This is not an artistically rounded off ghost story, and nothing is explained in it, and there seems to be no reason why any of it should have happened. But that is no reason why it should not be told. You must have noticed that all the real ghost stories you have ever come close to, are like this in these respects – no explanation, no logical coherence. Here is the story.

※

There were three of us and another, but she had fainted suddenly at the second extra of the Christmas Dance, and had been put to bed in the dressing-room next to the room which we three shared. It had been one of those jolly, old-fashioned dances where nearly everybody stays the night, and the big country house is stretched to its utmost containing – guests harbouring on sofas, couches, settles, and even mattresses on floors. Some of the young men actually, I believe, slept on the great dining-table. We had talked of our partners, as girls will, and then the stillness of the manor house, broken only by the whisper of the wind in the cedar branches, and the scraping of their harsh fingers against our window panes, had pricked us to such a luxurious confidence in our surroundings of bright chintz and candle-flame and fire-light, that we had dared to talk of ghosts – in which, said we all, we did not believe one bit. We had told the story of the phantom coach, and the horribly strange bed, and the lady in the sacque, and the house in Berkeley Square.

We none of us believed in ghosts, but my heart, at least, seemed to leap to my throat and choke me there, when a tap came to our door – a tap faint, not to be mistaken.

'Who's there?' said the youngest of us, craning a lean neck towards the door. It opened slowly, and I give you my word the instant of suspense that followed is still reckoned among my life's least confident moments. Almost at once the door opened fully, and Miss Eastwich, my aunt's housekeeper, companion and general stand-by, looked in on us.

We all said 'Come in,' but she stood there. She was, at all normal hours, the most silent woman I have ever known. She stood and looked at us, and shivered a little. So did we – for in those days corridors were not warmed by hot-water pipes, and the air from the door was keen.

'I saw your light,' she said at last, 'and I thought it was late for you to be up – after all this gaiety. I thought perhaps –' her glance turned towards the door of the dressing-room.

'No,' I said, 'she's fast asleep.' I should have added a good-night, but the youngest of us forestalled my speech. She did not know Miss Eastwich as we others did; did not know how her persistent silence had built a wall round her – a wall that no one dared to break down with the commonplaces of talk, or the littlenesses of mere human relationship. Miss Eastwich's silence had taught us to treat her as a machine; and as other than a machine we never dreamed of treating her. But the youngest of us had seen Miss Eastwich for the first time that day. She was young, crude, ill-balanced, subject to blind, calf-like impulses. She was also the heiress of a rich tallow-chandler, but that has nothing to do with this part of the story. She jumped up from the hearth-rug, her unsuitably rich silk lace-trimmed dressing-gown falling back from her thin collar-bones, and ran to the door and put an arm round Miss Eastwich's prim, lisse-encircled neck. I gasped. I should as soon have dared to embrace Cleopatra's

Needle. 'Come in,' said the youngest of us – 'come in and get warm. There's lots of cocoa left.' She drew Miss Eastwich in and shut the door.

The vivid light of pleasure in the housekeeper's pale eyes went through my heart like a knife. It would have been so easy to put an arm round her neck, if one had only thought she wanted an arm there. But it was not I who had thought that – and indeed, my arm might not have brought the light envoked by the thin arm of the youngest of us.

'Now,' the youngest went on eagerly, 'you shall have the very biggest, nicest chair, and the cocoa-pot's here on the hob as hot as hot – and we've all been telling ghost stories, only we don't believe in them a bit; and when you get warm you ought to tell one too.'

Miss Eastwich – that model of decorum and decently done duties, tell a ghost story!

'You're sure I'm not in your way,' Miss Eastwich said, stretching her hands to the blaze. I wondered whether housekeepers have fires in their rooms even at Christmas time. 'Not a bit' – I said it, and I hope I said it as warmly as I felt it. 'I – Miss Eastwich – I'd have asked you to come in other times – only I didn't think you'd care for girls' chatter.'

The third girl, who was really of no account, and that's why I have not said anything about her before, poured cocoa for our guest. I put my fleecy Madeira shawl round her shoulders. I could not think of anything else to do for her, and I found myself wishing desperately to do something. The smiles she gave us were quite pretty. People can smile prettily at forty or fifty, or even later, though girls don't realise this. It occurred to me, and this was another knife-thrust, that I had never seen Miss Eastwich smile – a real smile, before. The pale smiles of dutiful acquiescence were not of the same blood as this dimpling, happy, transfiguring look.

'This is very pleasant,' she said, and it seemed to me that I had never before heard her real voice. It did not please me to think that at the cost of cocoa, a fire, and my arm round her neck, I might have heard this new voice any time these six years.

'We've been telling ghost stories,' I said. 'The worst of it is, we don't believe in ghosts. No one one knows has ever seen one.'

'It's always what somebody told somebody who told somebody you know,' said the youngest of us, 'and you can't believe that, can you?'

'What the soldier said, is not evidence,' said Miss Eastwich. Will it be believed that the little Dickens quotation pierced one more keenly than the new smile or the new voice?

'And all the ghost stories are so beautifully rounded off – a murder committed on the spot – or a hidden treasure, or a warning … I think that makes them harder to believe. The most horrid ghost-story I ever heard was one that was quite silly.'

'Tell it.'

'I can't – it doesn't sound anything to tell. Miss Eastwich ought to tell one.'

'Oh do,' said the youngest of us, and her salt cellars loomed dark, as she stretched her neck eagerly and laid an entreating arm on our guest's knee.

'The only thing that I ever knew of was – was hearsay,' she said slowly, 'till just the end.'

I knew she would tell her story, and I knew she had never before told it, and I knew she was only telling it now because she was proud, and this seemed the only way to pay for the fire and the cocoa, and the laying of that arm round her neck.

'Don't tell it,' I said suddenly, 'I know you'd rather not.'

'I daresay it would bore you,' she said meekly, and the youngest of us, who, after all, did not understand everything, glared resentfully at me.

'We should just *love* it,' she said. '*Do* tell us. Never mind if it isn't a real, proper, fixed up story. I'm certain anything *you* think ghostly would be quite too beautifully horrid for anything.'

Miss Eastwich finished her cocoa and reached up to set the cup on the mantelpiece.

'It can't do any harm,' she said to herself, 'they don't believe in ghosts, and it wasn't exactly a ghost either. And they're all over twenty – they're not babies.'

There was a breathing time of hush and expectancy. The fire crackled and the gas suddenly glared higher because the billiard lights had been put out. We heard the steps and voices of the men going along the corridors.

'It is really hardly worth telling,' Miss Eastwich said doubtfully, shading her faded face from the fire with her thin hand.

We all said 'Go on – oh, go on – do!'

'Well,' she said, 'twenty years ago – and more than that, I had two friends, and I loved them more than anything in the world. And they married each other –'

She paused, and I knew just in what way she had loved each of them. The youngest of us said –

'How awfully nice for you. Do go on.'

She patted the youngest's shoulder, and I was glad that I had understood, and that the youngest of all hadn't. She went on.

'Well, after they were married, I didn't see much of them for a year or two; and then he wrote and asked me to come and stay, because his wife was ill, and I should cheer her up, and cheer him up as well; for it was a gloomy house, and he himself was growing gloomy too.'

I knew, as she spoke, that she had every line of that letter by heart.

'Well, I went. The address was in Lee, near London; in

those days there were streets and streets of new villa-houses
growing up round old brick mansions standing in their own
grounds, with red walls round, you know, and a sort of
flavour of coaching days, and post-chaises, and Blackheath
highwaymen about them. He had said the house was gloomy,
and it was called "The Firs", and I imagined my cab going
through a dark, winding shrubbery, and drawing up in front
of one of these sedate, old, square houses. Instead, we drew
up in front of a large, smart villa, with iron railings, gay
encaustic tiles leading from the iron gate to the stained-glass-
panelled door, and for shrubbery only a few stunted cypresses
and aucubas in the tiny front garden. But inside it was all
warm and welcoming. He met me at the door.'

She was gazing into the fire, and I knew she had forgotten
us. But the youngest girl of all still thought it was to us she
was telling her story.

'He met me at the door,' she said again, 'and thanked me for
coming, and asked me to forgive the past.'

'What past?' said that high priestess of the *inapropos*, the
youngest of all.

'Oh – I suppose he meant because they hadn't invited me
before, or something,' said Miss Eastwich worriedly, 'but it's
a very dull story, I find, after all, and –'

'Do go on,' I said – then I kicked the youngest of us, and got
up to rearrange Miss Eastwich's shawl, and said in blatant
dumb show, over the shawled shoulder: 'Shut up, you little
idiot –'

After another silence, the housekeeper's new voice went on.

'They were very glad to see me, and I was very glad to be
there. You girls now have such troops of friends, but these
two were all I had, all I had ever had. Mabel wasn't exactly ill,
only weak and excitable. I thought he seemed more ill than
she did. She went to bed early and before she went, she asked
me to keep him company through his last pipe, so we went

into the dining-room and sat in the two arm chairs on each side of the fireplace. They were covered with green leather I remember. There were bronze groups of horses and a black marble clock on the mantelpiece – all wedding-presents. He poured out some whisky for himself, but he hardly touched it. He sat looking into the fire. At last I said: –

"What's wrong? Mabel looks as well as you could expect."

'He said, "Yes – but I don't know from one day to another that she won't begin to notice something wrong. That's why I wanted you to come. You were always so sensible and strong-minded, and Mabel's like a little bird on a flower."

'I said yes, of course, and waited for him to go on. I thought he must be in debt, or in trouble of some sort. So I just waited. Presently he said:

"Margaret, this is a very peculiar house –" he always called me Margaret. You see we'd been such old friends. I told him I thought the house was very pretty, and fresh, and homelike – only a little too new – but that fault would mend with time. He said: –

"It *is* new: that's just it. We're the first people who've ever lived in it. If it were an old house, Margaret, I should think it was haunted."

'I asked if he had seen anything. "No," he said "not yet."

"Heard then?" said I.

"No – not heard either," he said "but there's a sort of feeling: I can't describe it – I've seen nothing and I've heard nothing, but I've been so near to seeing and hearing, just near, that's all. And something follows me about – only when I turn round, there's never anything, only my shadow. And I always feel that I *shall* see the thing next minute – but I never do – not quite – it's always just not visible."

'I thought he'd been working rather hard – and tried to cheer him up by making light of all this. It was just nerves, I said. Then he said he had thought I could help him, and did

I think anyone he had wronged could have laid a curse on him, and did I believe in curses. I said I didn't – and the only person anyone could have said he had wronged forgave him freely, I knew, if there was anything to forgive. So I told him this too.'

It was I, not the youngest of us, who knew the name of that person, wronged and forgiving.

'So then I said he ought to take Mabel away from the house and have a complete change. But he said No; Mabel had got everything in order, and he could never manage to get her away just now without explaining everything – "and, above all," he said, "she mustn't guess there's anything wrong. I daresay I shan't feel quite such a lunatic now you're here."

'So we said good-night.'

'Is that all the story!' said the third girl, striving to convey that even as it stood it was a good story.

'That's only the beginning,' said Miss Eastwich. 'Whenever I was alone with him he used to tell me the same thing over and over again, and at first when I began to notice things, I tried to think that it was his talk that had upset my nerves. The odd thing was that it wasn't only at night – but in broad daylight – and particularly on the stairs and passages. On the staircase the feeling used to be so awful that I have had to bite my lips till they bled to keep myself from running upstairs at full speed. Only I knew if I did I should go mad at the top. There was always something behind me – exactly as he had said – something that one could just not see. And a sound that one could just not hear. There was a long corridor at the top of the house. I have sometimes almost seen something – you know how one sees things without looking – but if I turned round, it seemed as if the thing drooped and melted into my shadow. There was a little window at the end of the corridor.

'Downstairs there was another corridor, something like it, with a cupboard at one end and the kitchen at the other. One night I went down into the kitchen to heat some milk for Mabel. The servants had gone to bed. As I stood by the fire, waiting for the milk to boil, I glanced through the open door and along the passage. I never could keep my eyes on what I was doing in that house. The cupboard door was partly open; they used to keep empty boxes and things in it. And, as I looked, I knew that now it was not going to be "almost" any more. Yet I said, "Mabel?" not because I thought it could be Mabel who was crouching down there, half in and half out of the cupboard. The thing was grey at first, and then it was black. And when I whispered, "Mabel", it seemed to sink down till it lay like a pool of ink on the floor, and then its edges drew in, and it seemed to flow, like ink when you tilt up the paper you have spilt it on; and it flowed into the cupboard till it was all gathered into the shadow there. I saw it go quite plainly. The gas was full on in the kitchen. I screamed aloud, but even then, I'm thankful to say, I had enough sense to upset the boiling milk, so that when he came downstairs three steps at a time, I had the excuse for my scream of a scalded hand. The explanation satisfied Mabel, but next night he said: –

"Why didn't you tell me? It was that cupboard. All the horror of the house comes out of that. Tell me – have you seen anything yet? Or is it only the nearly seeing and nearly hearing still?"

'I said, "You must tell me first what you've seen." He told me, and his eyes wandered, as he spoke, to the shadows by the curtains, and I turned up all three gas lights, and lit the candles on the mantelpiece. Then we looked at each other and said we were both mad, and thanked God that Mabel at least was sane. For what he had seen was what I had seen.

'After that I hated to be alone with a shadow, because at any moment I might see something that would crouch, and sink, and lie like a black pool, and then slowly draw itself into the shadow that was nearest. Often that shadow was my own. The thing came first at night, but afterwards there was no hour safe from it. I saw it at dawn and at noon, in the dusk and in the firelight, and always it crouched and sank, and was a pool that flowed into some shadow and became part of it. And always I saw it with a straining of the eyes – a pricking and aching. It seemed as though I could only just see it, as if my sight, to see it, had to be strained to the uttermost. And still the sound was in the house – the sound that I could just not hear. At last, one morning early, I did hear it. It was close behind me, and it was only a sigh. It was worse than the thing that crept into the shadows.

'I don't know how I bore it. I couldn't have borne it, if I hadn't been so fond of them both. But I knew in my heart that, if he had no one to whom he could speak openly, he would go mad, or tell Mabel. His was not a very strong character; very sweet, and kind, and gentle, but not strong. He was always easily led. So I stayed on and bore up, and we were very cheerful, and made little jokes, and tried to be amusing when Mabel was with us. But when we were alone, we did not try to be amusing. And sometimes a day or two would go by without our seeing or hearing anything, and we should perhaps have fancied that we had fancied what we had seen and heard – only there was always the feeling of there being something about the house, that one could just not hear and not see. Sometimes we used to try not to talk about it, but generally we talked of nothing else at all. And the weeks went by, and Mabel's baby was born. The nurse and the doctor said that both mother and child were doing well. He and I sat late in the dining-room that night. We had neither of us seen or heard anything for three days; our anxiety about Mabel was lessened. We talked of the future – it seemed then so much brighter than the past.

We arranged that, the moment she was fit to be moved, he should take her away to the sea, and I should superintend the moving of their furniture into the new house he had already chosen. He was gayer than I had seen him since his marriage – almost like his old self. When I said good-night to him, he said a lot of things about my having been a comfort to them both. I hadn't done anything much, of course, but still I am glad he said them.

'Then I went upstairs, almost for the first time without that feeling of something following me. I listened at Mabel's door. Everything was quiet. I went on towards my own room, and in an instant I felt that there *was* something behind me. I turned. It was crouching there; it sank, and the black fluidness of it seemed to be sucked under the door of Mabel's room.

'I went back. I opened the door a listening inch. All was still. And then I heard a sigh close behind me. I opened the door and went in. The nurse and the baby were asleep. Mabel was asleep too – she looked so pretty – like a tired child – the baby was cuddled up into one of her arms with its tiny head against her side. I prayed then that Mabel might never know the terrors that he and I had known. That those little ears might never hear any but pretty sounds, those clear eyes never see any but pretty sights. I did not dare to pray for a long time after that. Because my prayer was answered. She never saw, never heard anything more in this world. And now I could do nothing more for him or for her.

'When they had put her in her coffin, I lighted wax candles round her, and laid the horrible white flowers that people will send near her, and then I saw he had followed me. I took his hand to lead him away.

'At the door we both turned. It seemed to us that we heard a sigh. He would have sprung to her side, in I don't know what mad, glad hope. But at that instant we both saw it. Between us and the coffin, first grey, then black, it crouched an instant, then sank and liquefied – and was gathered together and drawn till it ran into the nearest shadow. And the nearest shadow was the shadow of Mabel's coffin. I left the next day. His mother came. She had never liked me.'

Miss Eastwich paused. I think she had quite forgotten us.

'Didn't you see him again?' asked the youngest of us all.

'Only once,' Miss Eastwich answered, 'and something black crouched then between him and me. But it was only his second wife, crying beside his coffin. It's not a cheerful story is it? And it doesn't lead anywhere. I've never told anyone else. I think it was seeing his daughter that brought it all back.'

She looked towards the dressing-room door.

'Mabel's baby?'

'Yes – and exactly like Mabel, only with his eyes.'

The youngest of all had Miss Eastwich's hands, and was petting them.

Suddenly the woman wrenched her hands away, and stood at her gaunt height, her hands clenched, eyes straining. She was looking at something that we could not see, and I know what the man in the Bible meant when he said: 'The hair of my flesh stood up.'

What she saw seemed not quite to reach the height of the dressing-room door handle. Her eyes following it down, down – widening and widening. Mine followed them – all the nerves of them seemed strained to the uttermost – and I almost saw – or did I quite see? I can't be certain. But we all heard the long-drawn, quivering sigh. And to each of us it seemed to be breathed just behind each.

It was I who caught up the candle – it dripped wax all over my trembling hand – and was dragged by Miss Eastwich to the girl who had fainted during the second extra. But it was the youngest of all whose lean arms were round the housekeeper when we turned away, and that have been round her many a time since, in the new home where she keeps house for the youngest of us.

The doctor who came in the morning said that Mabel's daughter had died of heart disease – which she had inherited from her mother. It was that that made her faint during the second extra. But I have sometimes wondered whether she may not have inherited something from her father. I have never been able to forget the look on her dead face.

5 Kerfol

BY EDITH WHARTON

I

'You ought to buy it,' said my host; 'it's just the place for a solitary-minded devil like you. And it would be rather worthwhile to own the most romantic house in Brittany. The present people are dead broke, and it's going for a song – you ought to buy it.'

It was not with the least idea of living up to the character my friend Lanrivain ascribed to me (as a matter of fact, under my unsociable exterior I have always had secret yearnings for domesticity) that I took his hint one autumn afternoon and went to Kerfol. My friend was motoring over to Quimper on business: he dropped me on the way, at a cross-road on a heath, and said: 'First turn to the right and second to the left. Then straight ahead till you see an avenue. If you meet any peasants, don't ask your way. They don't understand French, and they would pretend they did and mix you up. I'll be back for you here by sunset – and don't forget the tombs in the chapel.'

I followed Lanrivain's directions with the hesitation occasioned by the usual difficulty of remembering whether he had said the first turn to the right and second to the left, or the contrary. If I had met a peasant I should certainly have asked, and probably been sent astray; but I had the desert landscape to myself, and so stumbled on the right turn and walked across the heath till I came to an avenue. It was so unlike any other avenue I have ever seen that I instantly knew it must be *the* avenue. The grey-trunked trees sprang up straight to a great height and then interwove their pale-grey branches in a long tunnel through which the autumn light fell faintly. I know most trees by name, but I haven't to this day been able to decide what those trees were. They had the tall curve of elms, the tenuity of poplars, the ashen colour of olives under a rainy sky; and they stretched ahead of me for half a mile or more without a break in their arch. If ever I saw an avenue that unmistakably led to something, it was the avenue at Kerfol. My heart beat a little as I began to walk down it.

Presently the trees ended and I came to a fortified gate in a long wall. Between me and the wall was an open space of grass, with other grey avenues radiating from it. Behind the wall were tall slate roofs mossed with silver, a chapel belfry, the top of a keep. A moat filled with wild shrubs and brambles surrounded the place; the drawbridge had been replaced by a stone arch, and the portcullis by an iron gate. I stood for a long time on the hither side of the moat, gazing about me, and letting the influence of the place sink in. I said to myself: 'If I wait long enough, the guardian will turn up and show me the tombs –' and I rather hoped he wouldn't turn up too soon.

I sat down on a stone and lit a cigarette. As soon as I had done it, it struck me as a puerile and portentous thing to do, with that great blind house looking down at me, and all the empty avenues converging on me. It may have been the depth of the silence that made me so conscious of my gesture. The squeak of my match sounded as loud as the scraping of a brake, and I almost fancied I heard it fall when I tossed it onto the grass. But there was more than that: a sense of irrelevance, of littleness, of futile bravado, in sitting there puffing my cigarette-smoke into the face of such a past.

I knew nothing of the history of Kerfol – I was new to Brittany, and Lanrivain had never mentioned the name to me till the day before – but one couldn't as much as glance at that pile without feeling in it a long accumulation of history. What kind of history I was not prepared to guess: perhaps only that sheer weight of many associated lives and deaths which gives a majesty to all old houses. But the aspect of Kerfol suggested something more – a perspective of stern and cruel memories stretching away, like its own grey avenues, into a blur of darkness.

Certainly no house had ever more completely and finally broken with the present. As it stood there, lifting its proud roofs and gables to the sky, it might have been its own funeral monument. 'Tombs in the chapel? The whole place is a tomb!' I reflected. I hoped more and more that the guardian would not come. The details of the place, however striking, would seem trivial compared with its collective impressiveness; and I wanted only to sit there and be penetrated by the weight of its silence.

'It's the very place for you!' Lanrivain had said; and I was overcome by the almost blasphemous frivolity of suggesting to any living being that Kerfol was the place for him. 'Is it possible that anyone could *not* see –?' I wondered. I did not finish the thought: what I meant was undefinable. I stood up and wandered toward the gate. I was beginning to want to know more; not to *see* more – I was by now so sure it was not a question of seeing – but to feel more: feel all the place had to communicate. 'But to get in one will have to rout out the keeper,' I thought reluctantly, and hesitated. Finally I crossed the bridge and tried the iron gate. It yielded, and I walked through the tunnel formed by the thickness of the *chemin de ronde*. At the farther end, a wooden barricade had been laid across the entrance, and beyond it was a court enclosed in noble architecture. The main building faced me; and I now saw that one half was a mere ruined front, with gaping windows through which the wild growths of the moat and the trees of the park were visible. The rest of the house was still in its robust beauty. One end abutted on the round tower, the other on the small traceried chapel, and in an angle of the building stood a graceful well-head crowned with mossy urns. A few roses grew against the walls, and on an upper window-sill I remember noticing a pot of fuchsias.

My sense of the pressure of the invisible began to yield to my architectural interest. The building was so fine that I felt a desire to explore it for its own sake. I looked about the court, wondering in which corner the guardian lodged. Then I pushed open the barrier and went in. As I did so, a dog barred my way. He was such a remarkably beautiful little dog that for a moment he made me forget the splendid place he was defending. I was not sure of his breed at the time, but have since learned that it was Chinese, and that he was of a rare variety called the 'Sleeve-dog'. He was very small and golden brown, with large brown eyes and a ruffled throat: he looked like a large tawny chrysanthemum. I said to myself: 'These little beasts always snap and scream, and somebody will be out in a minute.'

The little animal stood before me, forbidding, almost menacing: there was anger in his large brown eyes. But he made no sound, he came no nearer. Instead, as I advanced, he gradually fell back, and I noticed that another dog, a vague rough brindled thing, had limped up on a lame leg. 'There'll be a hubbub now,' I thought; for at the same moment a third dog, a long-haired white mongrel, slipped out of a doorway and joined the others. All three stood looking at me with grave eyes; but not a sound came from them. As I advanced they continued to fall back on muffled paws, still watching me. 'At a given point, they'll all charge at my ankles: it's one of the jokes that dogs who live together put up on one,' I thought. I was not alarmed, for they were neither large nor formidable. But they let me wander about the court as I pleased, following me at a little distance – always the same distance – and always keeping their eyes on me. Presently I looked across at the ruined facade, and saw that in one of its empty window-frames another dog stood: a white pointer with one brown ear. He was an old grave dog, much more experienced than the others; and he seemed to be observing me with a deeper intentness.

'I'll hear from *him*,' I said to myself; but he stood in the window-frame, against the trees of the park, and continued to watch me without moving. I stared back at him for a time, to see if the sense that he was being watched would not rouse him. Half the width of the court lay between us, and we gazed at each other silently across it. But he did not stir, and at last I turned away. Behind me I found the rest of the pack, with a newcomer added: a small black greyhound with pale agate-coloured eyes. He was shivering a little, and his expression was more timid than that of the others. I noticed that he kept a little behind them. And still there was not a sound.

I stood there for fully five minutes, the circle about me – waiting, as they seemed to be waiting. At last I went up to the little golden-brown dog and stooped to pat him. As I did so, I heard myself give a nervous laugh. The little dog did not start, or growl, or take his eyes from me – he simply slipped back about a yard, and then paused and continued to look at me. 'Oh, hang it!' I exclaimed, and walked across the court toward the well.

As I advanced, the dogs separated and slid away into different corners of the court. I examined the urns on the well, tried a locked door or two, and looked up and down the dumb facade; then I faced about toward the chapel. When I turned I perceived that all the dogs had disappeared except the old pointer, who still watched me from the window. It was rather a relief to be rid of that cloud of witnesses; and I began to look about me for a way to the back of the house. 'Perhaps there'll be somebody in the garden,' I thought. I found a way across the moat, scrambled over a wall smothered in brambles, and got into the garden. A few lean hydrangeas and geraniums pined in the flower-beds, and the ancient house looked down on them indifferently. Its garden side was plainer and severer than the other: the long granite front, with its few windows and steep roof, looked like a fortress-prison. I walked around the farther wing, went up some disjointed steps, and entered the deep twilight of a narrow and incredibly old box-walk. The walk was just wide enough for one person to slip through, and its branches met overhead. It was like the ghost of a box-walk, its lustrous green all turning to the shadowy greyness of the avenues. I walked on and on, the branches hitting me in the face and springing back with a dry rattle; and at length I came out on the grassy top of the *chemin de ronde*. I walked along it to the gate-tower, looking down into the court, which was just below me. Not a human being was in sight; and neither were the dogs. I found a flight of steps in the thickness of the wall and went down them; and when I emerged again into the court, there stood the circle of dogs, the golden-brown one a little ahead of the others, the black greyhound shivering in the rear.

'Oh, hang it – you uncomfortable beasts, you!' I exclaimed, my voice startling me with a sudden echo. The dogs stood motionless, watching me. I knew by this time that they would not try to prevent my approaching the house, and the knowledge left me free to examine them. I had a feeling that they must be horribly cowed to be so silent and inert. Yet they did not look hungry or ill-treated. Their coats were smooth and they were not thin, except the shivering greyhound. It was more as if they had lived a long time with people who never spoke to them or looked at them: as though the silence of the place had gradually benumbed their busy inquisitive natures. And this strange passivity, this almost human lassitude, seemed to me sadder than the misery of starved and beaten animals. I should have liked to rouse them for a minute, to coax them into a game or a scamper; but the longer I looked into their fixed and weary eyes the more preposterous the idea became. With the windows of that house looking down on us, how could I have imagined such a thing? The dogs knew better: *they* knew what the house would tolerate and what it would not. I even fancied that they knew what was passing through my mind, and pitied me for my frivolity. But even that feeling probably reached them through a thick fog of listlessness. I had an idea that their distance from me was as nothing to my remoteness from them. The impression they produced was that of having in common one memory so deep and dark that nothing that had happened since was worth either a growl or a wag.

'I say,' I broke out abruptly, addressing myself to the dumb circle, 'do you know what you look like, the whole lot of you? You look as if you'd seen a ghost – that's how you look! I wonder if there *is* a ghost here, and nobody but you left for it to appear to?' The dogs continued to gaze at me without moving ...

It was dark when I saw Lanrivain's motor lamps at the cross-roads – and I wasn't exactly sorry to see them. I had the sense of having escaped from the loneliest place in the whole world, and of not liking loneliness – to that degree – as much as I had imagined I should. My friend had brought his solicitor back from Quimper for the night, and seated beside a fat and affable stranger I felt no inclination to talk of Kerfol ...

But that evening, when Lanrivain and the solicitor were closeted in the study, Madame de Lanrivain began to question me in the drawing-room.

'Well – are you going to buy Kerfol?' she asked, tilting up her gay chin from her embroidery.

'I haven't decided yet. The fact is, I couldn't get into the house,' I said, as if I had simply postponed my decision, and meant to go back for another look.

'You couldn't get in? Why, what happened? The family are mad to sell the place, and the old guardian has orders –'

'Very likely. But the old guardian wasn't there.'

'What a pity! He must have gone to market. But his daughter –?'

'There was nobody about. At least I saw no one.'

'How extraordinary! Literally nobody?'

'Nobody but a lot of dogs – a whole pack of them – who seemed to have the place to themselves.'

Madame de Lanrivain let the embroidery slip to her knee and folded her hands on it. For several minutes she looked at me thoughtfully.

'A pack of dogs – you *saw* them?'

'Saw them? I saw nothing else!'

'How many?' She dropped her voice a little. 'I've always wondered –'

I looked at her with surprise: I had supposed the place to be familiar to her. 'Have you never been to Kerfol?' I asked.

'Oh, yes: often. But never on that day.'

'What day?'

'I'd quite forgotten – and so had Hervé, I'm sure. If we'd remembered, we never should have sent you to-day – but then, after all, one doesn't half believe that sort of thing, does one?'

'What sort of thing?' I asked, involuntarily sinking my voice to the level of hers. Inwardly I was thinking: 'I *knew* there was something ...'

Madame de Lanrivain cleared her throat and produced a reassuring smile. 'Didn't Hervé tell you the story of Kerfol? An ancestor of his was mixed up in it. You know every Breton house has its ghost-story; and some of them are rather unpleasant.'

'Yes – but those dogs?'

'Well, those dogs are the ghosts of Kerfol. At least, the peasants say there's one day in the year when a lot of dogs appear there; and that day the keeper and his daughter go off to Morlaix and get drunk. The women in Brittany drink dreadfully.' She stooped to match a silk; then she lifted her charming inquisitive Parisian face. 'Did you *really* see a lot of dogs? There isn't one at Kerfol,' she said.

II

Lanrivain, the next day, hunted out a shabby calf volume from the back of an upper shelf of his library.

'Yes – here it is. What does it call itself? *A History of the Assizes of the Duchy of Brittany. Quimper, 1702.* The book was written about a hundred years later than the Kerfol affair; but I believe the account is transcribed pretty literally from the judicial records. Anyhow, it's queer reading. And there's a Hervé de Lanrivain mixed up in it – not exactly *my* style, as you'll see. But then he's only a collateral. Here, take the book up to bed with you. I don't exactly remember the details; but after you've read it I'll bet anything you'll leave your light burning all night!'

I left my light burning all night, as he had predicted; but it was chiefly because, till near dawn, I was absorbed in my reading. The account of the trial of Anne de Cornault, wife of the lord of Kerfol, was long and closely printed. It was, as my friend had said, probably an almost literal transcription of what took place in the court-room; and the trial lasted nearly a month. Besides, the type of the book was very bad ...

At first I thought of translating the old record. But it is full of wearisome repetitions, and the main lines of the story are forever straying off into side issues. So I have tried to disentangle it, and give it here in a simpler form. At times, however, I have reverted to the text because no other words could have conveyed so exactly the sense of what I felt at Kerfol; and nowhere have I added anything of my own.

III

It was in the year 16— that Yves de Cornault, lord of the domain of Kerfol, went to the *pardon* of Locronan to perform his religious duties. He was a rich and powerful noble, then in his sixty-second year, but hale and sturdy, a great horseman and hunter and a pious man. So all his neighbours attested. In appearance he was short and broad, with a swarthy face, legs slightly bowed from the saddle, a hanging nose and broad hands with black hairs on them. He had married young and lost his wife and son soon after, and since then had lived alone at Kerfol. Twice a year he went to Morlaix, where he had a handsome house by the river, and spent a week or ten days there; and occasionally he rode to Rennes on business. Witnesses were found to declare that during these absences he led a life different from the one he was known to lead at Kerfol, where he busied himself with his estate, attended mass daily, and found his only amusement in hunting the wild boar and water-fowl. But these rumours are not particularly relevant, and it is certain that among people of his own class in the neighbourhood he passed for a stern and even austere man, observant of his religious obligations, and keeping strictly to himself. There was no talk of any familiarity with the women on his estate, though at that time the nobility were very free with their peasants. Some people said he had never looked at a woman since his wife's death; but such things are hard to prove, and the evidence on this point was not worth much.

Well, in his sixty-second year, Yves de Cornault went to the *pardon* at Locronan, and saw there a young lady of

Douarnenez, who had ridden over pillion behind her father to do her duty to the saint. Her name was Anne de Barrigan, and she came of good old Breton stock, but much less great and powerful than that of Yves de Cornault; and her father had squandered his fortune at cards, and lived almost like a peasant in his little granite manor on the moors ... I have said I would add nothing of my own to this bald statement of a strange case; but I must interrupt myself here to describe the young lady who rode up to the lych-gate of Locronan at the very moment when the Baron de Cornault was also dismounting there. I take my description from a faded drawing in red crayon, sober and truthful enough to be by a late pupil of the Clouets, which hangs in Lanrivain's study, and is said to be a portrait of Anne de Barrigan. It is unsigned and has no mark of identity but the initials A B, and the date 16—, the year after her marriage. It represents a young woman with a small oval face, almost pointed, yet wide enough for a full mouth with a tender depression at the corners. The nose is small, and the eyebrows are set rather high, far apart, and as lightly pencilled as the eyebrows in a Chinese painting. The forehead is high and serious, and the hair, which one feels to be fine and thick and fair, is drawn off it and lies close like a cap. The eyes are neither large nor small, hazel probably, with a look at once shy and steady. A pair of beautiful long hands are crossed below the lady's breast ...

The chaplain of Kerfol, and other witnesses, averred that when the Baron came back from Locronan he jumped from his horse, ordered another to be instantly saddled, called to a young page to come with him, and rode away that same evening to the south. His steward followed the next morning with coffers laden on a pair of pack mules. The following week Yves de Cornault rode back to Kerfol, sent for his vassals and tenants, and told them he was to be married at All Saints to

Anne de Barrigan of Douarnenez. And on All Saints' Day the marriage took place.

As to the next few years, the evidence on both sides seems to show that they passed happily for the couple. No one was found to say that Yves de Cornault had been unkind to his wife, and it was plain to all that he was content with his bargain. Indeed, it was admitted by the chaplain and other witnesses for the prosecution that the young lady had a softening influence on her husband, and that he became less exacting with his tenants, less harsh to peasants and dependents, and less subject to the fits of gloomy silence which had darkened his widowhood. As to his wife, the only grievance her champions could call up in her behalf was that Kerfol was a lonely place, and that when her husband was away on business at Rennes or Morlaix – whither she was never taken – she was not allowed so much as to walk in the park unaccompanied. But no one asserted that she was unhappy, though one servant-woman said she had surprised her crying, and had heard her say that she was a woman accursed to have no child, and nothing in life to call her own. But that was a natural enough feeling in a wife attached to her husband; and certainly it must have been a great grief to Yves de Cornault that she bore no son. Yet he never made her feel her childlessness as a reproach – she admits this in her evidence – but seemed to try to make her forget it by showering gifts and favours on her. Rich though he was, he had never been openhanded; but nothing was too fine for his wife, in the way of silks or gems or linen, or whatever else she fancied. Every wandering merchant was welcome at Kerfol, and when the master was called away he never came back without bringing his wife a handsome present – something curious and particular – from Morlaix or Rennes or Quimper. One of the waiting-women gave, in cross-examination, an interesting list of one year's gifts, which I copy. From Morlaix, a carved ivory junk, with Chinamen at the oars, that a strange sailor had brought back as a votive offering for Notre Dame de la Clarté, above Ploumanac'h; from Quimper, an embroidered gown, worked by the nuns of the Assumption; from Rennes, a silver rose that opened and showed an amber Virgin with a crown of garnets; from Morlaix, again, a length of Damascus velvet shot with gold, bought of a Jew from Syria; and for Michaelmas that same year, from Rennes, a necklet or bracelet of round stones – emeralds and pearls and rubies – strung like beads on a fine gold chain. This was the present that pleased the lady best, the woman said. Later on, as it happened, it was produced at the trial, and appears to have struck the Judges and the public as a curious and valuable jewel.

The very same winter, the Baron absented himself again, this time as far as Bordeaux, and on his return he brought his wife something even odder and prettier than the bracelet. It was a winter evening when he rode up to Kerfol and, walking into the hall, found her sitting by the hearth, her chin on her hand, looking into the fire. He carried a velvet box in his hand and, setting it down, lifted the lid and let out a little golden-brown dog.

Anne de Cornault exclaimed with pleasure as the little creature bounded toward her. 'Oh, it looks like a bird or a butterfly!' she cried as she picked it up; and the dog put its paws on her shoulders and looked at her with eyes 'like a Christian's'. After that she would never have it out of her sight, and petted and talked to it as if it had been a child – as indeed it was the nearest thing to a child she was to know. Yves de Cornault was much pleased with his purchase. The dog had been brought to him by a sailor from an East India merchantman, and the sailor had bought it of a pilgrim in a bazaar at Jaffa, who had stolen it from a nobleman's wife in

China: a perfectly permissible thing to do, since the pilgrim was a Christian and the nobleman a heathen doomed to hell-fire. Yves de Cornault had paid a long price for the dog, for they were beginning to be in demand at the French court, and the sailor knew he had got hold of a good thing; but Anne's pleasure was so great that, to see her laugh and play with the little animal, her husband would doubtless have given twice the sum.

So far, all the evidence is at one, and the narrative plain sailing; but now the steering becomes difficult. I will try to keep as nearly as possible to Anne's own statements; though toward the end, poor thing ...

Well, to go back. The very year after the little brown dog was brought to Kerfol, Yves de Cornault, one winter night, was found dead at the head of a narrow flight of stairs leading down from his wife's rooms to a door opening on the court. It was his wife who found him and gave the alarm, so distracted, poor wretch, with fear and horror – for his blood was all over her – that at first the roused household could not make out what she was saying, and thought she had suddenly gone mad. But there, sure enough, at the top of the stairs lay her husband, stone dead, and head foremost, the blood from his wounds dripping down to the steps below him. He had been dreadfully scratched and gashed about the face and throat, as if with curious pointed weapons; and one of his legs had a deep tear in it which had cut an artery, and probably caused his death. But how did he come there, and who had murdered him?

His wife declared that she had been asleep in her bed, and hearing his cry had rushed out to find him lying on the stairs; but this was immediately questioned. In the first place, it was proved that from her room she could not have heard the struggle on the stairs, owing to the thickness of the walls and the length of the intervening passage; then it was evident that she had not been in bed and asleep, since she was dressed when she roused the house, and her bed had not been slept in. Moreover, the door at the bottom of the stairs was ajar, and it was noticed by the chaplain (an observant man) that the dress she wore was stained with blood about the knees, and that there were traces of small blood-stained hands low down on the staircase walls, so that it was conjectured that she had really been at the postern-door when her husband fell and, feeling her way up to him in the darkness on her hands and knees, had been stained by his blood dripping down on her. Of course it was argued on the other side that the blood-marks on her dress might have been caused by her kneeling down by her husband when she rushed out of her room; but there was the open door below, and the fact that the finger-marks in the staircase all pointed upward.

The accused held to her statement for the first two days, in spite of its improbability; but on the third day word was brought to her that Hervé de Lanrivain, a young nobleman of the neighbourhood, had been arrested for complicity in the crime. Two or three witnesses thereupon came forward to say that it was known throughout the country that Lanrivain had formerly been on good terms with the lady of Cornault; but that he had been absent from Brittany for over a year, and people had ceased to associate their names. The witnesses who made this statement were not of a very reputable sort. One was an old herb-gatherer suspected of witchcraft, another a drunken clerk from a neighbouring parish, the third a half-witted shepherd who could be made to say anything; and it was clear that the prosecution was not satisfied with its case, and would have liked to find more definite proof of Lanrivain's complicity than the statement of the herb-gatherer, who swore to having seen him climbing the wall of the park on the night of the murder. One way of patching out incomplete proofs in those days was to put some sort of pressure, moral or physical, on the accused person. It is not clear what pressure was put on Anne de Cornault; but on the third day, when she was brought in court, she 'appeared weak and wandering', and after being encouraged to collect herself and speak the truth, on her honour and the wounds of her Blessed Redeemer, she confessed that she had in fact gone down the stairs to speak with Hervé de Lanrivain (who denied everything), and had been surprised there by the sound of her husband's fall. That was better; and the prosecution rubbed its hands with satisfaction. The satisfaction increased when various dependents living at Kerfol were induced to say – with apparent sincerity – that during the year or two preceding his death their master had once more grown uncertain and irascible, and subject to the fits of brooding silence which his household had learned to dread before his second marriage. This seemed to show that things had not been going well at Kerfol; though no one could be found to say that there had been any signs of open disagreement between husband and wife.

Anne de Cornault, when questioned as to her reason for going down at night to open the door to Hervé de Lanrivain, made an answer which must have sent a smile around the court. She said it was because she was lonely and wanted to talk with the young man. Was this the only reason? she was asked; and replied: 'Yes, by the Cross over your Lordships' heads.' 'But why at midnight?' the court asked. 'Because I could see him in no other way.' I can see the exchange of glances across the ermine collars under the Crucifix.

Anne de Cornault, further questioned, said that her married life had been extremely lonely: 'desolate' was the word she used. It was true that her husband seldom spoke harshly to her; but there were days when he did not speak at all. It was true that he had never struck or threatened her; but he kept her like a prisoner at Kerfol, and when he rode away to

Morlaix or Quimper or Rennes he set so close a watch on her that she could not pick a flower in the garden without having a waiting-woman at her heels. 'I am no Queen, to need such honours,' she once said to him; and he had answered that a man who has a treasure does not leave the key in the lock when he goes out. 'Then take me with you,' she urged; but to this he said that towns were pernicious places, and young wives better off at their own firesides.

'But what did you want to say to Hervé de Lanrivain?' the court asked; and she answered: 'To ask him to take me away.'

'Ah – you confess that you went down to him with adulterous thoughts?'

'No.'

'Then why did you want him to take you away?'

'Because I was afraid for my life.'

'Of whom were you afraid?'

'Of my husband.'

'Why were you afraid of your husband?'

'Because he had strangled my little dog.'

Another smile must have passed around the courtroom: in days when any nobleman had a right to hang his peasants – and most of them exercised it – pinching a pet animal's windpipe was nothing to make a fuss about.

At this point one of the Judges, who appears to have had a certain sympathy for the accused, suggested that she should be allowed to explain herself in her own way; and she thereupon made the following statement.

The first years of her marriage had been lonely; but her husband had not been unkind to her. If she had had a child she would not have been unhappy; but the days were long, and it rained too much.

It was true that her husband, whenever he went away and left her, brought her a handsome present on his return; but this did not make up for the loneliness. At least nothing had, till he brought her the little brown dog from the East: after that she was much less unhappy. Her husband seemed pleased that she was so fond of the dog; he gave her leave to put her jewelled bracelet around its neck, and to keep it always with her.

One day she had fallen asleep in her room, with the dog at her feet, as his habit was. Her feet were bare and resting on his back. Suddenly she was waked by her husband: he stood beside her, smiling not unkindly.

'You look like my great-grandmother, Juliane de Cornault, lying in the chapel with her feet on a little dog,' he said.

The analogy sent a chill through her, but she laughed and answered: 'Well, when I am dead you must put me beside her, carved in marble, with my dog at my feet.'

'Oho – we'll wait and see,' he said, laughing also, but with his black brows close together. 'The dog is the emblem of fidelity.'

'And do you doubt my right to lie with mine at my feet?'

'When I'm in doubt I find out,' he answered. 'I am an old man,' he added, 'and people say I make you lead a lonely life. But I swear you shall have your monument if you earn it.'

'And I swear to be faithful,' she returned, 'if only for the sake of having my little dog at my feet.'

Not long afterward he went on business to the Quimper Assizes; and while he was away his aunt, the widow of a great nobleman of the duchy, came to spend a night at Kerfol on her way to the *pardon* of Ste Barbe. She was a woman of piety and consequence, and much respected by Yves de Cornault, and when she proposed to Anne to go with her to Ste Barbe no one could object, and even the chaplain declared himself in favour of the pilgrimage. So Anne set out for Ste Barbe, and there for the first time she talked with Hervé de Lanrivain. He had come once or twice to Kerfol with his father, but she had never before exchanged a dozen words with him. They did not talk for more than five minutes now: it was under the chestnuts, as the procession was coming out of the chapel. He said: 'I pity you', and she was surprised, for she had not supposed that anyone thought her an object of pity. He added: 'Call for me when you need me,' and she smiled a little, but was glad afterward, and thought often of the meeting.

She confessed to having seen him three times afterward: not more. How or where she would not say – one had the impression that she feared to implicate someone. Their meetings had been rare and brief; and at the last he had told her that he was starting the next day for a foreign country, on a mission which was not without peril and might keep him for many months absent. He asked her for a remembrance, and she had none to give him but the collar about the little dog's neck. She was sorry afterward that she had given it, but he was so unhappy at going that she had not had the courage to refuse.

Her husband was away at the time. When he returned a few days later he picked up the animal to pet it, and noticed that its collar was missing. His wife told him that the dog had lost it in the undergrowth of the park, and that she and her maids had hunted a whole day for it. It was true, she explained to the court, that she had made the maids search for the necklet – they all believed the dog had lost it in the park …

Her husband made no comment, and that evening at supper he was in his usual mood, between good and bad: you could never tell which. He talked a good deal, describing what he had seen and done at Rennes; but now and then he stopped and looked hard at her, and when she went to bed she found her little dog strangled on her pillow. The little thing was dead, but still warm; she stooped to lift it, and her distress turned to horror when she discovered that it had been strangled by twisting twice round its throat the necklet she had given to Lanrivain.

The next morning at dawn she buried the dog in the garden, and hid the necklet in her breast. She said nothing to her husband, then or later, and he said nothing to her; but that day he had a peasant hanged for stealing a faggot in the park, and the next day he nearly beat to death a young horse he was breaking.

Winter set in, and the short days passed, and the long nights, one by one; and she heard nothing of Hervé de Lanrivain. It might be that her husband had killed him; or merely that he had been robbed of the necklet. Day after day by the hearth among the spinning maids, night after night alone on her bed, she wondered and trembled. Sometimes at table her husband looked across at her and smiled; and then she felt sure that Lanrivain was dead. She dared not try to get news of him, for she was sure her husband would find out if she did: she had an idea that he could find out anything. Even when a witch-woman who was a noted seer, and could show you the whole world in her crystal, came to the castle for a night's shelter, and the maids flocked to her, Anne held back.

The winter was long and black and rainy. One day, in Yves de Cornault's absence, some gypsies came to Kerfol with a troop of performing dogs. Anne bought the smallest and cleverest, a white dog with a feathery coat and one blue and one brown eye. It seemed to have been ill-treated by the gypsies, and clung to her plaintively when she took it from them. That evening her husband came back, and when she went to bed she found the dog strangled on her pillow.

After that she said to herself that she would never have another dog; but one bitter cold evening a poor lean greyhound was found whining at the castle-gate, and she took him in and forbade the maids to speak of him to her husband. She hid him in a room that no one went to, smuggled food to him from her own plate, made him a warm bed to lie on and petted him like a child.

Yves de Cornault came home, and the next day she found the greyhound strangled on her pillow. She wept in secret, but said nothing, and resolved that even if she met a dog dying of hunger she would never bring him into the castle; but one day she found a young sheepdog, a brindled puppy with good blue eyes, lying with a broken leg in the snow of the park. Yves de Cornault was at Rennes, and she brought the dog in, warmed and fed it, tied up its leg and hid it in the castle till her husband's return. The day before, she gave it to a peasant woman who lived a long way off, and paid her handsomely to care for it and say nothing; but that night she heard a whining and scratching at her door, and when she opened it the lame puppy, drenched and shivering, jumped up on her with little sobbing barks. She hid him in her bed, and the next morning was about to have him taken back to the peasant woman when she heard her husband ride into the court. She shut the dog in a chest, and went down to receive him. An hour or two later, when she returned to her room, the puppy lay strangled on her pillow …

After that she dared not make a pet of any other dog; and her loneliness became almost unendurable. Sometimes, when she crossed the court of the castle, and thought no one was looking, she stopped to pat the old pointer at the gate. But one day as she was caressing him her husband came out of the chapel; and the next day the old dog was gone …

This curious narrative was not told in one sitting of the court, or received without impatience and incredulous comment. It was plain that the Judges were surprised by its puerility, and that it did not help the accused in the eyes of the public. It was an odd tale, certainly; but what did it prove? That Yves de Cornault disliked dogs, and that his wife, to gratify her own fancy, persistently ignored this dislike. As for pleading this trivial disagreement as an excuse for her relations – whatever their nature – with her supposed accomplice, the argument was so absurd that her own lawyer manifestly regretted having let her make use of it, and tried several times to cut short her story. But she went on to the end, with a kind of hypnotized insistence, as though the scenes she evoked were so real to her that she had forgotten where she was and imagined herself to be re-living them.

At length the Judge who had previously shown a certain kindness to her said (leaning forward a little, one may suppose, from his row of dozing colleagues): 'Then you would have us believe that you murdered your husband because he would not let you keep a pet dog?'

'I did not murder my husband.'

'Who did, then? Hervé de Lanrivain?'

'No.'

'Who then? Can you tell us?'

'Yes, I can tell you. The dogs –' At that point she was carried out of the court in a swoon.

✕

It was evident that her lawyer tried to get her to abandon this line of defence. Possibly her explanation, whatever it was, had seemed convincing when she poured it out to him in the heat of their first private colloquy; but now that it was exposed to the cold daylight of judicial scrutiny, and the banter of the town, he was thoroughly ashamed of it, and would have sacrificed her without a scruple to save his professional reputation. But the obstinate Judge – who perhaps, after all, was more inquisitive than kindly – evidently wanted to hear the story out, and she was ordered, the next day, to continue her deposition.

She said that after the disappearance of the old watchdog nothing particular happened for a month or two. Her husband was much as usual: she did not remember any special incident. But one evening a pedlar woman came to the castle and was selling trinkets to the maids. She had no heart for trinkets, but she stood looking on while the women made their choice. And then, she did not know how, but the pedlar coaxed her into buying for herself a pear-shaped pomander with a strong scent in it – she had once seen something of the kind on a gypsy woman. She had no desire for the pomander, and did not know why she had bought it. The pedlar said that whoever wore it had the power to read the future; but she did not really believe that, or care much either. However, she bought the thing and took it up to her room, where she sat turning it about in her hand. Then the strange scent attracted her and she began to wonder what kind of spice was in the box. She opened it and found a grey bean rolled in a strip of paper; and on the paper she saw a sign she knew, and a message from Hervé de Lanrivain, saying that he was at home again and would be at the door in the court that night after the moon had set ...

She burned the paper and sat down to think. It was nightfall, and her husband was at home ... She had no way of warning Lanrivain, and there was nothing to do but to wait ...

At this point I fancy the drowsy court-room beginning to wake up. Even to the oldest hand on the bench there must have been a certain relish in picturing the feelings of a woman on receiving such a message at nightfall from a man living twenty miles away, to whom she had no means of sending a warning ...

She was not a clever woman, I imagine; and as the first result of her cogitation she appears to have made the mistake of being, that evening, too kind to her husband. She could not ply him with wine, according to the traditional expedient, for though he drank heavily at times he had a strong head; and when he drank beyond its strength it was because he chose to, and not because a woman coaxed him. Not his wife, at any rate – she was an old story by now. As I read the case, I fancy there was no feeling for her left in him but the hatred occasioned by his supposed dishonour.

At any rate, she tried to call up her old graces; but early in the evening he complained of pains and fever, and left the hall to go up to the closet where he sometimes slept. His servant carried him a cup of hot wine, and brought back word that he was sleeping and not to be disturbed; and an hour later, when Anne lifted the tapestry and listened at his door, she heard his loud regular breathing. She thought it might be a feint, and stayed a long time barefooted in the passage, her ear to the crack; but the breathing went on too steadily and naturally to be other than that of a man in a sound sleep. She crept back to her room reassured, and stood in the window watching the moon set through the trees of the park. The sky was misty and starless, and after the moon went down the night was black as pitch. She knew the time had come, and stole along the passage, past her husband's door – where she stopped again to listen to his breathing – to the top of the stairs. There she paused a moment, and assured herself that no one was following her; then she began to go down the stairs in the darkness. They were so steep and winding that she had to go very slowly, for fear of stumbling. Her one thought was to get the door unbolted, tell Lanrivain to make his escape, and hasten back to her room. She had tried the bolt earlier in the evening, and managed to put a little grease on it; but nevertheless, when she drew it, it gave a squeak ... not loud, but it made her heart stop; and the next minute, overhead, she heard a noise ...

'What noise?' the prosecution interposed.

'My husband's voice calling out my name and cursing me.'

'What did you hear after that?'

'A terrible scream and a fall.'

'Where was Hervé de Lanrivain at this time?'

'He was standing outside in the court. I just made him out in the darkness. I told him for God's sake to go, and then I pushed the door shut.'

'What did you do next?'

'I stood at the foot of the stairs and listened.'

'What did you hear?'

'I heard dogs snarling and panting.' (Visible discouragement of the bench, boredom of the public, and exasperation of the lawyer for the defense. Dogs again –! But the inquisitive Judge insisted.)

'What dogs?'

She bent her head and spoke so low that she had to be told to repeat her answer: 'I don't know.'

'How do you mean – you don't know?'

'I don't know what dogs ...'

The Judge again intervened: 'Try to tell us exactly what happened. How long did you remain at the foot of the stairs?'

'Only a few minutes.'

'And what was going on meanwhile overhead?'

'The dogs kept on snarling and panting. Once or twice he cried out. I think he moaned once. Then he was quiet.'

'Then what happened?'

'Then I heard a sound like the noise of a pack when the wolf is thrown to them – gulping and lapping.'

(There was a groan of disgust and repulsion through the court, and another attempted intervention by the distracted lawyer. But the inquisitive Judge was still inquisitive.)

'And all the while you did not go up?'

'Yes – I went up then – to drive them off.'

'The dogs?'

'Yes.'

'Well –?'

'When I got there it was quite dark. I found my husband's flint and steel and struck a spark. I saw him lying there. He was dead.'

'And the dogs?'

'The dogs were gone.'

'Gone – where to?'

'I don't know. There was no way out – and there were no dogs at Kerfol.'

She straightened herself to her full height, threw her arms above her head, and fell down on the stone floor with a long scream. There was a moment of confusion in the court-room. Someone on the bench was heard to say: 'This is clearly a case for the ecclesiastical authorities' – and the prisoner's lawyer doubtless jumped at the suggestion.

After this, the trial loses itself in a maze of cross-questioning and squabbling. Every witness who was called corroborated Anne de Cornault's statement that there were no dogs at Kerfol: had been none for several months. The master of the house had taken a dislike to dogs, there was no denying it. But, on the other hand, at the inquest, there had been long and bitter discussions as to the nature of the dead man's wounds. One of the surgeons called in had spoken of marks that looked like bites. The suggestion of witchcraft was revived, and the opposing lawyers hurled tomes of necromancy at each other.

At last Anne de Cornault was brought back into court – at the instance of the same Judge – and asked if she knew where the dogs she spoke of could have come from. On the body of her Redeemer she swore that she did not. Then the Judge put his final question: 'If the dogs you think you heard had been known to you, do you think you would have recognized them by their barking?'

'Yes.'

'Did you recognize them?'

'Yes.'

'What dogs do you take them to have been?'

'My dead dogs,' she said in a whisper ... She was taken out of court, not to reappear there again. There was some kind of ecclesiastical investigation, and the end of the business was that the Judges disagreed with each other, and with the ecclesiastical committee, and that Anne de Cornault was finally handed over to the keeping of her husband's family, who shut her up in the keep of Kerfol, where she is said to have died many years later, a harmless mad-woman.

So ends her story. As for that of Hervé de Lanrivain, I had only to apply to his collateral descendant for its subsequent details. The evidence against the young man being insufficient, and his family influence in the duchy considerable, he was set free, and left soon afterward for Paris. He was probably in no mood for a worldly life, and he appears to have come almost immediately under the influence of the famous M Arnauld d'Andilly and the gentlemen of Port Royal. A year or two later he was received into their Order, and without achieving any particular distinction he followed its good and evil fortunes till his death some twenty years later. Lanrivain showed me a portrait of him by a pupil of Philippe de Champaigne: sad eyes, an impulsive mouth and a narrow brow. Poor Hervé de Lanrivain: it was a grey ending. Yet as I looked at his stiff and sallow effigy, in the dark dress of the Jansenists, I almost found myself envying his fate. After all, in the course of his life two great things had happened to him: he had loved romantically, and he must have talked with Pascal ...

6 Unseen – Unfeared

BY FRANCIS STEVENS

I

I had been dining with my ever-interesting friend, Mark Jenkins, at a little Italian restaurant near South Street. It was a chance meeting. Jenkins is too busy, usually, to make dinner engagements. Over our highly seasoned food and sour, thin, red wine, he spoke of little odd incidents and adventures of his profession. Nothing very vital or important, of course. Jenkins is not the sort of detective who first detects and then pours the egotistical and revealing details of achievement in the ears of every acquaintance, however appreciative.

But when I spoke of something I had seen in the morning papers, he laughed. 'Poor old "Doc" Holt! Fascinating old codger, to any one who really knows him. I've had his friendship for years – since I was first on the city force and saved a young assistant of his from jail on a false charge. And they had to drag him into the poisoning of this young sport, Ralph Peeler!'

'Why are you so sure he couldn't have been implicated?' I asked.

But Jenkins only shook his head, with a quiet smile. 'I have reasons for believing otherwise,' was all I could get out of him on that score, 'But,' he added, 'the only reason he was suspected at all is the superstitious dread of these ignorant people around him. Can't see why he lives in such a place. I know for a fact he doesn't have to. Doc's got money of his own. He's an amateur chemist and dabbler in different sorts of research work, and I suspect he's been guilty of "showing off". Result, they all swear he has the evil eye and holds forbidden communion with invisible powers. Smoke?'

Jenkins offered me one of his invariably good cigars, which I accepted, saying thoughtfully: 'A man has no right to trifle with the superstitions of ignorant people. Sooner or later, it spells trouble.'

'Did in his case. They swore up and down that he sold love charms openly and poisons secretly, and that, together with his living so near to – somebody else – got him temporarily suspected. But my tongue's running away with me, as usual!'

'As usual,' I retorted impatiently, 'you open up with all the frankness of a Chinese diplomat.'

He beamed upon me engagingly and rose from the table, with a glance at his watch. 'Sorry to leave you, Blaisdell, but I have to meet Jimmy Brennan in ten minutes.'

He so clearly did not invite my further company that I remained seated for a little while after his departure; then took my own way homeward. Those streets always held for me a certain fascination, particularly at night. They are so unlike the rest of the city, so foreign in appearance, with their little shabby stores, always open until late evening, their unbelievably cheap goods, displayed as much outside the shops as in them, hung on the fronts and laid out on tables by the curb and in the street itself. To-night, however, neither people nor stores in any sense appealed to me. The mixture of Italians, Jews and a few negroes, mostly bareheaded, unkempt and generally unhygienic in appearance, struck me as merely revolting. They were all humans, and I, too, was human. Some way I did not like the idea.

Puzzled a trifle, for I am more inclined to sympathize with poverty than accuse it, I watched the faces that I passed. Never before had I observed how stupid, how bestial, how brutal were the countenances of the dwellers in this region. I actually shuddered when an old-clothes man, a gray-bearded

Hebrew, brushed me as he toiled past with his barrow.

There was a sense of evil in the air, a warning of things which it is wise for a clean man to shun and keep clear of. The impression became so strong that before I had walked two squares I began to feel physically ill. Then it occurred to me that the one glass of cheap Chianti I had drunk might have something to do with the feeling. Who knew how that stuff had been manufactured, or whether the juice of the grape entered at all into its ill-flavoured composition? Yet I doubted if that were the real cause of my discomfort.

By nature I am rather a sensitive, impressionable sort of chap. In some way to-night this neighbourhood, with its sordid sights and smells, had struck me wrong.

My sense of impending evil was merging into actual fear. This would never do. There is only one way to deal with an imaginative temperament like mine – conquer its vagaries. If I left South Street with this nameless dread upon me, I could never pass down it again without a recurrence of the feeling. I should simply have to stay here until I got the better of it – that was all.

I paused on a corner before a shabby but brightly lighted little drug store. Its gleaming windows and the luminous green of its conventional glass show jars made the brightest spot on the block. I realized that I was tired, but hardly wanted to go in there and rest. I knew what the company would be like at its shabby, sticky soda fountain. As I stood there, my eyes fell on a long white canvas sign across from me, and its black-and-red lettering caught my attention.

SEE THE GREAT UNSEEN!
Come in! This Means You!
Free to All!

A museum of fakes, I thought, but also reflected that if it were a show of some kind I could sit down for a while, rest, and fight off this increasing obsession of nonexistent evil. That side of the street was almost deserted, and the place itself might well be nearly empty.

II

I walked over, but with every step my sense of dread increased. Dread of I knew not what. Bodiless, inexplicable horror had me as in a net, whose strands, being intangible, without reason for existence, I could by no means throw off. It was not the people now. None of them were about me. There, in the open, lighted street, with no sight nor sound of terror to assail me, I was the shivering victim of such fear as I had never known was possible. Yet still I would not yield.

Setting my teeth, and fighting with myself as with some pet animal gone mad, I forced my steps to slowness and walked along the sidewalk, seeking entrance. Just here there were no shops, but several doors reached in each case by means of a few iron-railed stone steps. I chose the one in the middle beneath the sign. In that neighbourhood there are museums, shops and other commercial enterprises conducted in many shabby old residences, such as were these. Behind the glazing of the door I had chosen I could see a dim, pinkish light, but on either side the windows were quite dark.

Trying the door, I found it unlocked. As I opened it a party of Italians passed on the pavement below and I looked back at them over my shoulder. They were gaily dressed, men, women and children, laughing and chattering to one another; probably on their way to some wedding or other festivity.

In passing, one of the men glanced up at me and involuntarily I shuddered back against the door. He was a young man, handsome after the swarthy manner of his race, but never in my life had I seen a face so expressive of pure, malicious cruelty, naked and unashamed. Our eyes met and his seemed to light up with a vile gleaming, as if all the wickedness of his nature had come to a focus in the look of concentrated hate he gave me.

They went by, but for some distance I could see him watching me, chin on shoulder, till he and his party were swallowed up in the crowd of marketers farther down the street.

Sick and trembling from that encounter, merely of eyes though it had been, I threw aside my partly smoked cigar and entered. Within there was a small vestibule, whose ancient tessellated floor was grimy with the passing of many feet. I could feel the grit of dirt under my shoes, and it rasped on my rawly quivering nerves. The inner door stood partly open, and going on I found myself in a bare, dirty hallway, and was greeted by the sour, musty, poverty-stricken smell common to dwellings of the very ill-to-do. Beyond there was a stairway, carpeted with ragged grass matting. A gas jet, turned low inside a very dusty pink globe, was the light I had seen from without.

Listening, the house seemed entirely silent. Surely, this was no place of public amusement of any kind whatever. More likely it was a rooming house, and I had, after all, mistaken the entrance.

To my intense relief, since coming inside, the worst agony of my unreasonable terror had passed away. If I could only get in some place where I could sit down and be quiet, probably I should be rid of it for good. Determining to try another entrance, I was about to leave the bare hallway when one of several doors along the side of it suddenly opened and a man stepped out into the hall.

'Well?' he said, looking at me keenly, but with not the least show of surprise at my presence.

'I beg your pardon,' I replied. 'The door was unlocked and I came in here, thinking it was the entrance to the exhibit

– what do they call it? – the "Great Unseen". The one that is mentioned on that long white sign. Can you tell me which door is the right one?'

'I can.'

With that brief answer he stopped and stared at me again. He was a tall, lean man, somewhat stooped, but possessing considerable dignity of bearing. For that neighbourhood, he appeared uncommonly well dressed, and his long, smooth-shaven face was noticeable because, while his complexion was dark and his eyes coal-black, above them the heavy brows and his hair were almost silvery-white. His age might have been anything over the threescore mark.

I grew tired of being stared at. 'If you can and – won't, then never mind,' I observed a trifle irritably, and turned to go. But his sharp exclamation halted me.

'No!' he said. 'No – no! Forgive me for pausing – it was not hesitation, I assure you. To think that one – one, even, has come! All day they pass my sign up there – pass and fear to enter. But you are different. *You* are not of these timorous, ignorant foreign peasants. You ask me to tell you the right door? Here it is! Here!'

And he struck the panel of the door, which he had closed behind him, so that the sharp yet hollow sound of it echoed up through the silent house.

Now it may be thought that after all my senseless terror in the open street, so strange a welcome from so odd a showman would have brought the feeling back, full force. But there is an emotion stronger, to a certain point, than fear. This queer old fellow aroused my curiosity. What kind of museum could it be that he accused the passing public of fearing to enter? Nothing really terrible, surely, or it would have been closed by the police. And normally I am not an unduly timorous person. 'So it's in there, is it?' I asked, coming toward him.

'And I'm to be sole audience? Come, that will be an interesting experience.' I was half laughing now.

'The most interesting in the world,' said the old man, with a solemnity which rebuked my lightness.

With that he opened the door, passed inward and closed it again – in my very face. I stood staring at it blankly. The panels, I remember, had been originally painted white, but now the paint was flaked and blistered, gray with dirt and dirty finger marks. Suddenly it occurred to me that I had no wish to enter there. Whatever was behind it could be scarcely worth seeing, or he would not choose such a place for its exhibition. With the old man's vanishing my curiosity had cooled, but just as I again turned to leave, the door opened and this singular showman stuck his white-eyebrowed face through the aperture. He was frowning impatiently. 'Come in – come in!' he snapped, and promptly withdrawing his head, once more closed the door.

'He has something in there he doesn't want should get out,' was the very natural conclusion which I drew. 'Well, since it can hardly be anything dangerous, and he's so anxious I should see it – here goes!'

With that I turned the soiled white porcelain handle, and entered.

The room I came into was neither very large nor very brightly lighted. In no way did it resemble a museum or lecture room. On the contrary, it seemed to have been fitted up as a quite well-appointed laboratory. The floor was linoleum-covered, there were glass cases along the walls whose shelves were filled with bottles, specimen jars, graduates, and the like. A large table in one corner bore what looked like some odd sort of camera, and a larger one in the middle of the room was fitted with a long rack filled with bottles and test tubes, and was besides littered with papers, glass slides, and various paraphernalia which my ignorance failed to identify. There were several cases of books, a few plain wooden chairs, and in the corner a large iron sink with running water.

My host of the white hair and black eyes was awaiting me, standing near the larger table. He indicated one of the wooden chairs with a thin forefinger that shook a little, either from age or eagerness. 'Sit down – sit down! Have no fear but that you will be interested, my friend. Have no fear at all – of anything!'

As he said it he fixed his dark eyes upon me and stared harder than ever. But the effect of his words was the opposite of their meaning. I did sit down, because my knees gave under me, but if in the outer hall I had lost my terror, it now returned twofold upon me. Out there the light had been faint, dingily roseate, indefinite. By it I had not perceived how this old man's face was a mask of living malice – of cruelty, hate and a certain masterful contempt. Now I knew the meaning of my fear, whose warning I would not heed. Now I knew that I had walked into the very trap from which my abnormal sensitiveness had striven in vain to save me.

III

Again I struggled within me, bit at my lip till I tasted blood, and presently the blind paroxysm passed. It must have been longer in going than I thought, and the old man must have all that time been speaking, for when I could once more control my attention, hear and see him, he had taken up a position near the sink, about ten feet away, and was addressing me with a sort of 'platform' manner, as if I had been the large audience whose absence he had deplored.

'And so,' he was saying, 'I was forced to make these plates very carefully, to truly represent the characteristic hues of each separate organism. Now, in colour work of every kind the film is necessarily extremely sensitive. Doubtless you are familiar in a general way with the exquisite transparencies produced by color photography of the single-plate type.'

He paused, and trying to act like a normal human being, I observed: 'I saw some nice landscapes done in that way – last week at an illustrated lecture in Franklin Hall.'

He scowled, and made an impatient gesture at me with his hand. 'I can proceed better without interruptions,' he said. 'My pause was purely oratorical.'

I meekly subsided, and he went on in his original loud, clear voice. He would have made an excellent lecturer before a much larger audience – if only his voice could have lost that eerie, ringing note. Thinking of that I must have missed some more, and when I caught it again he was saying:

'As I have indicated, the original plate is the final picture. Now, many of these organisms are extremely hard to photograph, and microphotography in colour is particularly difficult. In consequence, to spoil a plate tries the patience of the photographer. They are so sensitive that the ordinary dark-room ruby lamp would instantly ruin them, and they must therefore be developed either in darkness or by a special light produced by interposing thin sheets of tissue of a particular shade of green and of yellow between lamp and plate, and even that will often cause ruinous fog. Now I, finding it hard to handle them so, made numerous experiments with a view to discovering some glass or fabric of a colour which should add to the safety of the green, without robbing it of all efficiency. All proved equally useless, but intermittently I persevered – until last week.'

His voice dropped to an almost confidential tone, and he leaned slightly toward me. I was cold from my neck to my feet, though my head was burning, but I tried to force an appreciative smile.

'Last week,' he continued impressively, 'I had a prescription filled at the corner drug store. The bottle was sent home to me wrapped in a piece of what I first took to be whitish, slightly opalescent paper. Later I decided that it was some kind of membrane. When I questioned the druggist, seeking its source, he said it was a sheet of 'paper' that was around a bundle of herbs from South America. That he had no more, and doubted if I could trace it. He had wrapped my bottle so, because he was in haste and the sheet was handy.

'I can hardly tell you what first inspired me to try that membrane in my photographic work. It was merely dull white with a faint hint of opalescence, except when held against the light. Then it became quite translucent and quite brightly prismatic. For some reason it occurred to me that this refractive effect might help in breaking up the actinic rays – the rays which affect the sensitive emulsion. So that night I inserted it behind the sheets of green and yellow tissue, next the lamp, prepared my trays and chemicals, laid my plate holders to hand, turned off the white light and – turned on the green!'

There was nothing in his words to inspire fear. It was a wearisomely detailed account of his struggles with photography. Yet, as he again paused impressively, I wished that he might never speak again. I was desperately, contemptibly in dread of the thing he might say next.

Suddenly, he drew himself erect, the stoop went out of his shoulders, he threw back his head and laughed. It was a hollow sound, as if he laughed into a trumpet. 'I won't tell you what I saw! Why should I? Your own eyes shall bear witness. But this much I'll say, so that you may better understand – later. When our poor, faultily sensitive vision can perceive a thing, we say that it is visible. When the nerves of touch can feel it, we say that it is tangible. Yet I tell you there are beings intangible to our physical sense, yet whose presence is felt by the spirit, and invisible to our eyes merely because those organs are not attuned to the light as reflected from their bodies. But light passed through the screen which we are about to use has a wavelength novel to the scientific world, and by it you shall see with the eyes of the flesh that which has been invisible since life began. Have no fear!'

He stopped to laugh again, and his mirth was yellow-toothed – menacing.

'*Have no fear!*' he reiterated, and with that stretched his hand toward the wall, there came a click and we were in black, impenetrable darkness. I wanted to spring up, to seek the door by which I had entered and rush out of it, but the paralysis of unreasoning terror held me fast.

I could hear him moving about in the darkness, and a moment later a faint green glimmer sprang up in the room. Its source was over the large sink, where I suppose he developed his precious 'colour plates'.

Every instant, as my eyes became accustomed to the dimness, I could see more clearly. Green light is peculiar. It may be far fainter than red, and at the same time far more illuminating. The old man was standing beneath it, and his face by that ghastly radiance had the exact look of a dead man's. Beside this, however, I could observe nothing appalling.

'That,' continued the man, 'is the simple developing light of which I have spoken – now watch, for what you are about to behold no mortal man but myself has ever seen before.'

For a moment he fussed with the green lamp over the sink. It was so constructed that all the direct rays struck downward. He opened a flap at the side, for a moment there was a streak of comforting white luminance from within, then he inserted something, slid it slowly in – and closed the flap.

The thing he put in—that South American 'membrane' it must have been – instead of decreasing the light increased it – amazingly. The hue was changed from green to greenish-gray, and the whole room sprang into view, a livid, ghastly chamber, filled with – overcrawled by – what?

My eyes fixed themselves, fascinated, on something that moved by the old man's feet. It writhed there on the floor like a huge, repulsive starfish, an immense, armed, legged thing, that twisted convulsively. It was smooth, as if made of rubber, was whitish-green in colour; and presently raised its great round blob of a body on tottering tentacles, crept toward my host and writhed upward – yes, climbed up his legs, his body. And he stood there, erect, arms folded, and stared sternly down at the thing which climbed.

But the room – the whole room was alive with other creatures than that. Everywhere I looked they were – centipedish things, with yard-long bodies, detestable, furry spiders that lurked in shadows, and sausage-shaped translucent horrors that moved – and floated through the air. They dived here and there between me and the light, and I could see its brighter greenness through their greenish bodies.

Worse, though, far worse than these were the *things with human faces*. Mask-like, monstrous, huge gaping mouths and slitlike eyes – I find I cannot write of them. There was that about them which makes their memory even now intolerable.

The old man was speaking again, and every word echoed in my brain like the ringing of a gong. 'Fear nothing! Among such as these do you move every hour of the day and the night. Only you and I have seen, for God is merciful and has spared our race from sight. But I am not merciful! I loathe the race which gave these creatures birth – the race which might be so surrounded by invisible, unguessed but blessed beings – and chooses these for its companions! All the world shall see and know. One by one shall they come here, learn the truth, and perish. For who can survive the ultimate of terror? Then I, too, shall find peace, and leave the earth to its heritage of man-created horrors. Do you know what these are – whence they come?'

His voice boomed now like a cathedral bell. I could not answer, him, but he waited for no reply. 'Out of the ether – out of the omnipresent ether from whose intangible substance the mind of God made the planets, all living things, and man – man has made these! By his evil thoughts, by his selfish panics, by his lusts and his interminable, never-ending hate he has made them, and they are everywhere! Fear nothing – they cannot harm your body – but let your spirit beware! Fear nothing – but see where there comes to you, its creator, the shape and the body of your FEAR!'

And as he said it I perceived a great Thing coming toward me – a Thing – but consciousness could endure no more. The ringing, threatening voice merged in a roar within my ears, there came a merciful dimming of the terrible, lurid vision, and blank nothingness succeeded upon horror too great for bearing.

IV

There was a dull, heavy pain above my eyes. I knew that they were closed, that I was dreaming, and that the rack full of coloured bottles which I seemed to see so clearly was no more than a part of the dream. There was some vague but imperative reason why I should rouse myself. I wanted to awaken, and thought that by staring very hard indeed I could dissolve this foolish vision of blue and yellow-brown bottles. But instead of dissolving they grew clearer, more solid and substantial of appearance, until suddenly the rest of my senses rushed to the support of sight, and I became aware that my eyes were open, the bottles were quite real, and that I was sitting in a chair, fallen sideways so that my cheek rested most uncomfortably on the table which held the rack.

I straightened up slowly and with difficulty, groping in my dulled brain for some clue to my presence in this unfamiliar place, this laboratory that was lighted only by the rays of an arc light in the street outside its three large windows. Here I sat, alone, and if the aching of cramped limbs meant anything, here I had sat for more than a little time.

Then, with the painful shock which accompanies awakening to the knowledge of some great catastrophe, came memory. It was this very room, shown by the street lamp's rays to be empty of life, which I had seen thronged with creatures too loathsome for description. I staggered to my feet, staring fearfully about. There were the glass-floored cases, the bookshelves, the two tables with their burdens, and the long iron sink above which, now only a dark blotch of shadow, hung the lamp from which had emanated that livid, terrifically revealing illumination. Then the experience had been no dream, but a frightful reality. I was alone here now. With callous indifference my strange host had allowed me to remain for hours unconscious, with not the least effort to aid or revive me. Perhaps, hating me so, he had hoped that I would die there.

At first I made no effort to leave the place. Its appearance filled me with reminiscent loathing. I longed to go, but as yet felt too weak and ill for the effort. Both mentally and physically my condition was deplorable, and for the first time I realized that a shock to the mind may react upon the body as vilely as any debauch of self-indulgence.

Quivering in every nerve and muscle, dizzy with headache and nausea, I dropped back into the chair, hoping that before the old man returned I might recover sufficient self-control to escape him. I knew that he hated me, and why. As I waited, sick, miserable, I understood the man. Shuddering, I recalled the loathsome horrors he had shown me. If the mere desires and emotions of mankind were daily carnified in such forms as those, no wonder that he viewed his fellow beings with detestation and longed only to destroy them.

I thought, too, of the cruel, sensuous faces I had seen in the streets outside – seen for the first time, as if a veil had been withdrawn from eyes hitherto blinded by self-delusion. Fatuously trustful as a month-old puppy, I had lived in a grim, evil world, where goodness is a word and crude selfishness the only actuality. Drearily my thoughts drifted back through my own life, its futile purposes, mistakes and activities. All of evil that I knew returned to overwhelm me. Our gropings toward divinity were a sham, a writhing sunward of slime-covered beasts who claimed sunlight as their heritage, but in their hearts preferred the foul and easy depths.

Even now, though I could neither see nor feel them, this room, the entire world, was acrawl with the beings created by our real natures. I recalled the cringing, contemptible fear to which my spirit had so readily yielded, and the faceless Thing to which the emotion had given birth.

Then abruptly, shockingly, I remembered that every moment I was adding to the horde. Since my mind could conceive only repulsive incubi, and since while I lived I must think, feel, and so continue to shape them, was there no way to check so abominable a succession? My eyes fell on the long shelves with their many-colored bottles. In the chemistry of photography there are deadly poisons – I knew that. Now was the time to end it – now! Let him return and find his desire accomplished. One good thing I could do, if one only. I could abolish my monster-creating self.

V

My friend Mark Jenkins is an intelligent and usually a very careful man. When he took from 'Smiler' Callahan a cigar which had every appearance of being excellent, innocent Havana, the act denoted both intelligence and caution. By very clever work he had traced the poisoning of young Ralph

Peeler to Mr Callahan's door, and he believed this particular cigar to be the mate of one smoked by Peeler just previous to his demise. And if, upon arresting Callahan, he had not confiscated this bit of evidence, it would have doubtless been destroyed by its regrettably unconscientious owner.

But when Jenkins shortly afterward gave me that cigar, as one of his own, he committed one of those almost inconceivable blunders which, I think, are occasionally forced upon clever men to keep them from overweening vanity. Discovering his slight mistake, my detective friend spent the night searching for his unintended victim, myself, and that his search was successful was due to Pietro Marini, a young Italian of Jenkins' acquaintance, whom he met about the hour of two a.m returning from a dance.

Now, Marini had seen me standing on the steps of the house where Doctor Frederick Holt had his laboratory and living rooms, and he had stared at me, not with any ill intent, but because he thought I was the sickest-looking, most ghastly specimen of humanity that he had ever beheld. And, sharing the superstition of his South Street neighbours, he wondered if the worthy doctor had poisoned me as well as Peeler. This suspicion he imparted to Jenkins, who, however, had the best of reasons for believing otherwise. Moreover, as he informed Marini, Holt was dead, having drowned himself late the previous afternoon. An hour or so after our talk in the restaurant news of his suicide reached Jenkins.

It seemed wise to search any place where a very sick-looking young man had been seen to enter, so Jenkins came straight to the laboratory. Across the fronts of those houses was the long sign with its mysterious inscription, 'See the Great Unseen', not at all mysterious to the detective. He knew that next door to Doctor Holt's the second floor had been thrown together into a lecture room, where at certain hours a young man employed by settlement workers displayed upon a screen stereopticon views of various deadly bacilli, the germs of diseases appropriate to dirt and indifference. He knew, too, that Doctor Holt himself had helped the educational effort along by providing some really wonderful lantern slides, done by micro-colour photography.

On the pavement outside, Jenkins found the two-thirds remnant of a cigar, which he gathered in and came up the steps, a very miserable and self-reproachful detective. Neither outer nor inner door was locked, and in the laboratory he found me, alive, but on the verge of death by another means than he had feared.

In the extreme physical depression following my awakening from drugged sleep, and knowing nothing of its cause, I believed my adventure fact in its entirety. My mentality was at too low an ebb to resist its dreadful suggestion. I was searching among Holt's various bottles when Jenkins burst in. At first I was merely annoyed at the interruption of my purpose, but before the anticlimax of his explanation the mists of obsession drifted away and left me still sick in body, but in spirit happy as any man may well be who has suffered a delusion that the world is wholly bad – and learned that its badness springs from his own poisoned brain.

The malice which I had observed in every face, including young Marini's, existed only in my drug-affected vision. Last week's 'popular-science' lecture had been recalled to my subconscious mind – the mind that rules dreams and delirium – by the photographic apparatus in Holt's workroom. 'See the Great Unseen' assisted materially, and even the corner drug store before which I had paused, with its green-lit show vases, had doubtless played a part. But presently, following something Jenkins told me, I was driven to one protest. 'If Holt was not here,' I demanded, 'if Holt is dead, as you say, how do you account for the fact that I, who have never seen the man, was able to give you an accurate description which you admit to be that of Doctor Frederick Holt?'

He pointed across the room. 'See that?' It was a life-size bust portrait, in crayons, the picture of a white-haired man with bushy eyebrows and the most piercing black eyes I had ever seen – until the previous evening. It hung facing the door and near the windows, and the features stood out with a strangely lifelike appearance in the white rays of the arc lamp just outside. 'Upon entering,' continued Jenkins, 'the first thing you saw was that portrait, and from it your delirium built a living, speaking man. So, there are your white-haired showman, your unnatural fear, your colour photography and your pretty green golliwogs all nicely explained for you, Blaisdell, and thank God you're alive to hear the explanation. If you had smoked the whole of that cigar – well, never mind. You didn't. And now, my very dear friend, I think it's high time that you interviewed a real, flesh-and-blood doctor. I'll phone for a taxi.'

'Don't,' I said. 'A walk in the fresh air will do me more good than fifty doctors.'

'Fresh air! There's no fresh air on South Street in July,' complained Jenkins, but reluctantly yielded.

I had a reason for my preference. I wished to see people, to meet face to face even such stray prowlers as might be about at this hour, nearer sunrise than midnight, and rejoice in the goodness and kindliness of the human countenance – particularly as found in the lower classes.

But even as we were leaving there occurred to me a curious inconsistency.

'Jenkins,' I said, 'you claim that the reason Holt, when I first met him in the hall, appeared to twice close the door in my face, was because the door never opened until I myself unlatched it.'

'Yes,' confirmed Jenkins, but he frowned, foreseeing my next question.

'Then why, if it was from that picture that I built so solid, so convincing a vision of the man, did I see Holt in the hall before the door was open?'

'You confuse your memories,' retorted Jenkins rather shortly.

'Do I? Holt was dead at that hour, but – *I tell you I saw Holt outside the door!* And what was his reason for committing suicide?'

Before my friend could reply I was across the room, fumbling in the dusk there at the electric lamp above the sink. I got the tin flap open and pulled out the sliding screen, which consisted of two sheets of glass with fabric between, dark on one side, yellow on the other. With it came the very thing I dreaded – a sheet of whitish, parchment-like, slightly opalescent stuff.

Jenkins was beside me as I held it at arm's length toward the windows. Through it the light of the arc lamp fell – divided into the most astonishingly brilliant rainbow hues. And instead of diminishing the light, it was perceptibly increased in the oddest way. Almost one thought that the sheet itself was luminous, and yet when held in shadow it gave off no light at all.

'Shall we – put it in the lamp again – and try it?' asked Jenkins slowly, and in his voice there was no hint of mockery.

I looked him straight in the eyes. 'No,' I said, 'we won't. I was drugged. Perhaps in that condition I received a merciless revelation of the discovery that caused Holt's suicide, but I don't believe it. Ghost or no ghost, I refuse to ever again believe in the depravity of the human race. If the air and the earth are teeming with invisible horrors, they are *not* of our making, and – the study of demonology is better let alone. Shall we burn this thing, or tear it up?'

'We have no right to do either,' returned Jenkins thoughtfully, 'but you know, Blaisdell, there's a little too darn much realism about some parts of your "dream". I haven't been smoking any doped cigars, but when you held that up to the light, I'll swear I saw – well, never mind. Burn it – send it back to the place it came from.'

'South America?' said I.

'A hotter place than that. Burn it.'

So he struck a match and we did. It was gone in one great white flash.

A large place was given by morning papers to the suicide of Doctor Frederick Holt, caused, it was surmised, by mental derangement brought about by his unjust implication in the Peeler murder. It seemed an inadequate reason, since he had never been arrested, but no other was ever discovered.

Of course, our action in destroying that 'membrane' was illegal and rather precipitate, but, though he won't talk about it, I know that Jenkins agrees with me – doubt is sometimes better than certainty, and there are marvels better left unproved. Those, for instance, which concern the Powers of Evil.

7 Hodge

BY ELINOR MORDAUNT

People are accustomed to think of Somerset as a county of
deep, bosky bays, sunny coves, woods, moorlands. The very
name conjures up a set picture in their mind's eye, as certain
Christian names have a knack of doing – we all know the
'Bobs,' 'Marys,' 'Lucys' of this world.

But Hemerton was in itself sufficient to blur this bland
illusion of Somerset. It lay a mile and a half back from the
sea, counting it at full tide; at low tide the sly, smooth waters,
unbroken by a single rock, slipped away for another mile or
more across a dreary ooze of black mud.

The village lay pasted flat upon the marsh, with no trees
worthy of the name in sight: a few twisted blackthorn bushes,
a few split willows, one wreck of a giant blighted ash in the
Rectory gardens, and that was all.

For months on end the place swam in vapours. There were
wonderful effects of sunrise and sunset, veils of crimson and
gold, of every shade of blue and purple. At times the grey
sea-lavender was like silver, the wet, black mud gleaming like
dark opals; while at high summer there was purple willow-
strife spilled thick along the ditches, giving the strange place
a transitory air of warm-blooded life; but for the most part it
was all as aloof and detached as a sleep-walker.

The birds fitted the place as a verger fits his quiet and
dusky church: herons and waders of all kinds; wild-crying
curlew; and here and there a hawk, hanging motionless high
overhead.

There were scarcely fifty houses in Hemerton, and these
were all alike, flat and brown and grey; where there had been
plaster it was flaked and ashen. The very church stooped,

as though shamed to a sort of poor-relation pose by the immense indifference of the mist-veiled sky – the drooping lids on a scornful face – for even at midday, in midsummer, the heavens were never quite clear, quite blue, but still veiled and apart.

The Rectory was a two-storied building, low at that, and patched with damp: small, with a narrow-chested air, tiny windows, a thin, grudging doorway, blistered paint, which gave it a leprous air; and just that one tree, with its pale, curled leaves in summer, its jangling keys in winter.

It was amazing to find that any creature so warmly vital as the Rector's daughter, Rhoda Fane, had been begotten, born, reared in such a place; spent her entire life there, apart from two years of school at Clifton, and six months in Brussels, cut short by her mother's death.

She was like a beech wood in September: ruddy, crisp, fragrant. Her hair, dark-brown, with copper lights, was so springing with life that it seemed more inclined to grow up than hang down; her face was almost round, her wide, brown eyes frank and eager. She was as good as any man with her leaping-pole: broad-shouldered, deep-breasted, with a soft, deep contralto voice.

Her only brother was four years younger than herself. Funds had run low, drained away by their mother's illness, before it was time for him to go to school; he was too delicate for the second-best, roughing it among lads of a lower class, and so he was kept at home, taught by his father: a thin trickle of distilled classics and wavering mathematics; a good deal of history, no geography.

He, in startling contrast to his sister, was a true child of the marshes: thin light hair, vellum-white, peaked face, pale grey eyes beneath an overhanging brow, large transparent ears: narrow-chested, long-armed, stooping, so that he seemed almost a hunchback.

In all ways he was the shadow of Rhoda, followed her
everywhere; and as there is no shadow without the sun, so
it seemed that he could scarcely have existed apart from her.
Small as he already was, he almost pulled himself out of life
while she was away at school; and after a bare week from
home she would get back to find him with the best part of his
substance peeled from him, white as a willow-wand.

Different as these two were, they were passionately attached
to each other. The Rector was a kind father when he drew
himself out of the morass of melancholy and disillusion into
which he had fallen since his wife died, wilting away with
damp and discontent, and sheer loathing of the soil in which
it had been his misfortune to plant her. But still, at the best,
he was a parent, and so apart, while there were no neighbours,
no playfellows.

Once or twice Rhoda's school-friends came to stay at the
Rectory, and for the first day or so it seemed delightful to talk
of dress, of a gayer world, possible lovers. But after a very little
while they began to pall upon her: they understood nothing
of what was her one absorbing interest – the natural life of
the place in which she lived: were discontented, disdainful
of the marshland, hated the mud, feared the fogs, shivered
in the damp. Apart from all this, Hector was madly jealous;
hated them.

Hector! No, I was wrong when I spoke as though names
gave a uniform impression of places or people: in this case the
boy's name expressed him as little as the slow, luscious, sweet
'Summerzetshire' expressed Hemerton, its mud and marshes.

Anyhow, the brother and sister were sufficient to each other,
for they shared a never-failing, or even diminishing, interest
– and what more can any two people wish for? – a passionate
absorption in, a minute knowledge of, the wild life of the
marshland; its legends and folk-lore; its habits and calls; the
mating seasons and manners of the birds; the place and habit

of every wild flower; the way of the wind with the sky, and all it portends; the changing seasons, seemingly so uneven from year to year, and yet working out so much the same in the end: balancing, mild early in the winter and cold later, or *vice versa*; a tardy summer and a sunny autumn; a snowless winter and an extra wet spring to make up for it.

They could not have said how they first came to hear of the Forest: they had always talked of it. To Hector, at least, it was so vivid that he seemed to have actually struggled through its immense depths, swung in its hanging creepers, smelt its sickly-sweet orchids, breathed its hot, damp air – so far real to both alike that they would find themselves saying, 'Do you remember?' in speaking of paths that they had never traversed.

Provisionally they had fixed their Forest at the Miocene Period. Or, rather, this is what it came to: the boy ceasing to protest against the winged monsters, the rhinoceros, the long-jawed mastodon which fascinated the girl's imagination; though there was one impassioned scene when he flamed out over his clear remembrance of a sabre-toothed tiger, putting all those others – stupid, hulking brutes! – out of court by many thousands of years.

'They couldn't have been there, couldn't – not with us and with 'It' – I saw it, I tell you – I tell you I saw it!' His pale face flamed, his eyes were as bright as steel. 'The mastodon! That's nothing – nothing! But the sabre-toothed tiger – I tell you I saw it. What are you grinning at now? – in our Forest – ours, mind you! – I saw it!'

'Oh, indeed, indeed!' Suddenly, because the day was so hot, because they were bored, because she was unwittingly impressed, as always, by her brother's heat of conviction, Rhoda's serene temper was gone. 'And did you see yourself? and what were you doing there, may I ask – *you*! Silly infant, don't you know that there weren't any men then? Phew! Everyone knows that – everyone. You and your old tiger!'

There was mockery in her laugh as she took him by the lapels of his coat; shook him.

Then, next moment, when he turned aside, sullen and pale, his brows in a pent-house above his eyes, she was filled with contrition. The rotten, thundery day had set her all on edge; it was a shame to tease him like this; and, after all, how often had she herself remembered back? Though there was a difference, and she knew it, a sense of fantasy, pretending; while Hector was as jealous of every detail of their Forest as a long-banished exile over every cherished memory of his own land.

And yet – perhaps because it *had* never meant so much to her as it did to her brother; perhaps because he had never definitely stood out against her before – she was persistent in her determination to have the Forest just as she wished: to get her brother to state his views clearly, then to refute them by the clear light of well-authenticated research; that was the way.

And, of course, there *were* no men contemporary with that wretched tiger: he knew that; he must know.

Lolling under their one tree, in the steamy, early afternoon, she coaxed him back to the subject, and was beaten upon it, as the half-hearted always are.

He was so amazingly clear about the whole thing ... Why, it might have happened yesterday!

He had been up in the trees, slinking along – not the hunting man, but the hunted – watchful, furtive; a picker-up of what other beasts had slain and taken their fill of: more watchful than usual because he had already come across a carcass left by the long-toothed terror, all the blood sucked out of it. Swinging from bough to bough by his hands – which, even when he stood upright, as upright as possible, dangled far below his knees – he had actually seen it: seen its gleaming tusks, its shining eyes; seen it and fled, wild with terror.

Was it likely that he could ever forget it? 'It and its beastly teeth!' he added; then fell silent, brooding; while even Rhoda was awed to silence.

It was that very evening that they found their Forest, or, rather, a part of it.

Something in the day – the sort of day when one feels that anything might, something *must*, happen; the intense heat; the veiled, metallic sky; the still, thunder-laden air; their incipient quarrel – had made the boy restless; while Rhoda would have done anything in the world to make up for that sort of gulf which she had seemed to open between them by her mockery.

The Rector had gone off to a farm three miles away; told them that he would not be back to tea until after five. At the time it had not seemed to matter, but gradually the idea of being chained close to the house for goodness knows how long became unendurable.

'After five! Why, it might as well be midnight,' as Hector said.

It seemed as though he must have known they were going to find something; had infected Rhoda with his own unrest; for, after a glass of milk at four, they started off, away to the sea, running and walking by turns, inexplicably hurried. They had meant to bathe, but for once their memories were at fault; and they found that the tide was out, a mere rim of molten lead on the far edge of the horizon.

They were both tired, but they could not rest. They cut inland for a bit, then out again; crossing the mud-flats until the mud oozed above their boots and drove them back again.

They must have wandered about a long time, for the light – although it did not actually go – became illusive; the air freshened with that salty scent which tells of a flowing tide.

Hector insisted that they ought to wait until it was full in and have their bathe by moonlight; but, as Rhoda pointed out, that would mean no supper, dawdling about for hours. After some time they compromised: they would go out and meet the tide; see what it was like.

Almost at the water's edge they found It – their Forest.

There it was, buried like a fly in amber: twisted trunks and boughs, matted creepers, all ash-grey and black.

How far it stretched up and down the shore they could not have said, the time was too short, the sea too near for any exploration, but not far, they thought, or they must have discovered it before. 'Nothing more than a fold out of the old world, squeezed up to the surface'; that was what they agreed upon.

They divided and ran in opposite directions – 'Just to try and find out,' as Rhoda said. But after a few yards, a couple of dozen, maybe, they called back to each other that they had lost it.

The darkness was gathering, the water almost to their feet; they were bitterly disappointed, but anyhow there was to-morrow, many 'to-morrows.'

All that evening they talked of nothing else. 'It's been there for thousands and tens of thousands of years! It will be there to-morrow,' they said.

It was towards two o'clock in the morning that Hector, restless with excitement and fear, padded into his sister's room; found her sleeping – stupidly sleeping – with the moonlight full upon her, and shook her awake; unreasonably angry, as wakeful people always are with the sleepers.

'Suppose we never find it again! Oh, Rhoda, supposing we never find it again!'

'Find what?'

'The Forest, you idiot! – our Forest.'

'Hector, don't be silly. Go back to bed; you'll get cold. Of course we'll find it.'

'Why of course? I've been thinking and thinking and thinking. There wasn't a tree or bush or landmark of any sort: we had pottered about all over the shop: supposing we've lost it for ever? Oh, supposing, Rhoda, Rhoda! What sillies we were! Why didn't we stay there, camp opposite to it until the tide went out? I feel it in my bones we'll never find it again – never – never – never! There might have been skulls, all sorts of things – long teeth – tigers' teeth! And now we've lost it. It's no good talking – we've lost it; I know we've lost it – after all these years! After thousands and thousands and thousands of years of remembering!'

The boy's forehead was glistening with sweat; the tears were running down his face, white as bone in the moonlight. Rhoda drew him into her bed, comforted him as best she could, very sleepy, and unperturbed – for, of course, they would find it. How could they help finding it? And after a while he fell asleep, still moaning and crying, searching for a lost path through his dreams.

He was right in his foreboding. They did not find it. Perhaps the tide had been out further than usual: they had walked farther than they thought; they had dreamt the whole thing; the light had deceived them – impossible to say.

At first, in the broad light of day, even Hector was incredulous of their misfortune. Then, as the completeness of their loss grew upon them, they became desperate – possessed by that terrible restlessness of the searcher after lost things. Day after day they would come back from the sea worn out, utterly hopeless; declaring that here was the end of the whole thing; sick at the very thought of the secret mud, the long black shore.

They gave it up. They would never go near 'the rotten thing' again.

Then, a few hours later, the thought of the freshly-receding tide began to work like madness in their veins, and they would be out and away.

It was easier for Rhoda; for she was of those who 'sleep o' nights'; easier until she found that her brother slipped off on moonlight nights while she slumbered: coming back at all hours, haggard and worn to fainting-point.

He stooped more than ever: his brow was more overhung, furrowed with horizontal lines. Sometimes, furious with herself for her sleepiness, Rhoda would awake, jump out of bed and run to the window in the fresh dawn, to see the boy dragging himself home, old as the ages, his hands hanging loose to his knees.

At last the breaking-point came. He was very ill: after a long convalescence money was collected from numerous relations, family treasures were sold, and he was sent away to school.

He came back for his holidays a changed creature, talking of footer, then of cricket; of boys and masters; of school – school – school – nothing but school; blunt and practical.

But all this was at the front of him, deliberately displayed in the shop-windows.

At the back of him, buried out of sight, there was still the visionary rememberer. Rhoda, who loved him, realized this.

At first she did not dare to speak of the Forest. Then, trying to get at something of the old Hector, she pressed the point; pressed it and pressed it. It was she now who kept on with that eternal, 'Don't you remember?'

The worst of the whole thing was that he did not even pretend to forget. He did worse – he laughed. And in her own pain she now realized how often and how deeply she must have hurt him.

'Oh, that rot! What silly idiots we were! Such rot!'

And yet, at the back of him, at the back of his too-direct

gaze, his laughter, there was *something*. Oh yes, there was something. She was certain of that.

Deep, deep, hidden away at the back of him, at the back of that most imperturbable of all reserves, a boy's reserve, he remembered, felt as he had always felt. He shut her out of it, that was all: her – Rhoda.

At the end of a year they ceased to talk of the Forest; all those far-back things dropped away from their intercourse. To outward seeming their love for the countryside, their strange, unyouthful interest in geology, the age-buried world, was a thing of the past.

And it went on, too. Each holiday they seemed to have less in common, less to talk about. They took to glancing at each other curiously, as though each were a stranger whom the other was trying in vain to place.

Hector had a bicycle now: he was often away for hours at a time. He never even spoke of where he had been, what he had been doing. It was always: 'Nowhere in particular; nothing in particular.'

Then, two years later, upon just such a breathless mid-summer day, he burst in upon his sister, his face crimson with excitement.

'I've found it! I never gave up – never for a moment! I pretended – I thought you thought it rot – were drawing me on – but it's there. We were right. It's there – there! Quick! quick! Now the tide's just almost full out … Oh, by Jingo! to think I've found it! Rhoda, hurry up – quick!' He was dancing with impatience.

'I can ride the bike – you on the step,' breathed Rhoda, and snatched up a hat.

They flew. The village shot past them: the flat country swirled like a top. At last they came to a place where there was a tiny rag of torn handkerchief tied to a stick stuck upright in the ground. Here they left the road, laid the bicycle in a dry ditch, and cut away across the marsh, guided by more signals – scraps of cambric, then paper; towards the end, one every ten yards or less, until Rhoda wondered how in the world the boy had curbed himself to such care!

Then – there it was.

They stepped it: just on fifty yards long, indefinitely wide, running out into little bays, here and there tailing off so that it was impossible to discover any definite edge, sinking away out of sight like a dream.

The sun was blazing hot and the top of the mud dry. In places they went down upon their hands and knees, peering; but really one saw most standing a little way off, with one's head bent, eyeing it sideways.

It was in this way that Rhoda found It – Him!

'Look – look! Oh, I say – there's something … A thing – an animal! No – no – a – a –'

'Sabre-toothed tiger!' The boy's wild shriek of triumph showed how he had hugged that old conjecture.

He came running, but till he got his head at exactly the same slant as hers he could see nothing, and was furiously petulant.

'Idiot! Silly fool! – nothing but a bough. You –' A lucky angle, and, 'Oh, I say, by Jove! I've got it now! A man – a man!'

'A monkey – a great ape; there were no men, then, with "It".' There, it seemed, she conceded him his tiger. 'A little nearer – now again, there!'

They crept towards it. It was clear enough at a little distance; but nearer, what with the blazing sun and the queer incandescent lights on the mud, they found difficulty in exactly placing it. At last they had it, found themselves immediately over it; were able, kneeling side by side, to gaze down at the strange, age-old figure, lying huddled together, face forward.

It was not more than a couple of feet down; the semi-transparent mud must have been silting over it for years and years: silted away again through centuries. And all for them – just for them. What a thought!

Hector raced off for his bicycle, and so on to the nearest cottage to borrow a spade.

The mental picture of the 'man' and the sabre-toothed tiger met and clashed in his brain. If he was so certain of the man he must concede the tiger, give in to Rhoda and her later period. Unless – unless ... Suddenly he clapped his hands to his ears as though someone were shouting: his eyes closed, shutting out sight and sound. There *was* a tiger, he remembered – of course he remembered! And if he were there, others were there also – not one tiger, not one man, but tigers and men; both, both!

By the time he got back to where he had left his sister, the water was above her knees, the tide racing inwards.

They were not going to be done this time, however.

It was five o'clock in the afternoon, and their father was away from home. Rhoda went back and ordered the household with as much sobriety as possible; collected a supply of food and a couple of blankets – they had camped out before; there was nothing so very amazing in their behaviour; to the old servant's mind they couldn't possibly be more crazed than they had always been, and this is the truly comfortable estimate in which to find oneself – then returned to the shore, the shrine.

Hector was sitting at the edge of the water, staring fixedly, white as a sheet.

Rhoda collected driftwood and built a fire; almost fed him, for he took nothing but what was put into his hand.

'It will still be there, even if we go to sleep,' she said: then, 'Anyhow, we'll watch turn and turn about.'

But it was all of no use. The boy might lie down in his turn, but he still faced the sea with steady, staring eyes.

Soon after three he woke his sister, shaking her in a frenzy of impatience. Oh, these sleepers!

'Sleeping! Sleeping! You great stupid, you! I never! I … Just look at the tide – only look!'

The tide was pretty far out, the whole world a mist of pinkish-grey. Step by step they followed the retreating lap of water.

Hector's very lips were white; he was trembling from head to foot with anxiety, damp with sweat.

He had been certain of the place; but even when they reached it he had to wipe his blurred eyes; was too on edge to get his head at the proper angle, and it was Rhoda who saw it first, crying:

'It's there, old boy! It's all right – all right!' – while he was forced to turn aside, retching from sheer relief.

By six o'clock they had the heavy body out, and were dragging it across the rapidly-drying mud.

It was not as big as Hector: five-foot-one at the most, but almost incredibly heavy, with immense rounded shoulders.

By the time they reached the true shore they were done, and flung themselves down, panting, exhausted. But they could not rest. A few minutes more and they were up again, turning the creature over, rubbing the mud away from the hairy body with bunches of grass; parting the long, matted locks which hung over its lowering face, with the overhung brow, flat nose, almost non-existent chin.

'I declare to goodness it's like you, old chap,' cried Rhoda, and they rolled upon the ground, laughing hysterically.

'A little more chin, I should hope!' protested the boy. 'But the forehead … Oh, Lord!'

'Exactly – exactly like, only … I say, I wonder how he'd look after a shave.'

'Like me! My hat! Trust you!'

They had the thing on its back, and the hairy face was pretty well clear of mud. The eyes were shut, but oddly unsunken: it smelt of marsh slime, of decayed vegetation, but nothing more.

Hector poked forward a finger to see if he could push up one eyelid, and drew back sharply.

'Why – hang it all – the thing's warm!'

'No wonder, with this sun. I'm dripping from head to foot. Hector, we must go home. Matty will tell; there'll be the eyes of a row.'

For all her insistence it was another hour before Rhoda could get her brother away. Again and again he met the returning tide with her hat, bringing it back full of water; washing their find from head to foot, combing its matted hair with a chipped fragment of driftwood. But at last they dragged it to a dry dyke, covered it with dry yellow grass, and were off, Rhoda on the step this time, Hector draped limply over the handle of the bicycle.

He slept like a dead thing for the best part of that day. But soon after three they were away again: no use for Rhoda to raise objections; the unrest of an intense excitement was in her bones as in his, and he knew it.

It had been a cloudless day, the veil of mist fainter than usual, the sky bluer.

As they left the bicycle and cut across the rough foreshore the sun beat down upon them with an almost unbearable fierceness. There was a shimmer like a mirage across the marshes: the sea was the colour of burnt steel.

They dog-trotted half the way, arguing as they ran, Hector, still fixed, pivoting upon his sabre-toothed tiger, and yet insistent that *this* was a man – a real man – contemporary with it: the first absolute proof of human existence anterior to the First Glacial Age.

'An ape – a sort of ape – nearish to a man, but – well, look at its hair.' She'd give him his tiger, but not his man.

'By Gad, you'd grow hair, running wild as he did – a man –'

'Hector, what rot! Why, anyone – anyone could see –' She thought of her father, the smooth curate, the rubicund farmers … A man!

'Well, stick to it – stick to it! But I bet you anything – anything …'

Hector's words were jerked out of him as he padded on: 'We'll get hundreds and hundreds of pounds for him! Travel – see the world – go to Java, where that other chap – what's-his-name – was found. Why, he's older than the Heidelberg Johnny – a thousand thousand times great-grandfather to that Pitcairn thing – older – older – oh, older than any!'

Panting, stumbling, half-blind with exhaustion, the boy was still a good six yards in front of his sister as he reached the dry dyke where they had left their treasure.

Rhoda saw him stand for a moment, staring, then spin round as though he had been shot, throwing up his arms with a hoarse scream.

By the time she had her own arms about him, he could only point, trembling from head to foot.

There was nothing there! Torn grass where they had pulled it to rub down their find; the very shape of the body distinct upon the sandy, sparsely-covered soil; the stick with the pennant of blue ribbon which Rhoda had taken from her hat to mark the spot … Nothing more, nothing whatever.

Up and down the girl ran, circling like a plover, her head bent. It must be somewhere, it must – it must!

She glanced at her brother, who stood as though turned to stone: this was the sort of thing which sent people mad, killed them – to be so frightfully disappointed, and yet to stand still, to say nothing.

She caught at his arm and faced him, the tears streaming down her cheeks.

'Oh, my dear, my dear –' she began; then broke off, staring beyond him.

'Why … why – Hector – I say –' Her voice broke to a whisper: she had a feeling as though she must be taking part in some mad dream. Quite inconsequently the thought of Balaam came to her. How did Balaam feel when the ass spoke to him? As she did – with eye more amazed than any ears could ever be.

'Hector – look … It – It …'

As her brother still stood speechless, with bent head and ashen face, she dropped to silence: too terrified of It, of her plainly deluded self, of everything on earth, to say more …

One simply could not trust one's own eyes: that's what it came to.

Her legs were trembling; she could feel her knees touching each other, cold and clammy.

It would have been impossible to say a word, even if she had dared to reveal her own insanity; she could only pluck the lapels of her brother's coat, running her dry tongue along her lips.

Something in her unusual silence must have stirred through the boy's own misery, for after a moment or so he looked up, at first dimly, as though scarcely recognizing her. Then – slowly realizing her intent glance fixed on something beyond his own shoulder, he turned – and saw.

Twenty yards or more off, on a mound of coarse grass and sand just above the high-tide mark, 'It' was sitting, its long arms wound round its knees, staring out to sea.

For a moment or so they hung, open-mouthed, wide-eyed.

For the life of her, Rhoda could not have moved a step nearer. The creature's heavy shoulders were rounded, its head thrust forward. Silhouetted against the sea and sky, white

in contrast to its darkness, it had the aloofness of incredible
age; drawn apart, almost sanctified by its immeasurable
remoteness, its detachment from all that meant life to the
men and women of the twentieth century: the web of fancied
necessities, trivial possessions, absorptions.

'There was no sea – of course, there was no sea anywhere
near here then!' The boy's whisper opened an incalculable
panorama of world-wide change.

There had been no sea here then; no Bristol Channel, no
Irish Sea. Valley and river, that was all!

This alien being who had lived, and more than half-died,
in this very spot, was gazing at something altogether strange:
a vast, uneasy sheet of water with but one visible bank; no
golden-brown lights, no shadows, no reflections: a strange,
restless and indifferent god.

'Well – anyhow ... Oh, blazes! here goes! If –' Young Fane
broke off with a decision that cut his doubts, and moved
forward.

In a moment the creature was alert, its head flung sideways
and up, sniffing the air like a dog.

It half-turned, as though to run; then, as the boy stopped
short, it paused.

'Rhoda – get the grub – go quietly – don't run ... Bread-
and-butter – anything!'

They had flung down the frail with the bottle of milk, cake,
bread-and-butter that they had brought with them – enough
for tea and supper – heedless in their despair. Rhoda moved
a step or two away, picked up a packet, unfolded it and thrust
the food into her brother's hand – cake, a propitiation!

The strange figure, upright – and yet not upright as it is
counted in these days – remained stationary; there was one
quick turn of the head following her, then the poise of it
showed eyes immovably fixed upon the male.

Rhoda remembered her skirt, and almost tittered. 'It knows

by ...' she thought; then broke off, appalled at the immensity of the differences. There had been no skirts then; as there had been no sea, where it now washed, creeping in across the mud. The creature's evident realization of her as the female creature, lesser of the two to be feared, was based upon an instinct deeper and truer than all deductions of dress or long hair.

Hector moved forward very slowly, one smooth step after another. Rhoda had seen him like that with wild birds and rabbits. He wore an old suit of shrunken flannels, faded to a yellowish-grey, which blurred him into the landscape. Far enough off to catch his outline against the molten glare of the sea, she noted that his shoulders were almost as bent as those of that Other ... Other what? – man? – ape? The speculation zigzagged to and fro like lightning through her mind. She could scarcely breathe for anxiety.

As the boy drew quite near to the dull, brownish figure it jerked its head uneasily aside – she knew what Hector's eyes were like, a steady, luminous grey under the bent brows – made a swinging movement with its arms, half-turned; then stopped, stared sideways, crouching, sniffing.

The boy's arm was held out at its fullest stretch in front of him. Heaven – the old, old gods – only knew upon what beast-torn carrion the creature had once fed; but it was famished, and some instinct must have told it that here was food, for it snatched and crammed its mouth.

Hector turned, and Rhoda's heart was in her throat, for there was no knowing what it might do at that. But as he moved steadily away, without so much as a glance behind him, it hesitated, threw up its hand, as though to strike or throw; then followed.

That was the beginning of it. During those first days it would have followed him to the end of the world. Later on, he told himself bitterly that he had been a fool not to have seen further; gone off anywhere – oh, anywhere so long as it was far enough – dragging the brute after him while his leadership still held.

It was with difficulty that they prevented it from dogging them back to the Rectory – just imagine it tailing through the village at their heels! But once it understood that it must stay where it was, it sat down on a grassy hummock, crouching with its arms round its knees, one hand tightly clenched, its small, light eyes, overhung by that portentous brow, following them with a look of desolate loneliness.

Again and again the boy and girl glanced back, but it still sat there staring after them, immovable in the spot which Hector had indicated to it. They had left it all the food they had with them, and one of the blankets which they had been too hot to carry home that morning. As it plainly had not known what to do with the thing, Rhoda, overcome by a sort of motherliness, had thrown it over its shoulders. Thus it sat, shrouded like an Arab, its shaggy head cut like a giant burr against the pale primrose sky.

'A beastly shame leaving it alone like that!' They both felt it; scarcely liked to meet each other's eyes over it. And yet, pity it as they might, engrossed in it as they were, they couldn't stay there with it after dark. No reason, no fear – just couldn't! Why? Oh, well, for all its new-found life, it was as far away as any ghost.

'Poor brute!' said Rhoda.

'Poor chap!' Hector's under-lip was thrust out, his look aggressive. But there was no argument; and when he treated her – 'Don't be silly; of course it's not a man; any duffer could see that' – with contemptuous silence, Rhoda knew that he was absolutely fixed in his convictions.

He proved it, too, next morning, leading the creature out

into the half-dried mud and back again to where his sister sat, following his apparently aimless movements with puzzled eyes.

'Now, look,' he crowed. 'Just you look, Miss Blooming-Cocksure!'

He was right. There was the mark of his own heavy nailed boot, and beside it the track of other feet; oddly-shaped enough, but with the weight distinctly thrown upon the heel and great-toe, as no beast save man has ever yet thrown it – that fine developed great-toe, the emblem of leadership. Hardly a trace of such pressure as the three greater apes show, all on the outer edge of the foot; not even flat and even as the baboon throws his.

✕

It was after this that – without another word said – Rhoda, meek for once, followed her brother's example, and began to speak of the creature as 'He.'

They even gave him a name. They called him Hodge; only in fun, and yet with a feeling that here was one of the first of all countrymen: less learned, and yet in some ways so much more observant, self-sufficing, than his machine-made successors.

He could run at an almost incredible rate, bent as he was; climb any tree; out-throw either of them, doubling the distance. It was there that they got at the meaning of that closed fist; for at least three days he had never let go of his stone – his one weapon.

'He didn't trust us.' Rhoda was hurt, her vanity touched; and when they had seemed to be making such progress, too!

'Not that – a sort of ingrained habit; the poor devil didn't feel dressed without it,' protested Hector. 'Of course he trusts us as much as a perfectly natural creature ever trusts anything or anybody.'

That was enough for the boy, but not for his sister. In absolute innocence, still thinking – despite that 'He' – of their new acquisition as an animal, a strange, uncouth sort of pet, she wanted him to be 'really fond' of her, to trust her completely; as much hers as any dog domesticated through the ages.

And this was the beginning of the trouble.

※

The Rector had gone on a visit to their only relative, an old aunt, who was dying in as leisurely a fashion as she had lived, and was unable to leave her. A neighbouring curate took that next Sunday's service.

It had been a Monday when Hector found Hodge, and a very great deal can happen in that time.

From the first it had seemed clear that nothing in the way of communicating with authorities, experts, could be done until their father was there to back them, adding his own testimony. It was no good just writing – Hector did, indeed, begin a letter to Sir Ray Lankester, but tore it up, appalled by his own formless, boyish handwriting. 'He'd think we were just getting at him – a couple of silly kids,' was his reflection.

He knew a lot for his age; was very certain of his own knowledge; felt no personal fear of this wild man of his. But ordinary grown-up people! That was altogether a different matter. And here he touched the primitive mistrust of all real youth for anything too completely finished and sophisticated.

Of course, from the very beginning, there were all sorts of minor troubles with Matty over their continued thefts of food; difficulties in keeping the creature away from the house and village.

But all that was nothing to what followed.

The first dim, unformulated sense of fear began on the night when Hector, awakened by a loud rustling among the leaves of that one tree, discovered Hodge there, climbing along a bough which ended close against Rhoda's window.

Rhoda's, not his – that was the queer part of it!

The boy felt half huffed as he drove him off. But when he came again, some instinct, something far less plain than thought, began to worry him: something which seemed ludicrous, until it gathered and grew to a feeling of nausea so horrible that the cold sweat pricked out upon his breast and forehead.

At the third visit the fear was more defined. But still … That brute 'smitten' with Rhoda! He tried to laugh it off. Anyhow, what did it matter? And yet … Hang it all! there was something sickening about it all. It was impossible to sleep at night, listening, always listening.

He was only thirteen. Of course he had heard other chaps talking, but he had no real idea of the fierce drive of physical desire. And yet it was plain enough that here was something 'beastly' beyond all words.

He told Rhoda to keep her window bolted, and when she protested against such 'fugging', touched on his own fears, tried, awkwardly enough, to explain without explaining.

'I'm funky about Hodge – he's taken to following us. He might get in – bag something.'

'The darling!' cried Rhoda. 'Look here, old chap, I really believe he's fond of me; fonder of me than of you!'

She persisted in putting it to the test next day; left Hodge sitting by her brother, and walked away.

The creature moved his head uneasily from side to side, glanced at Hector, and his glance was full of hatred, malevolence; then, scrambling furtively to his feet, helping himself up with his hands, one fist tight-closed, in the old fashion, he passed round the back of the boy, and followed her.

For a minute or two Hector sat hunched together, staring doggedly out to sea. If Rhoda chose to make an ass of herself

– well, let her. After all, what could the brute do? She was bigger than he was, had nothing on her worth stealing; nothing of any use to Hodge, anyhow, he told himself.

Then, of a sudden, that half-formulated dread, that sick panic seized him afresh. He glanced round; both Hodge and his sister were out of sight, and he started to run with all his might, shouting.

There was an answering cry from Rhoda, shriller than usual, with a note of panic in it. This gave him the direction; and, plunging off among a group of shallow sand-dunes, he found himself almost upon them.

Rhoda was drawn up very straight, laughing nervously, her shoulders back, flushed to the eyes, while Hodge stood close in front of her, gabbling – they had tried him with their own words, but the oddly-angled jaw had seemed to cramp the tongue beyond hope of articulate speech – gabbling, gesticulating.

'Oh, Hector!' The girl's cry was full of relief as she swung sideways toward him; while Hodge, glancing round, saw him, raised his hand, and threw.

The stone just grazed the boy's cheek, drawing a spurt of blood; but this was enough for Rhoda, who forgot her own panic in a flame of indignation.

The creature could not have understood a word of what she said: her denunciation, abuse, 'the wigging' she gave him. But her look was enough, and he shrank aside, shamed as a beaten dog.

They did not bid him good-night. They had taught him to shake hands; but now he was in disgrace all that was over, and they turned aside with the set severity of youth: bent brows and straightened, hard mouths.

Rhoda was the first to relent, halfway home, breaking their silence with a laugh: 'Poor old Hodge! I don't know why I was so scared – I must have got him rattled, or he'd never have thrown that stone. Why, it was always you he liked best, followed,' she added magnanimously.

And yet she was puzzled, all on edge, as she had never been before. The look Hodge had cast at her brother was unmistakable; but why? – why? What had changed him? She never even thought of that passion common to man and beast, interwoven with all desire, hatred – the lees of love – jealousy.

All that evening Hector scarcely spoke. He was not so much scared as gravely anxious in a man's way. If that brute got him with a stone, what would happen to Rhoda? Even supposing that there had been anyone to consult, he could not, for the life of him, have put his fear into words. So much a man, he was yet too much a boy for that. Terrified of ridicule, incredulity, he hugged his secret, as that strange man-beast hugged his – the highest and lowest – the most primitive and the most cultured – forever uncommunicative; those in the midway the babblers.

He was so firm in his insistence upon Rhoda changing her room that night that she gave way, without argument, overawed by his gravity, by an odd, chill sense of fear which hung about her. 'I must have got a cold. I've a sort of feeling of a goose walking over my grave,' was what she said laughingly, half-shamefaced, accustomed as she was to attribute every feeling to some natural cause.

That night, soon after midnight, the brute was back in the tree. Hector heard the rustling, then the spring and swish of a released bough. Before he lay down he had unbolted one of the long bars from the underneath part of his old-fashioned iron bedstead; and now, taking it in his hand, he ran to Rhoda's room.

The white-washed walls and ceiling were so flooded with moonlight that it was almost as light as day.

Hodge was already in the room: the clothes were torn from

the bed; the cupboard doors wide open; the whole place littered with feminine attire.

He – It – the impersonal pronoun slid into its place in the boy's mind, and no words of self-reproach or condemnation could have said more – stood at the foot of the empty bed, with something white – it might have been a chemise – in its hand, held up to its face. Hector could not catch its expression, but there was something inexpressibly bestial in the silhouette of its head, bent, sniffing; he could actually hear the whistling breath.

He would have given anything if only it had stayed, fought it out then. But it belonged to a state too far away for that – defensive, at times aggressive, but forever running, hiding, slinking: a thrower among thick boughs behind tree-trunks – and in a moment it was out of the window, bundling over the sill, so clumsy and yet so amazingly quick.

He could hear the swing of a bough as it caught it. There was a loud rustle of leaves, and a stone hurtled in through the window; but that was all.

Hector tidied the room, tossed the scattered garments into the bottom of the wardrobe, and re-made the bed in his awkward boy-fashion, moving mechanically, as if in a dream; his hands busied over his petty tasks, his mind engrossed with something so tremendous that he seemed to be two separate people, of which the one, the greater, revolved slowly and certainly in an unalterable orbit, quite apart from his old everyday life, from that of Hector Fane whom he had always known, thought of, spoken of as 'myself.'

※

He went to his own room, put on his collar and coat – for he had lain down upon his bed without undressing, every nerve on edge – laced up his boots with meticulous care. He was no longer frightened or hurried; he knew exactly what he was going to do, and that alone hung him – moving slowly, surely – as upon a pivot.

The moonlight was so clear that there was no need for a candle, flooding the stairway, the study with its shabby book-shelves.

Easy enough to take the old shot-gun from the nails over the mantelshelf; only last holiday – years and years ago, while he was still a child – he had been allowed to use it for wild-duck shooting – and run his hand along the back of the writing-table drawer in search of those three or four cartridges which he had seen there a couple of days earlier.

The cartridges in his pocket swung against his hip as he mounted his bicycle and rode away – guiding himself with one hand, the gun lying heavily along his left arm; it was like someone nudging, reminding.

The scene was entirely familiar; but what was so strange in himself lent it an air of something new and uncanny. The winding road had a swing, drawing him with it; the mingled mist and moonlight were sentient, watchful, holding their breath.

Once or twice he seemed to catch sight of a low, stooping figure amid the rough grass and rush-tufted hollows to the left of him; but he could not be sure until he reached the very shore, left his bicycle in the old place.

Then a stone grazed his shoulder, and there was a blurred scurry of brown, from hummock to hummock, low as a hare to the ground.

Once in the open he got a clear sight of Hodge. The far-away tide was on the flow, but there was still a good half-mile of mud, like lead in the silvery dawn.

The man-beast bundled down the sandy strip of shore and out on to the mud: ungainly, stumbling; the boy behind it – 'It'. Hector held to that: the pronoun was altogether reassuring now – something to hold to, hard as a bone in his brain.

On the edge of the tide it tried to turn, double; then paused, fascinated, amazed: numb with fear of the strange level pipe pointing, oddly threatening, the first ray of sunlight running like an arrow of gold along the top of it.

There was something utterly naïve and piteous in the misplaced creature's gesture: the way in which it stood – long arms, short, bandy legs – moving its head uneasily from side to side; bewildered, yet fascinated.

'Poor beggar!' muttered Hector. He could not have said why, but he was horribly sorry, ashamed, saddened.

Years later he thought more clearly – 'Poor beggar! After all, what did he want but life – more life – the complete life of any man – or animal, either, come to that!'

As he pressed his finger to the trigger he saw the rough brown figure throw up its arms, leap high in the air, and drop.

Something like a red-hot iron burnt up the back of his own neck; his head throbbed. After all, what did death matter when life was so rotten, so inexplicable? It wasn't that, only – only … Well, it was beastly to feel so tired, so altogether gone to pieces.

With bent head he made his way, ploughing through the mud and sand, back to the shore; sat down rather suddenly, with a feeling as though the ground had risen up to meet him, and winding his arms round his knees, stared out to sea; washed through and through, swept by an immense sense of grief, a desperate regret which had nothing whatever to do with immediate action – the death of Hodge.

That was something which had to be gone through with; it wasn't that – not exactly that … But, oh, the futility, the waste of … well, of everything!

With a sense of appalling weariness he seemed to see the centuries which had passed sweep by him, wave upon wave, era upon era, each so superficially different, and yet so tragically, so stupidly alike: man driven like a dry leaf before the wind of destiny; man the soul-burdened brute.

'Rotten luck!' He shuddered as he dragged himself wearily to his feet. He could not have gone before: not while there was the mud with 'that' on it; not even so long as the shining sands were bare. It would have seemed too hurried, almost indecent. But now that an unbroken, glittering sheet of water lapped the very edge of the shore, the funeral ceremony – with all its pomp of sunrise – was over; and, turning aside, he stumbled wearily through the rough grass to the place where he had left his bicycle.

8 Where Their Fire Is Not Quenched

BY MAY SINCLAIR

There was nobody in the orchard. Harriott Leigh went out, carefully, through the iron gate into the field. She had made the latch slip into its notch without a sound.

The path slanted widely up the field from the orchard gate to the stile under the elder tree. George Waring waited for her there.

Years afterwards, when she thought of George Waring she smelt the sweet, hot, wine-scent of the elder flowers. Years afterwards, when she smelt elder flowers she saw George Waring, with his beautiful, gentle face, like a poet's or a musician's, his black-blue eyes, and sleek, olive-brown hair. He was a naval lieutenant.

Yesterday he had asked her to marry him and she had consented. But her father hadn't, and she had come to tell him that and say good-bye before he left her. His ship was to sail the next day.

He was eager and excited. He couldn't believe that anything could stop their happiness, that anything he didn't want to happen could happen.

'Well?' he said.

'He's a perfect beast, George. He won't let us. He says we're too young.'

'I was twenty last August,' he said, aggrieved.

'And I shall be seventeen in September.'

'And this is June. We're quite old, really. How long does he mean us to wait?'

'Three years.'

'Three years before we can be engaged even – Why, we might be dead.'

She put her arms round him to make him feel safe. They kissed; and the sweet, hot, wine-scent of the elder flowers mixed with their kisses. They stood, pressed close together, under the elder tree.

Across the yellow fields of charlock they heard the village clock strike seven. Up in the house a gong clanged.

'Darling, I must go,' she said.

'Oh stay – Stay *five* minutes.'

He pressed her close. It lasted five minutes, and five more. Then he was running fast down the road to the station, while Harriott went along the field-path, slowly, struggling with her tears.

'He'll be back in three months,' she said. 'I can live through three months.'

But he never came back. There was something wrong with the engines of his ship, the *Alexandra*. Three weeks later she went down in the Mediterranean, and George with her.

Harriott said she didn't care how soon she died now. She was quite sure it would be soon, because she couldn't live without him.

Five years passed.

The two lines of beech trees stretched on and on, the whole length of the Park, a broad green drive between. When you came to the middle they branched off right and left in the form of a cross, and at the end of the right arm there was a white stucco pavilion with pillars and a three-cornered pediment like a Greek temple. At the end of the left arm, the west entrance to the Park, double gates and a side door.

Harriott, on her stone seat at the back of the pavilion, could see Stephen Philpotts the very minute he came through the side door.

He had asked her to wait for him there. It was the place he always chose to read his poems aloud in. The poems were a pretext. She knew what he was going to say. And she knew what she would answer.

There were elder bushes in flower at the back of the pavilion, and Harriott thought of George Waring. She told herself that George was nearer to her now than he could ever have been, living. If she married Stephen she would not be unfaithful, because she loved him with another part of herself. It was not as though Stephen were taking George's place. She loved Stephen with her soul, in an unearthly way.

But her body quivered like a stretched wire when the door opened and the young man came towards her down the drive under the beech trees.

She loved him; she loved his slenderness, his darkness and sallow whiteness, his black eyes lighting up with the intellectual flame, the way his black hair swept back from his forehead, the way he walked, tiptoe, as if his feet were lifted with wings.

He sat down beside her. She could see his hands tremble. She felt that her moment was coming; it had come.

'I wanted to see you alone because there's something I must say to you. I don't quite know how to begin …'

Her lips parted. She panted lightly.

'You've heard me speak of Sybill Foster?'

Her voice came stammering, 'N-no, Stephen. Did you?'

'Well, I didn't mean to, till I knew it was all right. I only heard yesterday.'

'Heard what?'

'Why, that she'll have me. Oh, Harriott – do you know what it's like to be terribly happy?'

She knew. She had known just now, the moment before he told her. She sat there, stone-cold and stiff, listening to his raptures; listening to her own voice saying she was glad.

Ten years passed.

Harriott Leigh sat waiting in the drawing-room of a small house in Maida Vale. She had lived there ever since her father's death two years before.

She was restless. She kept on looking at the clock to see if it was four, the hour that Oscar Wade had appointed. She was not sure that he would come, after she had sent him away yesterday.

She now asked herself, why, when she had sent him away yesterday, she had let him come to-day. Her motives were not altogether clear. If she really meant what she had said then, she oughtn't to let him come to her again. Never again.

She had shown him plainly what she meant. She could see herself, sitting very straight in her chair, uplifted by a passionate integrity, while he stood before her, hanging his head, ashamed and beaten; she could feel again the throb in her voice as she kept on saying that she couldn't, she couldn't; he must see that she couldn't; that no, nothing would make her change her mind; she couldn't forget he had a wife; that he must think of Muriel.

To which he had answered savagely: 'I needn't. That's all over. We only live together for the look of the thing.'

And she, serenely, with great dignity: 'And for the look of the thing, Oscar, we must leave off seeing each other. Please go.'

'Do you mean it?'

'Yes. We must never see each other again.'

And he had gone then, ashamed and beaten.

She could see him, squaring his broad shoulders to meet the blow. And she was sorry for him. She told herself she had been unnecessarily hard. Why shouldn't they see each other again, now he understood where they must draw the line? Until yesterday the line had never been very clearly drawn. To-day she meant to ask him to forget what he had said to her. Once it was forgotten, they could go on being friends as if nothing had happened.

It was four o'clock. Half-past. Five. She had finished tea and given him up when, between the half-hour and six o'clock, he came.

He came as he had come a dozen times, with his measured, deliberate, thoughtful tread, carrying himself well braced, with a sort of held-in arrogance, his great shoulders heaving. He was a man of about forty, broad and tall, lean-flanked and short-necked, his straight, handsome features showing small and even in the big square face and in the flush that swamped it. The close-clipped, reddish-brown moustache bristled forwards from the pushed-out upper lip. His small, flat eyes shone, reddish-brown, eager and animal.

She liked to think of him when he was not there, but always at the first sight of him she felt a slight shock. Physically, he was very far from her admired ideal. So different from George Waring and Stephen Philpotts.

He sat down, facing her.

There was an embarrassed silence, broken by Oscar Wade.

'Well, Harriott, you said I could come.' He seemed to be throwing the responsibility on her.

'So I suppose you've forgiven me,' he said.

'Oh, yes, Oscar, I've forgiven you.'

He said she'd better show it by coming to dine with him somewhere that evening.

She could give no reason to herself for going. She simply went.

He took her to a restaurant in Soho. Oscar Wade dined well, even extravagantly, giving each dish its importance. She liked his extravagance. He had none of the mean virtues.

It was over. His flushed, embarrassed silence told her what he was thinking. But when he had seen her home he left her at her garden gate. He had thought better of it.

She was not sure whether she were glad or sorry. She had had her moment of righteous exaltation and she had enjoyed it. But there was no joy in the weeks that followed it. She had given up Oscar Wade because she didn't want him very much; and now she wanted him furiously, perversely, because she had given him up. Though he had no resemblance to her ideal, she couldn't live without him.

She dined with him again and again, till she knew Schnebler's Restaurant by heart, the white panelled walls picked out with gold; the white pillars, and the curling gold fronds of their capitals; the Turkey carpets, blue and crimson, soft under her feet; the thick crimson velvet cushions, that clung to her skirts; the glitter of silver and glass on the innumerable white circles of the tables. And the faces of the diners, red, white, pink, brown, grey and sallow, distorted and excited; the curled mouths that twisted as they ate; the convoluted electric bulbs pointing, pointing down at them, under the red, crinkled shades. All shimmering in a thick air that the red light stained as wine stains water.

And Oscar's face, flushed with his dinner. Always, when he leaned back from the table and brooded in silence she knew what he was thinking. His heavy eyelids would lift; she would find his eyes fixed on hers, wondering, considering.

She knew now what the end would be. She thought of George Waring, and Stephen Philpotts, and of her life, cheated. She hadn't chosen Oscar, she hadn't really wanted him; but now he had forced himself on her she couldn't afford to let him go. Since George died no man had loved her, no other man ever would. And she was sorry for him when she thought of him going from her, beaten and ashamed.

She was certain, before he was, of the end. Only she didn't know when and where and how it would come. That was what Oscar knew.

It came at the close of one of their evenings when they had

dined in a private sitting-room. He said he couldn't stand the heat and noise of the public restaurant.

She went before him, up a steep, red-carpeted stair to a white door on the second landing.

From time to time they repeated the furtive, hidden adventure. Sometimes she met him in the room above Schnebler's. Sometimes, when her maid was out, she received him at her house in Maida Vale. But that was dangerous, not to be risked too often.

Oscar declared himself unspeakably happy. Harriott was not quite sure. This was love, the thing she had never had, that she had dreamed of, hungered and thirsted for; but now she had it she was not satisfied. Always she looked for something just beyond it, some mystic, heavenly rapture, always beginning to come, that never came. There was something about Oscar that repelled her. But because she had taken him for her lover, she couldn't bring herself to admit that it was a certain coarseness. She looked another way and pretended it wasn't there. To justify herself, she fixed her mind on his good qualities, his generosity, his strength, the way he had built up his engineering business. She made him take her over his works and show her his great dynamos. She made him lend her the books he read. But always, when she tried to talk to him, he let her see that *that* wasn't what she was there for.

'My dear girl, we haven't time,' he said. 'It's waste of our priceless moments.'

She persisted. 'There's something wrong about it all if we can't talk to each other.'

He was irritated. 'Women never seem to consider that a man can get all the talk he wants from other men. What's wrong is our meeting in this unsatisfactory way. We ought to live together. It's the only sane thing. I would, only I don't want to break up Muriel's home and make her miserable.'

'I thought you said she wouldn't care.'

'My dear, she cares for her home and her position and the children. You forget the children.'

Yes. She had forgotten the children. She had forgotten Muriel. She had left off thinking of Oscar as a man with a wife and children and a home.

He had a plan. His mother-in-law was coming to stay with Muriel in October and he would get away. He would go to Paris, and Harriott should come to him there. He could say he went on business. No need to lie about it; he *had* business in Paris.

He engaged rooms in an hotel in the rue de Rivoli. They spent two weeks there.

For three days Oscar was madly in love with Harriott and Harriott with him. As she lay awake she would turn on the light and look at him as he slept at her side. Sleep made him beautiful and innocent; it laid a fine, smooth tissue over his coarseness; it made his mouth gentle; it entirely hid his eyes.

In six days reaction had set in. At the end of the tenth day, Harriott, returning with Oscar from Montmartre, burst into a fit of crying. When questioned, she answered wildly that the Hotel Saint Pierre was too hideously ugly; it was getting on her nerves. Mercifully Oscar explained her state as fatigue following excitement. She tried hard to believe that she was miserable because her love was purer and more spiritual than Oscar's; but all the time she knew perfectly well she had cried from pure boredom. She was in love with Oscar, and Oscar bored her. Oscar was in love with her, and she bored him. At close quarters, day in and day out, each was revealed to the other as an incredible bore.

At the end of the second week she began to doubt whether she had ever been really in love with him.

Her passion returned for a little while after they got back to London. Freed from the unnatural strain which Paris had put on them, they persuaded themselves that their romantic temperaments were better fitted to the old life of casual adventure.

Then, gradually, the sense of danger began to wake in them. They lived in perpetual fear, face to face with all the chances of discovery. They tormented themselves and each other by imagining possibilities that they would never have considered in their first fine moments. It was as though they were beginning to ask themselves if it were, after all, worthwhile running such awful risks, for all they got out of it. Oscar still swore that if he had been free he would have married her. He pointed out that his intentions at any rate were regular. But she asked herself: Would I marry *him?* Marriage would be the Hotel Saint Pierre all over again, without any possibility of escape. But, if she wouldn't marry him, was she in love with him? That was the test. Perhaps it was a good thing he wasn't free. Then she told herself that these doubts were morbid, and that the question wouldn't arise.

One evening Oscar called to see her. He had come to tell her that Muriel was ill.

'Seriously ill?'

'I'm afraid so. It's pleurisy. May turn to pneumonia. We shall know one way or another in the next few days.'

A terrible fear seized upon Harriott. Muriel might die of her pleurisy; and if Muriel died, she would have to marry Oscar. He was looking at her queerly, as if he knew what she was thinking, and she could see that the same thought had occurred to him and that he was frightened too.

Muriel got well again; but their danger had enlightened them. Muriel's life was now inconceivably precious to them both; she stood between them and that permanent union, which they dreaded and yet would not have the courage to refuse.

After enlightenment the rupture.

It came from Oscar, one evening when he sat with her in her drawing-room.

'Harriott,' he said, 'do you know I'm thinking seriously of settling down?'

'How do you mean, settling down?'

'Patching it up with Muriel, poor girl ... Has it never occurred to you that this little affair of ours can't go on forever?'

'You don't want it to go on?'

'I don't want to have any humbug about it. For God's sake, let's be straight. If it's done, it's done. Let's end it decently.'

'I see. You want to get rid of me.'

'That's a beastly way of putting it.'

'Is there any way that isn't beastly? The whole thing's beastly. I should have thought you'd have stuck to it now you've made it what you wanted. When I haven't an ideal, I haven't a single illusion, when you've destroyed everything you didn't want.'

'What didn't I want?'

'The clean, beautiful part of it. The part I wanted.'

'My part at least was real. It was cleaner and more beautiful than all that putrid stuff you wrapped it up in. You were a hypocrite, Harriott, and I wasn't. You're a hypocrite now if you say you weren't happy with me.'

'I was never really happy. Never for one moment. There was always something I missed. Something you didn't give me. Perhaps you couldn't.'

'No. I wasn't spiritual enough,' he sneered.

'You were not. And you made me what you were.'

'Oh, I noticed that you were always very spiritual *after* you'd got what you wanted.'

'What I wanted?' she cried. 'Oh, my God –'

'If you ever knew what you wanted.'

'What – I – wanted,' she repeated, drawing out her bitterness.

'Come,' he said, 'why not be honest? Face facts. I was

awfully gone on you. You were awfully gone on me – once. We got tired of each other and it's over. But at least you might own we had a good time while it lasted.'

'A good time?'

'Good enough for me.'

'For you, because for you love only means one thing. Everything that's high and noble in it you dragged down to that, till there's nothing left for us but that. *That's* what you made of love.'

Twenty years passed.

⁂

It was Oscar who died first, three years after the rupture. He did it suddenly one evening, falling down in a fit of apoplexy.

His death was an immense relief to Harriott. Perfect security had been impossible as long as he was alive. But now there wasn't a living soul who knew her secret.

Still, in the first moment of shock Harriott told herself that Oscar dead would be nearer to her than ever. She forgot how little she had wanted him to be near her, alive. And long before the twenty years had passed she had contrived to persuade herself that he had never been near to her at all. It was incredible that she had ever known such a person as Oscar Wade. As for their affair, she couldn't think of Harriott Leigh as the sort of woman to whom such a thing could happen. Schnebler's and the Hotel Saint Pierre ceased to figure among prominent images of her past. Her memories, if she had allowed herself to remember, would have clashed disagreeably with the reputation for sanctity which she had now acquired.

For Harriott at fifty-two was the friend and helper of the Reverend Clement Farmer, Vicar of St Mary the Virgin, Maida Vale. She worked as a deaconess in his parish, wearing the uniform of a deaconess, the semi-religious gown, the cloak, the bonnet and veil, the cross and rosary, the holy smile. She was also secretary to the Maida Vale and Kilburn Home for Fallen Girls.

Her moments of excitement came when Clement Farmer, the lean, austere likeness of Stephen Philpotts, in his cassock and lace-bordered surplice, issued from the vestry, when he mounted the pulpit, when he stood before the altar rails and lifted up his arms in the Benediction; her moments of ecstasy when she received the Sacrament from his hands. And she had moments of calm happiness when his study door closed on their communion. All these moments were saturated with a solemn holiness.

And they were insignificant compared with the moment of her dying.

She lay dozing in her white bed under the black crucifix with the ivory Christ. The basins and medicine bottles had been cleared from the table by her pillow; it was spread for the last rites. The priest moved quietly about the room, arranging the candles, the Prayer Book and the Holy Sacrament. Then he drew a chair to her bedside and watched with her, waiting for her to come up out of her doze.

She woke suddenly. Her eyes were fixed upon him. She had a flash of lucidity. She was dying, and her dying made her supremely important to Clement Farmer.

'Are you ready?' he asked.

'Not yet. I think I'm afraid. Make me not afraid.'

He rose and lit the two candles on the altar. He took down the crucifix from the wall and stood it against the foot-rail of the bed.

She sighed. That was not what she had wanted.

'You will not be afraid now,' he said.

'I'm not afraid of the hereafter. I suppose you get used to it. Only it may be terrible just at first.'

'Our first state will depend very much on what we are thinking of at our last hour.'

'There'll be my – confession,' she said.

'And after it you will receive the Sacrament. Then you will have your mind fixed firmly upon God and your Redeemer … Do you feel able to make your confession now, Sister? Everything is ready.'

Her mind went back over her past and found Oscar Wade there. She wondered: Should she confess to him about Oscar Wade? One moment she thought it was possible; the next she knew that she couldn't. She could not. It wasn't necessary. For twenty years he had not been part of her life. No. She wouldn't confess about Oscar Wade. She had been guilty of other sins.

She made a careful selection.

'I have cared too much for the beauty of this world … I have failed in charity to my poor girls. Because of my intense repugnance to their sin … I have thought, often, about – people I love, when I should have been thinking about God.'

After that she received the Sacrament.

'Now,' he said, 'there is nothing to be afraid of.'

'I won't be afraid if – if you would hold my hand.'

He held it. And she lay still a long time, with her eyes shut. Then he heard her murmuring something. He stooped close.

'This – is – dying. I thought it would be horrible. And it's bliss … Bliss.'

The priest's hand slackened, as if at the bidding of some wonder. She gave a weak cry.

'Oh – don't let me go.'

His grasp tightened.

'Try,' he said, 'to think about God. Keep on looking at the crucifix.'

'If I look,' she whispered, 'you won't let go my hand?'

'I will not let you go.'

He held it till it was wrenched from him in the last agony.

✕

She lingered for some hours in the room where these things had happened.

Its aspect was familiar and yet unfamiliar, and slightly repugnant to her. The altar, the crucifix, the lighted candles, suggested some tremendous and awful experience the details of which she was not able to recall. She seemed to remember that they had been connected in some way with the sheeted body on the bed; but the nature of the connection was not clear; and she did not associate the dead body with herself. When the nurse came in and laid it out, she saw that it was the body of a middle-aged woman. Her own living body was that of a young woman of about thirty-two.

Her mind had no past and no future, no sharp-edged, coherent memories, and no idea of anything to be done next.

Then, suddenly, the room began to come apart before her eyes, to split into shafts of floor and furniture and ceiling that shifted and were thrown by their commotion into different planes. They leaned slanting at every possible angle; they crossed and overlaid each other with a transparent mingling of dislocated perspectives, like reflections fallen on an interior seen behind glass.

The bed and the sheeted body slid away somewhere out of sight. She was standing by the door that still remained in position.

She opened it and found herself in the street, outside a building of yellowish-grey brick and freestone, with a tall slated spire. Her mind came together with a palpable click of recognition. This object was the Church of St Mary the Virgin, Maida Vale. She could hear the droning of the organ.

She opened the door and slipped in.

She had gone back into a definite space and time, and recovered a certain limited section of coherent memory. She remembered the rows of pitch-pine benches, with their Gothic peaks and mouldings; the stone-coloured walls and pillars with their chocolate stencilling; the hanging rings of lights along the aisles of the nave; the high altar with its lighted candles, and the polished brass cross, twinkling. These things were somehow permanent and real, adjusted to the image that now took possession of her.

She knew what she had come there for. The service was over. The choir had gone from the chancel; the sacristan moved before the altar, putting out the candles. She walked up the middle aisle to a seat that she knew under the pulpit. She knelt down and covered her face with her hands. Peeping sideways through her fingers, she could see the door of the vestry on her left at the end of the north aisle. She watched it steadily.

Up in the organ loft the organist drew out the Recessional, slowly and softly, to its end in the two solemn, vibrating chords.

The vestry door opened and Clement Farmer came out, dressed in his black cassock. He passed before her, close, close outside the bench where she knelt. He paused at the opening. He was waiting for her. There was something he had to say.

She stood up and went towards him. He still waited. He didn't move to make way for her. She came close, closer than she had ever come to him, so close that his features grew indistinct. She bent her head back, peering, short-sightedly, and found herself looking into Oscar Wade's face.

He stood still, horribly still, and close, barring her passage. She drew back; his heaving shoulders followed her. He leaned forward, covering her with his eyes. She opened her mouth to scream and no sound came.

She was afraid to move lest he should move with her. The heaving of his shoulders terrified her.

One by one the lights in the side aisles were going out. The lights in the middle aisle would go next. They had gone. If she didn't get away she would be shut up with him there, in the appalling darkness.

She turned and moved towards the north aisle, groping, steadying herself by the book ledge.

When she looked back, Oscar Wade was not there.

Then she remembered that Oscar Wade was dead. Therefore, what she had seen was not Oscar; it was his ghost. He was dead; dead seventeen years ago. She was safe from him forever.

✕

When she came out on to the steps of the church she saw that the road it stood in had changed. It was not the road she remembered. The pavement on this side was raised slightly and covered in. It ran under a succession of arches. It was a long gallery walled with glittering shop windows on one side; on the other a line of tall grey columns divided it from the street.

She was going along the arcades of the rue de Rivoli. Ahead of her she could see the edge of an immense grey pillar jutting out. That was the porch of the Hotel Saint Pierre. The revolving glass doors swung forward to receive her; she crossed the grey, sultry vestibule under the pillared arches. She knew it. She knew the porter's shining, wine-coloured mahogany pen on her left, and the shining, wine-coloured mahogany barrier on the clerk's bureau on her right; she made straight for the great grey carpeted staircase; she climbed the endless flights that turned round and round the caged-in shaft of the well, past the latticed doors of the lift, and came up on to a landing that she knew, and into the long, ash-grey, foreign corridor lit by a dull window at one end.

It was there that the horror of the place came on her. She had no longer any memory of St Mary's Church, so that she was unaware of her backward course through time. All space and time were here.

She remembered she had to go to the left, the left.

But there was something there; where the corridor turned by the window; at the end of all the corridors. If she went the other way she would escape it.

The corridor stopped there. A blank wall. She was driven back past the stairhead to the left.

At the corner, by the window, she turned down another long ash-grey corridor on her right, and to the right again where the night-light sputtered on the table-flap at the turn.

This third corridor was dark and secret and depraved. She knew the soiled walls and the warped door at the end. There was a sharp-pointed streak of light at the top. She could see the number on it now, 107.

Something had happened there. If she went in it would happen again.

Oscar Wade was in the room waiting for her behind the closed door. She felt him moving about in there. She leaned forward, her ear to the key-hole, and listened. She could hear the measured, deliberate, thoughtful footsteps. They were coming from the bed to the door.

She turned and ran; her knees gave way under her; she sank and ran on, down the long grey corridors and the stairs, quick and blind, a hunted beast seeking for cover, hearing his feet coming after her.

The revolving doors caught her and pushed her out into the street.

✖

The strange quality of her state was this, that it had no time. She remembered dimly that there had once been a thing called time; but she had forgotten altogether what it was like. She was aware of things happening and about to happen; she fixed them by the place they occupied, and measured their duration by the space she went through.

So now she thought: If I could only go back and get to the place where it hadn't happened.

To get back farther –

She was walking now on a white road that went between broad grass borders. To the right and left were the long raking lines of the hills, curve after curve, shimmering in a thin mist.

The road dropped to the green valley. It mounted the humped bridge over the river. Beyond it she saw the twin gables of the grey house pricked up over the high, grey garden wall. The tall iron gate stood in front of it between the ball-topped stone pillars.

And now she was in a large, low-ceilinged room with drawn blinds. She was standing before the wide double bed. It was her father's bed. The dead body, stretched out in the middle under the drawn white sheet, was her father's body.

The outline of the sheet sank from the peak of the upturned toes to the shin-bone, and from the high bridge of the nose to the chin.

She lifted the sheet and folded it back across the breast of the dead man. The face she saw then was Oscar Wade's face, stilled and smoothed in the innocence of sleep, the supreme innocence of death. She stared at it, fascinated, in a cold, pitiless joy.

Oscar was dead.

She remembered how he used to lie like that beside her in the room in the Hotel Saint Pierre, on his back with his hands folded on his waist, his mouth half open, his big chest rising and falling. If he was dead, it would never happen again. She would be safe.

The dead face frightened her, and she was about to cover it up again when she was aware of a light heaving, a rhythmical rise and fall. As she drew the sheet up tighter, the hands under it began to struggle convulsively, the broad ends of the fingers appeared above the edge, clutching it to keep it down. The mouth opened; the eyes opened; the whole face stared back at her in a look of agony and horror.

Then the body drew itself forward from the hips and sat up, its eyes peering into her eyes; he and she remained for an instant motionless, each held there by the other's fear.

Suddenly she broke away, turned and ran, out of the room, out of the house.

She stood at the gate, looking up and down the road, not knowing by which way she must go to escape Oscar. To the right, over the bridge and up the hill and across the downs she would come to the arcades of the rue de Rivoli and the dreadful grey corridors of the hotel. To the left the road went through the village.

If she could get further back she would be safe, out of Oscar's reach. Standing by her father's death-bed she had been young, but not young enough. She must get back to the place where she was younger still, to the Park and the green drive under the beech trees and the white pavilion at the cross. She knew how to find it. At the end of the village the high road ran right and left, east and west, under the Park walls; the south gate stood there at the top, looking down the narrow street.

She ran towards it through the village, past the long grey barns of Goodyer's farm, past the grocer's shop, past the yellow front and blue sign of the 'Queen's Head', past the post office, with its one black window blinking under its vine, past the church and the yew-trees in the churchyard, to where the south gate made a delicate black pattern on the green grass.

These things appeared insubstantial, drawn back behind a sheet of air that shimmered over them like thin glass. They opened out, floated past and away from her; and instead of the high road and park walls she saw a London street of dingy white facades, and instead of the south gate the swinging glass doors of Schnebler's Restaurant.

✕

The glass doors swung open and she passed into the restaurant. The scene beat on her with the hard impact of reality: the white and gold panels, the white pillars and their curling gold capitals, the white circles of the tables, glittering, the flushed faces of the diners, moving mechanically.

She was driven forward by some irresistible compulsion to a table in the corner, where a man sat alone. The table napkin he was using hid his mouth, and jaw, and chest; and she was not sure of the upper part of the face above the straight, drawn edge. It dropped; and she saw Oscar Wade's face. She came to him, dragged, without power to resist; she sat down beside him, and he leaned to her over the table; she could feel the warmth of his red, congested face; the smell of wine floated towards her on his thick whisper.

'I knew you would come.'

She ate and drank with him in silence, nibbling and sipping slowly, staving off the abominable moment it would end in.

At last they got up and faced each other. His long bulk stood before her, above her; she could almost feel the vibration of its power.

'Come,' he said. 'Come.'

And she went before him, slowly, slipping out through the maze of the tables, hearing behind her Oscar's measured, deliberate, thoughtful tread. The steep, red-carpeted staircase rose up before her.

She swerved from it, but he turned her back.

'You know the way,' he said.

At the top of the flight she found the white door of the room she knew. She knew the long windows guarded by drawn muslin blinds; the gilt looking-glass over the chimney-piece that reflected Oscar's head and shoulders grotesquely between two white porcelain babies with bulbous limbs and garlanded loins, she knew the sprawling stain on the drab carpet by the table, the shabby, infamous couch behind the screen.

They moved about the room, turning and turning in it like beasts in a cage, uneasy, inimical, avoiding each other.

At last they stood still, he at the window, she at the door, the length of the room between.

'It's no good your getting away like that,' he said. 'There couldn't be any other end to it – to what we did.'

'But that *was* ended.'

'Ended there, but not here.'

'Ended for ever. We've done with it for ever.'

'We haven't. We've got to begin again. And go on. And go on.'

'Oh, no. No. Anything but that.'

'There isn't anything else.'

'We can't. We can't. Don't you remember how it bored us?'

'Remember? Do you suppose I'd touch you if I could help it? ... That's what we're here for. We must. We must.'

'No. No. I shall get away – now.'

She turned to the door to open it.

'You can't,' he said. 'The door's locked.'

'Oscar – what did you do that for?'

'We always did it. Don't you remember?'

She turned to the door again and shook it; she beat on it with her hands.

'It's no use, Harriott. If you got out now you'd only have to come back again. You might stave it off for an hour or so, but what's that in an immortality?'

'Immortality?'

'That's what we're in for.'

'Time enough to talk about immortality when we're dead ... Ah –'

They were being drawn towards each other across the room, moving slowly, like figures in some monstrous and appalling dance, their heads thrown back over their shoulders, their faces turned from the horrible approach. Their arms rose slowly, heavy with intolerable reluctance; they stretched them out towards each other, aching, as if they held up an overpowering weight. Their feet dragged and were drawn.

Suddenly her knees sank under her; she shut her eyes; all her being went down before him in darkness and terror.

✖

It was over. She had got away, she was going back, back, to the green drive of the Park, between the beech trees, where Oscar had never been, where he would never find her. When she passed through the south gate her memory became suddenly young and clean. She forgot the rue de Rivoli and the Hotel Saint Pierre; she forgot Schnebler's Restaurant and the room at the top of the stairs. She was back in her youth. She was Harriott Leigh going to wait for Stephen Philpotts in the pavilion opposite the west gate. She could feel herself, a slender figure moving fast over the grass between the lines of the great beech trees. The freshness of her youth was upon her.

She came to the heart of the drive where it branched right and left in the form of a cross. At the end of the right arm the white Greek temple, with its pediment and pillars, gleamed against the wood.

She was sitting on their seat at the back of the pavilion,

watching the side door that Stephen would come in by.

The door was pushed open; he came towards her, light and young, skimming between the beech trees with his eager, tiptoeing stride. She rose up to meet him. She gave a cry.

'Stephen!'

It had been Stephen. She had seen him coming. But the man who stood before her between the pillars of the pavilion was Oscar Wade.

And now she was walking along the field-path that slanted from the orchard door to the stile; further and further back, to where young George Waring waited for her under the elder tree. The smell of the elder flowers came to her over the field. She could feel on her lips and in all her body the sweet, innocent excitement of her youth.

'George, oh, George!'

As she went along the field-path she had seen him. But the man who stood waiting for her under the elder tree was Oscar Wade.

'I told you it's no use getting away, Harriott. Every path brings you back to me. You'll find me at every turn.'

'But how did you get *here*?'

'As I got into the pavilion. As I got into your father's room, on to his death bed. Because I *was* there. I am in all your memories.'

'My memories are innocent. How could you take my father's place, and Stephen's, and George Waring's? You?'

'Because I did take them.'

'Never. My love for *them* was innocent.'

'Your love for me was part of it. You think the past affects the future. Has it never struck you that the future may affect the past? In your innocence there was the beginning of your sin. You *were* what you *were to be*.'

'I shall get away,' she said.

'And, this time, I shall go with you.'

The stile, the elder tree, and the field floated away from her. She was going under the beech trees down the Park drive towards the south gate and the village, slinking close to the right-hand row of trees. She was aware that Oscar Wade was going with her under the left-hand row, keeping even with her, step by step, and tree by tree. And presently there was grey pavement under her feet and a row of grey pillars on her right hand. They were walking side by side down the rue de Rivoli towards the hotel.

They were sitting together now on the edge of the dingy white bed. Their arms hung by their sides, heavy and limp, their heads drooped, averted. Their passion weighed on them with the unbearable, unescapable boredom of immortality.

'Oscar – how long will it last?'

'I can't tell you. I don't know whether *this* is one moment of eternity, or the eternity of one moment.'

'It must end some time,' she said. 'Life doesn't go on forever. We shall die.'

'Die? We *have* died. Don't you know what this is? Don't you know where you are? This is death. We're dead, Harriott. We're in hell.'

'Yes. There can't be anything worse than this.'

'This isn't the worst. We're not quite dead yet, as long as we've life in us to turn and run and get away from each other; as long as we can escape into our memories. But when you've got back to the farthest memory of all and there's nothing beyond it – When there's no memory but this –

'In the last hell we shall not run away any longer; we shall find no more roads, no more passages, no more open doors. We shall have no need to look for each other.

'In the last death we shall be shut up in this room, behind that locked door, together. We shall lie here together, for ever and ever, joined so fast that even God can't put us asunder. We shall be one flesh and one spirit, one sin repeated forever, and ever; spirit loathing flesh, flesh loathing spirit; you and I loathing each other.'

'Why? Why?' she cried.

'Because that's all that's left us. That's what you made of love.'

⋇

The darkness came down swamping, it blotted out the room. She was walking along a garden path between high borders of phlox and larkspur and lupin. They were taller than she was, their flowers swayed and nodded above her head. She tugged at the tall stems and had no strength to break them. She was a little thing.

She said to herself then that she was safe. She had gone back so far that she was a child again; she had the blank innocence of childhood. To be a child, to go small under the heads of the lupins, to be blank and innocent, without memory, was to be safe.

The walk led her out through a yew hedge on to a bright green lawn. In the middle of the lawn there was a shallow round pond in a ring of rockery cushioned with small flowers, yellow and white and purple. Gold-fish swam in the olive brown water. She would be safe when she saw the gold-fish swimming towards her. The old one with the white scales would come up first, pushing up his nose, making bubbles in the water.

At the bottom of the lawn there was a privet hedge cut by a broad path that went through the orchard. She knew what she would find there; her mother was in the orchard. She would lift her up in her arms to play with the hard red balls of the apples that hung from the tree. She had got back to the farthest memory of all; there was nothing beyond it.

There would be an iron gate in the wall of the orchard. It would lead into a field.

Something was different here, something that frightened her. An ash-grey door instead of an iron gate.

She pushed it open and came into the last corridor of the Hotel Saint Pierre.

9 The Haunted Saucepan

BY MARGERY LAWRENCE

'Yes,' said the long lean man in the corner, 'I have had one odd
experience that I suppose certainly comes under the heading
of 'Spook' stories. Not that I ever *saw* the ghost – I never saw
a real ghost in my life. But this was odd. Yes. Odd ... tell you?
Yes, of course, if you like, Saunderson! Ask that youngster by
the drinks to pour me out another whisky-and-splash, if she
will – thanks, Laurie! Now then. Here's the yarn, and don't
interrupt ...'

I was hunting for a flat in London say about three seasons
ago – a furnished flat, as I didn't know how long I was going
to stay in England, and it wasn't worth getting my furniture
out of store. Rents were pretty high in the district I wanted
– somewhere about St James's or thereabouts – and I didn't
want to go out far, as it was essential that I kept in touch with
my business interests. I had almost given up in despair and
concluded that I should have to go either to a hotel or my
Club, when an agent rang me up and said he had a flat for me,
he thought. The owner, a woman, was abroad – he thought
I might find it just the thing. The address was just what I
wanted, the rent almost incredibly low – I jumped into a taxi
and rushed round to see it, feeling sure there must be a catch
somewhere, but it was a delightful flat, nicely furnished and
as complete in every detail as you could wish. I was cautious
and asked all sorts of questions – but as far as the agent knew
it was a straightforward deal enough – the lady was staying
abroad indefinitely, the previous tenants had gone ... Why did

they leave? I wanted to know ... but the agent played with his pencil and assured me he didn't know. Illness in the family made them decide to leave very suddenly, he believed ... Well, at any rate, a week's time saw me settled in, with my faithful man Strutt to do for me – you know Strutt, of course – one of the best fellows that ever lived? He plays an important part in the remarkable story I'm going to tell you.

The first evening I spent there seemed too delightful for words after the discomfort and inconvenience I had been enduring in various hotels for the last six months, and I drew a sigh of enjoyment as I stretched out my legs before the fire and sipped the excellent coffee at my elbow. Strutt had found me a woman of sorts to do the cooking – marvellous fellow Strutt! – and certainly she could cook, though the glimpse I had caught of her through the kitchen door as I went into the dining-room proved her a dour and in truth most ill-favoured looking old lady, with a chenille net, a thing I had thought as dead as the Dodo, holding up her back hair. I rang for some more coffee, and as usual, Strutt was at my elbow almost as my finger left the bell-push.

'More coffee, please Strutt – and, by the way, a very good dinner,' I said carelessly. 'Where did you find this cook – she seems an excellent one?' Strutt took up my empty cup as he replied in his usual even voice – is there anything quite so woodenly self-contained as the well-trained valet's voice, I wonder?

'She came one day to fetch something – day or so before you came in, sir, and I was here getting a few things ready for you. We got talking, sir, and I found she was servant to the lady who owns the flat, and caretaker when she left; she seemed a sensible useful sort of body, sir, and I engaged her – after trying to get references from the lady, sir, and failing, as nobody seemed to know her address, I took the liberty of exercising my own judgment, sir, and took her for a month on trial. I hope you think I did right, sir?'

'Oh, of course,' I said hastily – as indeed Strutt's judgment is invariably better than my own! 'I should say she's a find, if she can keep up this standard of cooking. All right – tell her I'm pleased ...'

The door closed noiselessly and I sank into a brown study. The flat was very silent and the pleasant crackle of the flames sounded loud in the stillness, like little pistol-shots – the deep leather chair was comfortable, and beneath the red lampshade rested three books I particularly wanted to read. With a sigh of satisfaction I reached for one, and was in five minutes so deep in it that the entrance of Strutt with my second cup of coffee passed almost unnoticed, and I gulped it down heedlessly as I read. Buried civilisations have always been my hobby, though I've never had the money to go and explore in person – this book was a new and thrilling account of some recent diggings and discoveries, and I devoured the thing till I woke with a start to realise that it was after twelve and the fire out!

With a laugh and a shiver I struggled out of my chair, flipped on the full light and poured myself out a whisky – the syphon hissed as I pressed down the jet, and I cursed Strutt's forgetfulness (most unlike him it was, too!) as I saw it was empty. Perhaps there was another in the kitchen – I went along there to look, feeling rather peevish and very sleepy. The kitchen was flooded with moonlight and all the pots and pans and bottles and things struck little highlights of silver – it was quite a pretty effect; there were several things on the stove, and I remember now that one, a little saucepan, had its lid not quite on – not fitted on levelly, I mean – and it had the oddest look for a moment, just as if it had cocked up its lid to take a sly look at me! I found a fresh syphon on the dresser, had a drink and went to bed; my last thought as I curled luxuriously between the cool linen sheets was that the woman who had had this flat furnished and fitted it up so perfectly must have been a sybarite in her tastes, since I had yet to find the article in her flat that did not show the true lover of luxury. I wondered idly why she had left it, with all its contents, even to linen, plate, pots and pans ... then sleep came, and I sank into unconsciousness, my query unanswered.

I must have slept some two hours, I think, when I was awakened by a sudden attack of pain, of all extraordinary things! I awoke shaking and gasping, my hands alternately clutching my throat and stomach as the most awful gripping agonies seized me, throwing me into convulsive writhings as the pain twisted me into knots and the sweat poured down my face, or fits of frantic coughing that I thought must surely split my lungs – I felt as though I had swallowed some ghastly acid that was burning my very vitals out! ... Feebly I reached for the bell, but before I touched it Strutt was in the room, awakened by my coughing, and bending anxiously over me.

'My God, sir, what's the matter? You waked me coughing! Wait a second, sir, and I'll get you a drop of brandy ...'

The spirit spilled against my chattering teeth, for I was shaking like a man with ague, and my staring eyes were glazed with pain – poor old Strutt's face was a study – he's always been very devoted to me. A few drops went down my throat, however, and after another dose of it I seemed to feel a shade better, and lay back against the pillows panting and shivering. My pyjamas were damp and streaked with perspiration, and now my perceptions were coming back to me and I began to wonder – why this attack, and what on earth had happened to cause it? Strutt bustled about my room getting out a fresh pair of pyjamas, his anxious eye flitting back to me every minute. No need to worry any further though, as I was rapidly returning to my normal healthy self – but this only made it stranger.

Strutt approached the bed. 'You feeling better now, sir? If you'll take my advice you'll change them damp things and let me rub you down before you go to sleep again.'

Feeling almost sound again, though still shaken from the memory of that ghastly ten minutes, I slipped out of bed and stood lost in speculation as Strutt rubbed me – certainly, back in bed in a few minutes in clean pyjamas, with a stiff brandy-and-soda inside me, I could not understand what on earth could have attacked me so terribly, yet passed away so entirely, leaving no trace – for I felt as well as before the attack.

'Strutt,' I said, 'Heaven only knows what was the matter with me – it can't have been anything I've eaten, since you've probably had the same, and you're all right. But it was the most damnable attack – fever's nothing to it. Besides, it *wasn't* fever; I've had too many bouts of that not to know it. Wonder if my heart's all right?'

'I should have said so, sir, but it might be as well to see the doctor tomorrow. What sort of pain was it? You'll forgive me saying so, sir, but you looked simply ghastly. Never seen fever make you look so – never, sir!' Strutt's voice held conviction – moreover, the fellow had seen me through enough fever to know.

I knitted my brows: 'What did I have? Clear soup – a sole – piece of steak and vegetables. All well cooked – oh, and a savoury – mushrooms on toast. Mushrooms!'

I looked at Strutt triumphantly – for a minute I thought I'd hit it.

'Mushrooms – she must have got hold of some poisonous stuff, not real mushrooms. It's easily done –'

'Beg your pardon, sir,' said Strutt firmly, 'but that can't be it. Being rather partial to mushrooms myself, sir, I took a few – and Mrs Barker she did, too ... so that can't be the reason. There's nothing else you had, sir, barring your coffee, which I made myself – the second lot at least, as Mrs Barker had gone home when you rang.'

I lay back on my pillows silenced, but more puzzled than ever – however, I was too thankful to feel well again to worry very much over the cause of my strange attack.

'Well, I can't worry any more over it, Strutt. Turn out the lights. I shall see the doctor in the morning.'

I did, and his report confirmed my own opinion and added not a little to my puzzlement – I was as sound as a bell in every respect; even the trace of occasional fever left by my long sojourn in the East seemed to have vanished. Old Macdonald punched me in the ribs as he said goodbye, and grinned.

'Don't you come flying to me next time you get a pain under your pinny from a whisky or two too many, young fellow-me-lad – go for a good long tramp and blow it away. You're as strong as a young horse, and as for heart – don't you try to pull any of that stuff on me. You've got a heart that'll work like a drayhorse, and never turn a hair...'

I walked up St James's more puzzled than ever – what on earth had happened to me last night? In the light of my present feeling of supreme health and well-being my last night's agonies seemed more inexplicable than ever – obviously old Mac thought I had been more or less tight and exaggerated a nightmare into this ... It was very irritating – yet I still had the vivid memory of that terrible, choking, burning sensation, the torturing pains that had gripped my frame, tearing and wrenching me, it seemed, till my very bones groaned and quivered within me. Good Lord! – a dream? Still lost in thought about the whole curious affair I ran full tilt into an old chum of mine on the steps of the Club – George Trevanion, who seized me delightedly by the hand and poured forth questions. We dined together that night at the Club and spent a long time yarning over the fire afterwards – when we parted Trevanion had promised to dine with me the next night – I was, I admit, rather keen on showing him my new quarters. I had been so engrossed in talking shop – we're both engineers – and there had been so many things to say that I had forgotten to tell him, as I had meant, about my remarkable attack of pain, an omission that annoyed me a little, as having spent thirty years knocking about the world he might have been able to put his finger at once on the cause of it.

There were some letters lying on the table in the dark little hall of my flat as I let myself in. I picked them up; nothing interesting, only some bills and an invitation or two. I dropped them again and turned to hang up my coat. The kitchen door opened into the hall, and when I entered it had been shut – now I saw when I turned that it had swung noiselessly open, and I could see into the moonlit kitchen, the usual little place one finds in these small flats. The gas stove was in line with the door, with various utensils upon it ready for use in the morning – I think there was a large kettle and two saucepans, a big one and a little enamel one. The open door made me jump for a second, but of course I said 'draughts' and thought so – I paused a second to light a cigarette – and the match dropped from my fingers and sputtered out upon the carpet. I held the unlighted cigarette between my fingers as I stared. As I am a living man, this is what I saw – or thought I saw. The saucepan – the little one on the stove, nearest the door – seemed to lift its lid a shade – it seemed to tilt, ever so slightly, cautiously, and from beneath its tilted lid, it looked at me! Yes, I suppose it doesn't sound as horrible as I want it to, but I swear to you that was the most eerie thing I ever saw, or want to see ... For a second I stood cold and dumb, my mouth sticky with fright – somehow the utter banality of the thing made it more terrifying – then I swore at myself, strode into the kitchen and seized the saucepan, holding it to the light.

It was, of course, a mere trick of light – I remember noticing the previous night how brilliantly the moonlight streamed into the kitchen – but good heavens, it had shaken me for a minute, positively! That attack last night must have upset my nerves more than I knew – Lord, what a fool! I put the saucepan back, laughing heartily, and going into the hall, picked up my letters again, still grinning at my own folly. I glanced back at the kitchen as I went along to my room – I could still see the stove and the silent row of pans upon it. The lid of the little saucepan was still askew – it still had the absurd air of watching me stealthily from beneath it! There almost seemed a menace in its very stillness ... I laughed again as I got into bed. It seemed so lunatic – fancy being scared of a saucepan ... good Lord, a chunk of tin, an absurd piece of ironmongery – it just shows you what light and a few jangled nerves can do for one!...

I slept splendidly, and awoke hungry as a hunter, and flung myself into work that day like a giant refreshed. Trevanion and I met at the Club about six-thirty for a cocktail, and had several cocktails – it was good to see the old man again; we'd been boon companions in all sorts of odd places, and I really didn't know how much I'd missed him till we met again. We walked back to the flat about seven fifteen and found a rattling good dinner awaiting us – I'd told Strutt to put Mrs Barker on her mettle, and, by Jove! she turned us out a feed fit for a king. Cream soup, oysters done with cheese – marvellous things they were – roast chicken and salad and a soufflé that melted in your mouth; we were too occupied appreciating flavours to talk much at first, but at last Trevanion sat back, regarding me with reverence, and drew a long breath of repletion.

'Man, you must be a perfect Croesus! Where on earth did you strike the cash to pay for this place, this feeding, and your *cordon bleu* in the kitchen, I should like to know?'

I grinned with triumph, sipping the last drops of my claret.

'Why, sheer luck, dear boy – the rent of this flat is a mere flea-bite – the cook fell into my hands with the flat, and being a bit of an epicure I feel justified in spreading myself a trifle in the feeding line – especially when an old companion in crime like you turns up!'

Trevanion's brow wrinkled. 'A flat in St James's – for a flea-bite rental? Are you sure you're not being done somehow, old man? It seems to me almost impossible.'

I shrugged as I rose and we sought our armchairs by the smoke-room fire; the reason why was still as obscure to me as ever, and after a while we dismissed the subject and began to talk of other things. Strutt brought in coffee and liqueurs, and the hours passed imperceptibly as we chewed our pipes and yarned over old times, adventures old and new. At last Trevanion looked at the clock and laughed, putting down his pipe.

'Good Lord, look at the time! Time I got along to my place, though I don't boast palatial quarters like these of yours, you lucky devil. Come and dine with me one night next week anyway, and I'll see if I can't raise a good drink or two for you, though I can't promise a dinner anywhere near your standard...' He was standing by the door, his hand on the handle, and I was on the hearthrug knocking out the dottle of my pipe; suddenly we both fell silent, and his sentence broke off short as we stood listening. In the silence, down the passage came the sound of something boiling – on the cold stove, black and silent since Mrs Barker left two hours ago! We looked at each other, our mouths open with astonishment, then Trevanion laughed.

'What an odd noise – just like a kettle or something boiling. Suppose your man's been making a drop of toddy for himself on the Q.T. and left the thing on...' For some reason we stared at each other, hard, as he spoke. I know that I, for one, knew somehow that Strutt had not left the gas burning – the kitchen door was open, but from where we stood we could not see into it: the smoke-room door was round an angle. The moonlight streamed into the dark passage through the invisible open door, and with the moonlight came the distant sound of bubbling and boiling – like water in a kettle – or saucepan ... In the silence there seemed, however ridiculous it may sound, a sort of quiet menace in the sound – with a jerk I slewed round from the hearth and made towards the door.

'Probably it's only a draught – wind bubbling through a crevice or something of the sort. Come on, let's see at all events.'

Personally, the last thing I really wanted to do was to go into that kitchen – that beastly kitchen, as mentally I had already begun to call it; here was the door open again – Strutt assured me he had shut it when Mrs Darker left, and always did – there was something in the atmosphere of the whole flat now that I didn't like at all. But my funk was as yet not even definitely acknowledged even to myself, and I strode down the passage with my chin set, and round the angle into the kitchen. The bubbling sounds, clear and distinct till the second I turned the corner, ceased on the instant, and dead silence succeeded. In the moonlit kitchen Trevanion and I stared at each other blankly. The stove held only one utensil, the little enamel saucepan I had noticed before, but the gas beneath it was unlit; its lid was close down ... Trevanion was rattling the window, examining the catch, a frown of bewilderment on his brow – I took up the saucepan, vaguely disturbed, and peered inside it; empty of course.

'Well, upon my soul, this is rum!' said Trevanion, scratching his head. 'There doesn't seem to be a chink anywhere that could let in a draught – air bubbling through a knot-hole *might* make a noise like that ... I suppose there isn't another gas-jet left alight anywhere that might make a sound like water boiling – is the geyser on?'

The geyser was not on, nor was there any other gas-jet, the flat being lighted by electricity – at last we gave it up as a bad job, and gaped at each other, completely floored. Trevanion scratched his head again, then laughed and shrugged his shoulders as he reached for his hat.

'Well – it's the most extraordinary thing I ever knew – still, there's probably some perfectly simple reason for it. 'Phone me when you find out, Connor, old man; it's left me guessing for the present, and I'd really like to know what it is. Never heard anything so clearly – nor so odd, confound it! Think you must have some spook that boils water for its ghostly toddy!...'

Trevanion's cheery laugh died away down the street, and I slammed the door of the flat and stood for a minute, chin in hand, thinking. Damn it, something *had* been boiling, I'd take my oath – but what? As if in answer to my thought, a faint sound broke the stillness of the flat again – the bubbling of a boiling kettle – or saucepan? Why was it that somehow I always thought of a saucepan when that sound started? It was faint at first, but grew more distinct as I listened, every muscle taut with strain – now whatever the damned thing was, I *would* catch it!

The kitchen door stood ajar, of course – I had shut it when we went to look at the geyser, but it was open again when we came out of the bathroom – undoubtedly the sound came from the kitchen … cautious, I took a step forward, though my back crept unaccountably as I did so, and craning forward, I peered round the door. The little saucepan stood where I had put it, on the stove, still cold and unlit – but it was boiling! The lid was rakishly aslant, and tilted a shade every second or so as the liquid, whatever it was, bubbled inside, and gusts of steam came out as I gaped, dumbfounded – somehow as I listened, the noise of the bubbling shaped itself into a devilish little song, almost as if the thing was singing to itself, secretly and abominably ... chortling to itself in a disgusting sort of hidden way, if you know what I mean! I gave a half-gasp of sheer fright, and do you know, instantly the saucepan was ... just an ordinary saucepan again, silent on the stove! I made myself go in, though I admit I was shaking with nerves – I took it up; cold and empty ... Well, cursing myself for a fool, I took a stiff drink and despite a horrible little shivery feeling that there was more in this than I liked, told myself sternly that I must have had one whisky too many and mistaken light and the noise of a stray mouse might have made, for the whole thing, I knew, of course, inside me, that it wasn't so, and I *had* seen that abominable saucepan boiling some infernal brew – but I wouldn't admit it, and scrambled into bed with, I confess, considerable speed, and not a few glances over my shoulder into the dark.

However, I slept well again, and awoke laughing at myself not a little, but with sneaking thankfulness that Trevanion had also made a bit of an ass of himself over the mysterious noise! I lay for a few minutes blinking in the shaft of sunlight that filtered through my blinds, and reached for my watch – it was nine o'clock! Cursing Strutt for his laziness – I always had my bath at eight-thirty, confound him – I rang the bell. A shuffling step came along the passage, and the sullen lined face of Mrs Barker peeped in. I stared at her, then snapped:

'What on earth's the matter with Strutt? It's nine o'clock!'

The woman studied me in silence with her narrow, secret eyes for a few seconds – what an old hag she was, really, I thought impatiently – then jerked her thumb over her shoulder.

'E's took bad with summat – dunno what. Bin writhin' and cursin' like a good 'un...' Her lips wreathed themselves into a mirthless grin, and I eyed her with even less favour than before.

As she spoke I heard a faint moaning coming from poor old Strutt's room – curtly ordering Mrs Barker back to her kitchen I scrambled out of bed and went down the passage – poor Strutt was lying fully dressed on the bed, his lips blue and dry with pain, his limbs twitching convulsively – he was quite beyond speech, but his eyes implored help. I tore off his collar and shouted to Mrs Barker for brandy – the poor fellow's looks really frightened me to death. Bit by bit we pulled him round – though it struck me at the time that the woman's help was given none too willingly; and at last Strutt sat up, shaky, but himself. I sat on the bed staring at him, more concerned than I liked to say.

'What on earth happened, Strutt? It seemed much the same sort of attack I had the other night – you'd better go and see my doctor, I can't have you cracking up like this. When did it come on?'

Strutt cleared his throat, his voice still husky and strained with pain.

'I got up about seven, sir, as usual, or perhaps a little before – Mrs Barker was late, so I made myself some tea and boiled an egg. I hadn't eaten it so very long, sir, before I began to feel as if something was on fire inside me – awful the pain was, I couldn't move nor cry out – not a word. I dunno what it was, sir, but I'll take my oath it's the same sort of thing you was taken with the other night.'

I frowned and meditated. 'Well, you'd better see Macdonald. This is beyond me...'

Strutt was duly overhauled by the doctor and reported sound in wind and limb – this fresh puzzle made me feel almost as if there must be something in superstitions after all, and there must be a curse on my new flat. I was still lost in speculation about it when I met Trevanion in Bond Street, very spruce and dapper from lunching with the lady he happened to favour at the moment. He buttonholed me at once.

'Hullo, Connor, spotted the ghost yet?' I shook my head.

'Spotted it – I wish I could! Listen– there seems no end to the extraordinary things that are coming my way lately...' And I plunged into the story, beginning with my own attack of illness and winding up with what I had seen – or thought I had seen – in the kitchen after he had left, and Strutt's mysterious collapse this morning. Trevanion listened intently, not laughing as I half-expected ... it seems a queer place to discuss a bogey-tale, the corner of Bond Street on a fine spring morning, but it struck neither of us at the time.

'It's certainly odd,' Trevanion said at last. 'It's the oddest yarn I've heard for a long time. Frankly, if it wasn't you – and if I hadn't heard that noise myself last night – I'd of course say it was too much whisky and you were seeing things – But ... look here, I'll come up to your place tonight, say about eleven-thirty, and we'll try an experiment – I've got an idea slowly working its way out! So long, old man.'

I was relieved he had not laughed, and guessed, from his serious attitude towards the whole incomprehensible thing, that he must have been more impressed than I had thought with the episode of the mysterious bubbling – what connection had that, if any, with the equally mysterious attacks of pain that had seized both Strutt and myself? The whole thing obtruded itself upon my work, which did not go particularly well in consequence, and I was still cogitating when the bell rang that night, and Strutt let in Trevanion, accompanied by a dog, to my great astonishment. We shook hands warmly.

'Didn't know you'd got a dog,' I said, 'but while you were about it couldn't you have found a better specimen than this mouldy old semi-demi-collie?' Trevanion grinned at me mysteriously. When Strutt had gone out of the room he bent forward and whispered: 'This is the experiment!'

I gasped, and Trevanion went on, as the old beast settled himself down in front of the blazing fire.

'First and foremost, may I give this old beast a feed? – he's rather hungry, I'm afraid. It's the porter's dog from the Club. I borrowed him for tonight. Yes – as you say, he's a bit of a cheesehound, but not a bad old beast. What about that feed?'

'Of course,' I said, 'I daresay there are some bones in the kitchen – I'll tell Strutt.' Trevanion stopped my upraised hand on the way to the bell.

'I don't want Strutt, thanks old man. I want to give this myself – warm up some scraps for him; you know the sort of thing.' I stared rather, then shrugged my shoulders; I knew Trevanion too well to ask him too many questions at the start of a thing.

'Oh, all right, my dear fellow, though I really don't see why this fuss about warm stuff – you sound as if the beast was a Derby winner!'

'I'm not as cracked as I seem,' asserted Trevanion, going into the kitchen now brightly lighted and as cheerful as could well be imagined, 'You leave this to your Uncle Stalky – it's all part of the experiment!' I left him rummaging among pots and pans and betook myself to an armchair and my book on Egypt, till the entrance of my friend, the dog at his heels licking his lips after his feed, interrupted me. Throwing himself down in the opposite armchair, Trevanion reached for the whisky – I cocked an amused eyebrow at him.

'Finished your incantations over the kitchen stove, Trev?' I said, using my old abbreviation of his name. Trevanion laughed as he filled his pipe.

'You can pull my leg as much as you like, my dear chap, when we're through with this thing. It may be capable of an ordinary explanation – nine out of ten times it is – but there's always the faint possibility of the tenth time cropping up. D'you remember that case of the Box that Wouldn't keep Shut – when you and I were working on that road near Lahore? That was creepy if you like...' I nodded, silenced – for the moment I had forgotten that odd story, never fully explained. Trevanion went on:

'Well, I believe, from what I felt here the other night, and from various other little things – more than ever if the little experiment I've just tried on Ben here succeeds – I believe that we've got here one of the few cases of genuine "queerness". Something really uncanny, I mean.' I interrupted him, my back creeping uncomfortably.

'What have you tried on the dog, then?' Trevanion looked at me oddly.

'Fed him out of the saucepan – the saucepan that bubbled!' he said at last.

My back crept again, though I did not quite get what he was driving at – I stared, puzzled. 'But what – I don't quite see your drift, Trev. What should that show you?'

'If I'm right we shall soon see,' Trevanion returned, 'but I don't want to tell you all my ideas entirely before we've got through the end of this sitting, as they might colour your impressions, and I want to leave your mind as open as possible tonight ... Now about twelve I propose that you and I and old Ben shut ourselves up in the kitchen – and see if anything happens. I believe if we're right, and there *is* something more to this than the things of everyday life, the dog's behaviour will show it. Beasts are much more susceptible to psychic influence than we are, especially dogs and cats ... At any rate, it's worth trying to see if he *does* seem to sense anything – if he does that will prove that you and I are not both slightly off our chumps' ... A strangled gasp from Ben interrupted him, and like a flash we turned – the poor old dog was in convulsions of mortal agony, his eyes starting from his head, writhing and twisting, and snapping wildly at our hands as we tried to help him! I rushed for brandy and warm milk, and between us we got him round, and sat back staring at each other, our skins prickling faintly with a horrid little fright – at least mine was.

'I'm dead right in my first guess, I think,' Trevanion said soberly, stroking the head of the still panting and exhausted dog. 'Poor old Ben then! I boiled some scraps in that infernal saucepan – it was hard on Ben, but I had to find out somehow whether my idea was right, and by Jove it is! Everything cooked in that thing half-poisons people – or gives them an attack like poisoning ...'

'D'you think there's something in the paint?' I hazarded. Trevanion was not sure – it was only an ordinary enamel saucepan – he didn't think so. Ben lay panting on the rug before the fire, still rather a wreck, but regaining his strength every minute – I stooped down and patted him.

'We shall have to give him another five minutes or so to recover,' said Trevanion, 'poor old brute – never mind, he'll be all right in a jiff. I don't mind telling you, though, that it will take us all our nerve to face that kitchen, and that infernal saucepan ... that bubbling noise was quite the most unpleasant and disturbing thing I ever heard. The actual homeliness of it seeming to hide a sort of sinister meaning – and the purr of a boiling kettle is such a jolly thing as a rule ...'

I nodded – I didn't want to think about it overmuch just then to tell the truth, so I resolutely hunted out cards and we played poker for half an hour or so, till Strutt came in with a fresh syphon, and with his usual correct 'Anything more, sir? Good night, sir,' went off to his own quarters.

Trevanion, with a glance at the clock – it marked just twelve, or a few minutes before – got up and waked the old dog, who was sleeping by this time with his chin on his

paws. It was twelve o'clock ... in silence we turned the lights
low and tiptoed along to the kitchen. The door was open,
of course, but otherwise the whole place looked demure to
a degree. We had brought cushions and rugs with us, and
threw them into a corner, the furthest away from the stove,
near the window, from where we could watch both door and
stove – and saucepan – without being too close. I felt, as usual,
a horrid little reluctance to enter the room, but Trevanion's
large presence went a long way towards scotching that –
besides, I meant to see what we might see, however I funked
it. Settling ourselves down, I rummaged in my pocket for
my pipe, and realised the dog was not with us. Trevanion
craned out from his corner, calling softly – the old beast's
eyes gleamed from the shadows in the hall beyond ... he put
a cautious nose across the threshold, and retreated at once,
ears flat. Trevanion looked at me and nodded.

'You see? There *is* a funny atmosphere here. Come on, Ben,
old man – come on ...'

By dint of much coaxing the dog crept into the room,
unwilling enough but obedient, and we made room for him
beside us. But he would not lie down, and kept raising his
head and sniffing the air, his eyes watchful, puzzled, and
full of a vaguely stirring fear. The silence grew steadily as the
minutes passed – even the occasional low-toned remarks we
exchanged to start with died into the all-enveloping silence,
and we puffed our pipes solemnly, our eyes glued to Ben's
shaggy head. The air seemed to grow steadily colder, too, as
we sat there, despite the warmth of the spring night air that
stole through the slightly opened window. As the silence
deepened the cold seemed to intensify too – there seemed
to come a cold, dumb menace into the atmosphere, that
fastened upon us so gradually that we scarcely perceived its
beginnings till we were surrounded, soaked in it. My hands
were frozen, and my mind, too, seemed to have grown cold

and numbed: Trevanion told me later he felt just the same. Ben's yellow hair was fluffed out into a ruff round his head, his wary eyes, old, but alert, wandering ceaselessly round and round the little kitchen. The moonlight, flooding the whole place with eerie white light, helped the general uncanny effect – the shadows lay sharp-edged, black, behind every piece of furniture – the grandfather clock seemed to hide a long lean thing that peered furtively at us with narrow horrible eyes … Trevanion moved his leg and coughed – our eyes met and I read the same thought in his mind – was the silence, helped by our vivid imagination, already over-excited by the episode of poor old Ben, going to work on our nerves till we made shapes and sounds out of mere shadows and the silence of the night?

At this moment, the dog suddenly decided for us – with a faint wuff of uneasiness he sat up, his eyes on the open door; I could hear nothing, but obviously his ears, more finely attuned to degrees of sound, had caught something in the dark flat that vaguely distressed him. Ordinarily any dog would have promptly gone out to investigate, but Ben remained, stiff-poised, his head held forwards, his paws braced against the floor – Trevanion nudged me to watch him, but I did not need it – then suddenly the dog flattened himself down between us, his head low, his eyes fixed on the door, shivering in every limb. At the same moment it seemed to me that I heard a faint movement in the darkness beyond the door – very faint, but definite. The sound, it seemed to me, of a door being shut with the most delicate care so as to avoid any possible creaking or snap of the latch. The exquisite caution of the sound made it peculiarly horrible – I felt my hair rise as I strained my ears, wondering if the sound could possibly be my imagination? … The pause of silence that followed was almost worse – it was like the pause made by someone, having shut the door, waiting outside to be certain they were not heard ... I took a firm grip of myself, glanced at Trevanion – his hand was cold too, but we were both steady enough ... we waited – as a matter of fact I doubt if we could either of us have moved then, we were held in the fascination of fear.

Suddenly Ben gave a terrified whimper and burrowed wildly into the rugs – another sound broke the awesome stillness. A faint movement in the passage, at the far end – on tiptoe, pausing for greater stealth, *Something* stole towards the kitchen door! The cold draught seemed to grow even colder, it lifted our hair and stirred Ben's rough coat ... my flesh crept softly and horribly on my bones as I gripped Trev's clammy hand and stared at the door, setting my teeth as the Thing in the passage trailed softly nearer and nearer. I say trailed because that so neatly describes the sound – a faint footstep accompanied by a soft rustle like a trailing skirt. At this moment I became aware of another phenomenon – there grew a heavy scent in the air, like patchouli, I think ... at any rate a definite perfume that seemed to herald Whatever approached. Our throats dry with fright, we shrank close to each other, staring at the dog as he moaned and whimpered – and the steps drew near, and paused outside the kitchen door, as if Whoever walked that night stood still to peer at us through the crack of the door ... and laughed at us through the chink! For sheer terror, that beat all I had ever known, yet still the spell held us both motionless, staring, as Ben, shaking, his eyes bulging, slowly raised himself as if to face something. Dead silence – neither Trevanion nor I could see a thing – but the dog's eyes, fixed about five feet from the floor, followed – Someone – who entered. The moonlight lay white and sheer unbroken across the kitchen floor, yet Someone entered – paused – and walked towards the stove. As our terrified eyes followed Ben's, fixed on the Invisible, there came the faint click of a cautious hand moving among the pots and pans on the stove – and suddenly, upon the silence broke a sinister little sound – the clink of a saucepan lid, carefully lifted. My eyes bolting, dumb, I gaped – as I dreaded, the lid of the little saucepan was just raised, and from beneath it, there seemed to steal a faint curl of steam, thin and blue and horrible; it seems an absurd thing, but this just finished me – the spell of sheer terror that had held us both broke, and with a yell of mortal fear I flung aside the rugs and bolted past that horrible stove like a maniac, Trevanion at my heels, blundering madly over poor old Ben as he ran.

We gained the smoke-room, and slamming the door upon the Horror that ruled that uncanny kitchen, we sank into two chairs, sweating with fright. I was white and clammy, and Trevanion's hand shook against the glasses as he poured us out each a stiff tot of whisky … even now in the silence there stole upon the air that vile sound of bubbling; there was almost a note of meditation in it now, as if the soul behind that hateful little purring noise was pleased, and sat grinning to itself, planning new evil – a mocking, threatening little note. Oh, it was beyond words vile and awful, that sound – and to know, as now we did know, that Something – Someone – did actually, *sans* human light, gas or anything of that sort, set a-boiling in that horrible little saucepan some devil's brew of some sort, every night of the Lord I'd spent in that flat! My skin crept again as I thought of it, and I took a hasty gulp of whisky. Trevanion's voice broke the silence, still rather shaky.

'Well!—I said you had a spook, Connor – and by Jove, you've got a beauty! I frankly admit I'm not going past the door of that kitchen again tonight – I'm claiming a shakedown on the floor if you can't sleep two in your bed!'

His laugh was rather harsh, but it served its purpose, and I shook myself together. Putting down my glass, I patted Ben, his rough hair now beginning to lie down and the light of terror fading from his eyes.

In the distance, but more faintly, still purred that infernal sound.

'What is it, in the name of the Lord?' I ejaculated. Trevanion's normal senses were rapidly returning – he lit a cigarette.

'I don't know, for certain, but we must interrogate your man Strutt. I think you'll find he knows more about this than you think – he passed the door of the kitchen when I was feeding Ben, and I saw him jump and look at the saucepan in a furtive sort of way – I pretended not to see him. Then he glanced at the shelf where it sometimes stands, and looked puzzled ... I'm going to pump him. Obviously the whole thing centres round that infernal saucepan ... Anyway, we're both too knocked up to do any more tonight – let's turn in, and we'll thrash the whole thing out tomorrow.'

We slept like logs, Trevanion on the couch in my room, buried in rugs and pillows. I woke to broad daylight and Strutt at my shoulder with a cup of tea. I always had a weakness for early tea, feminine though it sounds. Trevanion was already awake. As my man turned to hand him his tea, Trevanion looked up at him.

'Strutt,' he said, 'did you boil the water for the tea in the – saucepan?'

There was a pause, and Strutt's eyes, first blank, then full of a passionate relief, stared back at Trevanion's intent blue ones.

'You – know, sir? Then, thank God, I'm not mad ...'

I turned sharply. 'What, Strutt, you must have seen something, too!'

'Seen something, sir! ... Well, gentlemen, if you knew what a relief it is to know you know, and don't think me crazy nor drunk – well, I can't tell you what it is. The last two days have been fair hell – beg your pardon, sir, but it's true – and I didn't dare tell you, sir, for fear you'd think I was mad or I'd bin drinking!' ... Strutt's strained eyes, blue circled, told their own tale, and the passionate, almost tearful relief in his voice was nakedly real – I felt a very definite admiration for Strutt as I realised what terrors he must have fought down all alone during the past few days. Trevanion nodded, his eyes alert with interest.

'Go on, Strutt—this is most interesting. Now tell me; when you made the coffee for Mr Connor the first night he was here, did you use this saucepan for boiling – or a kettle?'

Strutt's eyes looked back unflinchingly at Trevanion's – I think we both knew his answer before he said it though.

'The saucepan, sir. The kettle was leaking. The little enamel saucepan – the – the – one that *boils*, sir.'

Strutt's voice suddenly sank to a dreadful whisper, and although it was broad daylight, we involuntarily shuddered. 'And the day you were taken ill?'

My man nodded. 'Yessir – I'd boiled an egg for my breakfast in it … I've … wanted to speak to you about all this before, sir, but it all seemed so crazy I didn't like … I was afraid if I told you all I seen and heard you'd think I'd taken to drink, sir…'

'Lord, not now!' I said fervently. 'After last night I'd believe anything of this infernal flat! Go on, Strutt, for goodness' sake. Tell us all you know about the thing – don't keep anything back.'

'Well, sir – the first night I come in here, the night you were taken ill, I left your room to see if everything was all right, and I heard something singing in the kitchen, like a kettle on the boil – bubbling and steaming like. I thought, well I must have left something on, or Mrs Barker, but I went in, and blest if everything wasn't quiet, and as cold and dark as Egypt! Not a sign … well, I was scared, but I thought I must have bin half asleep – but I got back to my room and left the door open, and in a few minutes the same noise come again. I tiptoed out then, sir, you may bet, to try and catch whatever made that noise – and round the corner I could see that little saucepan boiling away like fury … You don't think I'm drunk, sir?'

'By George, we don't – I don't. Go on – what did you do?'

'I went in, sir – don't mind saying it took a lot of doing – I'd a given a month's salary not to – but I didn't want to feel done, and I still thought I *must* be seeing things … Well, sir, the minute I stepped round that door that blamed thing stopped dead – as true as I'm standing here. Wasn't even warm – well, I bolted back to my room, and that's a fact. Well, in the morning I thought I *must* have been mad or seeing things – but I didn't like the look of that saucepan till I got to feel it was behaving silly to act so, and I boiled that egg in it to show I didn't care … Well, after I was took ill like you, sir, I said I wasn't going to meddle any more with the beastly thing, and I took and threw it into the dustbin. But last night it was back again – and begging your pardon, sirs, I wouldn't touch the … thing if I was you. There's something about it's not right – don't you touch it.'

Strutt's troubled voice ceased, and Trevanion's eyes met mine. He nodded.

'You're right, Strutt. All you say goes to prove my theory. Obviously everything cooked in that thing produces acute symptoms of some sort of poisoning – arsenical, I should say, but we can find out the details later. Now what in the world is the story connected with this saucepan – I take it all the things here belonged to the woman who had this flat before?'

'Yessir – so I understand. Mrs Barker was with her a long time, and took care of the place when she left – I heard yesterday what we didn't know when you put in for this flat, sir; that three lots of tenants had had it and left very sudden. I did hear that one or two of them fell ill all of a sudden – I'm certain this saucepan'll be at the bottom of their going, sir – anyway they none of them stayed more than a month or so.'

'Mrs Barker – Mrs Barker –' mused Trevanion. 'Now I wonder whether that old soul knows anything ...' As he spoke there seemed a faint shuffle outside the door, and bouncing out of bed, I flung it open; Mrs Barker herself was outside, her wrinkled, wicked old face alive with rage and fear, her knotted hands twisted in her apron. We all stared, then Trevanion seized her wrist as she tried to glide away.

'No, you don't, old lady! What were you listening for, I should like to know?' She eyed him sullenly and venomously, but vouchsafed no reply; dragging her into the room, Trevanion shut the door determinedly.

'Look here, there's something here I don't like, Connor. Do you suppose this is all a plant by this old hag, for reasons of her own?'

I shook my head, still blank – evil old woman as she looked now, her face all twisted with hate, I did not see how in the world she could have been responsible for all the strange things we had, the three of us, witnessed the last few days.

'You know – something!' Trevanion said sternly, 'now you tell us the whole truth about this beastly business and it'll be all right for you ... if not –'

'I shan't tell you – besides, there ain't nothin' to tell,' the old woman answered sullenly – Strutt suddenly interrupted her.

'You're lying – beg your pardon, sir, but I seen her laugh when Mr Connor was took ill. Now, you wicked old sinner, you tell all you know about this, as you're told – or I'll make you eat something cooked in that saucepan ...'

It was horrible – the hag crumpled like a shot rabbit at the threat, and put up her trembling, gnarled hands – her deadly terror was dreadfully sincere ... I put up my hand.

'All right, Strutt – let her go, Trev. She'll tell us.'

Her voice shaky and strained, sullen, but vanquished, the old woman began her story. Shall I ever forget that scene, the untidy room, Trevanion and me in pyjamas, drinking it in, while Strutt, immovably correct as ever, with his back to the door as she talked? The story was incomplete; much had to be taken for granted, but it was a sufficiently grim picture that she conjured up before us of her late mistress. Young, beautiful, hard as marble; an old husband standing between her and her own ends ... A lover – lovers – and riches to be gained by his death. One lover a doctor, a mysterious packet of powder seen to be given by him to the woman one day when the old woman was prying round – then the empty paper, found thrown away, with a few grains of white powder in the creases. Afterwards, gradually weakening health of the husband, only helped by the constant solicitude of his young wife, the apple of his eye ... she was tireless in her goodness to him – how many times did she not rise in the middle of the night, to brew soup or tea or anything he fancied? At last he grew so that he would take nothing she had not prepared ... his attacks of pain were terrible, folks said – seemed to twist him all to pieces – heart, the doctor said – the young doctor that was Madam's friend was attending him, and he and Madam used to laugh together on the stairs when he left the old man – then the death of the husband, and hasty burial ... The doctor was crazy about Madam, and one night Mrs Barker heard them planning to be married very soon – she told him she was making her will in his favour and laughingly insisted he should return the compliment ... He did, and Mrs Barker was called in to witness it; they were very merry together, and Madam insisted on making some of her special punch for him to drink to their happiness in ... Madam came laughing into the kitchen, and seemed to talk and laugh even to the saucepan as she boiled the water for the punch. She sent Mrs Barker away then – but the doctor never got his honeymoon. Next day he was found dead in the flat, and Madam was away with another man, a Spaniard she was

running an affair with at the same time ... No – they said it
was heart failure, but Mrs Barker – well, she thought a lot of
things she didn't say. What was the use? and Madam left her
instructions to take care of the place till it was let, and it was
a good job; but she never fancied anything cooked in that
saucepan somehow – put it up on a shelf till one day the new
tenants used it and got sick and left ... Same thing happened
again with the next people, and they used to say they saw
things and heard the kettle or something boiling when there
was nothing there. Yes, Madam used a funny scent – began
with 'p' but she couldn't say the word – all over the place
it was some nights ... Couldn't say she'd ever actually seen
anything – she took good care to go to bed early when she
was living in the flat, and, anyway, it never come further than
the kitchen ... Yes ... (defiantly) she 'ad used the thing on
purpose once or twice! She was a poor woman, and caretakin'
was a good job when you got a post like this and no one
to interfere; yes, she 'ad used it before to scare out tenants
'cos she wanted to stick to her job, and she didn't care. There
were lots of other flats in London. No – She – It – never
came unless that there saucepan was there on the stove as it
used to be – yes, she'd missed it the day Strutt threw it into
the dustbin, and looked about there till she had found and
reinstated it. Of course she wanted us to go, like the rest – the
agents were so sick of tenants leaving that they'd said if we
went they shouldn't bother to let the place again ... Sorry –
why should she be? Nobody never died of it that she heard
of – on'y got attacks like the old man used to get ...

The door closed on her dismissed figure, and Trevanion's
stare met mine.

Gingerly we went into the kitchen and picked up the
saucepan, smooth and harmless-looking instrument of a
ruthless woman's crimes. Gingerly I handed it to Strutt.

'For heaven's sake tie a stone to the vile thing, Strutt, and sink it in the Thames or burn it – get rid of it somehow. We seem to have struck one of the most unpleasant stories I ever heard – however, once rid of this I don't think we shall be bothered any further, as obviously this horrible little thing is the "germ" of the haunting ...' which indeed was true, the ghostly bubbling and boiling never troubled the flat more, nor did the kitchen door persist in opening. The ghost was laid – but I often speculate on the fate probably in store for the unfortunate wretch now in love with the woman whose white hands once brewed death for her husband and lover in that uncanny saucepan.

10 The Twelve Apostles

BY ELEANOR SCOTT

The American visitor looked up from the specification book.

'That seems all square,' he said; 'genuine old English stuff. But there's one thing, sir, you haven't mentioned that I've just got to have.'

He looked at the house agent with a paternal smile.

'Well, sir, I think I've told you all details,' said Mr Gibson. He would not entrust this wealthy client to the tender care of a mere clerk; he was too rare a find. 'Still, I'm sure,' he went on persuasively, 'that Mr Langtre, the owner of the Manor, would be glad to meet you in any reasonable alterations or repairs.'

Mr Matthews smiled a little and his nice eyes twinkled.

'I'm sure, from what you tell me, that's so,' he replied. 'Only I'm afraid he couldn't have anyone put in just the detail I'm thinking of. Mr Gibson, I want a real good ghost.'

Mr Gibson looked distinctly less rubicund.

'A-a ghost?' he stammered, his eyes wandering.

'What? You don't mean to say there is one?' cried the shrewd client.

'Well, sir – with an old place like the Manor – genuine sixteenth century … What I mean to say is, there's always fools about in a country place …'

'But there is – well, a story? I warn you, sir, I shan't buy the place unless there is.'

Poor Mr Gibson fidgeted uneasily. Who could have foreseen such a difficulty as this?

'Well, you see, sir, how it is,' he said at last, 'Mr Langtre did give me most strict orders as nothing was to be said. Most strict. Still, sir, seeing what your conditions are, I don't mind saying that things – well, things are said about the Manor as had better not be said.'

'That's a bit vague,' said the American. 'I don't want any doubts about this thing. I want a real good Old English slap-up ghost, and I don't mind paying a bit for it. Why, who'd give two rows of pins for an Elizabethan manor without a ghost in it?'

Mr Gibson was understood to mutter something about 'a matter of opinion.' Then, taking his courage in both hands, he said desperately:

'I tell you what, sir. You come along with me to the Vicar. He's what they call an antiquarian, and he knows all about the Manor. You see, I'm bound not to tell anything; and truth to tell I don't know much. But Mr Molyneux, he'll tell you everything there is to know about Sir Jerome's room.'

The worthy house agent took his respectable bowler, and the two men went up the broad tree-lined main street of Much Barton, Gibson discoursing the while on the old-world atmosphere of the place. The American was certainly nibbling: it wouldn't be the agent's fault if Barton Cross Manor remained unsold.

The Vicar was in, and received his visitors in a book-lined study that might have come out of one of Trollope's novels: and Mr Matthews, summing him up with a businessman's acumen, came to his topic at once.

'Ghost at the Manor?' said Mr Molyneux, fingering his chin. 'Well, it wouldn't be surprising if there were. In fact, if one can rely on the evidence of an ignorant soldier and a jealous parish priest, there certainly were once some very – er – peculiar happenings in the priest's room.'

Mr Matthews preserved an intelligent silence, and the Vicar continued:

'The story goes that early in the reign of Elizabeth Mr

Everard Langtre, the then Squire of the Manor, had in his household a private chaplain, commonly called Sir Jerome, or Jeremy. 'Sir' was then, as you doubtless know, a courtesy title of Priests of the – er – Roman persuasion.'

'Sir – I mean, Mr – Everard Langtre was a Roman, then?' asked the American.

'He was,' answered the Vicar, 'and had, as was then customary, his private oratory and his private chaplain. Now this chaplain, Jeremy Lindall, seems to have been a man of very curious disposition. He was, like many another private chaplain of the time, a chemist of no little originality and skill. Stories about him were rife, of course – he does not seem to have been popular – and he was credited with witchcraft, demonology, traffic with the powers of evil, and so on. He certainly did go in for some very curious experiments, in which gold seems to have been a necessary ingredient: and it was said that he used in this way all his private stock of gold until at last he became so ragged that he had to keep within doors. This, one gathers, was no loss. His early – er – Mass over, he had the whole day free to conduct his chemical experiments or work his spells in the large chamber that was given up to him. The fact that he asked to be given a room facing north told against him greatly with the villagers.'

'Why?' asked Mr Matthews.

'Why, because it was considered the best aspect for devil-worship. Have you never noticed that in country churchyards there are no graves on the north side of the church? – Well, to continue. Sir Jerome seems to have gradually become quite a recluse; and when he died, which was in the year 1562, there was a curious scene at his burial. All sorts of things were said, as is always the case in these stories of chemists, misunderstood and maligned, their actions and words distorted through generations of rustic folk.'

'Such as – ?'

'Oh, that his dead face wore a look of terror and pain beyond human endurance: and the beldame who laid out the corpse for burial was so powerfully affected that she was stricken dumb, and died a few weeks later. No one could be persuaded to carry the body to the grave for some time, but at last four stout men were bribed into doing it. The story goes – But wait: I'll read it to you – '

He turned to a large desk and pulled out a drawer.

'This is an account of the burial written at the time by the parish priest of Much Barton,' he said. 'The original manuscript is in Mr Langtre's possession: but I made the copy myself, and I will vouch for its accuracy.'

He spread the sheets out before him.

'Of course,' he interpolated, looking up with his *pince-nez* in his hand, 'you will understand that the parish priest, a hard-working and humble person enough, was no doubt a little jealous of the gentleman of leisure up at the Manor. You must take his account *cum grano*. Well, then – the beginning is torn away, but the context is clear enough.

"…did with utmoste payne perswayd foure stoute Carles to ye Worke, and soe didd enforce Kit Harcott, Hodge Payne with his bro, Willm. and Ned Greene to engage to carrye ye Coffre to ye Churche, where I hadde all Thinges needefull for ye Buriall. But when these came, lo they bore no Coffre, but they were alle sweatinge and Tremblinge in suche Fearfulle wise that I was faine to Conforte them, saying that verelie Sir Hiereme must be a Starke Mann and Stoute when his deade Bodie gar'd Stronge Carles soe to Shake and to Sweate, Whereat Kit, Tis not his Weyghte, goode father, quoth he, for a man to be heavie is no suche mattere. But ye Coffre is lighte as it were emptie; and in soothe we had almost opend it,

fearinge we shou'de be att oure paynes for no goode;
but thatt (And here he soe Shooke that his voyce dy'd
in his Throote.)

"Come mann a Goddes mercie, quoth I to hearten
him, there is noughte to Tremble att in thatt youre
worke hath beene so lyghte. Ay but, (quoth he) there
came a sounde in ye Boxe lyke to a litel whisperyng
or rustelyng, soe thatt we didd put it downe in feare.
And soe we kneel'd and sayd a Pater and an Aue: and
Ned (who is an Acolyth and deuoute) wou'd saye the
De Profundis: but when we sayd *Requiem aeternam
dona ei Dñe* there came soe dreadfull a Laughe that
we felle forwarde in greate feare. But when after a
space we didd lifte our selues, lo we sawe a slimie
trayl as of an huge Slugge or Snayl coming out from
ye Coffre."

'The story goes on,' said Mr Molyneux, 'with an account, of
more interest to a cleric than a layman, of the burial rites.
No doubt the slight mystery surrounding the life of the
recluse, his chemical experiments, his retirement and so on,
had pre-disposed the simple folk, both priest and people, to
see signs and wonders; anyhow, the parish priest. Sir Edgar
Knox, gives quite a lurid account of the burial service: how
the holy water left a trail as of slime across the coffin: how the
holy candles went out and a heavy smoke dragged across the
church: and how the terrified boys serving at the altar saw in
the thick greasy vapour dim shapes twisting about the coffin;
and he says that in answer to each prayer he heard, instead of
"Amen", a devilish laugh, "highe and shrille like a Peeuishe
Shrewe". In fine, he could not take it on himself to bury Sir
Jerome in the consecrated ground, where lay the bodies of the
simple village folk; and so he laid the poor corpse in that dim
and unhallowed region that lies north of the church, "that he

who had Choasen ye northe in his Lyfe myghte have it alsoe in his Deth". And there he lies, I have no doubt, to this day.'

Mr Molyneux laid down the manuscript and took off his glasses. His face was flushed with the enthusiasm of the antiquarian.

'It's a good story,' commented the American. 'But it seems to me that Sir Jerome's ghost, if he has run to one, would walk in the 'dim and unhallowed region' – if I may use your words, sir – in the churchyard, rather than in the Manor.'

'No doubt,' answered the Vicar, 'if that were all. But there is more to come. Later in Elizabeth's reign the Langtres came into bad odour in connection with the Throgmorton Plot. The Manor, like many another Roman Catholic mansion, was ransacked for evidence. Little enough was found in the house except the plate in the chapel; and even that proved not to be genuine gold and silver. But among the soldiers who searched the house was one Job Harcott, who was a descendant or connection of the Kit Harcott who had carried Sir Jerome's coffin. This man remembered the tales of the chaplain's chemical experiments: and it occurred to him, sacrilegious as it sounds, that the gold plate of the chapel might have been taken for some such experiment. So he secretly left the party of soldiers and went back alone to the Manor to search for the treasure, which he believed (for so the tradition went) to be hidden in the priest's own room.

'What exactly happened to Job Harcott no one will ever know. He was missed after dusk. A crony of his, one Ezra Minshull, then remembered a conversation he had had with the miserable man. He reports it thus:

"This Minshull remember'd him that Harcott whyl he was yet with us had sayd that he was but litel astonied that ye Playt was contrefeyt: for (quoth he) when a Mann lusteth after Golde (as I haue herd

this Hierime didd) he leaueth not his Luste, but
hathe it euer in his Presence. Soe that when aftre
longe seekyng we cou'd by noe means find Harcott,
Minshull perswayding us, we return'd to ye Manour
to see what shou'd be in Sir Hierime's room where
he abode."

'Well?' interjected the American.

Mr Molyneux looked up, arrested by the tone of his visitor.

'They found Harcott. His body was lying in the passage that
leads from the priest's room: he seemed to have been running
away from the room down the passage. He was quite dead.'

There was a moment's silence, and then the Vicar continued:
'Sir, I am an old man. I have read many curious books and
seen many curious things. I ask you with all the earnestness
of which I am capable not to pry into this matter. Buy the
house if you will – you will be doing a kindness to my old
friend Godfrey Langtre and taking a step that you will not, I
think, regret: but, as you value your life and your sanity, avoid
that accursed room.'

He paused, flushed with the embarrassment of a shy man
who interferes in another's affairs.

'Sir, I'm grateful, real grateful, to you,' said the American,
'and I'll bear in mind what you've said. You've impressed me.
But I'm interested, and I'll buy that house right now, lock,
stock and barrel. And I hope, sir, that you'll do me the great
kindness to come and see me sometimes, I won't trespass on
your time any more now. Goodbye, sir, and thank you.'

So Mr Matthews became the owner of Barton Cross
Manor.

If the house was not quite as attractive seen in the dusk of a
drizzling October afternoon as it had appeared in the mellow
sunshine of September, certainly Mr Gibson could not be
blamed for the fact. Nor could Mr Langtre. Yet Mr Matthews

felt that he wanted to blame someone for the discomfort of the chill rooms with their stiff and unwelcoming air and suspicious atmosphere. Presently he put it down to the attitude of a couple, mother and son, who had been caretakers at the Manor, and who no doubt objected to having to do a little work, besides opening windows and airing rooms, in exchange for the wages the Langtre family allowed them. In fact, thought the American, sniffing the close air of the passages, they didn't seem really keen on doing even that.

He ordered a fire in the library and another in his bedroom, and, when these were well alight and snapping and blazing cheerily, he opened the windows wide and let in waves of cool rainy air, laden with faint scents of late roses and dying leaves and wet earth. The panelled walls shone in the warm firelight; the well-filled bookcases invited him. He began to feel really comfortable and at home, and went for a little psycho-analytic speculation on the subject of Atmosphere and its Influence on Human Sensation. Mr Matthews was the type of man who likes such phrases, especially when written with capital letters. They made him feel profound.

This comfortable mood lasted him until ten the next morning, when, warm and contented after a 'real English' breakfast followed by an indisputable cigar, he decided to spend the morning in a survey of the house.

The morning was dark, with a threatening sky; though the rain was not actually falling, it looked as though the lowering clouds were only allowing a respite to the garden battered by yesterday's downpour, and might stream again at any minute. It seemed a most suitable day to re-examine his property, which, like many Tudor manor-houses, needed much exploration before its plan was really known.

Mr Matthews wandered about over the ground floor, very contentedly losing his way in passages and communicating rooms, until he knew it thoroughly. He then proceeded to the next. This was easier, since it had suffered less from later incongruous additions. It was roughly in the shape of a cross, the arms of which were composed of four passages running north, south, east and west, and radiating from a square well which looked down to the hall below. The south passage was so short as hardly to be a passage at all, and the north corridor was correspondingly long. Mr Matthews' own bedroom was at the junction of the north and west corridors, with a door leading into each; and by the door in the north passage there was a kind of small shrine – a large crucifix, a prie-dieu chair, some candles and flowers. The whole house, in fact, bore signs of the religion of its late owners: Mr Matthews had never before seen so many holy water stoups, for instance. There was one outside every door, and even one on the wall opposite the shrine – a blank wall with no door in it.

Going along the north passage, Mr Matthews soon discovered the reason for the absence of doors in the east wall. It was the wall of the old chapel, which ran the whole length of the corridor, and whose door was in the northern end of the east wall. It was dismantled now, and all the decorations gone; and the American thought he could still see traces of the scars left by the soldiers who had ransacked the chapel for the lost treasure. He stood at the door, picturing the scene to himself; and then, as the whole story filtered back into his mind, he realised that he must be standing near, if not on, the very spot where the returning band had found the body of Job Harcott.

That door, at the end of the passage, must lead into the priest's room. Mr Matthews felt quite a thrill as he thought of the lonely chemist, labouring in that remote chamber at his terrible experiments, abandoned and feared by his neighbours, dying at last, desolate even in his death. Mr Matthews was not an imaginative man; but somehow, standing there in the dim passage, the melancholy rain pattering faintly outside, he could enter into the mind of the long-dead priest, fanatical with his dreadful enthusiasms, his mad, soul-destroying experiments, renouncing a happiness in this world or a possible next in exchange for that power which it is unlawful to possess. And the modern American thought he could understand some of the ambition, the horror, the enthusiasm, the desolation and despair, which had made up that man's soul.

Closing the door of the chapel, he continued his investigations. The door at the end of the north passage was locked, and he made a mental note to ask Mrs Sharpe, the caretaker, for the key. The other doors in the passage, that is those in the west wall, led to rooms whose close air and antique style of furnishing led him to the conclusion that they had not been used for many years; in fact the first room that gave signs of recent use was his own bedroom at the corner of the square well.

'That's queer,' thought the American. 'It's not as if that set of rooms faced north, for naturally they face west. I'd have understood it if the rooms in the west corridor, now, had been neglected; but they're quite fresh. Guess they're odd folk, these Langtres.' And with that he dismissed the matter from his mind. He remembered, however, to ask for the missing key of the locked door; and, meeting Sharpe himself on the stairs, he mentioned it there and then.

Sharpe changed colour, apparently confused at having been discovered remiss in his duty, and insisted on accompanying the new tenant back to the north passage.

'This room ain't much used, sir, 'aving a north aspeck,' he said apologetically as he turned the key. It squealed rustily in the lock, and Matthews, happening to glance at the man's face, was startled to see it white and wet with sweat.

'Why, man, what's wrong?' he cried.

The colour crept back to Sharpe's face.

'It's me 'eart, sir,' he panted. 'Any effort'll make me go all any'ow for a minute. But it goes off, sir, straight away. It don't last.' He glanced anxiously in the direction of his employer. Mr Matthews grunted and said no more.

The locked room was indeed in need of airing. A whiff of dank air with a curiously mouldy smell greeted them: so earthy a smell that the American looked instinctively at the walls for traces of damp.

'I suppose it's because of the damp that they don't use the room,' he said with a glance around him.

It was very obviously unused. It had very little furniture, and what there was looked old. There was an oak chair, a heavy table, and a kind of desk or cabinet, with a cupboard rising from a flat tabletop. The walls, however, showed no signs of damp: the panels were not warped or cracked, nor were the rather odd carvings on them at all defaced.

'I believe, if it were regularly warmed and aired, it would be as good a room as any, and most interesting,' declared the American. Anyway, we'll try. It's a real unique room. Do as you did with the other rooms, Sharpe – light a real good fire and open the windows and door to get a through draught. I've regularly taken to this room,' he went on as he examined the panelling more closely. 'Shouldn't wonder if I move in here when you get it fixed right.'

'The fam'ly don't consider it 'ealthy, sir, not this room,' muttered Sharpe.

He had to clear his throat before he could make his voice sound at all; and Mr Matthews, struck by the man's agitation, was suddenly seized by a suspicion. Why were the Sharpes so keen to keep him out of the room? Had they some motive for wishing to deny access to it to anyone but themselves?

'You do as I say,' he said, not peremptorily, but quite firmly.

'I don't take back my orders without a good reason,' he added.

Halfway down the corridor, he heard the grating of the key in the rusty lock of the closed door.

'Here, Sharpe! I said that room was to be left open and aired,' he said, turning sharply.

'Beg pardon, sir … I thought, seein' as it was wet. I'd best leave it shut till I got a fire goin', sir,' muttered the servant.

'Well… But, hang it, man, why lock the door when it's so stiff? Go back and – No, never mind. Give me the key.'

Taking it from the man's shaking hand, Mr Matthews went back down the corridor, and, with some difficulty, opened the door.

'There,' he said as he rejoined Sharpe. 'Get a fire on in there when you've time, and leave it open all day. I bet we'll get rid of that rank smell …' He stopped short, startled by the extraordinary expression in Sharpe's eyes. 'Why, Sharpe!' he began; but even as he spoke the man dropped his eyes and with an effort regained his composure.

'Very good, sir,' he murmured; and the baffled American went back to the library.

The rain lifted in the afternoon, with a sky that gave promise of a fine morrow: and Mr Matthews went out for a long walk to visit certain places of local interest. It was not until he had finished a cosy tea and a cigarette that it occurred to him to wonder whether his instructions with regard to the north room had been carried out.

He decided that, comfortable though the library was, it was worthwhile to go up to the passage and see whether the door of the north room was open and the fire lit. He was a determined man. He was really very much annoyed when he saw no gleam of light at the further end of the passage. Still, perhaps the door had swung to. He walked down the passage and tried it. It was locked.

Mr Matthews seldom allowed his temper, which was a hot

one, to get the better of him. He stood a moment, waiting for it to cool; and, as he paused in the dim corridor, he heard a faint sound. It was like a faint *thud*, as if some soft object had fallen to the ground; then came a very faint light rustling sliding sound.

He was almost sure that the sound came from the other side of the closed door. He thought perhaps the lock had merely stuck, and that Sharpe was within, closing windows or whatnot: but a second try at the door convinced him that it was locked fast. The sounds, then, must be an echo from some other part of the winding house. In any case, what really mattered was that his orders had been disobeyed.

He paid a visit to the Sharpes in the kitchen and made this quite clear.

The next morning, Wednesday, the sun rose apparently refreshed by the previous day's holiday. It was a magnificent day, with a sky of so deep and serene a blue that it seemed impossible that it could really have existed behind yesterday's rain. Mr Matthews interviewed Sharpe and repeated his instructions with regard to the airing of all the rooms, irrespective of their history, aspect, or any other peculiarity. He thought it unlikely that he would be again disobeyed: and he was right, for chance visits to the meeting of the four passages always found a cool breeze blowing and showed four rows of open doors and glimpses of open windows.

In the afternoon the sun streamed out so invitingly that Mr Matthews felt a desire to revisit his domain under these new conditions. He particularly wanted to see the effect of the golden light on the carved panelling of the north room, and to examine its design more closely.

This proved to be ordinary enough. There were plain panels reaching from the floor to a height of about three feet; then came a band of carving, ornament and scriptural texts intermingled; then twelve large panels, each four or five feet high. Each of these was surrounded by a frame of carved ornament, and they were separated from one another by narrower panels of plain wood. On the twelve panels were roughly carved twelve figures; and Mr Matthews, noticing one with keys and another bearing an eagle, put them down as representations of the twelve apostles. All the carving was rough and amateurish, lacking the exquisite finish and proportion of skilled Tudor workmanship; yet Mr Matthews felt little doubt in his mind that the curious designs, odd and archaic in conception, conventional to a degree, were of the sixteenth century.

'I'll get Mr Molyneux up to have a look at them,' he decided. 'He'll know if they're fake or genuine antique.'

An examination of the furniture yielded little beyond the bare wood of which they were made. Only in the desk did the American see anything at all interesting. This was a portrait – a rough but powerful sketch done on parchment; it was like a strong, though untaught, copy of a Dürer portrait; and yet it had the impress of originality.

It was the head of a man, apparently a priest, in the dress of the sixteenth century. The forehead was high and narrow, the cheeks sunken, the line of the jaw long and prominent. The mouth, thin-lipped and drooping, showed faintly through a straggling beard; the ears were singularly fine and sensitive. The eyes were so sunken under the overhanging, almost hairless, brows that it was difficult to see how the artist had managed to give them their expression of brooding horror. They were like the eyes of a haunted man.

Mr Matthews felt strangely stirred by the portrait. He could hardly take his eyes from the fascinating, fascinated gaze of the picture.

'If it's not valuable, it ought to be,' he muttered. 'The thing looks alive! He might speak any minute – and I guess he'd have some pretty awful things to tell.'

The light was fading now, and the American, wishing to study his find more carefully, carried it downstairs with him. As he examined the drawing by the newly-lit lamp, it occurred to him to look for a signature on the back of the portrait. There was, however, no mention of the artist; all he could see were words written in the crabbed and angular print often used in ecclesiastical documents of the period. 'Dom: Hierime Lindalle: 1562. Eccles. XIV, 121,' he read: and lower down two texts in full – 'Have regard unto My Name; for it shalle be to thee for greate Treasures of golde. Eccles XLI, 15,' and 'And he finisht alle the worke that he didd in ye Hous of ye Lorde and browght in ye thinges that were Dedicated, ye Golde and ye Siluere and ye Vesells, and layd up ye Treasoure in ye House. 1 Kings VII, 51.'

These did not interest Mr Matthews greatly, and when he had studied the curious, painful drawing a little longer, he put it away. It was about nine that evening when, having nothing to do, he decided to get on with the sorting of some papers he intended to arrange in the form of a pamphlet on the Colour Question in the United States. They were in his bedroom, and he went up at once for them.

As he reached the head of the stairs he noticed Sharpe in the north passage. He could not quite see what he was doing; but he noticed that the door of the north room was shut.

'Sharpe,' he said quietly, 'have you just shut that door?'

The man jumped violently, and dropped, with a crash and a spatter of liquid, something that he had been carrying in his hand.

'What's that?' asked the American, his suspicions at once aroused.

'It's – I-I've just been fillin' up the 'oly water stoups, sir,' stammered Sharpe. 'It's a thing we never leave undone, sir, and I'd nearly forgot it. They've been kep' filled ever since the 'ouse was built, so they say, and I promised Mr Langtre as I would see to it.'

The American bent down to the splash that spread right across the passage from wall to wall. It certainly had no scent. A glance assured him that the little receptacles on the walls had been recently filled.

'Right,' he said, 'and can you give me as good a reason for shutting that door? I said it was to be left open.'

Sharpe muttered something by which he gave his employer to understand that he 'adn't understood as the door was to be left open at night', that it didn't do the rooms no good, and that he hoped Mr Matthews wouldn't insist. It was all very incoherent and very rapidly spoken, and the American again entertained doubts as to the man's *bona fides*: but he contented himself with repeating his orders to Sharpe to open the door of the north room, and standing to watch him do it.

The man went with infinite reluctance, like one walking to a torture chamber. He turned the key – Mr Matthews noted grimly that the door was locked – and then, flinging open the door, fairly ran down the passage to the place where his employer stood awaiting him. He was white-lipped and shaking, and suddenly the American saw – the man was afraid! He had, of course, been brought up on village traditions of the haunted room, and he had intended to keep that door locked at all costs. Matthews half thought of reassuring him by going and relocking the door: but no, he wouldn't pander to these superstitions. He fetched his papers and spent a long evening in their classification and arrangement; then, happily conscious of time well spent, he went up to bed.

He woke once or twice in the night, and once thought he heard a faint scraping rustling sound, such as he had heard while waiting in the passage the day before. He listened intently, but heard nothing; and attributing the impression either to a dream or to the same natural cause that had occasioned it before, he curled up comfortably and went to sleep.

He woke vigorous and cheerful, full of the determination to call on Mr Molyneux and ask him about the picture and the panels. He dressed with speed and energy, and went out of his room with happy anticipations of breakfast.

As he came out on the landing he noticed that the dark splash caused by the fallen holy water still stained the floor; and then he saw that another stain – a bright glistening trail – led from the open door of the north room to the splash on the floor.

It was the long slimy trail that a snail leaves, only it was quite unusually large. It was as if a slug or snail thirty or forty times bigger than the usual variety had crawled from the room along the passage until it came to the splash of water on the floor.

'Very curious,' he thought.' I never knew before that slugs got up so high into a house. Thought it was the ground floor for theirs … By gosh!' he added, struck by an idea, 'that was the sound I heard! Of course it was. But, my word, it must be some snail to make a noise you can hear! Only one trail, too.'

After breakfast, Mr Matthews decided that, raw and damp as the morning was, he would stroll down to the Vicarage with his newly-discovered picture: and he accordingly went, the portrait under his arm.

The Vicar was in, and pleased to see him. They exchanged civilities, and then Mr Matthews, producing the portrait, broached the subject of his call.

'Well?' he asked, when the other had studied the drawing for some minutes in silence, 'what do you think of it?'

'It's an extraordinary thing,' said the Vicar slowly. 'Quite unique, and, I should say, valuable. And yet, Mr Matthews,' he went on, taking off his *pince-nez* and laying down the picture, 'if that portrait were mine, I declare to you I should burn it here and now. It is the picture of a fiend,' he added with energy. 'I consider it to be an unholy thing.'

The American was considerably surprised at this outburst of fanatical superstition – for so he could not help thinking it from a man as shy and reserved as the Vicar.

'Oh, come, sir,' he said, laughing a little. 'It's not as bad as that. It's odd, I admit, and it has a trick of haunting one; but after all the poor chap's dead, and I guess he had to pay for what he did.'

'That's true,' said the Vicar. Repugnance and antiquarian enthusiasm struggled within him as he picked up the drawing again.

'Oh, by the way,' said Matthews, 'I wanted to ask you about those texts on the back. What Book do they come from? I thought I knew my Bible tolerably well – New England, you know – but I don't just get the ones he's copied out.'

The Vicar turned over the portrait and read the inscription.

'"Dom. Hierime Lindalle, 1562". That would be about the year of his death,' he remarked. 'Then a text from Ecclesiasticus. Then here, lower down, another text from the same Book – "Have regard unto My Name, for it shall be unto thee for a Treasure of gold". Then a third, from the Book of Kings. It's not surprising you didn't recognise it, Mr Matthews: Ecclesiasticus is an apocryphal Book, admitted by the Romans. It's not in the Anglican Bible at all. Still, the text from Kings doesn't strike me as quite accurate. Stay, I have the Latin Vulgate here somewhere.'

He turned to his bookshelf.

'Here we are. Let's see, what's the first? Eccles, XIV, 121, copied just after the date.'

'Will you translate?' asked the American. 'Latin wasn't included in my schooling.'

'Well, it's roughly this: "Remember that death is not slow and the covenant of hell hath been shown to thee." That was in the year of his death. No doubt the poor man, poring alone over his books and incantations, allowed the idea of his seven years' pact with the devil so to prey on his mind that he did in fact die in the given year.'

'And left this as a kind of warning to other necromancers? I dare say you're right, sir. And the other reference, the one from Kings?'

Slowly the Vicar translated. '"And he finished all the work that he did in the house of the Lord, and brought in the things that were dedicated, the gold and the silver and the vessels, and laid them up in the treasures of the house of the Lord." He hasn't copied it accurately, you see. He has "and laid up the treasure in the house". And he has left out the reference to David.'

'And what's the other from Eccle-what's-his-name?'

'That, again, is inaccurately copied,' said the Vicar, turning over the leaves of his book. 'It should be, "Have regard to *thy* name: for it shall abide with thee for a great and precious treasure".'

'It's queer, isn't it, that when he went to the trouble of copying out the whole texts he should have done it wrong? Say, Mr Molyneux, I can't help sort of wondering –'

Their eyes met.

'The same thought occurred to me,' said the Vicar quietly. 'I believe the misquotations are intentional. I believe it's a clue to the place where he concealed the treasure – the stolen gold and jewelled plate of the chapel. You see,' he went on with growing excitement, 'the first of the misquoted texts concerns church vessels, and implies, or so I take it, that the plate was not melted down in his chemical experiments, but that he "laid up the treasure in the house".'

'That's what I make of it,' said the American. 'But the other one does me. Let's see: "Have regard unto My Name, for it shall be unto thee for a treasure of gold"? Why, say, Vicar, that's it – the clue to the hiding-place is in the man's name!'

'I believe you're right!' cried the Vicar. 'Some hint – perhaps a cipher –'

'"Dom: Hierime Lindalle". Hm. This needs some brain. Say, sir, what's wrong with you coming up to the Manor to lunch and working it out? We might find another clue in the room.'

The Vicar agreed, and the two men set out for the Manor. They found a distinctly good meal awaiting them, and, after a quiet smoke, went up together to the north room.

'I guess Dom. What's-his-name did these himself,' said Mr Matthews, looking round the rough carvings. 'These gentlemen are the twelve apostles I take it. I'm going by Peter here,' and he indicated the figure bearing a key.

'Yes, and that's St John with the eagle; and St Andrew with the bread. Why, of course, they're rough copies of the apostles in the Langtre Psalter,' he continued with increasing enthusiasm. 'They are quite unique in design and conception, and in the Psalter each has a text attached. So against St James, who is drawn as you see with his head half severed, is the text "And James the brother of John he killed with the sword." Each one can be identified in the same way. But *the* curiosity of the set is the representation of Judas: an extraordinary drawing, showing him falling out of the tree in which he is attempting to hang himself. You must see that.'

And he began to make the circuit of the room.

'Pity the light is so bad,' said Matthews. 'I can only just see the figures. But I don't see one such as you describe.'

'Neither do I,' admitted the Vicar in some perplexity. 'He has the Twelve, too.'

'Perhaps Judas touched him a little too near,' suggested the American. 'He may count his twelve after the Acts.'

'Let's see,' said Mr. Molyneux. 'I ought to be able to identify them all from the Psalter.'

He again went slowly round the room, murmuring the names of the apostles.

'Philip, Thomas with his finger outstretched; and this, with the book and the lion, of course is Mark. Now that's very odd,' he said, turning to the American. 'I wonder why he included Mark?'

'To make up the dozen, I guess,' said Mr Matthews. 'After all, he was an evangelist, if he wasn't an apostle. Now, sir, before the light quite goes, let's just copy down these texts he has in the band round the wall, and then we'll see what we can make of 'em.'

'The first,' said the Vicar, 'is Psalms cxx, 6 – "The sun shall not smite it by day, nor the moon by night".'

Mr Matthews wrote rapidly.

'Next, just a reference – Ecclesiasticus xxxi, 7. Then St Matthew vi, 21 – "Where the treasure is, there will the heart be also." Then another reference to Ecclesiasticus xxii, 12. That's all.'

Matthews shut his notebook and slipped it into his pocket. 'Now we'll go down to the library and have a go at the puzzle,' he said genially.

'Of course,' said the Vicar as they descended the stairs, 'that first text is another misquotation. In the Authorised Version, at any rate, the verse is "The sun shall not smite *thee* by day".'

'Why, you're right,' said Matthews. 'We'll just see what the Papists say. But it strikes me, sir, that any text that's copied in full is wrong and that's the clue.'

In the library, established in armchairs, one with the paper of texts, the other with his Latin Vulgate, they traced out the references. The first was, as the Vicar had said, wrong.

'That don't tell us much,' complained the American. 'It applies to the treasure, I guess, but it's not much help to know that "the sun will not smite it by day nor the moon by night".'

'It may refer to the hiding place,' said the Vicar. 'That would suggest some hole or cellar or vault.'

'That's so,' admitted the American. 'Now, Ecclesiasticus xxxi, 7.'

The Vicar read aloud. '"Gold is a stumbling block to them that sacrifice for it; woe to them that eagerly follow after it: every fool shall perish by it." At once a lamentation and a warning from the dead devil-worshipper,' he said. Then, with some hesitation, 'Mr Matthews, it's evident the man had some horrible experience. Don't you think it would be wiser to abandon the search?'

'Abandon it. Vicar? What, when were just getting on the track? Not if I know it,' cried Matthews. 'Why, this is just the biggest thrill that ever happened! And if there's any risk, why, that makes it all the better. Come on, what's next? Matthew vi, 11.'

'That's from the Sermon on the Mount ... Yes, I thought so. It really reads, "Where *thy* treasure is, there shall *thy* heart be also." Another deliberate misquotation.'

'And the last? Ecclesiasticus again, xxii, 12.'

The Vicar read it with a certain solemnity. '"The wicked life of a wicked fool is worse than death".'

'He certainly didn't get much hilarious pleasure out of the sacrilege,' commented the American.

The Vicar said nothing. Somehow they both felt a little uncomfortable.

'Well, now, let's get down to work,' said Matthews, throwing off his momentary discomfort. 'We've got three clues. "Have regard unto my name, for it shall be unto thee for a great treasure." "The sun shall not smite it by day nor the moon by night." "Where the treasure is, there shall the heart be also." Let's get on to the name. "Dom: Hierime Lindalle." Now what's wrong with that as a name?'

They puzzled over this for some time, replacing letters by figures, rearranging the letters to form anagrams, seeking for some principle to guide them to the clue. Tea was served and eaten almost silently as the two men badgered their brains over the riddle of the priest's name.

At last the American looked up.

'No good,' he said; and the Vicar shook his head.

'"Hierime" strikes me as being a bit of a freak in the way of a name,' commented Matthews. 'Was he a saint?'

'Why, yes,' said Mr Molyneux. 'Saint Hiereme, or Jerome, was a Father of the Church, a hermit who translated the Bible into Latin.'

'Perhaps that accounts for this chap's attention to the text,' suggested Matthews.

'Perhaps. St Jerome was a great scholar. No doubt you know Dürer's famous pictures of him – in the desert, and at work in his room, with his lion at his feet.'

'What's that?' cried the American. 'A *lion*, did you say?'

'Why, yes, but – '

'What about that twelfth panel – the one with the book and the lion? What's the betting it's not Mark at all, but *Jerome*? The sly beggar! He slips in a figure he knows we'll take for Mark, and all the time –'

'I declare I believe you're right!' exclaimed Mr Molyneux, flushed with excitement. 'That's the clue – the panel in the north room.'

'And, look here, the next fits,' cried Matthews. '"The sun shall not smite it by day nor the moon by night." Do you remember just where that panel is? It's between the windows in the north wall. No direct light ever touches it.'

'You're right!' cried the Vicar, almost as much excited as the American. 'And the last clue – the heart?'

'This is where we go and look,' declared Mr Matthews.

The day was nearly ended, but a few rays of light struggled dimly into the north passage. As they hurried along, a small gleaming object lying on the floor met their eyes. Matthews stooped and picked it up. It was a thin silver chain to which was attached a tiny crucifix – a trinket such as is worn by a large majority of Catholics.

'One of the Sharpes dropped it, I reckon,' said the American. 'I'll take it down when I go.' And he dropped it into his pocket.

In the north room the light had almost gone; but enough remained to direct the two men to the panel. 'See here, the book *is* the Vulgate!' cried Matthews, peering closely at the carving. 'We're right on the trail.'

'"Where the treasure is, there the heart is also",' murmured the Vicar. 'Now, what can that mean?'

They tried the breast of the carved figure in all possible ways, with no result.

'Well, if that's not plumb annoying!' cried the American, pausing in his efforts. 'I guess it must be another of his tricks. The wall's hollow here, too, I'd take my oath,' and he rapped the panel with his knuckles. It certainly was not solid. It gave a queer echo, and Mr Matthews thought he detected a faint sound, as of something stirring within the wall.

'Something moved!' he cried excitedly. 'Guess it might've been machinery ...' But further knockings produced no result.

'Let's try the decorated border,' suggested Mr Molyneux. 'There may be some hint there.'

The border was made up of wreaths of fruit and flowers, broken at intervals by shields so small that the quarterings were almost invisible. In some the arms could only be guessed from the crest, which was generally cut more deeply and with greater care than the shield.

'That's a queer crest,' said Matthews, pointing to one of these. 'Looks more like a setting sun than anything.'

'I daresay it is,' said the Vicar. 'There was a lady of the Wigram family, whose crest is a rising sun, who intermarried with the Langtres. The arms are quite gone from the shield, though. It is perfectly smooth.'

The light was now so bad that by common consent they abandoned their hunt till next day, and went down again to the lamp-lit library.

'Why, Mr Molyneux, I'm afraid I've tired you by my treasure hunt,' said Matthews, penitently, as he saw the Vicar's pale face.

'It's nothing – nothing at all,' protested the other. 'Just a little headache – my eyes are not strong. And I found that north room very close.'

'You look as if bed was the place for you,' declared Matthews; and the Vicar needed little urging, after dinner, to retire early. The American followed at eleven: not because he felt inclined for sleep, but because he wished to wake in the morning with a brain clear to tackle the problem of the panel. He was excited, and undressed with rapid, untidy movements, flinging down his discarded garments with utter disregard for neatness. The result of this was that his coat, thrown carelessly, fell upside-down, scattering the contents of the pockets over the floor. It was only then that he saw and remembered the silver chain and cross he had picked up.

'I must remember to give that back to the Sharpes,' he thought. 'Where'll I put it?' Then a queer fancy came into his head, and he slipped the chain round his neck.

'Guess I shan't forget it now,' he chuckled, as he slid between the sheets.

The clocks had struck midnight, and still Mr Matthews lay awake. The riddle of the panel bothered him. Try as he would, he could not see what the hint about the heart was intended to convey. He ran over the carving again and again in his mind – the draped figure with the book, the conventional lion beside it, placed on a perfectly plain background, and below it the thickly decorated border with its scrolls and shields.

He grew sleepy, and his thoughts began to stray. He thought of the chain, of Sharpe, of the holy-water stoups, of the shrine in the passage, of the many plaster statues about the house, and of one in particular that he had noticed in Mrs Sharpe's room – a Christ with outstretched arms and a crimson heart emitting rays showing on the breast …

Mr Matthews sat up, wide awake. That thing in the border that they had taken for a crested shield – that smooth triangle with the rays springing from it – it was not a shield at all: it represented a *heart*! He had solved the puzzle.

He leapt out of bed, armed himself with an electric torch, and fairly ran down the corridor to the north room. The single beam of light from his torch made the surrounding darkness seem almost opaque. In a dim subconscious way Matthews associated the dense gloom with the clammy, earthy smell that now seemed intensified; but he paid no conscious attention to either.

He walked with a quick, resolute stride to the panel, and soon found the smooth triangle in the decoration of the border. Of course, it was a heart – the conventional representation! He put his finger on it and pressed. He felt the panel slowly move.

He could not wait for it to swing fully open; he thrust his hand into the widening chink between the wall and the wood. There *was* something there, down in the bottom of the hole in the wall. Eagerly he reached for it.

It was piled up, and felt slimy to his touch. Then he dropped his torch with a hoarse cry; for, as he touched it, it moved, and a long slimy arm slid up his wrist.

Frantically he tore at his hand. He got it free for a second, and, turning, rushed to the door. He heard, as he ran, a heavy *flop*, and then a whispering, scratching sound. He knew that the thing had dropped from its lair and was dragging its loathsome length in pursuit. As he reached the door a tentacle, both slimy and hairy, curved round one ankle: another pawed at his left arm: and with a sickening thrill of disgust he felt something cold and slimy touch the back of his neck.

He gave a shriek of loathing and terror as he fell his length in the passage.

✳

It was three weeks before Mr Matthews, now installed at the Vicarage, could bring himself to speak of the end of that night. Then he asked, quite abruptly.

'How do you account for my escape, Molyneux? It – it was at my throat. I-I felt it …'

'One can't really account for any of these things,' replied the Vicar, gravely. 'Only – there is this. You had round your neck the image of Christ. I think the – thing – had touched it, for it – it was retreating when I heard you scream and came out. I-I saw it – dimly – and its trail … And I can't tell you how much I wished that I had read you a passage out of the manuscript about the room – a passage I left out. It might have warned you.'

'Will you tell me now?'

'It describes the finding of the body of Job Harcott. It reads like this – I almost know it by heart since … since you so nearly …' He gulped, and then went on in grave tones – "We found him indeede in ye passage wh. leadeth to yt. accursed roome. He was Starke Naked and his Bodie fearsomelie swolne, longe Trayls of Slyme compassing him aboute as it were in a Nett."

11 The Book

BY MARGARET IRWIN

On a foggy night in November, Mr Corbett, having guessed the murderer by the third chapter of his detective story, arose in disappointment from his bed and went downstairs in search of something more satisfactory to send him to sleep.

The fog had crept through the closed and curtained windows of the dining-room and hung thick on the air in a silence that seemed as heavy and breathless as the fog. The atmosphere was more choking than in his room, and very chill, although the remains of a large fire still burned in the grate.

The dining-room bookcase was the only considerable one in the house and held a careless unselected collection to suit all the tastes of the household, together with a few dull and obscure old theological books that had been left over from the sale of a learned uncle's library. Cheap red novels, bought on railway stalls by Mrs Corbett, who thought a journey the only time to read, were thrust in like pert, undersized intruders among the respectable nineteenth-century works of culture, chastely bound in dark blue or green, which Mr Corbett had considered the right thing to buy during his Oxford days; beside these there swaggered the children's large gaily bound story-books and collections of Fairy Tales in every colour.

From among this neat new cloth-bound crowd there towered here and there a musty sepulchre of learning, brown with the colour of dust rather than leather, with no trace of gilded letters, however faded, on its crumbling back to tell what lay inside. A few of these moribund survivors from the Dean's library were inhospitably fastened with rusty clasps;

all remained closed, and appeared impenetrable, their blank, forbidding backs uplifted above their frivolous surroundings with the air of scorn that belongs to a private and concealed knowledge. For only the worm of corruption now bored his way through their evil-smelling pages.

It was an unusual flight of fancy for Mr Corbett to imagine that the vaporous and fog-ridden air that seemed to hang more thickly about the bookcase was like a dank and poisonous breath exhaled by one or other of these slowly rotting volumes. Discomfort in this pervasive and impalpable presence came on him more acutely than at any time that day; in an attempt to clear his throat of it he choked most unpleasantly.

He hurriedly chose a Dickens from the second shelf as appropriate to a London fog, and had returned to the foot of the stairs when he decided that his reading to-night should by contrast be of blue Italian skies and white statues, in beautiful rhythmic sentences. He went back for a Walter Pater.

He found *Marius the Epicurean* tipped sideways across the gap left by his withdrawal of *The Old Curiosity Shop*. It was a very wide gap to have been left by a single volume, for the books on that shelf had been closely wedged together. He put the Dickens back into it and saw that there was still space for a large book. He said to himself in careful and precise words: 'This is nonsense. No one can possibly have gone into the dining-room and removed a book while I was crossing the hall. There must have been a gap before in the second shelf.' But another part of his mind kept saying in a hurried, tumbled torrent: 'There was no gap in the second shelf. There was no gap in the second shelf.'

He snatched at both the *Marius* and *The Old Curiosity Shop*, and went to his room in a haste that was unnecessary and absurd, since even if he believed in ghosts, which he did not, no one had the smallest reason for suspecting any in the modern Kensington house wherein he and his family had lived for the last fifteen years. Reading was the best thing to calm the nerves, and Dickens a pleasant, wholesome and robust author.

To-night, however, Dickens struck him in a different light. Beneath the author's sentimental pity for the weak and helpless, he could discern a revolting pleasure in cruelty and suffering, while the grotesque figures of the people in Cruikshank's illustrations revealed too clearly the hideous distortions of their souls. What had seemed humorous now appeared diabolic, and in disgust at these two favourites he turned to Walter Pater for the repose and dignity of a classic spirit.

But presently he wondered if this spirit were not in itself of a marble quality, frigid and lifeless, contrary to the purpose of nature. 'I have often thought', he said to himself, 'that there is something evil in the austere worship of beauty for its own sake.' He had never thought so before, but he liked to think that this impulse of fancy was the result of mature consideration, and with this satisfaction he composed himself for sleep.

He woke two or three times in the night, an unusual occurrence, but he was glad of it, for each time he had been dreaming horribly of these blameless Victorian works. Sprightly devils in whiskers and peg-top trousers tortured a lovely maiden and leered in delight at her anguish; the gods and heroes of classic fable acted deeds whose naked crime and shame Mr Corbett had never appreciated in Latin and Greek Unseens. When he had woken in a cold sweat from the spectacle of the ravished Philomel's torn and bleeding tongue, he decided there was nothing for it but to go down and get another book that would turn his thoughts in some more pleasant direction. But his increasing reluctance to do this found a hundred excuses. The recollection of the gap in the shelf now occurred to him with a sense of unnatural importance; in the troubled dozes that followed, this gap between two books seemed the most hideous deformity, like a gap between the front teeth of some grinning monster.

But in the clear daylight of the morning Mr Corbett came down to the pleasant dining-room, its sunny windows and smell of coffee and toast, and ate an undiminished breakfast with a mind chiefly occupied in self-congratulation that the wind had blown the fog away in time for his Saturday game of golf. Whistling happily, he was pouring out his final cup of coffee when his hand remained arrested in the act as his glance, roving across the bookcase, noticed that there was now no gap at all in the second shelf. He asked who had been at the bookcase already, but neither of the girls had, nor Dicky, and Mrs Corbett was not yet down. The maid never touched the books. They wanted to know what book he missed in it, which made him look foolish, as he could not say. The things that disturb us at midnight are negligible at 9 am.

'I thought there was a gap in the second shelf,' he said, 'but it doesn't matter.'

'There never is a gap in the second shelf,' said little Jean brightly. 'You can take out lots of books from it and when you go back the gap's always filled up. Haven't you noticed that? I have.'

Nora, the middle one in age, said Jean was always being silly; she had been found crying over the funny pictures in the *Rose and the Ring* because she said all the people in them had such wicked faces, and the picture of a black cat had upset her because she thought it was a witch. Mr Corbett did not like to think of such fancies for his Jeannie. She retaliated briskly by saying Dicky was just as bad, and he was a big boy. He had kicked a book across the room and said, 'Filthy stuff,' just like that. Jean was a good mimic; her tone expressed a venom of disgust, and she made the gesture of dropping a book as though the very touch of it were loathsome. Dicky, who had been making violent signs at her, now told her she was a beastly little sneak and he would never again take her for rides on the step of his bicycle. Mr Corbett was disturbed. Unpleasant housemaids and bad school-friends passed through his head, as he gravely asked his son how he had got hold of this book.

'Took it out of that bookcase of course,' said Dicky furiously.

It turned out to be the *Boy's Gulliver's Travels* that Granny had given him, and Dicky had at last to explain his rage with the devil who wrote it to show that men were worse than beasts and the human race a wash-out. A boy who never had good school reports had no right to be so morbidly sensitive as to penetrate to the underlying cynicism of Swift's delightful fable, and that moreover in the bright and carefully expurgated edition they bring out nowadays. Mr Corbett could not say he had ever noticed the cynicism himself, though he knew from the critical books it must be there, and with some annoyance he advised his son to take out a nice bright modern boy's adventure story that could not depress anybody. It appeared, however, that Dicky was 'off reading just now', and the girls echoed this.

Mr Corbett soon found that he too was 'off reading'. Every new book seemed to him weak, tasteless and insipid; while his old and familiar books were depressing or even, in some obscure way, disgusting. Authors must all be filthy-minded; they probably wrote what they dared not express in their lives. Stevenson had said that literature was a morbid secretion; he read Stevenson again to discover his peculiar morbidity, and detected in his essays a self-pity masquerading as courage, and in *Treasure Island* an invalid's sickly attraction to brutality.

This gave him a zest to find out what he disliked so much, and his taste for reading revived as he explored with relish the hidden infirmities of minds that had been valued by fools as great and noble. He saw Jane Austen and Charlotte Brontë as two unpleasant examples of spinsterhood; the one as a prying, sub-acid busybody in everyone else's flirtations, the other as a raving, craving maenad seeking self-immolation on the altar of her frustrated passions. He compared Wordsworth's love of nature to the monstrous egoism of an ancient bell-wether, isolated from the flock.

These powers of penetration astonished him. With a mind so acute and original he should have achieved greatness, yet he was a mere solicitor and not prosperous at that. If he had but the money, he might do something with those ivory shares, but it would be a pure gamble, and he had no luck. His natural envy of his wealthier acquaintances now mingled with a contempt for their stupidity that approached loathing. The digestion of his lunch in the City was ruined by meeting sentimental yet successful dotards whom he had once regarded as pleasant fellows. The very sight of them spoiled his game of golf, so that he came to prefer reading alone in the dining-room even on sunny afternoons.

He discovered also and with a slight shock that Mrs Corbett had always bored him. Dicky he began actively to dislike as an impudent blockhead, and the two girls were as insipidly alike as white mice; it was a relief when he abolished their tiresome habit of coming in to say good-night.

In the now unbroken silence and seclusion of the dining-room, he read with feverish haste as though he were seeking for some clue to knowledge, some secret key to existence which would quicken and inflame it, transform it from its present dull torpor to a life worthy of him and his powers.

He even explored the few decaying remains of his uncle's

theological library. Bored and baffled, he yet persisted, and had the occasional relief of an ugly woodcut of Adam and Eve with figures like bolsters and hair like dahlias, or a map of the Cosmos with Hell-mouth in the corner, belching forth demons. One of these books had diagrams and symbols in the margin which he took to be mathematical formulae of a kind he did not know. He presently discovered that they were drawn, not printed, and that the book was in manuscript, in a very neat, crabbed black writing that resembled black-letter printing. It was moreover in Latin, a fact that gave Mr Corbett a shock of unreasoning disappointment. For while examining the signs in the margin, he had been filled with an extraordinary exultation as though he knew himself to be on the edge of a discovery that should alter his whole life. But he had forgotten his Latin.

With a secret and guilty air which would have looked absurd to anyone who knew his harmless purpose, he stole to the schoolroom for Dicky's Latin dictionary and grammar and hurried back to the dining-room, where he tried to discover what the book was about with an anxious industry that surprised himself. There was no name to it, nor of the author. Several blank pages had been left at the end, and the writing ended at the bottom of a page, with no flourish or superscription, as though the book had been left unfinished. From what sentences he could translate, it seemed to be a work on theology rather than mathematics. There were constant references to the Master, to his wishes and injunctions, which appeared to be of a complicated kind. Mr Corbett began by skipping these as mere accounts of ceremonial, but a word caught his eye as one unlikely to occur in such an account. He read this passage attentively, looking up each word in the dictionary, and could hardly believe the result of his translation. 'Clearly,' he decided, 'this book must be by some early missionary, and the passage I have just read the account of some horrible rite practised by a savage tribe of devil-worshippers.' Though he called it 'horrible', he reflected on it, committing each detail to memory. He then amused himself by copying the signs in the margin near it and trying to discover their significance. But a sensation of sickly cold came over him, his head swam, and he could hardly see the figures before his eyes. He suspected a sudden attack of influenza, and went to ask his wife for medicine.

They were all in the drawing-room, Mrs Corbett helping Nora and Jean with a new game, Dicky playing the pianola, and Mike, the Irish terrier, who had lately deserted his accustomed place on the dining-room hearthrug, stretched by the fire. Mr Corbett had an instant's impression of this peaceful and cheerful scene, before his family turned towards him and asked in scared tones what was the matter. He thought how like sheep they looked and sounded; nothing in his appearance in the mirror struck him as odd; it was their gaping faces that were unfamiliar. He then noticed the extraordinary behaviour of Mike, who had sprung from the hearthrug and was crouched in the furthest corner, uttering no sound, but with his eyes distended and foam round his bared teeth. Under Mr Corbett's glance, he slunk towards the door, whimpering in a faint and abject manner, and then as his master called him, he snarled horribly, and the hair bristled on the scruff of his neck. Dicky let him out, and they heard him scuffling at a frantic rate down the stairs to the kitchen, and then, again and again, a long-drawn howl.

'What *can* be the matter with Mike?' asked Mrs Corbett.

Her question broke a silence that seemed to have lasted a long time. Jean began to cry. Mr Corbett said irritably that he did not know what was the matter with any of them.

Then Nora asked, 'What is that red mark on your face?'

He looked again in the glass and could see nothing.

'It's quite clear from here,' said Dicky; 'I can see the lines in the finger print.'

'Yes, that's what it is,' said Mrs Corbett in her brisk staccato voice; 'the print of a finger on your forehead. Have you been writing in red ink?'

Mr Corbett precipitately left the room for his own, where he sent down a message that he was suffering from headache and would have his dinner in bed. He wanted no one fussing round him. By next morning he was amazed at his fancies of influenza, for he had never felt so well in his life.

No one commented on his looks at breakfast, so he concluded that the mark had disappeared. The old Latin book he had been translating on the previous night had been moved from the writing bureau, although Dicky's grammar and dictionary were still there. The second shelf was, as always in the day-time, closely packed; the book had, he remembered, been in the second shelf. But this time he did not ask who had put it back.

That day he had an unexpected stroke of luck in a new client of the name of Crab, who entrusted him with large sums of money: nor was he irritated by the sight of his more prosperous acquaintances, but with difficulty refrained from grinning in their faces, so confident was he that his remarkable ability must soon place him higher than any of them. At dinner he chaffed his family with what he felt to be the gaiety of a schoolboy. But on them it had a contrary effect, for they stared, either at him in stupid astonishment, or at their plates, depressed and nervous. Did they think him drunk? he wondered, and a fury came on him at their low and bestial suspicions and heavy dullness of mind. Why, he was younger than any of them!

But in spite of this new alertness he could not attend to the

letters he should have written that evening and drifted to the
bookcase for a little light distraction, but found that for the
first time there was nothing he wished to read. He pulled out
a book from above his head at random, and saw that it was the
old Latin book in manuscript. As he turned over its stiff and
yellow pages, he noticed with pleasure the smell of corruption
that had first repelled him in these decaying volumes, a smell,
he now thought, of ancient and secret knowledge.

This idea of secrecy seemed to affect him personally, for on
hearing a step in the hall he hastily closed the book and put
it back in its place. He went to the schoolroom where Dicky
was doing his home-work, and told him he required his Latin
grammar and dictionary again for an old law report. To his
annoyance he stammered and put his words awkwardly; he
thought that the boy looked oddly at him and he cursed him
in his heart for a suspicious young devil, though of what he
should be suspicious he could not say. Nevertheless, when
back in the dining-room, he listened at the door and then
softly turned the lock before he opened the books on the
writing bureau.

The script and Latin seemed much clearer than on the
previous evening, and he was able to read at random a
passage relating to a trial of a German midwife in 1620 for
the murder and dissection of 783 children. Even allowing
for the opportunities afforded by her profession, the number
appeared excessive, nor could he discover any motive for
the slaughter. He decided to translate the book from the
beginning.

It appeared to be an account of some secret society whose
activities and ritual were of a nature so obscure, and when not,
so vile and terrible, that Mr Corbett would not at first believe
that this could be a record of any human mind, although his
deep interest in it should have convinced him that from his

humanity at least it was not altogether alien.

He read until far later than his usual hour for bed and when at last he rose, it was with the book in his hands. To defer his parting with it, he stood turning over the pages until he reached the end of the writing, and was struck by a new peculiarity.

The ink was much fresher and of a far poorer quality than the thick rusted ink in the bulk of the book; on close inspection he would have said that it was of modern manufacture and written quite recently were it not for the fact that it was in the same crabbed late seventeenth-century handwriting.

This however did not explain the perplexity, even dismay and fear, he now felt as he stared at the last sentence. It ran: 'Contine te in perennibus studiis,' and he had at once recognised it as a Ciceronian tag that had been dinned into him at school. He could not understand how he had failed to notice it yesterday.

Then he remembered that the book had ended at the bottom of a page. But now, the last two sentences were written at the very top of a page. However long he looked at them, he could come to no other conclusion than that they had been added since the previous evening.

He now read the sentence before the last: 'Re imperfecta mortuus sum,' and translated the whole as: 'I died with my purpose unachieved. Continue, thou, the never-ending studies.'

With his eyes still fixed upon it, Mr Corbett replaced the book on the writing bureau and stepped back from it to the door, his hand outstretched behind him, groping and then tugging at the door-handle. As the door failed to open, his breath came in a faint, hardly articulate scream. Then he remembered that he had himself locked it, and he fumbled with the key in frantic ineffectual movements until at last he opened it and banged it after him as he plunged backwards into the hall.

For a moment he stood there looking at the door-handle; then with a stealthy, sneaking movement, his hand crept out towards it, touched it, began to turn it, when suddenly he pulled his hand away and went up to his bedroom, three steps at a time.

There he behaved in a manner only comparable with the way he had lost his head after losing his innocence when a schoolboy of sixteen. He hid his face in the pillow, he cried, he raved in meaningless words, repeating: 'Never, never, never. I will never do it again. Help me never to do it again.' With the words, 'Help me,' he noticed what he was saying, they reminded him of other words, and he began to pray aloud. But the words sounded jumbled, they persisted in coming into his head in a reverse order so that he found he was saying his prayers backwards, and at this final absurdity he suddenly began to laugh very loud. He sat up on the bed, delighted at this return to sanity, common sense and humour, when the door leading into Mrs Corbett's room opened, and he saw his wife staring at him with a strange, grey, drawn face that made her seem like the terror-stricken ghost of her usually smug and placid self.

'It's not burglars,' he said irritably. 'I've come to bed late, that is all, and must have waked you.'

'Henry,' said Mrs Corbett, and he noticed that she had not heard him, 'Henry, didn't you hear it?'

'What?'

'That laugh.'

He was silent, an instinctive caution warning him to wait until she spoke again. And this she did, imploring him with her eyes to reassure her.

'It was not a human laugh. It was like the laugh of a devil.'

235

He checked his violent inclination to laugh again. It was wiser not to let her know that it was only his laughter she had heard. He told her to stop being fanciful, and Mrs Corbett, gradually recovering her docility, returned to obey an impossible command, since she could not stop being what she had never been.

The next morning, Mr Corbett rose before any of the servants and crept down to the dining-room. As before, the dictionary and grammar alone remained on the writing bureau; the book was back in the second shelf. He opened it at the end. Two more lines had been added, carrying the writing down to the middle of the page. They ran:

> Ex auro canceris
> In dentem elephantis.

which he translated as:

> Out of the money of the crab
> Into the tooth of the elephant.

From this time on, his acquaintances in the City noticed a change in the mediocre, rather flabby and unenterprising 'old Corbett'. His recent sour depression dropped from him: he seemed to have grown twenty years younger, strong, brisk and cheerful, and with a self-confidence in business that struck them as lunacy. They waited with a not unpleasant excitement for the inevitable crash, but his every speculation, however wild and hare-brained, turned out successful. He no longer avoided them, but went out of his way to display his consciousness of luck, daring and vigour, and to chaff them in a manner that began to make him actively disliked. This he welcomed with delight as a sign of others' envy and his superiority.

He never stayed in town for dinners or theatres, for he was always now in a hurry to get home, where, as soon as he was sure of being undisturbed, he would take down the manuscript book from the second shelf of the dining-room and turn to the last pages.

Every morning he found that a few words had been added since the evening before, and always they formed, as he considered, injunctions to himself. These were at first only with regard to his money transactions, giving assurance to his boldest fancies, and since the brilliant and unforeseen success that had attended his gamble with Mr Crab's money in African ivory, he followed all such advice unhesitatingly.

But presently, interspersed with these commands, were others of a meaningless, childish, yet revolting character, such as might be invented by a decadent imbecile, or, it must be admitted, by the idle fancies of any ordinary man who permits his imagination to wander unbridled. Mr Corbett was startled to recognise one or two such fancies of his own, which had occurred to him during his frequent boredom in church, and which he had not thought any other mind could conceive.

He at first paid no attention to these directions, but found that his new speculations declined so rapidly that he became terrified not merely for his fortune but for his reputation and even safety, since the money of various of his clients was involved. It was made clear to him that he must follow the commands in the book altogether or not at all, and he began to carry out their puerile and grotesque blasphemies with a contemptuous amusement, which however gradually changed to a sense of their monstrous significance. They became more capricious and difficult of execution, but he now never hesitated to obey blindly, urged by a fear that he could not understand, but knew only that it was not of mere financial failure.

By now he understood the effect of this book on the others near it, and the reason that had impelled its mysterious agent to move the books into the second shelf so that all in turn should come under the influence of that ancient and secret knowledge.

In respect to it, he encouraged his children, with jeers at their stupidity, to read more, but he could not observe that they ever now took a book from the dining-room bookcase. He himself no longer needed to read, but went to bed early and slept sound. The things that all his life he had longed to do when he should have enough money now seemed to him insipid. His most exciting pleasure was the smell and touch of these mouldering pages as he turned them to find the last message inscribed to him.

One evening it was in two words only: 'Canem occide.'

He laughed at this simple and pleasant request to kill the dog, for he bore Mike a grudge for his change from devotion to slinking aversion. Moreover, it could not have come more opportunely, since in turning out an old desk he had just discovered some packets of rat poison bought years ago and forgotten. No one therefore knew of its existence and it would be easy to poison Mike without any further suspicion than that of a neighbour's carelessness. He whistled light-heartedly as he ran upstairs to rummage for the packets, and returned to empty one in the dog's dish of water in the hall.

That night the household was awakened by terrified screams proceeding from the stairs. Mr Corbett was the first to hasten there, prompted by the instinctive caution that was always with him these days. He saw Jean, in her nightdress, scrambling up on to the landing on her hands and knees, clutching at anything that afforded support and screaming in a choking, tearless, unnatural manner. He carried her to the room she shared with Nora, where they were quickly followed by Mrs Corbett.

Nothing coherent could be got from Jean. Nora said that

she must have been having her old dream again; when her father demanded what this was, she said that Jean sometimes woke in the night, crying, because she had dreamed of a hand passing backwards and forwards over the dining-room bookcase, until it found a certain book and took it out of the shelf. At this point she was always so frightened that she woke up.

On hearing this, Jean broke into fresh screams, and Mrs Corbett would have no more explanations. Mr Corbett went out on to the stairs to find what had brought the child there from her bed. On looking down into the lighted hall, he saw Mike's dish overturned. He went down to examine it and saw that the water he had poisoned must have been upset and absorbed by the rough doormat which was quite wet.

He went back to the little girls' room, told his wife that she was tired and must go to bed, and he would take his turn at comforting Jean. She was now much quieter. He took her on his knee where at first she shrank from him. Mr Corbett remembered with an angry sense of injury that she never now sat on his knee, and would have liked to pay her out for it by mocking and frightening her. But he had to coax her into telling him what he wanted, and with this object he soothed her, calling her by pet names that he thought he had forgotten, telling her that nothing could hurt her now he was with her.

At first his cleverness amused him; he chuckled softly when Jean buried her head in his dressing-gown. But presently an uncomfortable sensation came over him, he gripped at Jean as though for her protection, while he was so smoothly assuring her of his. With difficulty he listened to what he had at last induced her to tell him.

She and Nora had kept Mike with them all the evening and taken him to sleep in their room for a treat. He had lain at the foot of Jean's bed and they had all gone to sleep. Then Jean began her old dream of the hand moving over the books in the dining-room bookcase; but instead of taking out a book, it came across the dining-room and out on to the stairs. It came up over the banisters and to the door of their room, and turned their door-handle very softly and opened it. At this point she jumped up wide awake and turned on the light, calling to Nora. The door, which had been shut when they went to sleep, was wide open, and Mike was gone.

She told Nora that she was sure something dreadful would happen to him if she did not go and bring him back, and ran down into the hall where she saw him just about to drink from his dish. She called to him and he looked up, but did not come, so she ran to him, and began to pull him along with her, when her nightdress was clutched from behind and then she felt a hand seize her arm. She fell down, and then clambered upstairs as fast as she could, screaming all the way.

It was now clear to Mr Corbett that Mike's dish must have been upset in the scuffle. She was again crying, but this time he felt himself unable to comfort her. He retired to his room, where he walked up and down in an agitation he could not understand, for he found his thoughts perpetually arguing on a point that had never troubled him before.

'I am not a bad man,' he kept saying to himself. 'I have never done anything actually wrong. My clients are none the worse for my speculations, only the better. Nor have I spent my new wealth on gross and sensual pleasures; these now have even no attraction for me.

Presently he added: 'It is not wrong to try and kill a dog, an ill-tempered brute. It turned against me. It might have bitten Jeannie.'

He noticed that he had thought of her as Jeannie, which he had not done for some time; it must have been because he had called her that to-night. He must forbid her ever to leave her room at night, he could not have her meddling. It would be safer for him if she were not there at all.

Again that sick and cold sensation of fear swept over him: he seized the bed-post as though he were falling, and held on to it for some minutes. 'I was thinking of a boarding school,' he told himself, and then, 'I must go down and find out – find out –' He would not think what it was he must find out.

He opened his door and listened. The house was quiet. He crept on to the landing and along to Nora's and Jean's door where again he stood, listening. There was no sound, and at that he was again overcome with unreasonable terror. He imagined Jean lying very still in her bed, too still. He hastened away from the door, shuffling in his bedroom slippers along the passage and down the stairs.

A bright fire still burned in the dining-room grate. A glance at the clock told him it was not yet twelve. He stared at the bookcase. In the second shelf was a gap which had not been there when he had left. On the writing bureau lay a large open book. He knew that he must cross the room and see what was written in it. Then, as before, words that he did not intend came sobbing and crying to his lips, muttering, 'No, no, not that. Never, never, never.' But he crossed the room and looked down at the book. As last time, the message was in only two words: 'Infantem occide.'

He slipped and fell forward against the bureau. His hands clutched at the book, lifted it as he recovered himself and with his finger he traced out the words that had been written. The smell of corruption crept into his nostrils. He told himself that he was not a snivelling dotard, but a man stronger and wiser than his fellows, superior to the common emotions of humanity, who held in his hands the sources of ancient and secret power.

He had known what the message would be. It was after all the only safe and logical thing to do. Jean had acquired dangerous knowledge. She was a spy, an antagonist. That she was so unconsciously, that she was eight years old, his youngest and favourite child, were sentimental appeals that could make no difference to a man of sane reasoning power such as his own. Jean had sided with Mike against him. 'All that are not with me are against me,' he repeated softly. He would kill both dog and child with the white powder that no one knew to be in his possession. It would be quite safe.

He laid down the book and went to the door. What he had to do, he would do quickly, for again that sensation of deadly cold was sweeping over him. He wished he had not to do it to-night; last night it would have been easier, but to-night she had sat on his knee and made him afraid. He imagined her lying very still in her bed, too still. But it would be she who would lie there, not he, so why should he be afraid? He was protected by ancient and secret powers. He held on to the door-handle, but his fingers seemed to have grown numb, for he could not turn it. He clung to it, crouched and shivering, bending over it until he knelt on the ground, his head beneath the handle which he still clutched with upraised hands. Suddenly the hands were loosened and flung outwards with the frantic gesture of a man falling from a great height, and he stumbled to his feet. He seized the book and threw it on the fire. A violent sensation of choking overcame him, he felt he was being strangled, as in a nightmare he tried again and again to shriek aloud, but his breath would make no sound. His breath would not come at all. He fell backwards heavily, down on the floor, where he lay very still.

In the morning, the maid who came to open the dining-room windows found her master dead. The sensation caused by this was scarcely so great in the City as that given by the simultaneous collapse of all Mr Corbett's recent speculations. It was instantly assumed that he must have had previous knowledge of this and so committed suicide.

The stumbling-block of this theory was that the medical report defined the cause of Mr Corbett's death as strangulation of the windpipe by the pressure of a hand which had left the marks of its fingers on his throat.

12 Couching at the Door

BY D K BROSTER

I

The first inkling which Augustine Marchant had of the matter was on one fine summer morning about three weeks after his visit to Prague – that is to say, in June, 1898. He was reclining, as his custom was when writing his poetry, on the very comfortable sofa in his library at Abbot's Medding, near the French windows, one of which was open to the garden. Pausing for inspiration – he was nearly at the end of his poem, *Salutation to All Unbeliefs* – he let his eyes wander round the beautifully appointed room, with its cloisonné and Satsuma, Buhl and first editions, and then allowed them to stray towards the sunlight outside. And so, between the edge of the costly Herat carpet and the sill of the open window, across the strip of polished oak flooring, he observed what he took to be a small piece of dark fluff blowing in the draught; and instantly made a note to speak to his housekeeper about it. There was slackness somewhere; and in Augustine Marchant's house no one was allowed to be slack but himself.

There had been a time when the poet would not for a moment have been received, as he was now, in country and even county society – those days, even before the advent of *The Yellow Book* and *The Savoy*, when he had lived in London, writing the plays and poems which had so startled and shocked all but the 'decadent' and the 'advanced,' *Pomegranates of Sin*, *Queen Theodora and Queen Marozia*, *The Nights of the Tour de Nesle*, *Amor Cypriacus* and the rest. But when, as the 'nineties began to wane, he inherited Abbot's Medding from a distant

244

cousin and came to live there, being then at the height of an almost international reputation, Wiltshire society at first tolerated him for his kinship with the late Lord Medding, and then, placated by the excellence of his dinners and further mollified by the patent staidness of his private life, decided that, in his personal conduct at any rate, he must have turned over a new leaf. Perhaps indeed he had never been as bad as he was painted, and if his writings continued to be no less scandalously free and free-thinking than before, and needed to be just as rigidly kept out of the hands of daughters, well, no country gentleman in the neighbourhood was obliged to read them!

And indeed Augustine Marchant in his fifty-first year was too keenly alive to the value of the good opinion of county society to risk shocking it by any overt doings of his. He kept his licence for his pen. When he went abroad, as he did at least twice a year – but that was another matter altogether. The nose of Mrs Grundy was not sharp enough to smell out his occupations in Warsaw or Berlin or Naples, her eyes long-sighted enough to discern what kind of society he frequented even so near home as Paris. At Abbot's Medding his reputation for being 'wicked' was fast declining into just enough of a sensation to titillate a croquet party. He had charming manners, could be witty at moments (though he could not keep it up), still retained his hyacinthine locks (by means of hair restorers), wore his excellently cut velvet coats and flowing ties with just the right air – half poet, half man of the world – and really had, at Abbot's Medding, no dark secret to hide beyond the fact, sedulously concealed by him for five-and-twenty years, that he had never been christened Augustine. Between Augustus and Augustine, what a gulf! But he had crossed it, and his French poems (which had to be smuggled into his native land) were signed Augustin – Augustin Lemarchant.

Removing his gaze from the objectionable evidence of domestic carelessness upon the floor, Mr Marchant now fixed it meditatively upon the ruby-set end of the gold pencil which he was using. Rossell & Ward, his publishers, were about to bring out an édition de luxe of *Queen Theodora and Queen Marozia* with illustrations by a hitherto unknown young artist – if they were not too daring. It would be a sumptuous affair in a limited edition. And, as he thought of this, the remembrance of his recent stay in Prague returned to the poet. He smiled to himself, as a man smiles when he looks at a rare wine, and thought: 'Yes, if these blunt-witted Pharisees round Abbott's Medding only knew!' It was a good thing that the upholders of British petty morality were seldom great travellers; a dispensation of … ahem, Providence!

Twiddling his gold pencil between plump fingers, Augustine Marchant returned to his ode, weighing one epithet against another. Except in summer he was no advocate of open windows, and even in summer he considered that to get the most out of that delicate and precious instrument, his brain, his feet must always be kept thoroughly warm; he had therefore cast over them, before settling into his semi-reclining position, a beautiful rose-coloured Indian *sari* of the purest and thickest silk, leaving the ends trailing on the floor. And he became aware, with surprise and annoyance, that the piece of brown fluff or whatever it was down there, travelling in the draught from the window, had reached the nearest end of the *sari* and was now, impelled by the same current, travelling up it.

The master of Abbot's Medding reached out for the silver hand-bell on the table by his side. There must be more breeze coming in than he had realized, and he might take cold, a catastrophe against which he guarded himself as against the plague. Then he saw that the upward progress of the dark blot – it was about the size of a farthing – could not by any possibility be assigned to any other agency than its own. It was *climbing* up – some horrible insect, plainly, some disgusting kind of almost legless and very hairy spider, round and vague in outline. The poet sat up and shook the *sari* violently. When he looked again the invader was gone. He had obviously shaken it on to the floor, and on the floor somewhere it must still be. The idea perturbed him, and he decided to take his writing out to the summer-house, and give orders later that the library was to be thoroughly swept.

Ah! it was good to be out of doors, and in a pleasance so delightfully laid out, so exquisitely kept, as his! In the basin of the fountain the sea-nymphs of rosy-veined marble clustered round a Thetis as beautiful as Aphrodite herself; the lightest and featheriest of acacia trees swayed near. And as the owner of all this went past over the weedless turf he repeated snatches of Verlaine to himself about 'sveltes jets d'eau' and 'sanglots d'exstase.'

Then, turning his head to look back at the fountain, he became aware of a little dark-brown object about the size of a halfpenny running towards him over the velvet-smooth sward ...

He believed afterwards that he must first have had a glimpse of the truth at that instant in the garden, or he would not have acted so instinctively as he did, and so promptly. For a moment later he was standing at the edge of the basin of Thetis, his face blanched in the sunshine, his hand firmly clenched. Inside that closed hand something feather-soft pulsated ... Holding back as best he could the disgust and the something more which clutched at him, Augustine Marchant stooped and plunged his whole fist into the bubbling water, and let the stream of the fountain whirl away what he had picked up. Then with uncertain steps he went and sat down on the nearest seat and shut his eyes. After a while he took out his lawn handkerchief and carefully dried his hand with the intaglio ring, dried it and then looked curiously at the palm. 'I did not know I had so much courage,' he was thinking; 'so much courage and good sense!' ... It would doubtless drown very quickly.

Burrows, his butler, was coming over the lawn. 'Mr and Mrs Morrison have arrived, sir.'

'Ah, yes; I had forgotten for the moment.' Augustine Marchant got up and walked towards the house and his guests, throwing back his shoulders and practising his famous enigmatic smile, for Mrs Morrison was a woman worth impressing.

(But what had it been exactly? Why, just what it had looked – a tuft of fur blowing over the grass, a tuft of fur! Sheer imagination that it had moved in his closed hand with a life of its own ... Then why had he shut his eyes as he stooped and made a grab at it? Thank God, thank God, it was nothing now but a drenched smear swirling round the nymphs of Thetis!)

'Ah, dear lady, you must forgive me! Unpardonable of me not to be in to receive you!' He was in the drawing-room now, fragrant with its bank of hothouse flowers, bending over the hand of the fashionably attired guest on the sofa, in her tight bodice and voluminous sleeves, with a fly-away hat perched at a rakish angle on her gold-brown hair.

'Your man told us that you were writing in the garden,' said her goggle-eyed husband reverentially.

'Cher maître, it is we who ought not to be interrupting your rendezvous with the Muse,' returned Mrs Morrison in her sweet, high voice. 'Terrible to bring you from such company into that of mere visitors!'

Running his hand through his carefully tended locks the cher maître replied: 'Between a visit from the Muse and one from Beauty's self no true poet would hesitate! – Moreover, luncheon awaits us, and I trust it is a good one.'

He liked faintly to shock fair admirers by admitting that he cared for the pleasures of the table; it was quite safe to do so, since none of them had sufficient acumen to see that it was true.

The luncheon was excellent, for Augustine kept an admirable cook. Afterwards he showed his guests over the library – yes, even though it had not received the sweeping which would now be unnecessary – and round the garden; and in the summer-house was prevailed upon to read some of *Amor Cypriacus* aloud. And Mrs Frances (nowadays Francesca) Morrison was thereafter able to recount to envious friends how the Poet himself had read her stanza after stanza from that most *daring* poem of his; and how poor Fred, fanning himself meanwhile with his straw hat – not from the torridity of the verse but because of the afternoon heat – said afterwards that he had not understood a single word. A good thing, perhaps …

When they had gone Augustine Marchant reflected rather cynically: 'All that was just so much bunkum when I wrote it.' For ten years ago, in spite of those audacious, glowing verses, he was an ignorant neophyte. Of course, since then … He smiled, a private, sly, self-satisfied smile. It was certainly pleasant to know oneself no longer a fraud!

Returning to the summer-house to fetch his poems he saw what he took to be Mrs Morrison's fur boa lying on the floor just by the basket chair which she had occupied. Odd of her not to have missed it on departure – a tribute to his verses perhaps. His housekeeper must send it after her by post. But just at that moment his head gardener approached, desiring some instructions, and when the matter was settled, and Augustine Marchant turned once more to enter the summer-house, he found that he had been mistaken about the dropped boa, for there was nothing on the floor.

Besides, he remembered now that Mrs Morrison's boa had

been a rope of grey feathers, not of dark fur. As he took up *Amor Cypriacus* he asked himself lazily what could have led him to imagine a woman's boa there at all, much less a fur one.

Suddenly he knew why. A lattice in the house of memory had opened, and he remained rigid, staring out at the jets of the fountain rising and falling in the afternoon sun. Yes; of that glamorous, wonderful, abominable night in Prague the part he least wished to recall was connected – incidentally but undeniably – with a fur boa … a long boa of dark fur …

He had to go up to town next day to a dinner in his honour. There and then he decided to go up that same night, by a late train, a most unusual proceeding, and most disturbing to his valet, who knew that it was doubtful whether he could at such short notice procure him a first-class carriage to himself. However, Augustine Marchant went, and even, to the man's amazement, deliberately chose a compartment with another occupant when he might, after all, have had an empty one.

The dinner was brilliant; Augustine had never spoken better. Next day he went round to the little street not far from the British Museum where he found Lawrence Storey, his new illustrator, working feverishly at his drawings for *Queen Theodora and Queen Marozia*, and quite overwhelmed at the honour of a personal visit. Augustine was very kind to him, and, while offering a few criticisms, highly praised his delineation of those two Messalinas of tenth-century Rome, their long supple hands, their heavy eyes, their full, almost repellent mouths. Storey had followed the same type for mother and daughter, but with a subtle difference.

'They were certainly two most evil women, especially the younger,' he observed ingenuously. 'But I suppose that, from an artistic point of view, that doesn't matter nowadays!'

Augustine, smoking one of his special cigarettes, made

a delicate little gesture. 'My dear fellow, Art has nothing whatever to do with what is called 'morality'; happily we know that at last! Show me how you thought of depicting the scene where Marozia orders the execution of her mother's papal paramour. Good, very good! Yes, the lines there, even the fall of that loose sleeve from the extended arm, express with clarity what I had in mind. You have great gifts!'

'I have tried to make her look wicked,' said the young man, reddening with pleasure. 'But,' he added deprecatingly, 'it is very hard for a ridiculously inexperienced person like myself to have the right artistic vision. For to you, Mr Marchant, who have penetrated into such wonderful arcana of the forbidden, it would be foolish to pretend to be other than I am.'

'How do you know that I have penetrated into any such arcana?' enquired the poet, half-shutting his eyes and looking (though not to the almost worshipping gaze of young Storey) like a great cat being stroked.

'Why, one has only to read you!'

'You must come down and stay with me soon,' were Augustine Marchant's parting words. (He would give the boy a few days' good living, for which he would be none the worse; let him drink some decent wine.) 'How soon do you think you will be able to finish the rough sketches for the rest, and the designs for the *culs de lampe*? A fortnight or three weeks? Good; I shall look to see you then. Good-bye, my dear fellow; I am very, very much pleased with what you have shown me!'

The worst of going up to London from the country was that one was apt to catch a cold in town. When he got back, Augustine Marchant was almost sure that this misfortune had befallen him, so he ordered a fire in his bedroom, despite the season, and consumed a recherché little supper in seclusion.

And, as the cold turned out to have been imaginary, he was very comfortable, sitting there in his silken dressing-gown, toasting his toes and holding up a glass of golden Tokay to the flames. Really *Theodora and Marozia* would make as much sensation when it came out with these illustrations as when it first appeared!

All at once he set down his glass. Not far away on his left stood a big cheval mirror, like a woman's, in which a good portion of the bed behind him was reflected. And, in this mirror, he had just seen the valance of the bed move. There could be no draught to speak of in this warm room, he never allowed a cat in the house, and it was quite impossible that there should be a rat about. If after all some stray cat should have got in it must be ejected at once. Augustine hitched round in his chair to look at the actual bed-hanging.

Yes, the topaz hued silk valance again swung very slightly outwards as though it were being pushed. Augustine bent forward to the bell-pull to summon his valet. Then the flask of Tokay rolled over on the table as he leapt from his chair instead. Something like a huge, dark caterpillar was emerging very slowly from under his bed, moving as a caterpillar moves, with undulations running over it. Where its head should have been was merely a tapering end smaller than the rest of it, but of like substance. It was a dark fur boa.

Augustine Marchant felt that he screamed, but he could not have done so, for his tongue clave to the roof of his mouth. He merely stood staring, staring, all the blood gone from his heart. Still very slowly, the thing continued to creep out from under the valance, waving that eyeless, tapering end to and fro, as though uncertain where to proceed. 'I am going mad, mad, mad!' thought Augustine, and then, with a revulsion: 'No, it can't be! It's a real snake of some kind!'

That could be dealt with. He snatched up the poker as the

boa-thing, still swaying the head which was no head, kept pouring steadily out from under the lifted yellow frill, until quite three feet were clear of the bed. Then he fell upon it furiously, with blow after blow.

But they had no effect on the furry, spineless thing; it merely gave under them and rippled up in another place. Augustine hit the bed, the floor; at last, really screaming, he threw down his weapon and fell upon the thick, hairy rope with both hands, crushing it together into a mass – there was little if any resistance in it – hurled it into the fire and, panting, kept it down with shovel and tongs. The flames licked up instantly and, with a roar, made short work of it, though there seemed to be some slight effort to escape, which was perhaps only the effect of the heat. A moment later there was a very strong smell of burnt hair, and that was all.

Augustine Marchant seized the fallen flask of Tokay and drained from its mouth what little was left in the bottom ere, staggering to the bed, he flung himself upon it and buried his face in the pillows, even heaping them over his head as if he could thus stifle the memory of what he had seen.

✶

He kept his bed next morning; the supposed cold afforded a good pretext. Long before the maid came in to re-lay the fire he had crawled out to make sure that there were no traces left of … what he had burnt there. There were none. A nightmare could not have left a trace, he told himself. But well he knew that it was not a nightmare.

And now he could think of nothing but that room in Prague and the long fur boa of the woman. Some department of his mind (he supposed) must have projected that thing, scarcely noticed at the time, scarcely remembered, into the present and the here. It was terrible to think that one's mind possessed such dark, unknown powers. But not so terrible as if the ... apparition ... had been endowed with an entirely separate objective existence. In a day or two he would consult his doctor and ask him to give him a tonic.

But, expostulated an uncomfortably lucid part of his brain, you are trying to run with the hare and hunt with the hounds. Is it not better to believe that the thing *had* an objective existence, for you have burnt it to nothing? Well and good! But if it is merely a projection from your own mind, what is to prevent it from reappearing, like the phoenix, from ashes?

There seemed no answer to that, save in an attempt to persuade himself that he had been feverish last night. Work was the best antidote. So Augustine Marchant rose, and was surprised and delighted to find the atmosphere of his study unusually soothing and inspiring; and that day, against all expectation, *Salutation to All Unbeliefs* was completed by some stanzas with which he was not too ill-pleased. Realizing nevertheless that he should be glad of company that evening, he had earlier sent round a note to the local solicitor, a good fellow, to come and dine with him; played a game of billiards with the lawyer afterwards, and retired to bed after some vintage port and a good stiff whisky and soda with scarcely a thought of the visitant of the previous night.

He woke at that hour when the thrushes in early summer punctually greet the new day – three o'clock. They were greeting it even vociferously, and Augustine Marchant was annoyed with their enthusiasm. His golden damask window-curtains kept out all but a glimmer of the new day, yet as, lying upon his back, the poet opened his eyes for a moment, his only half-awakened sense of vision reported something swinging to and fro in the dimness like a pendulum of rope. It was indistinct, but seemed to be hanging from the tester of the bed. And, wide awake in an instant, with an unspeakable anguish of premonition tearing through him, he felt, next moment, a light thud on the coverlet about the level of his knees. Something had arrived on the bed …

And Augustine Marchant neither shrieked nor leapt from his bed; he could not. Yet, now that his eyes were grown used to the twilight of the room, he saw it clearly, the fur rope which he had burnt to extinction two nights ago, dark and shining as before, rippling with a gentle movement as it coiled itself neatly together in the place where it had struck the bed, and subsided there in a symmetrical round, with only that tapering end a little raised, and, as it were, looking at him – only, eyeless and featureless, it could not look. One thought of disgusted relief, that it was not at any rate going to attack him, and Augustine Marchant fainted.

Yet his swoon must have merged into sleep, for he woke in a more or less ordinary fashion to find his man placing his early tea-tray beside him and enquiring when he should draw his bath. There was nothing on the bed.

'I shall change my bedroom,' thought Augustine to himself, looking at the haggard, fallen-eyed man who faced him in the mirror as he shaved. 'No, better still, I will go away for a change. Then I shall not have these … dreams. I'll go to old Edgar Fortescue for a few days; he begged me again not long ago to come any time.'

So to the house of that old Maecenas he went. He was much too great a man now to be in need of Sir Edgar's patronage. It was homage which he received there, both from host and guests. The stay did much to soothe his scarified nerves. Unfortunately the last day undid the good of all the foregoing ones.

Sir Edgar possessed a pretty young wife – his third – and, among other charms in his place in Somerset, an apple orchard under-planted with flowers. And in the cool of the evening Augustine walked there with his host and hostess almost as if he were the Almighty with the dwellers in

Eden. Presently they sat down upon a rustic seat (but a very comfortable one) under the shade of the apple boughs, amid the incongruous but pleasant parterres.

'You have come at the wrong season for these apple-trees, Marchant,' observed Sir Edgar after a while, taking out his cigar. 'Blossom-time or apple-time – they are showy at either, in spite of the underplanting. – What is attracting you on that tree – a tit? We have all kinds here, pretty, destructive little beggars!'

'I did not know that I was looking … it's nothing … thinking of something else,' stammered the poet. Surely, surely he had been mistaken in thinking that he had seen a sinuous, dark, furry thing undulating like a caterpillar down the stem of that particular apple-tree at a few yards' distance?

Talk went on, even his own; there was safety in it. It was only the breeze which faintly rustled that bed of heliotrope behind the seat. Augustine wanted desperately to get up and leave the orchard, but neither Sir Edgar nor his wife seemed disposed to move, and so the poet remained at his end of the seat, his left hand playing nervously with a long bent of grass which had escaped the scythe.

All at once he felt a tickling sensation on the back of his hand, looked down and saw that featureless snout of fur protruding upwards from underneath the rustic bench, and sweeping itself backwards and forwards against his hand with a movement which was almost caressing. He was on his feet in a flash.

'Do you mind if I go in?' he asked abruptly. 'I'm not … feeling very well.'

✖

If the thing could follow him it was of no use to go away. He returned to Abbot's Medding looking so much the worse for his change of air that Burrows expressed a respectful hope that he was not indisposed. And almost the first thing that occurred, when Augustine sat down at his writing-table to attend to his correspondence, was the unwinding of itself from one of its curved legs of a soft, brown, oscillating serpent which slowly waved an end at him as if in welcome ...

In welcome, yes, that was it! The creature, incredible though it was, the creature seemed glad to see him! Standing at the other end of the room, his hands pressed over his eyes – for what was the use of attempting to hurt or destroy it? – Augustine Marchant thought shudderingly that, like a witch's cat, a 'familiar' would not, presumably, be ill disposed towards its master. Its master! Oh God!

The hysteria which he had been trying to keep down began to mount uncontrollably when, removing his hands, Augustine glanced again towards his writing-table, and saw that the boa had coiled itself in his chair and was sweeping its end to and fro over the back, somewhat in the way that a cat, purring meanwhile, rubs itself against furniture or a human leg in real or simulated affection.

'Oh, go, go away from there!' he suddenly screamed at it, advancing with outstretched hand. 'In the devil's name, get out!'

To his utter amazement, he was obeyed. The rhythmic movements ceased, the fur snake poured itself down out of the chair and writhed towards the door. Venturing back to his writing-table after a moment Augustine saw it coiled on the threshold, the blind end turned towards him as usual, as though watching. And he began to laugh. What would happen if he rang and someone came; would the opening door scrape it aside ... would it vanish? Had it, in short, an existence for anyone else but himself?

But he dared not make the experiment. He left the room by the French window, feeling that he could never enter the house again. And perhaps, had it not been for the horrible knowledge just acquired that it could follow him, he might easily have gone away for good from Abbot's Medding and all his treasures and comforts. But of what use would that be – and how should he account for so extraordinary an action? No; he must think and plan while he yet remained sane.

To what, then, could he have recourse? The black magic in which he had dabbled with such disastrous consequences might possibly help him. Left to himself he was but an amateur, but he had a number of books ... There was also that other realm whose boundaries sometimes marched side by side with magic – religion. But how could he pray to a Deity in whom he did not believe? Rather pray to the Evil which had sent this curse upon him to show him how to banish it. Yet since he had deliberately followed what religion stigmatised as sin, what even the world would label as lust and necromancy, supplication to the dark powers was not likely to deliver him from them. They must somehow be outwitted, circumvented.

He kept his *grimoires* and books of the kind in a locked bookcase in another room, not in his study; in that room he sat up till midnight. But the spells which he read were useless; moreover, he did not really believe in them. The irony of the situation was that, in a sense, he had only played at sorcery; it had but lent a spice to sensuality. He wandered wretchedly about the room dreading at any moment to see his 'familiar' wreathed round some object in it. At last he stopped at a small bookcase which held some old forgotten books of his mother's – Longfellow and Mrs Hemans, *John Halifax, Gentleman,* and a good many volumes of sermons and mild essays. And when he looked at that blameless assembly a cloud seemed to pass over Augustine Marchant's vision, and he saw his mother, gentle and lace-capped, as years and years ago she used to sit, hearing his lessons, in an antimacassared chair. She had been everything to him then, the little boy whose soul was not smirched. He called silently to her now: 'Mamma, Mamma, can't you help me? Can't you send this thing away?'

When the cloud had passed he found that he had stretched out his hand and removed a big book. Looking at it he saw that it was her Bible, with 'Sarah Amelia Marchant' on the faded yellow fly-leaf. Her spirit *was* going to help him! He turned over a page or two, and out of the largish print there sprang instantly at him: *Now the serpent was more subtle than any beast of the field.* Augustine shuddered and almost put the Bible back, but the conviction that there was help there urged him to go on. He turned a few more pages of Genesis and his eyes were caught by this verse, which he had never seen before in his life.

'And if thou doest well, shalt thou not be accepted? And if thou doest not well, sin lieth at the door. And unto thee shall be his desire, and thou shalt rule over him.'

What strange words! What could they possibly mean? Was there light for him in them? 'Unto thee shall be his desire.' That Thing, the loathsome semblance of affection which hung about it ... 'Thou shalt rule over him.' It *had* obeyed him, up to a point ... Was this Book, of all others, showing him the way to be free? But the meaning of the verse was so obscure! He had not, naturally, such a thing as a commentary in the house. Yet, when he came to think of it, he remembered that some pious and anonymous person, soon after the publication of *Pomegranates of Sin*, had sent him a Bible in the Revised Version, with an inscription recommending him to read it. He had it somewhere, though he had always meant to get rid of it.

After twenty minutes' search through the sleeping house he found it in one of the spare bedrooms. But it gave him little enlightenment, for there was scant difference in the rendering, save that for, 'lieth at the door', this version had, 'coucheth', and that the margin held an alternative translation for the end of the verse: 'And unto thee is its desire, but thou shouldest rule over it'.

Nevertheless, Augustine Marchant stood after midnight in this silent, sheeted guest-chamber repeating: *'But thou shouldest rule over it.'*

And all at once he thought of a way of escape.

II

It was going to be a marvellous experience, staying with Augustine Marchant. Sometimes Lawrence Storey hoped there would be no other guests at Abbot's Medding; at other times he hoped there would be. A *tête-à-tête* of four days with the great poet – could he sustain his share worthily? For Lawrence, despite the remarkable artistic gifts which were finding their first real flowering in these illustrations to Augustine's poem, was still unspoilt, still capable of wonder and admiration, still humble and almost naïf. It was still astonishing to him that he, an architect's assistant, should have been snatched away, as Ganymede by the eagle, from the lower world of elevations and drains to serve on Olympus. It was not, indeed, Augustine Marchant who had first discovered him; but it was Augustine Marchant who was going to make him famous.

The telegraph-poles flitted past the second-class carriage window and more than one traveller glanced with a certain envy and admiration at the fair, good-looking young man who diffused such an impression of happiness and candour,

and had such a charming smile on his boyish lips. He
carried with him a portfolio which he never let out of reach
of his hand; the oldish couple opposite, speculating upon its
contents, might have changed their opinion of him had they
seen them.

But no shadow of the dark weariness of things unlawful
rested on Lawrence Storey; to know Augustine Marchant, to
be illustrating his great poem, to have learnt from him that
art and morality had no kinship, this was to plunge into a
new realm of freedom and enlarging experience. Augustine
Marchant's poetry, he felt, had already taught his hand what
his brain and heart knew nothing of.

There was a dog-cart to meet him at the station, and in the
scented June evening he was driven with a beating heart past
meadows and hayfields to his destination.

Mr Marchant, awaiting him in the hall, was at his most
charming. 'My dear fellow, are those the drawings? Come,
let us lock them away at once in my safe! If you had brought
me diamonds I should not be one quarter so concerned about
thieves. And did you have a comfortable journey? I have had
you put in the orange room; it is next to mine. There is no one
else staying here, but there are a few people coming to dinner
to meet you.'

There was only just time to dress for dinner, so that Lawrence
did not get an opportunity to study his host until he saw him
seated at the head of the table. Then he was immediately
struck by the fact that he looked curiously ill. His face –
ordinarily by no means attenuated – seemed to have fallen
in, there were dark circles under his eyes, and the perturbed
Lawrence, observing him as the meal progressed, thought
that his manner, too, seemed strange and once or twice quite
absent-minded. And there was one moment when, though
the lady on his right was addressing him, he sharply turned

his head away and looked down at the side of his chair just as if he saw something on the floor. Then he apologised, saying that he had a horror of cats, and that sometimes the tiresome animal from the stables ... But after that he continued to entertain his guests in his own inimitable way, and, even to the shy Lawrence, the evening proved very pleasant.

The three ensuing days were wonderful and exciting to the young artist – days of uninterrupted contact with a master mind which acknowledged, as the poet himself admitted, none of the petty barriers which man, for his own convenience, had set up between alleged right and wrong. Lawrence had learnt why his host did not look well; it was loss of sleep, the price exacted by inspiration. He had a new poetic drama shaping in his mind which would scale heights that he had not yet attempted.

There was almost a touch of fever in the young man's dreams to-night – his last night but one. He had several. First he was standing by the edge of a sort of mere, inexpressibly desolate and unfriendly, a place he had never seen in his life, which yet seemed in some way familiar; and something said to him: 'You will never go away from here!' He was alarmed, and woke, but went to sleep again almost immediately, and this time was back, oddly enough, in the church where in his earliest years he had been taken to service by the aunt who had brought him up – a large church full of pitch-pine pews with narrow ledges for hymn-books, which ledges he used surreptitiously to lick during the long dull periods of occultation upon his knees. But most of all he remembered the window with Adam and Eve in the Garden of Eden, on either side of an apple-tree round whose trunk was coiled a monstrous snake with a semi-human head. Lawrence had hated and dreaded that window, and because of it he would never go near an orchard and had no temptation to steal apples ... Now he was back in that church again, staring at the window, lit up with some infernal glow from behind. He woke again, little short of terrified – he, a grown man! But again he went to sleep quite quickly.

His third dream had for background, as sometimes happens in nightmares, the very room in which he lay. He dreamt that a door opened in the wall, and in the door-way, quite plain against the light from another room behind him, stood Augustine Marchant in his dressing-gown. He was looking down at something on the ground which Lawrence did not see, but his hand was pointing at Lawrence in the bed, and he was saying in a voice of command: 'Go to him, do you hear? Go to him! Go to *him!* Am I not your master?' And Lawrence, who could neither move nor utter a syllable, wondered uneasily what this could be which was thus commanded, but his attention was chiefly focused on Augustine Marchant's face. After he had said these words several times, and apparently without result, a dreadful change came upon it, a look of the most unutterable despair. It seemed visibly to age and wither; he said, in a loud, penetrating whisper: 'Is there no escape then?' covered his ravaged face a moment with his hands, and then went back and softly closed the door. At that Lawrence woke; but in the morning he had forgotten all three dreams.

The *tête-à-tête* dinner on the last night of his stay would have lingered in a gourmet's memory, so that it was a pity the young man did not know in the least what he was eating. At last there was happening what he had scarcely dared hope for; the great poet of the sensuous was revealing to him some of the unimaginably strange and secret sources of his inspiration. In the shaded rosy candle-light, his elbows on the table among trails of flowers he, who was not even a neophyte, listened like a man learning for the first time of some spell of spring which will make him more than mortal.

'Yes,' said Augustine Marchant, after a long pause, 'yes, it was a marvellous, an undying experience … one that is not given to many. It opened doors, it – but I despair of doing it justice in mere words.' His look was transfigured, almost dreamy.

'But she ... the woman ... how did you ...?' asked Lawrence Storey in a hushed voice.

'Oh, the woman?' said Augustine, suddenly finishing off his wine. 'The woman was only a common street-walker.'

A moment or two later Lawrence was looking at his host wonderingly and wistfully. 'But this was in Prague. Prague is a long way off.'

'One does not need to go so far, in reality. Even in Paris –'

'One could ... have that experience in Paris?'

'If you knew where to go. And, of course, it is necessary to have credentials. I mean that – like all such enlightenments – it has to be kept secret, most secret, from the vulgar minds who lay their restrictions on the finer. That is self-evident.'

'Of course,' said the young man, and sighed deeply. His host looked at him affectionately.

'You, my dear Lawrence – I may call you Lawrence? – want just that touch of ... what shall I call them – *les choses cachées* – to liberate your immense artistic gifts from the shackles which still bind them. Through that gateway you would find the possibility of their full fruition! It would fertilize your genius to a still finer blossoming ... But you would have scruples ... and you are very young.'

'You know,' said Lawrence in a low and trembling tone, 'what I feel about your poetry. You know how I ache to lay the best that is in me at your feet. If only I could make my drawings for the Two Queens more worthy – already it is an honour which overwhelms me that you should have selected me to do them – but they are not what they should be. I am *not* sufficiently liberated ...'

Augustine leant forward on the flower-decked table. His eyes were glowing.

'Do you truly desire to be?'

The young man nodded, too full of emotion to find his voice.

The poet got up, went over to a cabinet in a corner and unlocked it. Lawrence watched his fine figure in a sort of trance. Then he half-rose with an exclamation.

'What is it?' asked Augustine very sharply, facing round.

'Oh, nothing, sir – only that I believe you hate cats, and I thought I saw one, or rather its tail, disappearing into that corner.'

'There's no cat here,' said Augustine quickly. His face had become all shiny and mottled, but Lawrence did not notice it. The poet stood a moment looking at the carpet; one might almost have thought that he was gathering resolution to cross it; then he came swiftly back to the table.

'Sit down again,' he commanded. 'Have you a pocket-book with you, a pocket-book which you never leave about? Good! Then write *this* in one place; and *this* on another page ... write it small ... among other entries is best ... not on a blank page ... write it in Greek characters if you know them ...'

'What ... what is it?' asked Lawrence, all at once intolerably excited, his eyes fixed on the piece of paper in Augustine's hand.

'The two halves of the address in Paris.'

III

Augustine Marchant kept a diary in those days, a locked diary written in cipher. And for more than a month after Lawrence Storey's visit the tenor of the entries there was almost identical: 'No change ... Always with me ... How much longer can I endure it? The alteration in my looks is being remarked upon to my face. I shall have to get rid of Thornton [his man] on some pretext or other, for I begin to

think that he has seen It. No wonder, since It follows me
about like a dog. When It is visible to everyone it will be the
end … I found It in bed with me this morning, pressed up
against me as if for warmth …'

But there was a different class of entry also, appearing at
intervals with an ever-increasing note of impatience. 'Will
LS go there? … When shall I hear from LS? … Will the
experiment do what I think? It is my last hope.'

Then, suddenly, after five weeks had elapsed, an entry in a
trembling hand: 'For twenty-four hours I have seen no sign
of It! Can it be possible?'

And next day: 'Still nothing. I begin to live again – This
evening has come an ecstatic letter from LS, from Paris,
telling me that he had 'presented his credentials' and was
to have the experience next day. He has had it by now – by
yesterday, in fact. Have I really freed myself? It looks like it!'

In one week from the date of that last entry it was remarked
in Abbot's Medding how much better Mr Marchant was
looking again. Of late he had not seemed at all himself; his
cheeks had fallen in, his clothes seemed to hang loosely upon
him, who had generally filled them so well, and he appeared
nervous. Now he was as before, cheery, courtly, debonair.
And last Sunday, will you believe it, he went to church! The
Rector was so astonished when he first became aware of him
from the pulpit that he nearly forgot to give out his text. And
the poet joined in the hymns, too! Several observed this
amazing phenomenon.

It was the day after this unwonted appearance at St Peter's.
Augustine was strolling in his garden. The air had a new
savour, the sun a new light; he could look again with pleasure
at Thetis and her nymphs of the fountain, could work
undisturbed in the summer-house. Free, free! All the world
was good to the senses once again, and the hues and scents
of early autumn better, in truth, than the brilliance of that

summer month which had seen his curse descend upon him.

The butler brought him out a letter with a French stamp. From Lawrence Storey, of course; to tell him – what? Where had he caught his first glimpse of it? In one of those oppressively furnished French bedrooms? And how had he taken it?

At first, however, Augustine was not sure that the letter was from Storey. The writing was very different, cramped instead of flowing, and, in places, spluttering, the pen having dug into the paper as if the hand which held it had not been entirely under control – almost, thought Augustine, his eyes shining with excitement, almost as though something had been twined, liana-like, round the wrist. (He had a sudden sick recollection of a day when that had happened to him, quickly submerged in a gush of eager anticipation.) Sitting down upon the edge of the fountain he read – not quite what he had looked for.

'I don't know what is happening to me,' began the letter, without other opening. 'Yesterday I was in a café by myself, and had just ordered some absinthe – though I do not like it. And quite suddenly, although I knew that I was in the café, I realized that I was also back in *that room*. I could see every feature of it, but I could see the café too, with all the people in it; the one was, as it were, superimposed upon the other, the room, which was a good deal smaller than the café, being inside the latter, as a box may be within a larger box. And all the while the room was growing clearer, the café fading. I saw the glass of absinthe suddenly standing on nothing, as it were. All the furniture of the room, all the accessories you know of, were mixed up with the chairs and tables of the café. I do not know how I managed to find my way to the *comptoir*, pay and get out. I took a *fiacre* back to my hotel. By the time I arrived there I was all right. I suppose that it was only the after effects of a very strange and violent emotional experience. But I hope to God that it will not recur!'

'How interesting!' said Augustine Marchant, dabbling his hand in the swirling water where he had once drowned a piece of dark fluff. 'And why indeed should I have expected that It would couch at his door in the same form as at mine?'

Four days more of new-found peace and he was reading this: 'In God's name – or the Devil's – come over and help me! I have hardly an hour now by night or day when I am sure of my whereabouts. I could not risk the journey back to England alone. It is like being imprisoned in some kind of infernal half-transparent box, always growing a little smaller. Wherever I go now I carry it about with me; when I am in the street I hardly know which is the pavement and which is the roadway, because I am always treading on that black carpet with the cabalistic designs; if I speak to anyone they may suddenly disappear from sight. To attempt to work is naturally useless. I would consult a doctor, but that would mean telling him everything ...'

'I hope to God he won't do that!' muttered Augustine uneasily. 'He can't – he swore to absolute secrecy. I hadn't bargained, however, for his ceasing work. Suppose he finds himself unable to complete the designs for *Theodora and Marozia*! That would be serious ... However, to have freed myself is worth *any* sacrifice ... But Storey cannot, obviously, go on living indefinitely on two planes at once ... Artistically, though, it might inspire him to something quite unprecedented. I'll write to him and point that out; it might encourage him. But go near him in person – is it likely!'

The next day was one of great literary activity. Augustine was so deeply immersed in his new poetical drama that he neglected his correspondence and almost his meals – except his dinner, which seemed that evening to be shared most agreeably and excitingly by these new creations of his brain. Such, in fact, was his preoccupation with them that it was not until he had finished the savoury and poured out a glass of his superlative port that he remembered a telegram which had been handed to him as he came in to dinner. It still lay unopened by his plate. Now, tearing apart the envelope, he read with growing bewilderment these words above his publishers' names:

'Please inform us immediately what steps to take are prepared send to France recover drawings if possible what suggestions can you make as to successor Rossell and Ward.'

Augustine was more than bewildered; he was stupefied. Had some accident befallen Lawrence Storey of which he knew nothing? But he had opened all his letters this morning, though he had not answered any. A prey to a sudden very nasty anxiety he got up and rang the bell.

'Burrows, bring me *The Times* from the library.'

The newspaper came, unopened. Augustine, now in a frenzy of uneasiness, scanned the pages rapidly. But it was some seconds before he came upon the headline: 'Tragic Death of a Young English Artist,' and read the following, furnished by the Paris correspondent:

'Connoisseurs who were looking forward to the appearance of the superb illustrated edition of Mr Augustine Marchant's *Queen Theodora and Queen Marozia* will learn with great regret of the death by drowning of the gifted young artist, Mr Lawrence Storey, who was engaged upon the designs for it. Mr Storey had recently been staying in Paris, but left one day last week for a remote spot in Brittany, it was supposed in pursuance of his work. On Friday last his body was discovered floating in a lonely pool near Carhaix. It is hard to see how Mr Storey could have fallen in, since this piece of water – the Mare de Plougouven – has a completely level shore surrounded by reeds, and is not in itself very deep, nor is there any boat upon it. It is said that the unfortunate young Englishman had been somewhat strange in his manner recently and complained of hallucinations; it is therefore possible that under their influence he deliberately waded out into the Mare de Plougouven. A strange feature of the case is that he had fastened round him under his coat the finished drawings for Mr Marchant's book, which were, of course, completely spoilt by the water before the body was found. It is to be hoped that they were not the only –'

Augustine threw *The Times* furiously from him and struck the dinner-table with his clenched fist.

'Upon my soul, that is too much! It is criminal! My property – and I who had done so much for him! Fastened them round himself – he must have been crazy!'

But had he been so crazy? When his wrath had subsided a little, Augustine could not but ask himself whether the young artist had not in some awful moment of insight guessed the truth, or a part of it that his patron had deliberately corrupted him? It looked almost like it. But, if he had really taken all the finished drawings with him to this place in Brittany, what an unspeakably mean trick of revenge thus to destroy them! … Yet, even if it were so, their loss must be regarded as the price of deliverance, since, from his point of view, the desperate expedient of passing on his 'familiar' had been a complete success. By getting someone else to plunge even deeper than he had done into the unlawful (for he had seen to it that Lawrence Storey should do that) he had proved, as that verse in Genesis said, that he *had* rule over … what had pursued him in tangible form as a consequence of his own night in Prague. He could not be too thankful. The literary world might well be thankful too. For his own art was of infinitely more importance than the subservient, the parasitic art of an illustrator. He could with a little search find half a dozen just as gifted as that poor hallucination-ridden Storey to finish *Theodora and Marozia* – even, if necessary, to begin an entirely fresh set of drawings. And meanwhile, in the new lease of creative energy which this unfortunate but necessary sacrifice had made possible for him, he would begin to put on paper the masterpiece which was now taking brilliant shape in his liberated mind. A final glass, and then an evening in the workshop!

Augustine poured out some port, and was raising the glass, prepared to drink to his own success, when he thought he heard a sound near the door. He looked over his shoulder. Next instant the stem of the wineglass had snapped in his hand, and he had sprung back to the farthest limit of the room.

Reared up for quite five feet against the door, huge, dark, sleeked with wet and flecked with bits of green waterweed, was something half-python, half gigantic cobra, its head drawn back as if to strike – its head, for in its former featureless tapering end were now two reddish eyes, such as furriers put into the heads of stuffed creatures. And these eyes were fixed upon him in an unwavering and malevolent glare.

13 With and Without Buttons

BY MARY BUTTS

It is not only true, it is comforting, to say that incredulity is often no more than superstition turned inside out. But there can be a faith of disbelief as inaccurate as its excess, and in some ways more trying, for the right answers to it have not yet been thought up. It was only because Trenchard said at lunch that the Mass was a dramatized wish-fulfilment that what came after ever happened. At least I wish we did not think so. It was trying to get out anyhow, but if he had not irritated us and made us want to show off, we would not have made ourselves serviceable to it. And it was we who came off lightly. To him it has been something that he has not been able to shake off. When it happened he behaved so well about it, but that didn't save him. Now he cannot think what he used to think, and he does not know what else there is that he might think.

I am seeing him now, more vividly than I like. He was our next-door neighbour in a remote village in Kent. A nest of wasps had divided their attention between us, and we had met after sunset to return their calls with cyanide and squibs.

He was a sanguine man, positive, hearty, actually emotional. He had known and done a great many things, but when he came to give his account of them, all he had to say was a set of pseudo-rationalizations, calling the bluff, in inaccurate language, of God, the arts, the imagination, the emotions. That is not even chic science for laymen today. He might have thought that way as much as he liked, but there was no reason, we said, to try and prove it to us all one hot, sweet, blue-drawn summer, in a Kentish orchard; to sweat for our conversion; to shame us into agreement. Until the evening

I told him to stop boring us with his wish-fulfilments, for they weren't ours, and saw his healthy skin start to sweat and a stare come into his eyes. That ought to have warned me, as it did my sister, of whom I am sometimes afraid. It did warn us, but it wound us up also. We went home through the orchard in the starlight and sat downstairs in the midsummer night between lit candles, inviting in all that composed it, night hunting cries and scents of things that grow and ripen, cooled in the star-flow. A world visible, but not in terms of colour. With every door and every window open, the old house was no more than a frame, a set of screens to display night, midsummer, perfume, the threaded stillness, the stars strung together, their spears glancing, penetrating an earth breathing silently, a female power asleep.

'All he hears is nature snoring,' said my sister. 'Let's give him a nightmare.' It was a good idea.

'How?' I said.

'We'll find out tomorrow. I can feel one about.'

I got up to close the doors before we mounted with our candles. Through walls and glass, through open doors or shut, a tide poured in, not of air or any light or dark or scent or sound or heat or coolness. Tide. Without distinction from north or south or without or within; without flow or ebb, a Becoming; without stir or departure or stay: without radiance or pace. Star-tide. Has not Science had wind of rays poured in from interstellar space?

There is no kind of ill-doing more fascinating than one which has a moral object, a result in view which will justify the means without taking the fun out of them. All that is implied when one says that one will give someone something to cry about. It was that line which we took at breakfast.

'We'll try this simple faith,' we said. 'We'll scare him stiff and see how he stands the strain. We'll haunt him.' And asked each other if either of us knew of a practising vampire in the neighbourhood or a were-cow.

It was several days before we hit on a suitable technique, examining and rejecting every known variety of apparition, realizing that apparatus must be reduced to a minimum, and that when nothing will bear scrutiny, there must be very little given to scrutinize. In fact, what we meant to do was to suggest him into an experience – the worse the better – wholly incompatible with the incredulities of his faith. That it would be easy to do, we guessed; that it would be dangerous to him – that appeared at the moment as part of the fun. Not because we did not like him, because we wanted to have power over him, the power women sometimes want to have over men, the pure, not erotic power, whose point is that it shall have nothing to do with sex. We could have made him make love, to either or both of us, any day of the week.

This is what we planned, understanding that, like a work of art, once it had started, its development could be left to look after itself.

'Suppose,' said my sister, 'that we have heard a ridiculous superstition in the village that there is Something Wrong with the house. We will tell him that, and when he has gone through his reaction exercises – it may take a day or so and will depend on our hints, and if we make the right ones, the battle's won – he will ask us what the story is?'

'What is it to be?' I said, who can rarely attain to my sister's breadth of mind.

'That does not matter. Because before we begin we'll *do* something. Anything. A last year's leaf for a start, so long as it can go into a series – on his blotter or his pillow. We're always in and out. We'll put them there and get asked round for the evening and start when we see one, and that's where our village story begins. All that he has to get out of us is that there *is* a story, and that wet leaves or whatever it is we choose are found about. Signatures, you know. If he doesn't rise the first night, he'll find that leaf when he goes to bed. It depends on how well we do it –'

I recognized a master's direction, but it all seemed to depend on our choice of stimulants. Last year's leaves, delicate damp articulations; coloured pebbles, dead flies, scraps of torn paper with half a word decipherable ... A mixture of these or a selection?

'Keep it tangible,' my sister said – 'that's the way. Our only difficulty is the planting of them.'

'Which,' I asked, 'are suitable to what?'

It seemed to be necessary in laying our train to determine the kind of unpleasantness for which they were ominous. But I could not get my sister to attend.

'It's not that way round,' she said at length – 'dead bees, feathers, drops of candle-grease? Old kid gloves? With and Without Buttons. That will do.'

I felt a trifle queer. 'Well,' I said, 'they're the sort of things a man never has in his house, so that's sound so far. But women do. Not the sort of things we wear, but he'd not know that. And how do we get hold of them?'

'There's a shoe-box in the loft full of them, by the door into his place when these houses were one.' (Our cottages were very old, side by side, with a common wall, our orchards divided by a hedge.) We had rented ours from a friend who had recently bought it as it stood from a local family which had died out, and of which very little seemed known. My sister said:

'Shiny black kid and brown, with little white glass buttons and cross stitching and braid. All one size, and I suppose for one pair of hands. Some have all the buttons and some have none and some have some –' I listened to this rune until I was not sure how many times my sister had said it.

'With and without buttons,' I repeated, and could not remember how often I had said that.

After that we said nothing more about it, and it was three days later that he asked us to supper, and we walked round through the gap in the hedge in the pure daylight, and sat in his little verandah, whose wooden pillars spread as they met the roof in fans of plaited green laths. Prim fantasy, with its French windows behind it, knocked out of walls of flint rubble three feet thick. Roses trailed up it. A tidy little home, with something behind it of monstrous old age one did as well to forget.

'By the way,' he said. (As I have said before, his name was Trenchard, and he had come back to his own part of England to rest, after a long time spent in looking after something in East Africa.) 'By the way, have either of you two lost a glove?'

'So she's got busy already and didn't tell me, the spoilsport,' I thought.

'No,' we said, 'but one always does. What sort of a glove?'

'A funny little thing of brown kid with no buttons. I didn't think it could be yours. I found it on the top of the loft stairs. Outside the door. Here it is.' He went inside and came out on to the verandah where we were having supper, a moment later, puzzled.

'Here it is,' he said. 'I put it in the bureau, and the odd thing is that when I went to look for it I found another. Not its pair either. This one's black.'

Two little ladylike shiny kid gloves, the kind worn by one's aunts when one was a child. I had not yet seen our collection. The black had three of its buttons missing. We told him that they were not the kind that women wore now.

'My landlady bought the place unfurnished,' he said. 'Must have come out of the things the old owners left behind when they died.' My sister gave a slight start, a slight frown and bit her lip. I shook my head at her.

'What's up?' he asked, simply.

'Nothing,' we said.

'I'm not going to be laughed at by you,' said my sister.

'I'm not laughing,' he said, his goodwill beaming at us, prepared even to be tolerant.

'Oh, but you'd have the right to –'

After that, he wanted to know at once.

'It's playing into your hands,' she said, 'but don't you know that your half of the house is the Village Haunt? And that it's all about gloves? With and without buttons?'

It was ridiculously easy. He was amiable rather than irritated at her story, while I was still hurt that she had not first rehearsed it with me. She began to tell him a story about old Miss Blacken, who had lived here with her brother, a musty old maid in horrible clothes, but nice about her hands; and how there was something – no, not a ghost – but something which happened that was always preceded by gloves being found about. This we told him and he behaved very prettily about it, sparing us a lecture.

'But it's not quite fair,' he said. 'I mustn't be selfish. She must leave some at your place. Remember, in her day, it was all one house.'

Then we talked about other things, but when we had gone home I found my sister a little pensive. I began on my grievance.

'Why didn't you tell me you had begun? Why didn't you coach me?'

Then she said: 'To tell you the truth, I hadn't meant to begin. What I said I made up on the spot. All I'd done was that just before we left I ran up to the loft and snatched a glove from the box and left it on his bureau. That's the second one he found.'

'Then what about the one he found outside the loft door?'

'It's that that's odd. That's why he never thought it was us. I haven't had a chance to get to that part of his house. I didn't put it there.'

✕

Well, now that the affair was launched, we felt it had better go on. Though I am not sure if we were quite so keen about it. It was as though – and we had known this to be possible before – it had already started itself. One sometimes feels this has happened. Anyhow, it was two days later before I thought it was my turn to lay a glove on his premises, and went up to our loft and took one out of the box. There was nothing in it but gloves. I took a white one, a little cracked, with only two buttons, and having made sure he was out, slipped through the hedge and dropped it at the foot of the stair. He startled me considerably by returning at that instant. I said I had come for a book. He saw the thing.

'Hallo,' he said, 'there's another. It's beginning. That makes four.'

'Four?' I said. 'There were only two the other night.'

'I found one in my bedroom. A grey. Are we never going to get a pair?'

Then it occurred to me that he'd seen through us all along, and was getting in ahead with gloves. I took my book and returned to my sister.

'That won't do,' she said, 'he's sharp, but we didn't begin it. He found his first.'

I said: 'I'm beginning to wonder if it mightn't be a good thing to find out in the village if anything is known about Miss Blacken and her brother.'

'You go,' said my sister, still pensive.

I went to the pub when it opened and drew blank. I heard about diseases of bees and chickens and the neighbours. The Post Office was no good. I was returning by a detour, along a remote lane, when a voice said:

'You *were* asking about Miss Blacken along at Stone Cottages?'

It was only a keeper who had been in the pub, come up suddenly through a gate, out of a dark fir planting. ' – Seeing as you have the uses of her furniture,' said he. We passed into step. I learned that after fifty years' odd residence in the place there was nothing that you might have to tell about her and waited.

' – Now her brother, he was not what you might call ordinary.' Again that stopped at that.

' – Regular old maid she was. If maid she'd ever been. Not that you could be saying regular old man for him, for he wasn't either, if you take my meaning, Miss.'

I did. Finally I learned – and I am not quite sure how I learned – it was certainly not all by direct statement – that Miss Blacken had been a little grey creature, who had never seemed naturally to be living or dying; whose clothes were little bits and pieces, as you might say. Anyhow, she'd dropped something – an excuse me, Miss, petticoat, his wife had said – on the green, and run away without stopping to pick it up, opening and shutting her mouth. It was then it had begun. If you could call *that* beginning. I was asking to know what that was? In a manner of speaking he couldn't rightly say. It was the women took it to heart. What became of the petticoat? That was the meaning of it. 'Twasn't rightly speaking a petticoat at all. There weren't no wind, and when they came to pick it up, it upped and sailed as if there were a gale of wind behind it, right out of sight along the sky. And one day it had come back; hung down from the top of an elm and waved at them, and the women had it there were holes in it, like a face. And no wonder, seeing it had passed half a winter blowing about in the tops of the trees. Did it never come down to earth? Not it they said. Nor old Miss Blacken start to look for it, except that it was then that people remembered her about at nights.

A little pensive now myself, I asked about gloves and was told and no more than that 'they say that she's left her gloves about.'

I returned to my sister and we spent the evening doing a reconstruction of Miss Blacken out of Victorian oddments. It was most amusing and not in the least convincing.

'Tomorrow, shall we feed him a glove?' I said. It was then that it came across our minds, like a full statement to that effect, that it was no longer necessary. The gloves would feed themselves.

'I know what it is we've done,' said my sister, 'we've wound it up.'

'Wound up what?' I answered. 'Ghost of a village eccentric, who was careful about her hands?'

'Oh no,' said my sister. 'I don't know. Oh no.'

✖

After another three days, I said:

'Nothing more has happened over there. I mean he's found no more gloves. Hadn't we better help things along a bit?'

'There was one yesterday in my room, unbuttoned,' she said. 'I didn't drop it.'

I was seriously annoyed. This seemed to be going too far. And in what direction? What does one do when this sort of thing happens? I was looking as one does when one has heard one's best friend talking about oneself, when the shadow of a heavy man fell across our floor. It was Trenchard. My sister looked up and said quickly:

'I've found one now.'

'Have you?' he said. 'So have I.' He hesitated. There was something very direct and somehow comforting in the way he was taking it, piece by piece as it happened, not as what he would think it ought to mean. It was then that we began to be ashamed of ourselves. He went on:

'You know my cat. She's her kittens hidden somewhere in the loft and I wanted to have a look at them. I went up softly not to scare her. You know it's dark on that top stair. I got there, and then I heard – well – a little thing falling off a step. Thought it was a kitten trying to explore. Peered and felt and picked up a glove.'

He pulled it out of his pocket and held it up by a finger with slight distaste. A brown one this time.

'One button,' he said. 'The kittens aren't big enough to have been playing with it and the cat wasn't about. There's no draught. Funny, isn't it? Reminded me of one of those humpty-dumpty toys we had, a little silk man with arms and legs and a painted face, and a loose marble inside him to make him turn over and fall about.'

My sister said:

'We've found a box of loose gloves in our attic close to your bricked-up door.'

His answer was that it was bricked up all right, and had we thought to count them in case either of our maids was up to some village trick. We hadn't, but I noticed that he mistrusted our maids as little as we did. Also that his behaviour was so reasonable because he had not yet thought that there was any cause for suspicion.

'Let's do it now,' he said. 'Put them all back, yours and mine. Count them and lock your door.'

He went back and fetched his five, and together we went upstairs. They sat on a basket trunk while I emptied the box.

'Twenty-seven. Eleven pairs in all and one missing.' I shovelled them back into the cardboard box, yellow with time and dust. I looked up at his broad straight nose and my sister's little one that turns up. Both were sniffing.

'There's a smell here,' they said. There was. Not the dust-camphor-mouse-and-apple smell proper to lofts.

'I know what it is,' Trenchard said, 'I smelt it in Africa in a damp place. Bad skins.'

The loft went suddenly darker. We looked up. There was no window, but someone had cut the thatch and let in a skylight.

Something was covering it, had suddenly blown across it, though outside there was no wind. I took the iron handle with holes in it to stick through the pin in the frame, and threw it up. The piece of stuff slid backwards into the thatch. I put my arm out, caught hold of it and pulled it in. A piece of calico with a stiff waxy surface, once used for linings, again some time ago. It seemed to have no shape, but there were holes in it. Holes not tears.

'Nasty slummy rag,' I said. 'I suppose it was lying about in the thatch.'

Our thatch was old and full of flowers. This thing went with dustbins and tin cans. One piece was clotted together. A large spider ran out of it. I dropped it on the floor beside the box and the gloves. I was surprised to see Trenchard look at it with disgust.

'Never could stand oooing things go bad,' he said. We left the attic, locking the door and went downstairs. We gave him the key. It seemed the decent thing to do.

Over a late and thoughtful tea, we talked of other things. We did not think it necessary to tell him what the keeper had said.

※

The evening was exquisite and the next day and the next night. Days refreshed with night-showers to draw out scent, and steady sun to ripen; a pattern on the world like the dry dew on a moth's wing, or the skin on a grape or a rose. And nothing more happened. The next evening Trenchard was to give a little party for his birthday, for some friends who would motor over; and my sister and I were to see that all was in order for it, flowers and fruit and wine and all the good cold things to eat. We had the delicate pleasant things to do; to slice the cucumbers and drench sprays of borage and balm-in-Gilead for the iced drinks. The almonds did not come, so we salted some ourselves, blanching them in the garden, getting hot in the kitchen over pans of burnt salt.

At about six o'clock we went back to dress. Trying, as was appropriate, to look like Paris, in compliment to Trenchard, but principally to the garden and to the weather and to the earth. There was a bump overhead from the attic.

'What's that?' said my sister, painting her face.

'I left the skylight open,' I said. 'It must have slipped. Let's leave it. Am I in a state of dress or undress to go up there?'

She was ready before I was, and said that she was going across to Trenchard's to have one more look to see if all was in order there. Half of our day's work had been to keep him out of the way. We had just sent him up to the village after more strawberries and hoped that he would be back in time – and there was still plenty of time – for him to dress. As she went, I heard his step at his front door, and a few moments later, my dressing finished, I went downstairs and out across the orchard to join them. He had gone upstairs to change, but just as I reached the verandah, I heard a short cry which must have come from him. I ran in with my sister, who was also outside, building a last pyramid of strawberries on a dish shaped like a green leaf. He came out of the dining room.

'Who's done this?' he said.

The supper table was set with food to be fetched and eaten when people pleased. There were little bowls of cut-glass set with sweets and almonds. One of these had been sprinkled with buttons, little white buttons that had been torn off, still ragged with red-brown threads.

'I filled it,' said my sister in a small weak voice, 'with those sugar rose leaves, and a real one on top.'

'Your servant –' I began, when he cried out again:

'What's that glove doing up the back of your dress?'

It was a little silver coat I had on to begin with. I pulled it off, and there fell off the collar, but with a tiny thud, another glove, a black one. It had no buttons on it and was open like a hand. Trenchard picked it up, and I thought I saw it collapse a little.

'No time to count them tonight,' he said, and looked round. It was too hot for a fire, but they were laid in all the rooms. He put the glove down and struck a match. The huge chimney used to roar with its draught, but the fire would not catch. He went out to the lavatory with the glove and the dish.

'Go up and dress,' we said when he came back; but instead he sniffed.

'It's what we smelt the other day,' he said. 'Up in the loft. Dead skin.'

Outside the air was hot and sweet and laced with coolness, but we noticed that here indoors it was cold, stale cold.

'Go and dress,' we said again, with the female instinct to keep the minutiae of things steady and in sequence.

'They won't be here till eight: there's plenty of time,' he said, feeling not fear or even much curiosity, but that it was not the proper thing to leave us alone with the inexplicable unpleasant.

'Your servant,' I began again.

'My servant's all right,' he said. 'Go out and wait in the verandah. I'll be down quickly.'

So he went up. We took a chair and sat each side of the open glass doors where we could see into the house. We remembered that his maid as well as ours had gone back to her cottage to get ready for company. So there was no one in either house.

'He's taking it well,' we said, and 'What is it?' And what we meant was: 'What have we stirred up?' And (for my sister and I cannot lie to one another) 'You did not do that with the buttons in the dish?' 'Dear God, I did not.'

'A dirty old woman,' said my sister, 'nice about her hands.'

I said: 'Dirty things done in a delicate way. There was that piece of stuff.'

The house and the little orchard were backed with tall trees. There was a hint of evening, and high branches black against strong gold. Was there something hanging high up, very high, that looked like a square of stuff that had holes in it?

Upstairs, Trenchard must have gone to the bathroom first. Then we heard him, moving about in his bedroom, just above the verandah roof. Then we heard him shout again, a cry he tried to stop. We ran out across the grass and called up at his window. He answered: 'No, don't come up.' Of course we ran up, in and through the sitting-room and up the stairs. The dining-room door was still open, and with a corner of my eye I saw a candle, guttering hideously in the windless room.

'Let us in,' we said at his door.

'Of all the filthy nonsense –' he was repeating: ' – Look at my shirt.'

On the top of the chest of drawers out of which he had taken it, his shirt was lying; and on its stiff white linen was what looked like a patch of grey jelly. Only it had spread out from a clot into five ribbons, like a hand or the fingers of a glove.

'Fine sort of beastliness,' he said, 'that won't let you dress for dinner.' I heard myself saying:

'Are all your shirts like that?'

'No,' he said grimly, 'and if you don't mind waiting here till I've finished, we'll go downstairs and see what this is about.'

He took another shirt and finished his dressing, wincing as he touched things; while we felt as if there were slugs about, the things of which we are most afraid; and that we must keep our long dresses tight about us.

We went down together into the dining-room and there my sister screamed. On the top of the centre strawberry pyramid, hanging over the berries like a cluster of slugs, was a glove, yellow-orange kid-skin, still and fat. A colour we had not seen in the box. The wrist and the fingers open and swollen. No buttons.

'What witches' trick is this?' he cried, and stared at us, for we were women. And like a wave moving towards us, rearing its head, came the knowledge that we were responsible for this; that our greed and vanity in devising this had evoked this: that we would now have to show courage, courage and intelligence to put an end to this, to lay this. And we had no idea how.

'The fire must burn,' I said. 'A great fire.' He turned towards the outhouse.

'What's the lovely scent you wear?' he said to my sister. 'I want to smell it. Get that.'

She ran away, and I stood still, aware of my shoulder-blades and the back of my neck, and all of my body that I couldn't see. Doors would not open easily. I heard him swearing and stumbling, the clang of a bucket tripped over and kicked away in the yard. My sister ran in, a scent-spray in her hand, crying:

'It's not scent any more. I tried it. It smells like the attic –'

She was squeezing the bulb and spraying us all violently; and I could not smell the dead smell of the loft, but the sweetness, like a ladylike animal, of old kid gloves.

Outside, the delicious evening was pouring in, to meet the original smell of the house; smell of flowers and tobacco, of polished furniture and wood-smoke and good things to eat. Trenchard had brought in a gallon jar of paraffin. He tipped and splashed it over the sitting-room fire.

'Get all the gloves,' he said, looking at our helpless skirts: 'I'll go across. I've got the loft key.'

We peered again into the dining-room, that the kitchen opened out of. The candle guttered in fat dripping folds; a spider ran across a plate. My sister said:

'It's got only five fingers. Like a glove.'

We waited. 'Let's have the fire ready,' we said, and I staggered with the can at arm's length to the sitting-room fire and drenched the piled wood. The ugly vulgar smell was sweet with reassurance. My sister threw in a match. A roar drowned the crackle of catching sticks.

'Now for it,' we said, and tore open the bureau drawer for the gloves. I ran up for Trenchard's shirt, and when I came back, my sister, her hands full of strawberries, threw them, yellow glove and all, on the leaping pillars of fire, I shook the guttering candle out of its stick; my sister unscrewed her spray and emptied the precious stuff, that waved blue and white fingers at us out of the fierce, shrill yellow flames.

'So much for that,' I said. 'Where is he?' said my sister. We looked at each other.

'This is our fault,' we said – 'We must go over. If it starts here again when we're gone, God knows what we're to do.' Then she said:

'The loft's the place. It started there.'

Outside, the orchard was full of bird-conversation. Inside, in half an hour we were to give a birthday party. We ran through the gap in the hedge and into our side of the house, which had become again part of one house.

Inside it we expected to find one large, troubled man, upstairs collecting things. Instead there was quiet, a kind of dead quiet that came to meet us down the steep stair. The loft door was open. On the flight that led up to it he was lying, feet down, his head upon the sill; his head invisible, wrapped up in what looked like a piece of dark green cotton, dirty and torn. We dragged it off.

'Burn. Burn,' my sister said.

Some of it was in his mouth. We pulled it out. His tongue and mouth were stained. We slid him down to the foot of the flight and got water.

'Draw it fresh,' she said. And 'Keep it tight in your hand,' for I wanted to drop the cloth, to pull it away, as if it were trying to wrap itself round me, to stick to me.

We threw water on him. ('Two shirts already; what an evening!' thought a bit of me.) By this time I had hold of the cloth like grim death, for it felt as though it was straining away in a wind that wasn't there. 'Gloves,' he said. We went into the loft. The skylight was open, and the cardboard box lay open and full. She put on the lid, and put it under her arm, and we left him on the stairs and made off again, across the orchard to the fire. It was dying down. The room stifling, the wood sulky with oil-black. My sister flung in the box, drenched it with the oil, and stiff grey smoke poured out on us. She tossed a match on it, and there was the grunt of an explosion, and, as we jumped back, the fire poured up again. I felt a smart in my hand, as if the cloth was raw between my fingers.

'It mustn't fly up the chimney,' she said. 'If it does, it will come back all over again.'

There was a box of cigars on the table. We turned them out, and thrust it in between the thin cedar boards and shut it up. Flung it into the fire wall and held it down. The box rose once or twice, bucked under the poker and the shovel.

Then we went back to Trenchard. He had come round, and was sitting at the foot of the loft stair.

'Everything's burned,' we said. 'Tell us what happened to you.'

'God knows,' he said. And then: 'I was stooping to get the box, and something flapped against the skylight. Blew in, I suppose, and the next thing I knew it had wrapped itself round my head and I couldn't get it off. I tore at it and I tried to get out. Then I couldn't bear it any more. It was winding itself tight. Then I must have passed out. But, oh God, it was the smell of it ...'

Notes

BY KATE MACDONALD

1 The Weird of the Walfords

Restoration: the accession of Charles II to the throne of England, Wales and Ireland in 1660.

murder of his royal father: Charles I was executed in 1649, after a trial that ended the Civil Wars in England, Wales, Scotland and Ireland.

saluted her: he kissed her: Charles II was a notable womaniser.

layings out: when a person dies, their body is washed, straightened, dressed and made ready for public viewing and then for burial: this was traditionally done by older women of the family or close attendants.

paper cap: carpenters traditionally wore a square paper cap.

knife-handles: before stainless steel became the standard metal for knives and forks, cutlery was made of pewter or silver, with bone handles.

mantelshelf and wainscot: the wooden mantelpiece above the fireplace, and the wooden panelling at the base of the walls around the edge of the floor.

engirt: surrounded by.

oriel windows: window embrasure on the first floor or above, extending out from the main wall of the house.

open carriage: parcels were normally delivered by the shop that supplied them, or collected by servants.

2 Let Loose

high, starched collar: men's collars in the nineteenth century were laundered separately from shirts, starched, and then buttoned to the neck of the shirt.

portmanteau: a large rigid case in two halves, with shelves and drawers inside to organise the contents. It thus functioned as a portable chest of drawers.

wold: chalk and limestone hills separated by steep valleys.

waste: dialect term for moorland, uncultivable land.

beck: the North-country term for a small stream.

mould: leaf litter and debris blown there by the wind.

groined: thin, buttressing raised strips of stone.

credence table: small table near the altar, used in Anglican church services.

reredos: a large devotional carving, painting or tapestry placed behind the altar in Anglican churches.

priests were proscribed: in the sixteenth century, during the reign of Henry VIII and the Dissolution of the monasteries, when the Anglican form of Christian worship became the established church in England and Wales.

family meal: the meal that all the staff were eating.

penny posts: some regional postal services, called the penny post, had been established in Britain since the seventeenth century, but the first universal postal scheme began in 1835.

pack road: a road created by travelling convoys of pack horses, carrying goods to market or to the ports.

the Reformation never reached it: an improbable circumstance that can be resolved by either a realist explanation that the Catholic Church merely remained or returned to that area after the Protestant Reformation, or a fantastical one that Dyke Fens is an otherworldly survival that the modern world has never touched.

Clementine Homilies: an early Christian text dating from the third century CE or earlier.

Asaph: in the Hebrew Bible Asaph is held to be the author of several of the Psalms.

even the Lord of the manor: he was the Lord of the manor; a Biblical phrasing for emphasis in identification.

MS: manuscript.

3 The Giant Wistaria

bromide: a sedative.

prohibition: the legal ban on selling alcohol that shaped US culture and society in the 1920s, which had been agitated for by temperance reformers since the 1870s.

repeater, Waterbury: a repeater watch chimed the hour and quarter hours. A Waterbury was a proprietary name for a watch, the original name of the present-day Timex company.

good mark: a good point to aim a gun at.

vide: Latin for see, see also.

4 The Shadow

second extra: the second of the extra dances put on at the end of a ball.

sacque: a distinctive eighteenth-century fashion of informal ladies' dress, suggesting that they're talking of a ghost.

Cleopatra's Needle: very large Pharaonic-era stone column with squared-off corners brought from Egypt and erected on the Victoria Embankment in central London in 1877.

salt cellars: referring to the hollow at the base of the girl's throat, showing how thin she is.

the gas suddenly glared higher: use of early gas supplies in a house affected different rooms. When the men had finished playing billiards, and turned out the gas, the release of that pressure back to the supply made other lights still in use burn brighter.

post-chaise: a two- or four-horse coach for hire, which would be ridden 'post', ie one set of horses would draw it at high speed to the next coaching inn or post-house, where the coachman would change horses and carry on with the journey.

encaustic tiles: colourful patterned tiles made using a medieval technique repopularised after the Victorian Gothic revival in architecture and design.

cypress, aucuba: these are both thick, light-obscuring evergreen shrubs.

inapropos: the inappropriate.

5 Kerfol

Quimper: a regional capital city in Brittany, north-west France.

'They don't understand French': the local people speak Breton, a language more like Welsh than French, a Romance language.

desert: in the sense that the soil is sandy and the low scrub is not verdant.

chemin de ronde: the raised walk alongside a battlement or high wall.

traceried: patterns made of thin strips of stone in the window spaces.

pardon: a Breton religious festival.

sleeve-dog: the Pekingese breed.

brindled: brown and grey or black hair making a subtle stripe in the animal's coat.

cloud of witnesses: reference to Hebrews 12.1. Here Wharton hints to the reader that the dogs have witnessed something in the past, while her usage can also be taken to mean that they are merely watching the narrator.

box-walk: a walk framed by the branches of the hedging shrub *buxus*, or box.

ridden over pillion: she had ridden over by sitting behind her father's saddle as he rode his horse.

the Clouets: fifteenth- and sixteenth-century French portrait painters.

Arnauld d'Andilly: a notable seventeenth-century Councillor of State, theologian and horticulturist.

6 Unseen – Unfeared

young sport: lively young man.

Chinese diplomat: in this period 'inscrutability' was frequently assigned as an identity marker for people of Chinese origin.

a few negroes: the story was written and published in a period when racial stereotyping was the norm for the white readership.

barrow: recycling discarded clothes for resale, or for the reclaimable value of their fabrics, was a common occupation, often carried out by Jewish tradesmen. Collecting them in a hand-barrow was efficient transportation in busy streets, despite its weight.

tessellated: tiled with tiny squares of stone.

threescore mark: over seventy years old.

graduate: a container with markings to show measurements.

settlement workers: church-sponsored mission workers established in poor urban areas.

stereopticon: a device for showing pairs of slides of the same subject, to give the impression of three-dimensionality.

7 Hodge

verger: church official in charge of the fabric of the church building.

waders: wading birds.

jangling keys: its seed-pods.

leaping-pole: a pole used for vaulting over streams or drainage ditches, essential for getting about a semi-flooded marshy area such as the Somerset Levels. A light person can travel as far and quickly as a stronger but heavier person.

pent-house: a ridge with a downward slope in one direction.

Java: modern Indonesia. Bones from an individual later identified as *Homo erectus* were found there in 1892.

Heidelberg: the first bones from an individual of *Homo heidelbergensis* were found in Heidelberg in 1907.

Pitcairn thing: Hector may have been muddled with the names, as the Piltdown Man 'discovery' took place in 1912 (and was not revealed as a hoax until 1953, long after this story was published). There are no known 'Pitcairn man' discoveries.

frail: the basket.

fugging: an unaired room has an atmosphere of 'fug'.

lees: the bitter particles that remain at the bottom of a bottle of wine, the unusable remainder.

9 The Haunted Saucepan

St James: the quarter between the Ritz, Piccadilly Circus and St James' Palace in the heart of Mayfair; traditionally the centre of London clubland.

chenille net: hairnet made of a soft woolly yarn.

brown study: a musing mood.

syphon: a soda syphon for whisky and soda.

dottle: the hardened tobacco debris remaining in a well-smoked pipe.

geyser: the gas boiler supplying hot water.

Uncle Stalky: reference to Rudyard's Kipling's character Stalky, ringleader of many ingenious and daring escapades.

10 The Twelve Apostles

pince-nez: glasses that grip the bridge of the nose.

cum grano: with a grain of salt, with some skepticism.

in fine: in the end, at the finish.

Throgmorton Plot: the plot to release the imprisoned Roman Catholic Mary Queen of Scots, assassinate the Protestant Queen Elizabeth, and crown Mary Queen of England and Scotland.

prie-dieu chair: upholstered chair suitable for kneeling at in prayer.

holy-water stoup: small niche or bowl inset into the wall to contain holy water, intended for people passing through the door to bless themselves with.

Dürer. Albrecht Durer, fifteenth-century German artist renowned for his skilled portraiture.

Colour Question: it is left vague as to whether Matthews is a eugenicist or an early campaigner for civil rights.

bona fides: good intentions.

quarterings: the four sections in the shield of a coat of arms.

11 The Book

Unseens: the section of an examination where candidates must translate or discuss a passage not seen before in their classes.

Philomel: character from Greek myth who is raped and her tongue torn out to prevent the rapist's discovery; she is later turned into a nightingale by the gods.

The Rose and the Ring: 1855 novel by Thackeray, one that often appeals to young girls for its romantic plot, though it is a satire.

maenad: from Classical myth, a female devotee of the Dionysian cult, given to ecstatic dances and riotous attacks on men while in a drunken frenzy.

bell-wether: the oldest male goat or sheep, the one who keeps watch for the safety of the flock.

12 Couching at the Door

couching: archaic verb for lying down, to recline.

cloisonné, Satsuma, Buhl: cloisonné is an enameled or decorated ornamental metalwork; Satsuma is a Japanese pottery style exported to the West in bulk in the nineteenth century: Buhl, or boulle, is a style of French cabinet furniture made famous in the seventeenth century. All these, with the first editions, are expensive collectables signifying money and taste.

Herat: carpets from Herat in Afghanistan are prized for their fine worksmanship and design.

The Yellow Book and *The Savoy*: two of the 'little' magazines of the fin de siècle, notable for their aesthetic qualities and tendency to publish scandalous literature and art.

Mrs Grundy: an invented name to personify social censoriousness and judging one's neighbours for what is nobody's business but their own.

pleasance: from *pleasaunce*, a pleasure-ground, garden, artificially constructed space for outdoor leisure.

'sveltes jets d'eau', 'sanglots d'exstase': quotations from Verlaine's poem *Clair de Lune* (1869).

sward: medieval term for a lawn of grass.

culs de lampe: typographical term for the ornamental designs that signify the end of the chapter.

Maecenas: after Gaius Cilnius Maecenas, friend of the future Emperor Augustus, and a wealthy patron and sponsor of the arts in pre-Christian Rome. The name is complimentary since it suggests taste and generosity.

scarified: scarred multiple times.

grimoire: a book of instruction in magic and the dark arts.

And if thou doest well: Genesis 4.7.

dog-cart: an open carriage drawn by one horse, with an open box at the rear to carry shooting dogs, or luggage.

mere: archaic term for a lake, usually a dark and gloomy one.

les choses cachées: hidden or concealed things.

comptoir: counter.

fiacre: horse-drawn cab.

13 With and Without Buttons

squibs: a firework used for illumination.

one always does: in this period women routinely wore gloves when visiting, travelling or on errands out of doors.